AN
AMISH
CHRISTMAS
BAKERY

OTHER NOVELS BY THE AUTHORS

AMY CLIPSTON

◆

AN AMISH MARKETPLACE NOVEL
The Bake Shop (available November 2019)

THE AMISH HOMESTEAD SERIES
A Place at Our Table
Room on the Porch Swing
A Seat by the Hearth
A Welcome at Our Door

THE AMISH HEIRLOOM SERIES
The Forgotten Recipe
The Courtship Basket
The Cherished Quilt
The Beloved Hope Chest

THE HEARTS OF THE LANCASTER GRAND HOTEL SERIES
A Hopeful Heart
A Mother's Secret
A Dream of Home
A Simple Prayer

THE KAUFFMAN AMISH BAKERY SERIES
A Gift of Grace
A Promise of Hope
A Place of Peace
A Life of Joy
A Season of Love

A Kauffman Amish Bakery YA Story
Reckless Heart

STORY COLLECTIONS
Amish Sweethearts
Seasons of an Amish Garden

STORIES
A Plain and Simple Christmas
Naomi's Gift included in *An Amish Christmas Gift*
A Spoonful of Love included in *An Amish Kitchen*
Love Birds included in *An Amish Market*
Love and Buggy Rides included in *An Amish Harvest*
Summer Storms included in *An Amish Summer*
The Christmas Cat included in *An Amish Christmas Love*
Home Sweet Home included in *An Amish Winter*
A Son for Always included in *An Amish Spring*
A Legacy of Love included in *An Amish Heirloom*
No Place Like Home included in *An Amish Homecoming*
Their True Home included in *An Amish Reunion*

NONFICTION
The Gift of Love

ROADSIDE ASSISTANCE YA SERIES
Roadside Assistance
Destination Unknown
Miles from Nowhere

BETH WISEMAN

◆

THE AMISH JOURNEY NOVELS
Hearts in Harmony
Listening to Love
A Beautiful Arrangement (available April 2020)

THE AMISH SECRETS NOVELS
Her Brother's Keeper
Love Bears All Things
Home All Along

THE DAUGHTERS OF THE PROMISE NOVELS
Plain Perfect
Plain Pursuit
Plain Promise
Plain Paradise
Plain Proposal
Plain Peace

THE LAND OF CANAAN NOVELS
Seek Me with All Your Heart
The Wonder of Your Love
His Love Endures Forever

OTHER NOVELS
Need You Now
The House that Love Built
The Promise

STORY COLLECTIONS
An Amish Year
Amish Celebrations

KATHLEEN FULLER

◇

The Middlefield Amish Novels
A Faith of Her Own

The Middlefield Family Novels
Treasuring Emma
Faithful to Laura
Letters to Katie

The Hearts of Middlefield Novels
A Man of His Word
An Honest Love
A Hand to Hold

Story Collection
An Amish Family

Stories
A Miracle for Miriam included in *An Amish Christmas*
A Place of His Own included in *An Amish Gathering*
What the Heart Sees included in *An Amish Love*
A Perfect Match included in *An Amish Wedding*
Flowers for Rachael included in *An Amish Garden*
A Gift for Anne Marie included in *An Amish Second Christmas*
A Heart Full of Love included in *An Amish Cradle*
A Bid for Love included in *An Amish Market*
A Quiet Love included in *An Amish Harvest*
Building Faith included in *An Amish Home*
Lakeside Love included in *An Amish Summer*
The Treasured Book included in *An Amish Heirloom*
What Love Built included in *An Amish Homecoming*
A Chance to Remember included in *An Amish Reunion*

KELLY IRVIN

◆

AMISH OF BIG SKY COUNTRY NOVELS
Mountains of Grace
A Long Bridge Home (available February 2020)

EVERY AMISH SEASON NOVELS
Upon a Spring Breeze
Beneath the Summer Sun
Through the Autumn Air
With Winter's First Frost

THE AMISH OF BEE COUNTY NOVELS
The Beekeeper's Son
The Bishop's Son
The Saddle Maker's Son

STORIES
A Christmas Visitor included in *An Amish Christmas Gift*
Sweeter than Honey included in *An Amish Market*
One Sweet Kiss included in *An Amish Summer*
Snow Angels included in *An Amish Christmas Love*
The Midwife's Dream included in *An Amish Heirloom*
Mended Hearts included in *An Amish Reunion*

ROMANTIC SUSPENSE
Tell Her No Lies
Over the Line

AN
AMISH
CHRISTMAS
BAKERY

FOUR STORIES

AMY CLIPSTON, BETH WISEMAN, KATHLEEN FULLER, AND KELLY IRVIN

ZONDERVAN®

ZONDERVAN

An Amish Christmas Bakery

Cookies and Cheer Copyright © 2019 by Amy Clipston
Loaves of Love Copyright © 2019 by Elizabeth Wiseman Mackey
Melting Hearts Copyright © 2019 by Kathleen Fuller
Cakes and Kisses Copyright © 2019 by Kelly Irvin

This title is also available as a Zondervan ebook.

This title is also available as a Zondervan audio book.

Requests for information should be addressed to:
Zondervan, *3900 Sparks Dr. SE, Grand Rapids, Michigan 49546*

ISBN 978-0-310-35281-5 (e-book)

Library of Congress Cataloging-in-Publication Data
Names: Clipston, Amy, author. | Wiseman, Beth, 1962- author. | Fuller,
Kathleen, author. | Irvin, Kelly, author.
Title: An Amish Christmas Bakery : four stories / Amy Clipston, Beth Wiseman,
Kathleen Fuller, and Kelly Irvin.
Description: Nashville : Zondervan Fiction, [2019]
Identifiers: LCCN 2019019147 | ISBN 9780310352808 (softcover)
Subjects: LCSH: Amish--Fiction. | GSAFD: Love stories. | Christian fiction.
Classification: LCC PS3603.L58 A6 2019 | DDC 813/.6--dc23 LC record available at https://
lccn.loc.gov/2019019147

Printed in the United States of America

19 20 21 22 23 LSC 10 9 8 7 6 5 4 3 2 1

CONTENTS

GLOSSARY

ab im kopp: addled in the head
ach: oh
aenti: aunt
appeditlich: delicious
boppli: baby
bruders: brothers
bu: boy
daadi: grandfather
daed/dat: dad
danki: thank you
dawdy haus/ daadi haus: grandparents' house
Deitsch: Dutch
dochder: daughter
dummkopf: foolish person
Englisch/Englischer: English or Non-Amish
fraa: wife
Frehlicher Grischtdaag!: Merry Christmas!
freind: friend
freinden: friends
froh: happy
gegisch: silly

geh: go

gern gschehne: you're welcome

Gmay: church district

Gott: God

groossmammi: grandma

gude mariye: good morning

gut: good

gut nacht/gute nacht: Good night

haus: house

hund: dog

Ich liebe dich: I love you

jah: yes

kaffee/kaffi: coffee

kapp: prayer cap or head covering worn by Amish women

kichli: cookie

kichlin: cookies

kinn: child

kinner: children

krank: ill

kuchen: cakes

liewe: love, a term of endearment

maed: young women, girls

maedel: young woman

mamm/mudder/mutter: mom

mammi: grandmother

mann: husband

mei: my

nee: no

nix: nothing

onkel: uncle

GLOSSARY

Ordnung: written and unwritten rules in an Amish district

rumspringa/rumschpringe: period of running around

schee: pretty

schtupp: family room

schweschder: sister

schweschders: sisters

sohn/suh: son

vatter: father

Was iss letz?: What's wrong?

Wie bischt: How are you?

Wie geht's: How do you do? or Good day!

wunderbaar: wonderful

ya: yes

yer: your

yerself: yourself

*The German dialect spoken by the Amish is not a written language and varies depending on the location and origin of the settlement. These spellings are approximations. Most Amish children learn English after they start school. They also learn high German, which is used in their Sunday services.

COOKIES AND CHEER

---◆---

AMY CLIPSTON

With love and appreciation for Zac Weikal
and the members of my Bakery Bunch

FEATURED CHARACTERS

LOUISE M. ROMAN BYLER
```
     ┌──────────┴──────────┐
  Alyssa            Jenne Lynn
```

MARIETTA M. ABRAM SMOKER
```
            │
          Kyle
```

1

"I CAN'T BELIEVE IT'S THE MIDDLE OF NOVEMBER already," Jenne Lynn Byler said after a lone customer walked out of Ronks Bakery, finally giving the staff a break. They'd been busy all afternoon. "We have to start thinking about decorating the store for Christmas."

"You're right." Alyssa turned from arranging two pies fresh from the bakery ovens and looked at her younger sister. "We do need to talk about that—especially the window display." She stepped over to the large window at the front of the store and took in the fall decorations she'd set up in early September. The design she'd created included orange donuts, several small pumpkins, two cakes and cookies all with orange icing, and orange whoopie pies, along with a flurry of paper leaves she'd cut out and painted before adding them to the background. This was one of her favorite window designs since coming to work for Denise Sherwood and her bakery five years ago, and she was grateful that Denise liked them.

Now she tapped her finger against her chin, contemplating possibilities for a Christmas design. The rest of the store would have lovely greenery as usual, but the window display needed to be unique. Inviting.

The bakery had originally been an Amish-owned business, and when Denise bought it nearly thirty years ago, she'd continued hiring young Amish women to preserve its theme. Now in her early sixties, and with graying dark-brown hair, Denise continued to enjoy a thriving business.

Alyssa was nineteen when she started her part-time job there, and she still worked the same three days a week. That gave her plenty of time to keep up with family chores, and the work was a good fit since she'd always loved to bake. Jenne Lynn joined Alyssa three years ago, when she turned eighteen. One of the other employees left to get married, and Denise needed a replacement. Alyssa had always appreciated that Denise gave her younger sister a chance. Not all Amish siblings had the opportunity to work together, and she cherished being able to do that.

Alyssa enjoyed baking and helping the customers, but her favorite part of the job was designing and decorating the display window.

"Are you contemplating your Christmas theme for the window?" Denise appeared behind her, and Alyssa turned around to see her boss's bright smile. Denise rested her hands on her hips and tilted her head as if eagerly awaiting Alyssa's response.

"*Ya.*" Alyssa twirled one ribbon from her prayer covering as she studied the window. "I think I have a good idea."

"What is it?" Jenne Lynn joined them.

"What if I created a nativity scene with some of the elements represented with sugar cookies?" Alyssa's lips spread into a wide smile as the idea took shape in her mind. "That's it! We'll bake cookies shaped like angels, shepherds, animals, and stars.

We already have figurines that represent Mary and Joseph, and one of baby Jesus in a manger. We can put the figurines in the middle and the cookies around it." She held out her hands in front of her as if she were already creating the display. "I can see it coming together." She met Denise's gaze. "What do you think?"

Denise nodded slowly. "It sounds good, but I'd like to know more before you start. Why don't you draw out the design and show it to me?"

"I can do that." Alyssa's heart did a little dance. Eager to get started, she rubbed her hands together and then looked up at her boss. "Are you going to hire one more baker to help us this season?"

"No. Why?"

"Last Christmas we had trouble keeping up with the baking, stocking inventory, running the cash register . . . Don't you think we need more help before we get another influx of tourists and even local customers after Thanksgiving?"

Denise seemed to consider this, but then she shook her head. "Even with the increase in sales, I can't afford more help. We'll just have to do the best we can." With that she turned and headed into the kitchen at the back of the store.

The front door opened, and the bell above it rang as three women dressed in jeans and winter coats came inside.

"Oh my. It smells heavenly in here! We heard this is the best bakery to purchase local baked goods," one of the women said.

Alyssa smiled. "How may we help you?"

As she stepped to the counter, Alyssa's mind spun with more details for her idea. She could hardly wait to sit down at her desk tonight and sketch out the designs. She wanted to make this year's Christmas display one of the best. After all, all the businesses on Lincoln Highway took their holiday decorating seriously.

———◇———

"How's the drawing coming?"

Alyssa looked up from her desk later that evening and found Jenne Lynn standing in her doorway. Alyssa had helped her sister and mother clean the kitchen after supper and then retreated to her bedroom to start sketching the window display.

"I think it's going pretty well." Alyssa motioned for Jenne Lynn to join her at the desk. "This is the whole design." She held up the drawing showing the entire nativity, and Jenne Lynn gasped.

"This is really *gut*, Alyssa!" Jenne Lynn pointed to the page. "I love the angels and the animals." Her fingers traced the different shapes, and then her brow furrowed. "Does Denise have all these *kichli* cutters?"

Alyssa shook her head. "No. I'm working on designing them now."

"But how are you going to make *kichli* cutters? We can't cut out those shapes with just paper or cardboard." Jenne Lynn scrunched her nose, and Alyssa bit back a laugh. Her sister always reminded her of a younger version of their mother with her bright blue eyes and light-brown hair—unlike her own hair, which was a medium brown, and her darker-blue eyes, so like their father's.

"I'm going to design them and then find someone to make them for us."

"Oh." Jenne Lynn continued to look confused. "Who would make them for you?"

Alyssa chewed her lower lip as her thoughts turned to the only metalworker she knew—Kyle Smoker. He'd been in school and youth group with her. But would he have time to make the cookie cutters? And how much would he charge her?

"Alyssa?" Jenne Lynn gave a little laugh. "Are you okay?"

"*Ya.*" Alyssa waved off the question. "I was thinking of someone who might be able to make the *kichli* cutters."

"Who?"

Alyssa looked down at the drawing of a cow cookie cutter. "Kyle Smoker."

"Ooh!" Jenne Lynne cooed. "He's handsome."

Alyssa shrugged as her cheeks heated. Her sister was correct. Kyle was easily the most handsome young man she knew, but Alyssa could count their conversations on one hand even though he lived just a block away and they both attended their district's church services. A few young men had asked her out over the years, but no relationship had developed from those dates. She wondered if Kyle had ever considered asking her out, but obviously he would have if he'd wanted to.

Alyssa looked at her sister, who still wore a wide smile. "His father owns that metalworking business down the street, right next to their *haus*, and Kyle works with him. I hope he has the time and interest to make these for me. If not, I'll ask him if he can recommend someone else."

"When are you going to ask him?"

"If Denise approves of my sketches, I'll walk over there tomorrow after work. Hopefully he'll be home on a Saturday."

"I'm sure Denise will love this." Jenne Lynn's eyes skimmed back across the paper. "You're so talented. I could never draw like this."

"You have your own talents." Alyssa gave her arm a nudge.

But talent or no, would Denise like the drawing as much as her sister did?

———— ❖ ————

"This is fantastic." Denise flipped through the drawings of the nativity and the cookie cutter shapes the following morning as she and Alyssa stood in the bakery's kitchen. "I love your creativity. I think this will be a hit with customers."

"Thank you." Alyssa grinned. "And what if we sell the cookies in boxes and tape Scripture verses on them?"

"I love that!" Jenne Lynn exclaimed. "I can help you write out the verses."

"That would be *wunderbaar*." Alyssa smiled at her sister, who was always generous with her time.

"Where do you think you can find the cookie cutters?" Denise asked.

"Alyssa is going to ask Kyle Smoker to make custom cutters." Jenne Lynn bumped her shoulder against Alyssa, who shot her a warning look. "He does metalworking for a living."

"And if he can't, he might be able to recommend someone." Alyssa worked to keep her tone even despite her frustration with her sister. "His father owns Smoker's Iron Works."

"He sounds like a good choice." Denise set the drawings on the counter.

"That's what I was thinking." Alyssa folded her hands and rested them next to her sketches. "They live about a block from us, and I'll go by there after work." She turned to Jenne Lynn. "Please explain to *Mamm* and *Dat* that I'll be home after I speak to him."

Jenne Lynn nodded. "*Ya*, I will."

Denise rubbed her chin. "I'll have to set a limit on how much I can spend on the cookie cutters. Our budget for decorations is tight."

"I understand." Alyssa held up her hands. "I don't want this to cost you much money."

They discussed the budget, and then Denise looked at the clock. "I'd better unlock the front door. It's time to open. We know how busy Saturdays can be."

As Alyssa started for the front of the store, excitement thrummed through her. Her fingers itched to get started on the window display, but she wouldn't be able to do that until she found someone to make the cookie cutters.

———————◆———————

Alyssa's hands trembled as she walked up the long rock driveway leading to the large workshop bearing the sign SMOKER'S IRON WORKS. When Kyle's mother answered Alyssa's knock on the back door of the house, she said Kyle was still working in the shop even though business hours were over.

What if Kyle thought asking him to make the cookie cutters was trivial—beneath his abilities and not worth his time? What if he even laughed at the idea? She swallowed a groan. This was a terrible idea.

From what little she knew of Kyle, though, he was a nice young man. She couldn't recall a time when he'd teased another student like some of the other boys who attended her school had. He'd always appeared to be quiet and respectful. She hoped he was still the person she remembered.

She reached the door and opened it, and a bell rang above her head, just like the one Denise had installed in her bakery. She scanned the shop. It was illuminated by skylights and propane lights, and she took in several workbenches cluttered with tools and a variety of metal projects. She gasped when she saw a metal coffee table sitting next to a metal propane lamp. It was beautiful! She also noticed a long railing she imagined would line porch steps, and then a metal shelving unit.

Turning to her right, Alyssa bumped into a metal chair that sat with five matching chairs and a table. She ran her fingers over it and silently marveled at the expert craftsmanship. Kyle and his father were truly talented.

"That's one of our most popular items."

Alyssa jumped with a start and sucked in a breath as she spun toward the voice. "I'm sorry. I didn't hear you walk over."

"No, I'm the one who should be sorry. I didn't mean to startle you." Kyle towered over her by at least five inches, standing close to six feet tall. His light-brown hair held flecks of gold as they stood under the skylights, and his honey-brown eyes seemed to sparkle. He folded his arms over his wide chest, and when he smiled at her, she felt a strange quiver start in her chest and spread to her arms and legs. "It's *gut* to see you, Alyssa. How are you?"

"I'm fine." She looked over at the table and chairs, hoping he wouldn't notice the blush that suddenly heated her cheeks. "This is your most popular item, huh?"

"*Ya.*" He gave a little laugh. "You'd be surprised how many stores want metal outdoor furniture. And they order it in fall and winter, so they'll have it for spring sales—believe it or not, starting right after Christmas."

"Oh." She nodded and cleared her throat. She glanced down at her sketches and again doubted coming to see Kyle. Why would he want to waste his time making cookie cutters if he had outdoor furniture to make?

"So what can I do for you?"

She looked up at him, and her words were trapped in her throat for a moment.

He lifted his eyebrows as his lips twitched. "Are you looking for outdoor furniture? Or maybe a railing?"

"No." She felt a smile break free on her lips as well. "I'm wondering if you could help me with a much smaller project."

"Okay. What is it?"

"I work at Ronks Bakery on Lincoln Highway," she began. "I'm sort of in charge of our window display, and we try to do something special for Christmas." She glanced down at the pile of papers in her hand. "I came up with an idea to do a sugar cookie nativity, but I need someone to make the *kichli* cutters for me."

He rubbed at his clean-shaven, strong jaw. "I can't say I've ever made *kichli* cutters before, but it can't be too difficult."

She felt some of the tension release in her shoulders. "I've drawn them all out. I even have the dimensions."

"Great." He clapped his hands. "Let's see your designs." He motioned for her to follow him to the closest workbench, where he moved some tools out of the way.

She handed him the designs and held her breath as he flipped through them.

When he got to the last page, he turned to her. "These are really *gut*."

"You think so?" She longed to remove the thread of desperation in her voice.

"*Ya*, I do." He looked down at them again and pursed his lips as if he were mentally making the cookie cutters. "How soon do you need them?"

"Does that mean you'll make them?" She swallowed back a squeal when he nodded.

"*Ya*, I can do it, but how much time would I have?"

"Is a week reasonable?"

"I think so." He jammed his thumb toward the back of the shop. "*Mei dat* and I are working on a big railing project besides the outdoor furniture, but I can work this in at the end of my day."

"*Danki* so much, Kyle." She folded her hands. "How much do you think all the *kichli* cutters will cost?"

"Not much." He shook his head. "We can talk about that later."

"Okay." She smiled up at him. "I really appreciate this."

"It's not a problem. I'm *froh* you thought of me."

He held out his hand, and when she shook it, she was certain she felt a spark skitter up her arm. Had he felt that too?

"I'll bring the *kichli* cutters to you at the bakery when I have them done, okay?" he asked.

"That would be perfect. I work there Thursday through Saturday."

"Great. I look forward to seeing you when I've finished them," he said as he walked with her to the front door. He pushed it open, and they stepped outside together. "Did you walk here?"

"*Ya*." She shrugged. "It's only a block."

"Do you need a ride home? It's getting dark."

"No, *danki*." She looked up at him and smiled again. "I appreciate your help."

"I'll see you soon."

With a spring in her step, Alyssa started down the driveway. Excitement spread through her at the thought of using the cookie cutters Kyle had just agreed to create.

And she wouldn't mind seeing their creator again either.

2

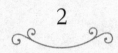

KYLE TIED HIS HORSE TO THE HITCHING POST BEHIND THE bakery and then retrieved the box of *kichli* cutters. As he walked around the side of the building toward the front, he glanced up at the crystal-blue, late-afternoon sky and shivered against the cold breeze seeping through his coat.

When he reached the front entrance, he stopped and peered into the display window, clearly designed for fall. He smiled as he recalled how Alyssa's pretty face had lit up and her eyes had twinkled as she told him about her plans for creating a Christmas display. She was talented, and not only had he seen the evidence in her drawings, but her creativity and flair sparkled in this spectacular autumn display.

He stepped toward the front entrance but then halted. Through the glass in the door he could see Alyssa. She was sweeping the floor, focused on her work, staring down as the ties from her prayer covering bobbed over her slight shoulders. When she glanced up to look at a clock on one wall, he couldn't help but notice that the dark blue of her dress brought out the deep blue of her eyes.

Although Kyle and Alyssa never talked much at school or youth group, he'd been aware of her and had admired her from afar. She lit up the room with her contagious laugh and her dazzling smile.

Why had he never had the confidence to ask her out?

Pushing away the thought, he ignored the CLOSED sign and tried turning the knob on the door. It was unlocked. He pushed it open, causing a bell to ring above his head. The sugary, inviting scent of fresh baked goods filled his nostrils as he glanced around. He'd never been here before, but he could see why customers would like the place. His mother mentioned the Amish bakery had been bought by an *Englischer* long ago, and she'd obviously retained its original charm. The walls were decorated with framed photos of picturesque Lancaster County, with horses and buggies; farms featuring large, white farmhouses with wraparound porches; red barns; and lush patchwork fields dotted with cows and horses.

"Sorry, but we're closed," Alyssa said. She had bent to sweep a small pile of crumbs into a dustpan, but when she straightened and faced him, her rosy lips formed an *O* and her cheeks flushed a bright shade of pink. She was adorable.

"Kyle. Hi." She set the dustpan and broom on the floor against a display case before brushing her hands over her apron and walking toward him.

"Hi." He held up the box. "I have your *kichli* cutters. I had hoped to get them to you sooner, but as I mentioned, *mei dat* and I have some big projects right now."

"Oh, that's *wunderbaar*. It's only Thursday. I wasn't expecting them before Saturday." She touched the box. "May I see them?"

"*Ya.*" He scanned the bakery, finding all the shelves and tables covered with baked goods. He looked up at the counter by the cash register and spotted an empty space. "Why don't we put the box up on that counter? Then you can spread them out to look at them."

"Okay." Alyssa followed him to the counter, where he set down the box and then stepped aside. She fished through the box and pulled out the cookie cutters, one by one, grinning and gasping as she examined each shape. "These are fantastic." She looked up at him, and her smile widened. "*Danki* so much, Kyle! They're perfect."

He shrugged. "*Gern gschehne*, but you made it easy."

Her brow furrowed. "What do you mean?"

"Your drawings were spot on, and that made it easier."

"How much do we owe you?"

"Alyssa?" An older *Englisch* woman wearing an apron stepped out from the back and gave Kyle a nod. "Hello."

"Denise, this is Kyle Smoker," Alyssa said. "Kyle, this is Denise Sherwood. She owns the bakery."

"It's nice to meet you." He shook her hand.

"You too." Denise glanced down at the counter. "These are the cookie cutters?"

"*Ya.*" Alyssa's expression brightened. "Aren't they perfect?"

Just as Alyssa had, Denise lifted each cookie cutter to examine it. "They certainly *are* perfect." She looked over at Kyle again. "Thank you for taking time to make these. You're talented, just like Alyssa said you were after seeing some of your work at your shop."

Kyle stood a little straighter. "Thank you." He turned to Alyssa and grinned. His grin widened when her cheeks again flushed pink.

A phone rang somewhere beyond the doorway Denise had come through, and she backed away. "Excuse me. Thank you again, Kyle. Alyssa, let me know if I didn't give you enough money."

"Okay."

Denise turned and disappeared.

Alyssa looked up at him. "So how much do we owe—"

"Alyssa!" A young woman Kyle knew was Alyssa's sister, Jenne Lynn, rushed in from the back. She stopped short when her gaze landed on him, and then she glanced at her sister. A smile spread on her lips. "I didn't realize you had company." She turned back to Kyle. "Hi, Kyle." Then she faced Alyssa again. "Our ride is here." She pointed toward the back. "I'll meet you outside?"

"I can give you a ride home, Alyssa," Kyle said, surprising himself. "We can, uh, finish our talk." When Alyssa's eyes widened, he added, "If that's okay."

"Oh." Alyssa glanced at her sister, and they seemed to share a knowing look. Then she turned back to Kyle. "That will be fine."

"Okay." Jenne Lynn motioned toward the front door. "Do you want to lock up in here before you leave, Alyssa? Denise is staying for a while, so she'll get the back door."

"*Ya*, of course. Tell *Mamm* and *Dat* I'm on my way."

"I will." Jenne Lynn grinned. "Bye, Kyle." She gave a little wave, and then she was gone.

Alyssa seemed embarrassed. "I'm sorry about that. We keep being interrupted."

"It's my fault. I didn't realize you'd be busy closing." He gestured toward the box. "Are you sure the *kichli* cutters are okay?"

"They're spectacular." She pulled a change purse from the pocket in her apron. "Now, again, what do we owe you?"

"Let's talk about it in the buggy, okay?" He'd already decided he wouldn't charge for the cookie cutters, but suddenly another idea popped into his head, an idea that seemed even better.

Alyssa hesitated, and then she held up a handful of bills. "But I want to make sure I have enough, so I can tell Denise if I don't."

"I'm sure you do. I'll help you lock up, and then we can talk in my buggy."

"Oh. Okay."

"What can I do?"

Alyssa directed him to the front door and told him how to lock it. After she'd turned off the propane lights Denise had also retained, Kyle picked up the box of cookie cutters and followed her into the kitchen. He noticed shelves full of ingredients and other supplies, a large island in the center of the room, and a wall of counters and cabinets. He counted three ovens.

"Should I leave the *kichli* cutters here?" Kyle set the box on the island.

"*Ya*, that's perfect," Alyssa said. "*Danki*. Do you like chocolate chip cookies?"

"*Ya*, I do," he said, and she handed him a box. "How much do I owe you for these?"

"They're free today," she said as she smiled brightly.

"*Danki*."

Denise stood by a desk in the corner, flipping through a ledger. "Are you getting ready to go?"

"*Ya*. I just need to grab my things." Alyssa retrieved her black coat from a peg on the wall, pulled it on, and buttoned it. Then she lifted a tote bag from another peg.

"Have a good night," Denise called.

"You too," Kyle said, waving at her.

Kyle went out the back door first and then held it open for Alyssa.

Alyssa glanced up at him as they walked to his buggy. "I was so surprised when you came into the bakery."

"Again, I'm sorry I got here so late. I didn't realize you close at five."

"It's fine." She motioned toward the bakery behind them. "The perfect time, really. We were busy most of the day, so it would have been even harder to talk."

"Do you like working here?"

A smile broke out on her face. "*Ya*, I do. I've always loved to bake, so I was thrilled when I saw the HELP WANTED sign in the window and Denise hired me. Jenne Lynn joined me when another *maedel* got married and had to quit. I really like working with *mei schweschder*. We have a lot of fun, and Denise is *wunderbaar*. She was a great help to my family when *mei daadi* was diagnosed with cancer. She and her husband took turns driving him to appointments and treatments and never charged us. They were also a *wunderbaar* source of strength when he passed away. They brought meals to us, and Denise prayed with us."

"She sounds like a special *freind*."

"She is. How about you? Do you like metalworking?"

"*Ya*, I do. I always knew I wanted to work with *mei dat*."

When they reached his buggy, he opened the door for her.

"*Danki*." She climbed in as he untied his horse, and then he hopped into the driver's side. "Tell me about the railing project you and your *dat* had to complete."

"Oh." Surprised that she would be interested, he glanced over at her before guiding the horse toward the road. "Well, we had to install a railing inside an *Englischer*'s *haus*. It's more like a mansion."

"Really?" Her eyes rounded as she angled her body toward him. "What does it look like?"

"It has six bedrooms and four bathrooms. It's probably three times the size of *mei dat*'s *haus*."

"No kidding!"

He smiled as he took in the excitement on her face. "It also has this sweeping staircase. And the kitchen is probably three times the size of the bakery's. They have stainless steel appliances, including a tremendous refrigerator and two ovens."

For the remainder of the drive Kyle answered Alyssa's questions about the house, and she listened with rapt attention. When they reached the road that led to her farm, she folded her hands and turned toward him once again.

"So," she began, "are you going to tell me what I owe you for the *kichli* cutters? Or do I have to keep asking?"

He chuckled. "You don't have to keep asking. And it really didn't cost me anything. I used some leftover metal from another project."

"But I have to owe you something for your time and effort." She tilted her head.

He swallowed against his suddenly dry throat. Now was his chance to ask her out, but would she say yes? He cleared his throat and pushed himself to find the confidence to ask the question burdening him. "I'm sure you've dated since we were in youth group together, but do you have a boyfriend?"

She paused and raised her eyebrows. "No. Why?"

"Could I take you out for supper one evening?"

"Uh . . . *ya*." She nodded. "That would be nice."

"How about tomorrow night? I can pick you up when the bakery closes."

"Sure." Her eyes widened. Was she stunned or excited?

"Great." A smile tugged on his lips as he guided the horse up the rock driveway leading to her white farmhouse. Perhaps he had a chance with Alyssa!

"I'm confused." Her statement broke through his mental celebration.

His stomach dipped as he halted the horse by her front porch. Was she going to change her mind? "Why are you confused?"

"Well, I asked you how much money we owe you, but you asked me out instead of giving me an answer."

"Going out with me is the payment."

Her brow furrowed as she studied him. "How is taking me out to supper a payment for the work you did?" She pulled out her change purse again. "Please take this money from Denise. It's only right that you're paid for your work. We don't give away *kichlin* or *kuchen* for free."

"You just *gave* me a box of chocolate chip *kichlin* for free, but that's beside the point. I can't accept payment from a *freind*." Without a second thought he reached over and covered her hands with his. Heat rushed from the place where their skin met, and he was surprised that she didn't pull away. He didn't want to be too forward. "I'm just *froh* you thought to ask me to make the *kichli* cutters for you."

"You were the first person who entered my mind." She seemed sheepish at her confession, and that made his smile broaden. "Are you certain you won't accept any money?"

"I'm absolutely positive." He gave her hands a quick squeeze and then sat up. "I look forward to seeing you tomorrow. May I pick you up at the bakery a little after closing time?"

"*Ya*. And I look forward to seeing you too. *Danki* for the ride." She pushed the door open. "Be safe going home."

"I will. *Gut nacht*."

"*Gut nacht*." She climbed out of the buggy, waved, and then hurried up the front steps.

Kyle sat up straighter as he guided the horse back down her driveway. He'd asked Alyssa to go out with him—and she'd said yes! How grateful he was for her cookie cutter project, giving him the perfect opportunity.

"So. Where is Kyle taking you to supper tonight?" Jenne Lynn asked as Alyssa set sampler boxes on the shelf below the counter at the back of the bakery.

"I don't know." Alyssa tried to keep her voice even despite the anticipation thrumming through her body. She was excited to spend more time with Kyle after discovering he was still the kind man she remembered.

"Why aren't you jumping up and down?" Jenne Lynn pressed. "Kyle Smoker asked you out! You should be dancing around the pie displays."

"I am excited, but I don't think it's appropriate to dance around the bakery." Alyssa had danced in the privacy of her room last night, but her younger sister didn't need to know that. If she allowed herself to get too worked up, she'd be tongue-tied when Kyle arrived. She had to keep her calm in public.

"Who's going on a date?" Denise appeared from the back

with another armload of samplers Alyssa knew contained some of the whoopie pies, shoofly pie, and assortment of cookies she'd baked that day.

"Alyssa didn't tell you?" Jenne Lynn gasped, and Alyssa rolled her eyes. "Kyle asked her out last night. He's taking her to supper after we close the bakery."

"Really?" Denise grinned. "I remember my first date with Greg. He took me to a movie and then for ice cream. We talked for hours, and I knew then that I wanted to marry him."

"Ooh," Jenne Lynn cooed as she turned back to her sister. "Maybe you and Kyle will get married."

"Stop, Jenn. It's just a date." Alyssa bit back a smile as she imagined a future with Kyle. After all, dates sometimes turned into more.

A timer buzzed in the kitchen, and Alyssa returned to reality. "I need to get more sugar cookies ready for the oven."

Denise followed her into the kitchen. "It looks like those cookie cutters are working out well."

"They are." Alyssa pulled on a mitt and opened the first oven. She took out a cookie sheet full of cow-shaped cookies. "These look spectacular." She set the sheet on hot pads and then slipped a cookie sheet full of angel cookies into the oven and set the timer. She moved to the second oven and pulled out a sheet of star cookies and then put in a sheet of cookies shaped like sheep.

"Thank you for giving me back the money. I still can't believe Kyle didn't charge us." Denise leaned against the counter beside Alyssa, and a smile turned up her lips. "He must really like you."

Alyssa couldn't hold back a smile as she began to mix more dough. "I guess so."

Denise surveyed the cookies. "I think your window display is going to be popular with the customers. I love this whole motif. I'm so proud of your creativity." She touched Alyssa's shoulder.

"Thank you." Alyssa stood a little taller and imagined her window. "I think the cookies in the display will last only a week or so since I'm going to ice them. I'll replace them as soon as they start to look a little old."

"It's going to be wonderful, Alyssa. I'm so glad you share your talent with me."

3

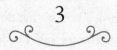

THE BELL RANG OVER THE BAKERY DOOR, AND ALYSSA'S heart seemed to trip over itself when Kyle walked in.

"Hi." He waved as he walked to the counter where she'd been closing out the cash register for the day.

"Hi." She slipped the stacks of money into a bank bag and zipped it. "How was your day?"

"*Mei dat* and I delivered furniture to a local store. We also took some rush orders, so we're staying busy." He leaned on the counter, and she admired the sparkle in his brown eyes. "How was yours?"

"Busy, but *gut*." She retrieved the zippered storage bag of Christmas sugar cookies she'd made for him from under the counter. "I have a gift for you." She handed him the bag. "Your *kichli* cutters are perfect."

"Wow." He studied the bag, shifting the cookies around. "You used all of them?"

"I did." She pointed to a display in the center of the store. "We're going to sell them in sampler boxes with Christmas Scripture verses on them."

"That's a great idea." He walked over to the display and picked up a box. "I'm going to buy a box for my parents."

Denise had just come in from the kitchen. "You can have them. It's the least I can do after you refused to take payment for the cookie cutters."

"Thank you." A smile lit up his handsome face.

"Would you like anything else?" Denise asked.

"No, this is perfect." He held up the box. "They'll really enjoy them."

"Good." Denise turned to Alyssa. "Why don't you get going? I'll finish up for you."

"Thank you." Alyssa handed her the bank bag. "I'll see you tomorrow."

"Have a good supper." Denise winked at Alyssa.

Alyssa hoped Kyle hadn't seen Denise's wink. Dismissing threatening embarrassment, she motioned for him to follow her. "I just have to get my things."

"Good night, Denise," Kyle said as he walked through the kitchen with Alyssa.

"Good night, Kyle." Jenne Lynn grinned from behind the counter where she was drying a cookie sheet.

"Good night," Kyle said with a smile.

"Have fun!" Jenne Lynn sang as Alyssa and Kyle headed out the back door.

Alyssa swallowed a groan at her younger sister's teasing and then smiled up at Kyle as they walked to his buggy. "Sorry about all the fuss from Denise and Jenne Lynn."

"It's no problem." Kyle opened the buggy door for her. "Where would you like to eat?"

"I don't know." She climbed into the buggy. "Do you have a spot in mind?"

"It's your choice." He closed her door, unhitched the horse from the post, and then slipped into the driver's seat beside her. "What sounds *gut*?"

She considered the options. "I haven't been to the Bird-in-Hand Family Restaurant in quite a while."

"Then that's where we'll go."

He guided the horse toward the road, and Alyssa settled back in her seat. She glanced over at Kyle's profile and once again wondered if she were dreaming. How had she wound up on a date with Kyle Smoker?

"Are you ready for Thanksgiving?" he asked as he guided the horse through an intersection.

"I suppose so. I can't believe it's next Thursday." She glanced out the window at passing traffic. "We already got our turkey. Are you ready?"

He shrugged and then smiled. "I think so. Do you celebrate with your extended family?"

"*Ya*, we do. *Mei aentis*, *onkels*, and cousins come to our *haus*. We have a *gut* time. How about you?"

"*Mei mammi*, *daadi*, *onkels*, *aentis*, and cousins all meet up at my grandparents' *haus*."

They talked more about their families as they made their way to the restaurant, and when they arrived Kyle tied up the horse in the parking lot. Inside they were seated at a table and then gave the waitress their order.

Alyssa sipped her water as she racked her brain for something to say.

"When will you start working on the window display?" Kyle lifted his own glass of water and took a long draw.

"The day after Thanksgiving. Denise thinks I should wait until then to take down the fall display." She reached into her apron pocket and fingered the sketch she'd worked on until late last night, trying to improve it. "I made some changes to the window design. Would you like to see them?"

"*Ya*, I'd love to." He moved his chair around the table so that their elbows brushed.

She pulled the drawing from her pocket and tried to focus on it instead of on his proximity. She took in a deep breath and inhaled his scent—sandalwood. She set the drawing on the table and smoothed out the creases in the paper. "I added more angels and a stable. *Mei dat* says he can build the stable for me out of some spare wood he has in his barn. I think I'll also add a fence here. I could make that out of Popsicle sticks from the craft store."

"Wow." He grinned. "You're so creative and talented."

"*Danki*." She looked up at him. "You are too."

"We both like being creative with our work, don't we?"

"*Ya*, we do." Their eyes locked, and her stomach took the flight of a thousand hummingbirds as his expression grew intensely . . . personal? She forced herself to look away for fear that her cheeks might catch on fire. "Do you have any suggestions for improving the display?"

"I think it's perfect." He pointed to one corner. "Although . . . What if you added more fence over here and maybe more sheep?" He shook his head. "What do I know? You're the artist."

"You're an artist too. I've seen your work." She pulled a pencil from her pocket and added more fencing and sheep. "That's a great idea. I think it's perfect now." She sat back and looked up at him. *"Danki."*

He laughed. "You act as if I designed the whole display. This is your work, Alyssa, not mine."

The waitress appeared behind them with their food, and Kyle scooted his chair around to the other side of the table as she set down their orders—Kyle's Salisbury steak and Alyssa's ham loaf. They bowed their heads in silent prayer before digging into their food, and then they spent the rest of the meal talking about their youth group days.

When they were finished eating, Kyle paid the bill and then they headed outside. Alyssa shivered and hugged her coat closer to her body as she climbed into the passenger side of the buggy. Kyle shut her door and then rushed around to the other side.

"Danki for supper," she told him as he guided the horse through the parking lot. "It was *appeditlich.* I've always enjoyed their ham loaf. It's the best."

"Gern gschehne. Danki for going with me." He glanced over at her. "You're cold."

"Ya." She gave a little smile as she pulled her coat tighter. "A little. But that's okay."

"I have something." He halted the horse at the parking lot exit, reached behind the seat, and pulled out a lap quilt. "Here you go."

"Danki." She ran her fingers over the cream-colored quilt that featured a beautiful gray-and-blue star in the center. "This Lone Star quilt is *schee.* Did your *mamm* make it?"

"No, *mei mammi* made it for me when I was about twelve. A bigger one she made for me is on my bed."

"I love it." She wrapped the quilt around her shoulders and breathed in the scent. It reminded her of Kyle's sandalwood. She tried to push away her growing attachment to him, but it was an impossible task. She was already falling for Kyle Smoker, and she wondered if he cared for her, too, or if this would be their only date. She had to be realistic. Maybe he was just being nice. Friendly.

Kyle guided the horse out onto Old Philadelphia Pike and then looked over at her. "Are you warming up?"

She smiled. "*Ya*. Do you have a big job planned for tomorrow?"

"I do." He blew out a sigh. "We have to get started on the first of the furniture orders we just got. It's going to keep us busy for the next month, maybe longer."

She settled back in her seat, silently admiring the streetlights decorated with pretty, lit wreaths. Soon her father's farm came into view, and she felt a frown overtake her lips. If only they had more time to get to know each other better. The evening had flown by too quickly.

He halted the horse and turned toward her. "Well, here we are. May I see you again?"

She smiled. This was what she'd been hoping for. "*Ya*, I'd like that. *Danki* again for a really nice evening." She removed the quilt from her shoulders, folded it, and then set it on the seat between them.

"*Gern gschehne*." He reached over the quilt and touched her hand. "Have a *gut nacht*."

Her heart skittered at the contact. "You too." She climbed out of the buggy and hurried through the cold, feeling as if she were walking on a cloud. When she reached the porch, she turned and waved at Kyle before rushing into her warm house.

As she pulled off her coat, she smiled again. Maybe, just maybe, she and Kyle would grow to be more than friends.

———◇———

Still full after yesterday's Thanksgiving meal, Alyssa hummed as she began work on the new display window. She was also still excited that Kyle had stopped by to see her on Sunday afternoon.

As they'd shared cookies and hot cocoa with her family, he'd been friendly and attentive with her parents. And then he'd held her hand when she walked out to his buggy with him when it was time for him to leave. He promised to see her again soon.

She smiled as she hung an iced angel cookie above the stable her father had built for her on Saturday. It seemed that this holiday season was going to be even more special than she'd expected. She might have a boyfriend by Christmas! Her stomach fluttered at the thought of calling Kyle Smoker her own.

She added sheep, a donkey, and two cows to the display. Then she concentrated on the fencing, extending it to the far end of the window. She added shepherds and more sheep by the fence and then placed hay inside the stable, along with the Mary, Joseph, and baby Jesus in the manger figurines.

When she heard voices, she turned toward the street. Three women stood pointing at the window and smiling. They waved at her, and she returned the gesture as the women walked into the bakery.

"I just love those cookies!" one of the women exclaimed as she walked over to where Alyssa worked. "Are you selling them?"

"Yes, we are. My sister can help you find them." Alyssa looked out toward the bakery displays. "Jenne Lynn!"

"Yes?" Jenne Lynn popped out from behind a bakery case.

"Would you please show these ladies where the Christmas cookies are?"

"Of course." Jenne Lynn motioned to them. "Please follow me."

Alyssa returned to working on the display, and she was adding the finishing touches when the women began talking again.

"Oh, my goodness! Annette! Bonnie! Look at this. The box has a Scripture verse on it. Listen to this: 'For to us a child is born, to us a son is given, and the government will be on his shoulders. And he will be called Wonderful Counselor, Mighty God, Everlasting Father, Prince of Peace.' Isaiah 9:6."

Alyssa bit back a smile as she kept working. She and Jenne Lynn had stayed up late one night writing the Scripture verses in their best handwriting. Then Denise had made photocopies, so they could tape one verse to the top of each box.

"Oh, Laurel. That is just lovely. Let me get a box too," one of the other women said. "This is what mine says: 'And there were shepherds living out in the fields nearby, keeping watch over their flocks at night. An angel of the Lord appeared to them, and the glory of the Lord shone around them, and they were terrified. But the angel said to them, "Do not be afraid. I bring you good news that will cause great joy for all the people. Today in the town of David a Savior has been born to you; he is the Messiah, the Lord. This will be a sign to you: You will find a baby wrapped in cloths and lying in a manger."' Luke 2:8–12."

The woman clicked her tongue. "Oh, I love it. I need to get a box for each of my grandchildren."

Alyssa looked up and found Jenne Lynn giving her a thumbs-up. The Christmas cookies were indeed a success!

Throughout the afternoon, customers complimented the window display and asked to buy some of the Christmas cookies. It seemed they were the most popular item.

At five o'clock Alyssa flipped the sign to CLOSED and walked past the display of Christmas sugar cookies. She gasped. The shelves were empty.

"*Was iss letz?*" Jenne Lynn skidded around the corner. "Are you okay?"

"I'm fine, but I can't believe we sold out of the Christmas cookies." Alyssa pointed to the empty shelf. "We sold them all today, Jenne."

"What?" Denise called from the counter. "We sold out of the Christmas cookies?"

"*Ya.*" Alyssa walked over to the counter. "I'll come in early tomorrow and make more." She turned to her sister. "Will you help me?"

"Of course I will."

"I suppose the Christmas season rush has started already." Denise pointed to the front window. "And I think your wonderful window display has helped jump-start that rush. So many customers complimented me on it. Thank you again for another fabulous design."

4

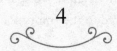

KYLE'S STOMACH FLIP-FLOPPED AS HE HELPED SET ONE OF the benches into a stand, converting it to a table for the noon meal. Then he searched the Blank family's barn for Alyssa's father, Roman. Kyle was nervous. He'd spent most of the church service sneaking glances at Alyssa and debating the best time to ask her father for permission to ask her to be his girlfriend.

The idea had been rolling around in his head ever since he'd taken her out for supper. He'd realized that night how much he was attracted to her. Alyssa was beautiful, funny, kind, and talented. But more than that, he already truly cared for her. Although he'd dated a few women, no one had seemed to capture his heart the way Alyssa had. His fondness for her and his attachment to her grew every time they talked. And now he hoped her father would allow him to see if Alyssa would make their dating official. It seemed that today was as good a day as any to ask him—if only he could find the confidence.

Kyle set another bench into a stand, and when he turned to

his left, he saw Roman talking to another member of the congregation. Squaring his shoulders, Kyle walked over to him and waited until he finished his conversation.

"Kyle. *Wie geht's?*" Roman shook his hand. Kyle surmised Roman was in his early to midfifties, and Kyle could tell Alyssa had inherited her eyes from him.

"I'm well. *Danki.*" Kyle cleared his throat and pointed to a bench seat. "I was wondering if I could have lunch with you today."

Roman nodded. "*Ya.* That would be nice."

"Great." Kyle followed Roman to the closest table and then sat down across from him. "How are things on your farm?"

Roman shrugged. "There's always something to do when you have a dairy farm. The work never stops."

"I can only imagine how challenging that is. Alyssa mentioned that you had a couple of farmhands working for you."

"That's right." Roman seemed to study Kyle for a moment, and Kyle shifted on the bench before Roman added, "Alyssa is still thrilled that you made those *kichli* cutters for her window display. She says they're fantastic."

"That's right." Kyle added quickly, "I mean, yes, that's right that I made them, but I don't know if they're fantastic. They seem to have worked out, though. She gave me some of the *kichlin* she made with the cutters, and they were *appeditlich.* She said she was going to start working on the display this past week. Do you know how it turned out?"

"She said it turned out well. She wants Louise and me to come and see it, and Jenne Lynn has been raving about how the customers love it. They're having trouble keeping the Christmas *kichlin* on the shelves."

"Wow. That's great." Kyle's chest warmed with pride for Alyssa's accomplishment. "I can't wait to see the finished product. I'll have to stop by soon."

"Has your *dat*'s shop been busy?"

Kyle told Roman about the orders his father and he were working on. But then a few young ladies walked past their table and caught his attention. As they delivered plates, cups, lunchmeat, bread, and peanut butter spread, Kyle searched among them for Alyssa. But he didn't see her.

Roman smiled at someone behind Kyle, and Kyle glanced up. Alyssa was approaching them.

"Hi there." Alyssa leaned over Kyle and set two bowls of pretzels on the table. She divided a look between her father and Kyle. "I didn't expect to see you two sitting together."

"Kyle asked me to join him today," Roman explained.

"Oh." Alyssa gave Kyle a curious look and then smiled. "Enjoy your lunch."

"*Danki.*" Kyle watched her walk away and then took a deep breath as he turned toward Roman, who gave him a curious expression. "I want to speak with you about something in particular."

Roman raised a dark eyebrow. "What's that?"

"I would be honored if you would allow me to ask Alyssa to be my girlfriend." Then he held his breath as he waited for Roman's response.

To his surprise, Roman smiled. "I think she would like that."

"Does that mean you give me your permission?" Kyle's voice was louder than he'd expected.

"*Ya, sohn,* it does."

"*Danki,* Roman. I really appreciate it."

Some other men joined them, and they all bowed their heads

AMY CLIPSTON

in silent prayer. Kyle smiled to himself when he finished his prayer. Roman had said yes. But now he had to ask Alyssa, and his heart pounded at the thought.

When he'd finished lunch, Kyle hopped up from the bench and shook Roman's hand. Then he scanned the barn for Alyssa. When he didn't find her, he headed to the Blanks' house.

He stepped inside the kitchen and found a knot of women milling about. Alyssa was loading a tray with cookies in one corner of the room, and he wove through the crowd to get to her.

"Alyssa." He sidled up to her.

"Kyle. Hi. I was just going to carry this to the barn."

He reached for the tray as she lifted it. "May I carry it for you?"

"No, but *danki*. I can do it. What do you need?"

"Would you come home with me today and visit with my family?"

"Oh." She seemed surprised by the question, and his hope deflated like a balloon.

"If you don't want to . . ."

"No, it's not that. I'll just need to ask *mei mamm*." Then she turned as her mother approached them with a hello. "Here she is."

"Hi, Louise." Kyle shook her mother's hand.

"How are you, Kyle?"

"Fine. You?"

"I'm great." Louise smiled at him and then turned to Alyssa. "Are you going to eat with Jenne Lynn and me in the barn?"

41

Alyssa nodded. "*Ya. Mamm*, Kyle has asked me to go home with him after lunch to visit with his family. Would that be okay?"

"*Ya*, of course." Was that a knowing smile she was giving her daughter?

"Then I'd love to," Alyssa told him with a bright smile.

"Great." Kyle felt his shoulders relax. "I'll wait for you to finish your lunch, and then we can head to *mei haus*."

———◆———

"How did your window display turn out?" Kyle's mother asked Alyssa as they sat at her kitchen table and drank coffee later that afternoon.

"I think it turned out well, Marietta, and I have Kyle to thank for that. Without the *kichli* cutters, I never could have put it together." Alyssa picked up her mug and took a sip as she glanced at Kyle, who sat beside her.

"I heard it's terrific." Kyle grinned at her. "I think you're being modest."

"Who told you that?" Alyssa asked him.

"Your *dat*. He said Jenne Lynn insists that it's amazing, and that she wants your parents to go see it."

Alyssa couldn't help but smile. "*Danki.*"

"I want to see it too," Marietta said. "Kyle told me about the sketch you did, and it sounds so creative and different from anything I've seen at any other store." She looked over at Kyle's father. "You need to take me to see it the next time you go to town."

"*Ya*, that sounds like a *gut* idea," Abram said. "I'm intrigued too."

"Maybe we can all go see it together," Marietta suggested. "Let us know when you work again."

"Jenne Lynn and I both work Thursday through Saturday. I'd love it if you came to visit."

"Those *kichlin* Kyle brought home to us were just fantastic," Marietta continued. "He said you made them."

"I did. I'm so glad you liked them. You can see how great the *kichli* cutters came out." She took another sip.

"They were really easy to make." Kyle seemed embarrassed by the praise. "They didn't take me much time at all."

"Are you ready for Christmas?" Marietta asked.

Alyssa shook her head. "No. We haven't started making our Christmas cards, and I need to make a list of what presents I want to buy. I've been so busy at the bakery. After I made the display on Friday, we ran out of the Christmas *kichlin* right away. I had to go in early on Saturday to make more. Then we sold out again. I have a feeling I may be working longer hours this week too."

"Wow. That does sound busy," Marietta said.

Alyssa enjoyed talking to Kyle's parents, and he never seemed to stop smiling as he listened to the conversation. She nearly lost herself in his eyes when their gazes tangled.

Alyssa helped Marietta wash the mugs when they were finished.

Kyle came up behind her as she dried the last one. "Alyssa, would you like to see our workshop before I take you home?"

"*Ya*, I would." She set the mug in a cabinet and then turned to Marietta. "*Danki* again for the *kaffi*."

Marietta touched Alyssa's arm. "*Gern gschehne.* I'm so *froh* you came to visit with us today."

Alyssa walked to the mudroom with Kyle, where he helped her pull on her coat. After he put on his, he led her outside and down the porch steps toward a large building.

"*Danki* for inviting me over today," she said as they walked together through the brisk air. It was colder than she'd expected for early December. "I really enjoyed talking with your parents."

"I'm glad you could come, and I could tell they enjoyed talking to you too." He opened the shop door, and she stepped through.

"I was surprised to see you eating lunch with *mei dat* today," she told him as he turned on the propane lights that hung next to the skylights.

"I had a nice talk with him."

She studied his expression. "Oh? What did you talk about?"

"Work." He shrugged, but his expression didn't seem casual. He looked a little . . . nervous.

He walked over to a workbench and lifted an object from it. "I made something for you."

She crossed the room, and then she gaped as he handed her a metal candleholder with a heart design. In it sat a purple candle. "Kyle. This is for me?"

"*Ya*, it is. Do you like it?" He seemed hesitant.

"I love it." She ran her fingers over the metal curves, taking in the heart in the center, and then looked up at him again. "This is amazing. I don't know what to say."

"The candle reminded me of the dress you wore when I visited you last week. I like that color purple on you. I was going to wait until Christmas to give this to you, but I couldn't wait."

She sucked in a breath as her insides warmed. She'd never received a more special gift. "This is so *schee*. But I feel bad because I don't have anything for you."

"Please, don't. Think of it as an early Christmas gift. I didn't expect anything in return." He leaned back on the bench. "I ate lunch with your *dat* today for a reason." He paused and folded his hands over his middle. "I asked his permission to ask you if you'll be my girlfriend. And he gave it."

Alyssa stared at him as her heartbeat began to drum in her chest and Kyle went on.

"I'm so grateful you asked me to make the *kichli* cutters," he told her. "It gave us a chance to get reacquainted." He reached over and took her hand in his. "You're already so special to me, Alyssa. You're *schee*, sweet, thoughtful, kind, and easy to talk to. I enjoy spending time with you, and I'd like to spend a lot more time with you and get to know you better." He paused and swallowed. "Will you be my girlfriend?"

She nodded vigorously. "*Ya.* I'd love to."

A smile broke out on his handsome face. "*Gut.*"

Cupping his hand to her cheek, he leaned down and gently kissed her. An unfamiliar quiver of wanting danced up her spine, and she closed her eyes and enjoyed the feel of his lips against hers.

When he lifted his head, he said, "I'll always regret not asking you out when we were in youth group. But I think God gave me a second chance when you asked me to make the *kichli* cutters." He moved his finger over her cheek with a featherlike touch that made her body shiver.

When he kissed her again, Alyssa was certain she was dreaming, but the heat rushing through her veins was as real as the feel of his lips.

No, she wasn't dreaming. She was enjoying the company of her new boyfriend. And she was certain life couldn't be better.

―――――◆―――――

Jenne Lynne turned the candleholder over in her hands later that evening. "He made this for you? It's so *schee*."

"I know." Alyssa rested her chin on her palm as she sat across from her mother and sister at the kitchen table. "I still can't believe it."

Mamm sighed. "And he asked you to be his girlfriend. I had a feeling that was coming."

"Why?" Alyssa asked.

"Please." Jenne Lynn rolled her eyes. "The level of his interest was so obvious from the way he came to see you at the bakery, refused payment for the *kichli* cutters, and then took you out for supper."

"And also when he came to visit us last week," *Mamm* added.

Alyssa absently drew a heart shape on the wooden tabletop. "I did sort of have a feeling, but I didn't expect him to ask me so soon."

"The Lord works in mysterious ways." *Mamm* picked up her mug of tea and sipped it before adding, "I'm *froh* for you. Kyle seems like a *gut* Christian man and a hard worker."

"I agree." Jenne Lynn held up her mug as if for a toast. "I think you and Kyle will have a *wunderbaar* future together."

Alyssa's chest fluttered as if with butterfly wings as she imagined a future with Kyle. That seemed more possible now than it had the first time Jenne Lynn suggested they could have a future.

Later that evening she lit the candle and set it on her dresser before sitting down at her desk and pulling out her sketchpad. The warm aroma of lilac filled her senses as her mind swirled with excitement and possibilities. She couldn't stop recalling the feel of Kyle's sweet kisses and his handsome face. Maybe he would come by to see her at the bakery on Thursday and then they could ride home together in his buggy. Perhaps his parents would stop by to see the window too. They'd all seemed interested in it.

She fiddled with a pencil as her thoughts turned to the Christmas display window. Kyle's mother had seemed so excited to hear about it. Would more people come to see it if they heard about it? And if so, how could Alyssa get the word out to bring those potential customers to the bakery? More business would be great for Denise.

The questions floated around her mind as she pushed herself up from her desk and retrieved her nightgown from her dresser. Sleep would help.

5

"GOOD MORNING!" ALYSSA CALLED AS SHE AND JENNE Lynn stepped into the bakery kitchen Thursday morning. "How are you, Denise?"

"I'm well, but I'm tired." Denise shook her head. "It's been so busy this week. We ran out of Christmas cookies again on Tuesday, so I stayed late to make more. I had Janie make even more yesterday morning, but they still weren't enough. The shelf is almost half empty already. I need you to start making more right away."

"Okay." Alyssa began to gather the ingredients.

"I'll get the pans and turn on the ovens," Jenne Lynn said, offering help as usual.

"I saw several customers take pictures of your window with their phones," Denise said. "Customers talked about it nearly all day yesterday. It's truly been a popular attraction."

"That's wonderful," Alyssa said over her shoulder as she poured flour into a large mixing bowl. "I was wondering if we should try to promote the display to bring in even more business."

"What do you mean by 'promote'?" Denise came to stand beside Alyssa.

"Well, I was over at Kyle's house on Sunday after church—"

"He's her boyfriend now," Jenne Lynn chimed in.

Alyssa shot her sister a look and then turned her attention back to the dough. "Anyway, I told Kyle's parents all about the window display, and his *mamm* was curious enough to want to see it. That got me thinking that maybe we could do something to pull in even more customers, and when I woke up this morning, I had an idea." She turned toward Denise. "What if I wrote a letter to the *Lancaster News* and told them about it? I think it might entice a reporter to come and do a story about the display."

Denise tapped her chin. "That's a fantastic idea."

"I agree," Jenne Lynn announced as she set a pile of cookie sheets on the counter.

Denise glanced around the kitchen. "But if they write an article for the paper and business really picks up, will we be able to keep up with the demand for the cookies? It's challenging to keep up now."

"I think we can," Alyssa said, insistent as she added egg to the flour.

"I might need you to work longer hours if it gets too crazy," Denise said. "Do you think your parents will agree to that?"

Alyssa looked at Jenne Lynn, who shrugged and said, "I think so." Then Alyssa turned back to Denise, whose expression had brightened.

"Great," Denise said. "Write that letter to the paper then. You'll find stationery, envelopes, and stamps in my office desk. I have a copy of the *Lancaster News* in there too. You'll need the address." Then she walked out to the front of the store to open for business.

After the cookies were baked and cooled, Alyssa assembled

them into boxes and attached Scripture verses. It was lunchtime by the time she'd finished filling the shelves.

She gathered everything she needed for the letter in Denise's office, and then she hopped onto a stool at the kitchen counter. After pulling her lunch out of her tote bag, she began writing the letter as she ate. She smiled as the words took shape.

Once finished with her turkey sandwich, she addressed the envelope and stuck the stamp on it. Then she slipped the letter inside before sealing it. Jumping off the stool, she pulled on her coat and rushed out the back door to the mailbox on the corner to make the next pickup.

Surely the newspaper would want to write an article about the window display, and surely the publicity would increase business. All the baking would be a challenge, but more customers would be a blessing to Denise. She worked so hard, and maybe more profit now would allow her to hire additional help next year.

———————◆———————

Kyle cupped his mug of hot cocoa with his hands as he sat beside Alyssa on her front porch glider the following evening. Then he gazed at the sky above them and said, *"Danki* again for inviting me over for supper tonight. It's the perfect December evening. Look at those stars!"

"Ya." She laughed as she hugged her coat closer to her body. "But I can't believe how the temperature has dropped this week. I should have brought a quilt outside for us."

"Do you want to go back inside?"

She shifted, and her leg brushed against his. "No. We can talk without interruption out here."

"That's true." He glanced at her and warmth filled his chest. He was so grateful she'd said yes when he'd asked her to be his girlfriend on Sunday. He couldn't stop smiling as thoughts of her kept his mood cheerful all week.

He had planned to stop by the bakery to visit her today, but then she'd called last night and invited him to pick her up after work, bring her home, and then stay for supper. He'd been delighted when he found the message on his father's voice mail. He just wished the evening would slow down so they could have more time together.

"So how are your furniture orders going?" Her question broke through his thoughts.

"We're making progress on some more metal patio furniture right now. We have to build four sets of them for one of the stores in Bird-in-Hand." He stretched his arm out on the back of the glider, brushing her shoulders.

"You'll have to show one to me before you deliver it to the store."

"Okay. I will." He tilted his head and looked at her. "How's the bakery?"

She laughed. "Crazy. The window display has been a success. We can't keep the Christmas *kichlin* on the shelves. I had to go in early again today to bake more before we even opened." She angled her body toward him, and her expression brightened. "I wrote a letter to the paper telling them about our cookie nativity. I thought some publicity might increase sales."

"Really?"

"*Ya.* I asked Denise's permission and she agreed to it. I mailed the letter at lunchtime today, so I'm hoping they'll get it tomorrow. I started thinking about seeking some publicity after your *mamm* was so excited to hear about the display. When your parents stopped by yesterday afternoon, they seemed impressed by it."

"*Ya*, they loved it. It was all *mei mamm* talked about when she got back to the *haus*." He rubbed her arm, and she shifted closer to him, resting her head on his shoulder, sending happiness coursing through him.

"*Danki*. I was so *froh* to see them. Your *mamm* bought quite a bit of *kichlin*."

"I know. I've been enjoying them."

"I'm so glad to hear it." Alyssa chuckled. "Denise said customers were even taking photos of the display with their phones. That's the other thing that gave me the idea to write to the newspaper. They usually take photos for stories like the one I hope they write for us. I guess we'll see if they're interested." She sipped her cocoa.

"I bet they will. I think it was a brilliant plan." Kyle kissed the top of her head. His heartbeat thudded when she smiled up at him. How blessed he was to call Alyssa his girlfriend.

"*Danki*. But we made it happen together."

He leaned down and brushed his mouth over hers, savoring the sweet, chocolaty taste of her lips.

When he broke the kiss, he wished he could not only slow time but freeze it, so they could enjoy this moment for hours and hours.

She snuggled against his shoulder once again. "I want to stay like this forever."

"Funny you should say that. I was just thinking the same thing." He looked again at the stars twinkling in the dark sky and sent up a silent prayer. *Thank you, God, for bringing Alyssa into my life.*

———————◆———————

"Is that all for you?" Alyssa asked a customer the next day as she rang up two boxes of Christmas cookies, two sampler boxes, and three loaves of bread.

"Yes, thank you." The woman pulled out her wallet.

Alyssa gave the woman her change before bagging the items. "Please come see us again soon," she said as she handed the woman her purchases.

"Oh, I will, honey. This is where I get the goodies for my holiday parties."

"Thank you. Have a great day." Alyssa waved as the woman headed out the door.

When the bell above the door sounded a few minutes later, Alyssa looked toward the front of the store and said, "Welcome to Ronks Bakery!"

A tall woman dressed in jeans, boots, and a black coat approached with a camera hanging around her neck. "Hi there. Are you Alyssa Byler?"

"Yes, I am. How may I help you?"

"I'm Jordyn Marshall. I'm a reporter with the *Lancaster News*." Jordyn shook Alyssa's hand. "We received your letter earlier today, and I'm here to see your display window."

Alyssa's stomach tumbled. "Oh my goodness. I'm so glad you came." She pointed toward the back room. "Let me introduce you to the bakery owner. Excuse me for a moment." She rushed into the kitchen, where Denise was filling more sampler boxes. "Denise! You have to come out front."

"What is it?" Sudden worry etched Denise's face. "Is everything all right?"

Alyssa grabbed Denise's hand and gave it a tug. "*Ya*, it is. A reporter is here from the *Lancaster News*. They received my letter."

"Fantastic! You mailed it only two days ago." Denise wiped her hands on a paper towel and smoothed out her apron.

"I know. Please come and meet her." Alyssa beckoned for Denise to follow her out to the front, where Jordyn stood perusing a shelf of baked breads as Jenne Lynn reviewed the various flavors for her.

"Jordyn," Alyssa said, "this is Denise Sherwood. She's owned the bakery for almost thirty years."

"Hi, Denise." Jordyn shook her hand. "It's so nice to meet you. I was intrigued by Alyssa's letter, and I hurried over to see your display window. It's spectacular." She pulled a notepad from her pocket. "I have some questions for you. Tell me how you came up with the idea and how it all came together."

"Well, it was all Alyssa's idea, so I'll let her explain." Denise smiled at Alyssa.

Alyssa shared her story, and Jordyn asked more questions and took notes. When a group of customers came into the bakery, Denise and Jenne Lynn excused themselves to help them.

"I just love how you laid out the nativity scene," Jordyn said as she and Alyssa walked over to the window. "It's so creative. And your boyfriend made the cookie cutters!"

Alyssa smiled to herself. She was still getting used to calling Kyle her boyfriend. "That's right. I drew the shapes I needed and gave him the dimensions, and then he made the cutters in his father's metalworking shop."

"I see." Jordyn scribbled on her notepad. "Did you build the stable?"

"My father built it for me out of some spare wood he had on our farm."

"Tell me more about the bakery. What baked goods do you sell here besides the sugar cookies and breads?"

Alyssa gave Jordyn a tour of the store, explaining what they offered, including locally made peanut butter, jelly, and jams.

Jordyn made more notes and then smiled at Alyssa. "This will be a great holiday story. I think I have everything I need. I'm just going to take some photos from the outside."

"Great." Alyssa clasped her hands together. "When do you think the story will run in the paper?"

"I'm hoping for Monday."

Alyssa's heart thudded. "Monday? That soon?"

"Yeah." Jordyn pushed back a tendril of her dark hair that had fallen into her face. "We're trying to feature a few holiday stories every week now since Christmas is only two and a half weeks away."

"That's wonderful. Thank you for coming to visit us." Alyssa shook Jordyn's hand again.

"You're welcome. Thank you for the letter." Jordyn waved goodbye to Denise and Jenne Lynn, and then she pushed open the door. "Take care. And do have a merry Christmas."

Alyssa watched Jordyn take several photos of the display window from different angles. She tried to imagine what the newspaper article might look like with the photos featured on the page.

"Alyssa," Denise called from the back of the store.

"*Ya?*" Alyssa spun to face her.

"We're running low on chocolate chip and macadamia nut cookies. Would you please make some more?"

"Of course." As Alyssa headed toward the kitchen, she imagined what the newspaper story could mean for the bakery. They might be busier than ever, but she was sure the extra work would be worth it.

———◇———

"The reporter received your letter yesterday and came right over?" Kyle asked as he and Alyssa sat at her kitchen table the following afternoon.

"*Ya*, can you believe it?" Alyssa brought a plate of oatmeal raisin and peanut butter cookies to the table. She was glad Kyle had decided to spend this off Sunday without a church service visiting her and her family. "I was so surprised when she walked in and introduced herself. I never expected someone to respond so quickly."

"I guess she knew it would be a fascinating story." Kyle winked at her, and her cheeks heated.

"*Ya*, I suppose so." She carried the coffee carafe to the table and filled his mug before filling hers. "She was really nice. She wanted to hear all about how I got the idea for the display, and I told her how you made the *kichli* cutters and *mei dat* built the stable." She set the carafe on the counter and then sat down across from him. "I even mentioned your *dat*'s business. Maybe she'll put its name in the article too."

Kyle reached across the table and set his hands on hers. "*Danki* for mentioning me and *mei dat*'s business, but the cutters were all your idea. You deserve the credit."

"I didn't do it alone." When he gave her hands a gentle squeeze, she relished the contact. "Without you and *mei dat*, the display wouldn't have come together."

He lifted his coffee mug. "I'm just glad it did. Now we'll have to see what kind of response the article brings."

"*Ya*, I know. The reporter said it might be in the paper tomorrow. She took so many photos. I keep trying to imagine what the article will look like."

"I can't wait to see it. I'll have to make sure I pick up a paper when I go out for supplies tomorrow."

"*Ya*, I'll ask *mei dat* to get a copy too."

Kyle handed her a peanut butter cookie. "By the way, would you please make more of these for me?"

"Who said I made them for you this time?" Alyssa said, teasing.

"Oh, you got me right in the heart." His smile crumbled as he grabbed at his chest. "It hurts."

Alyssa laughed as she popped up from the table. "I have a whole container you can take home, but you have to promise me one thing."

"What's that?"

"That I'll see you again this week."

"Are you kidding? Wild horses couldn't keep me away from you."

As Alyssa handed him the container of peanut butter cookies, she thanked God for the cookies and cheer she had to look forward to this Christmas season.

6

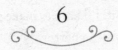

ON WEDNESDAY MORNING ALYSSA SHIVERED AS SHE stood on the back porch and pinned a pair of her father's trousers on the clothesline. She picked up another pair and then looked toward the barn just as Jenne Lynn stepped out its door and started toward her.

"Any voice mail messages?" Alyssa asked as she hung the trousers and then moved the line down.

Jenne Lynn climbed the porch steps. "*Ya*. Denise left a message asking if one or both of us could come to the bakery as soon as possible."

"She wants us to work today?" Alyssa studied her sister. "But it's Wednesday. We don't work until tomorrow."

"She said she can't keep up with the demand for the Christmas *kichlin*. The bakery has been busy nonstop since the article ran in the paper on Monday. She even had a line of customers waiting for her to open this morning." Jenne Lynn shook her head. "She needs someone to continue baking while she, Janie, and Ruby keep up with the crowds in the store. She said it would be a blessing if one or both of us could come and help out."

Guilt pummeled Alyssa. Had the article been a bad idea after all? "Did Denise sound upset?"

Jenne Lynn frowned. "She sounded desperate."

"But we have chores to do today." Alyssa pointed at the large basket of laundry she had to finish hanging before she started cleaning their two bathrooms.

"I know, but it sounds like Denise truly needs our help." Jenne Lynn gave her a palms up. "Maybe *Mamm* would understand?"

"What would I understand?" *Mamm* appeared from inside the house.

"We received a message from Denise asking if one or both of us can go in to help her today," Alyssa said.

"Is someone *krank*?"

"No."

"Then why would Denise need your help? She has two other workers on Wednesdays." *Mamm* divided a confused look between Alyssa and her sister.

"She said the bakery has been busy nonstop since the article ran in the paper on Monday." Jenne Lynn turned toward *Mamm*. "She needs someone to bake Christmas *kichlin* while the rest of them help the constant rush of customers."

"I should go since the article was my idea," Alyssa said.

"I don't think so," *Mamm* said. "If Denise has more business, she should hire more help."

"She said she can't afford that this year, *Mamm*."

"But you have chores to do today." *Mamm* gestured around the porch. "You were going to clean the bathrooms while Jenne Lynn cleaned the upstairs."

"I can clean the bathrooms for you," Jenne Lynn said.

"Danki." Alyssa smiled at her sister. As much as Jenne Lynn

frustrated her with her teasing at times, she appreciated her kind and giving heart.

Mamm frowned. "We also planned to start making our Christmas cards this afternoon, after our chores are done. That's why I had you pick up the supplies at the craft store yesterday, Alyssa."

Alyssa felt as though her stomach was tying itself into a tight knot. How could she help Denise and her family at the same time? She couldn't stand the idea of disappointing anyone.

"We still have time to make the cards," Jenne Lynn said as she looked at their mother. "You and I can start making them, *Mamm*, and then Alyssa can help us finish them and sign and address them." She cut her gaze to Alyssa. "Right?"

"*Ya*, that's right." Alyssa gnawed her lower lip as she considered a solution. "I could finish hanging out the laundry and then get *Dat*'s driver to take me to the bakery. I'll work only as long as Denise needs me, and then I'll come home and help with whatever still needs to be done. Would that work? I hate to see Denise struggling."

Mamm blew out a puff of air and then nodded. "*Ya*. You're right. We should help Denise. She's been a *gut freind* as well as a *gut* employer." She gestured toward the basket of laundry. "Finish up here. I'll let your *dat* know you need a ride to the bakery, and he can make the call."

"*Danki, Mamm*," Alyssa said as she pinned another pair of trousers to the line.

"I'll help you." Jenne Lynn picked up one of *Dat*'s shirts and handed it to Alyssa.

"*Danki*."

"Did you expect the article to make such an impact—and so quickly?"

Alyssa shook her head. "No. It was a nice article, and the photos were really *gut*, but I didn't think it would cause a problem for Denise. I truly thought we could keep up. I feel so guilty about this."

"Don't be *gegisch*." Jenne Lynn elbowed Alyssa in her arm as she gave her another one of *Dat*'s shirts. "More customers are *gut* for Denise's business."

But was the stress worth it?

Thirty minutes later Alyssa stepped through the front door of the bakery and sucked in a deep breath. The store was full of women—and a few men—filling their plastic shopping baskets with baked goods. One group congregated by the window, pointing at the nativity scene. Ruby stood by the display of jarred peanut butter and jellies, explaining the ingredients and differences in the local brands.

Alyssa excused herself as she wove through the crush of people and made her way to the counter, where Denise and Janie were checking out customers. A lengthy line of them were waiting to pay for their purchases.

Denise looked up, and her expression brightened. "Alyssa! You made it! I'm so grateful you could come in on one of your days off. It's been like this since Monday afternoon." She pointed toward the kitchen. "Would you please start making more Christmas cookies? We're nearly out, and we need them desperately."

"*Ya*, of course. I'll get right to work." Alyssa slipped past a few more customers and entered the kitchen, where she quickly hung up her coat before washing her hands. She gathered the ingredients she needed, and then set out mixing dough and cutting out cookie shapes. While the cookies baked, she assembled boxes.

"I'm so glad you came in today," Ruby told her as she walked into the kitchen later that afternoon. Alyssa liked Ruby. She was about Jenne Lynn's age, and just as nice. "We weren't sure what we were going to do for a while. It was just too crazy."

"I'm glad Denise called." Alyssa smiled up at Ruby as she closed the lid on another box of Christmas cookies.

Ruby washed her hands and started assembling boxes too. "One of the customers asked if she could buy a set of your *kichli* cutters."

Alyssa spun toward her. "What? Really?"

Ruby nodded. "*Ya.* When she asked, three more customers chimed in and said they'd like a set too. Do you think you could get Kyle to make some to sell?"

"I don't know." Alyssa paused, her hand on one of the Scripture verse tags. "He's awfully busy, but I could ask him. And I'll have to talk to Denise about how she'd like to handle the sales."

"Denise seemed to like the idea. She told the customers she'd see if she could get some."

"I'll talk to Kyle tonight and ask him if he even has time to make more."

"Great." Ruby taped a verse to the last box she'd assembled and then stacked several of the finished boxes one on top of the other before lifting them into her arms. "I'll get these out on the shelves. We've been selling them as quickly as we stock them. You really had a *wunderbaar* idea for this year's Christmas window display."

"*Danki.*"

At closing time Alyssa felt more guilt slithering through her.

She'd told her family she'd be home as soon as possible, but it was already five o'clock, and she'd just now cleaned the kitchen. She'd let them down, but she'd been trying to help Denise. She felt so torn!

"Thank you for your help today." Denise sidled up to her at the sink as Alyssa washed her hands. "I don't know how we could have kept the customers happy without your extra help back here."

Alyssa frowned. "I'm sorry it's so busy."

"Why are you apologizing?" Denise gently squeezed Alyssa's shoulder. "I love seeing so many satisfied customers in the store. We'll get through it. Christmas will be here soon, and then business will go back to normal—although I think we might have gained some new regular customers. That makes me happy too!"

Alyssa forced a smile. "Right. Denise, Ruby told me a few customers asked if they could buy a set of the cookie cutters."

Denise snapped her fingers. "I meant to ask you about that. Do you think Kyle would make some sets for us to sell? Would he be interested?" She pointed toward the front of the store. "Or we could sell them individually. I could separate them in bins, or I could just put them all in one big basket."

Alyssa shrugged as she dried her hands. "I don't know. I'll have to see if he even has time to make them."

"Let me know what he says, and then we can discuss terms. Whatever he'd like to charge is fine with me. I'll want the money he makes to be worth his time. I'll appreciate his considering this." Denise started back to the main area of the store. "I need to see what I'll have to bake tonight so we can restock tomorrow. I don't think my shelves have ever been this empty. And I'll have to buy more supplies . . ."

She halted and turned back to Alyssa, and Alyssa couldn't help but see the weariness in her employer's eyes along with her delight. "Do you think you and Jenne Lynn could come in early tomorrow?"

"We can try. We'll just need to get our mother's permission."

"Of course. Either way, please thank her for me."

Denise left the room.

Alyssa thought about when to ask Kyle if he'd make the cookie cutters, and then she stepped to the phone to call her father's driver.

She hoped that when she got home her mother would understand why she was so late—and that she needed to be back at work early tomorrow. She couldn't ignore Denise's predicament when she'd been the one to cause it. And after all, working extra hours was temporary.

If only she could shake the guilt that had taken hold of her . . .

———◇———

Kyle stepped out of his father's workshop when he heard the hum of an engine. It was suppertime, and the sign out at the street clearly stated that they closed at five. Who could this be?

When he spotted Alyssa climbing out of a blue van, his heartbeat ticked up a few notches. She'd been at the back of his thoughts throughout his exhausting day, and her beautiful smile was the balm his tired soul needed. He quickened his steps and rushed over to meet her.

"Alyssa!" He pulled her to him for a quick hug. "What a *wunderbaar* surprise! How are you?"

"I'm fine. Do you have a minute to talk?"

"*Ya*, I do." He nodded toward the van. "May I give you a ride home?"

"That would be great." She pulled out her change purse. "I'll pay him." She walked over to the driver's side and thanked him before handing him some bills. Then she joined Kyle at the top of the driveway. "I'm sorry to just show up without calling first."

He took her hand in his. "Are you kidding? This is the best kind of surprise." He gestured toward the shop. "Let's go inside, where it's warm."

"Okay. I need to ask you something."

They walked together into the workshop, where he flipped on the propane lights and then pulled up two stools.

"What's going on?" he asked as he gestured for her to sit down. "Where have you been today? Not at work, right?"

She hopped onto one of the stools. "Yes, at work. Jenne Lynn and I got a message from Denise asking for at least one of us to come to the bakery today. It's been so busy since the article ran in the paper that she needed someone to bake while she, Janie, and Ruby ran the front."

"Wow." He sat down on the other stool and rested his ankle on his opposite knee. "I thought the article was fantastic, but I didn't realize business would pick up so quickly."

"Neither did I. It was a madhouse." She hugged her arms to her middle. "I just hope we can keep up. Even before all this started Denise told me she can't afford to hire more help this year. I guess it's more economical to give extra hours to the employees she already has."

He studied her pretty blue eyes, finding what looked like anxiety there. What was troubling her? The extra hours? Or something else? "What do you need to ask me?"

"Some of the customers have asked if they can buy the *kichli* cutters. Could you possibly make more? Or are you even interested in selling them? Denise says she'll want the terms to fairly compensate you for your work and time."

"Oh." He glanced across the shop to the scrap metal pile. He and his *dat* had quite a stockpile, so he had the supplies. But did he have the time? That was the bigger question.

"Please, Kyle?" She folded her hands as if to say a prayer. "I know you're busy, and maybe you don't need the money, but I think the *kichli* cutters would be popular with the customers. The more they buy when they show up, the more profitable this crush will be for Denise. It's a lot to handle, but I'm hoping it will all be worth it."

Was that it? She was concerned for Denise? He rubbed at the back of his neck. If he came back out to the shop after supper every night, he could make a few each day. It would make for long days, but it would also help Alyssa, who clearly wanted to help Denise not just as her employee but as her friend. He'd do anything for Alyssa.

"*Ya*, I'll do it." He smiled at her, and her face brightened with a smile of her own as she clapped her hands. "I'll get started tonight."

"*Danki!*" She leapt off the stool and hugged him.

Kyle pulled her close and kissed her cheek. How he'd missed her since Sunday!

She looked up at him. "Do you still have my drawings of the cutters?"

He pointed to the workbench in a far corner. "I do. They're in a drawer with some of my tools."

"Perfect." She stepped back. "Denise will be so *froh* to hear it."

The shop door opened, and *Mamm* stepped inside.

"Kyle, are you coming in for sup—" She looked at Alyssa, and her expression brightened. "Alyssa! I didn't realize you were here. How are you?"

"I'm well. And you?" Alyssa stood up straighter.

"I'm great. How long have you been here?" *Mamm* looked from Alyssa to Kyle and raised her eyebrows.

Kyle stood. "She just stopped by a few minutes ago—to ask me if I could make more *kichli* cutters to sell at the bakery."

"*Ya*," Alyssa chimed in. "The customers are going crazy for the Christmas *kichlin*, and today a few asked if they could buy the cutters too."

"Oh my. I'm certain that's because of that article in the paper. What *wunderbaar* coverage you received. You must have been *froh* to see all those lovely photographs of your gorgeous *kichli* nativity," *Mamm* said.

"*Danki*, Marietta. I was excited by the article."

"Are you in hurry?" *Mamm* asked. "Could you stay for supper?"

"Oh. That's such a generous invitation." Alyssa glanced up at Kyle, and he nodded. "I'll have to call my parents and ask."

"You can use the phone over there." Kyle pointed to *Dat*'s desk across the shop.

"Okay. I'll call and see." She crossed the shop and picked up the phone and dialed. Soon she was speaking to someone on the other end of the line.

"What a pleasant surprise." *Mamm* grinned at Kyle.

"*Ya.*" Kyle was careful to keep his voice low. "*Danki* for inviting her to supper."

Mamm gave his arm a squeeze. "Of course. I'll always be *froh* when Alyssa comes to visit."

"I know the feeling."

After a few moments, Alyssa hung up and returned. "*Mei dat* said it was fine. *Danki* for the invitation."

"*Gern gschehne.*" *Mamm* made a sweeping gesture toward the door. "Let's get inside the *haus* before the food's cold."

Kyle took Alyssa's hand in his as they stepped out into the fading winter light.

———◆———

Kyle glanced at Alyssa as he guided his horse to her house later that evening. She cupped her hand to her mouth to cover a yawn.

"You okay?" He raised an eyebrow in concern yet failed to stop a smile. She was so adorable.

"*Ya.* I'm sorry. You caught me." She gave a little laugh, which sounded like a sweet hymn to his ears. "I'm just wiped out." She covered her mouth and yawned again. "Between doing the laundry and then baking all day, I wore myself out." She pulled his quilt around her body.

"But you got to see me."

She touched his arm. "*Ya,* that's true. That was the best part of my day. And your *mamm* makes the best roasted chicken and stuffing. Dinner was *appeditlich.*"

"I'm glad you could stay." He halted the horse at a stop sign. "I wanted to see you before the weekend, and God answered that prayer today."

He steered the horse onto her street.

"You should come to *mei haus* Tuesday evening," she said. "Then I can repay you for the *wunderbaar* supper—even if your *mamm* is the one who made it!"

He grinned at her. "You don't have to repay anyone. But I'd be honored to join you Tuesday."

"*Gut.*"

He directed the horse to her father's farm and up the long rock driveway. When they reached the back porch, he halted the horse and turned to her. "Let me walk you to the back door."

"That would be nice."

He climbed out of the buggy and met her in front of the horse. When he felt something cold and wet on his hand, he looked up and spotted snow flurries dancing down from the heavens.

He pointed up. "Look, Alyssa. It's snowing."

She gasped as a wide smile overtook her lips. "It is!"

He laughed. "Isn't it magical?"

"*Ya.*" She laced her fingers in his as they walked up the porch steps.

"I hope you get some rest tonight." He traced the tip of his finger down her cheek. "*Danki* for coming to see me." Then he leaned down and brushed his lips over hers, sending his heartbeat into a gallop.

"*Gut nacht.*" Her words came out in a breathy rush, as if she'd run the length of her father's back pasture. He felt a little breathless too.

"*Gut nacht.*" As he walked back to his buggy, he smiled up at the falling snow flurries and imagined a bright and blessed future with his beautiful girlfriend at his side.

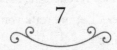

7

EXHAUSTION BOGGED ALYSSA'S STEPS AS SHE WRENCHED open the back door and entered the mudroom the following Tuesday evening. Her feet felt as if they were on fire as she pulled off her coat and hung it on a peg on the wall. When she heard laughter floating out from the kitchen, she froze. It sounded as if Kyle were with her parents and sister. Why was he here?

Alyssa swallowed a gasp. It was Tuesday night! She was supposed to come home on time to have supper with Kyle. How could she have forgotten? She cupped her hand to her forehead. Hopefully Kyle would forgive her for forgetting their plans. When he laughed again, her worry morphed into envy. Her boyfriend was enjoying time with her family without her. How had the pull of the bakery gotten so out of hand?

She took a deep breath and then stepped into the kitchen, where Kyle sat at the table across from Jenne Lynn.

"Alyssa!" Kyle announced. "You finally made it."

"I'm so sorry." She set her tote bag on the floor and then moved to wash her hands at the sink. "I completely forgot you were going to meet me here tonight." A yawn overtook her and she succumbed to it.

"You're forgiven," he said. But he sounded disappointed.

After drying her hands, Alyssa slipped into the chair beside Kyle. She bowed her head in silent prayer and then filled her plate with chicken and dumplings.

She turned toward Kyle. He seemed to study her. "How was your day?"

Alyssa shook her head. "Insane. My head and feet are throbbing."

"I was surprised you agreed to stay late tonight," Jenne Lynn commented.

"I really didn't have a choice." Alyssa shrugged. "Denise needed my help." She turned to Kyle. "Again, I'm so sorry I forgot you were coming tonight."

Kyle nodded, but this time his disappointment seemed almost palpable.

Guilt weighed heavily on Alyssa's chest as she turned her attention to her food.

"You look worn-out, Alyssa," *Dat* said. "You need to get your rest."

"That's right," *Mamm* added. "It's not your job to keep the bakery running. Denise needs to hire more help."

"I agree," Kyle said.

Alyssa covered her mouth to stifle another yawn. "I've explained before that hiring a seasonal employee isn't possible for Denise this year. And we just didn't expect the display and then the newspaper article to generate so much business. Today one of the customers told us the newspaper article was picked up by a website, which means even more people have heard about our display. I spoke to people who had come from as far as New Jersey and

New York to see it and buy the Christmas *kichlin*. We ran out of the *kichlin* again today, so I have to go in early tomorrow, and I might have to work late again."

Mamm shook her head. "You worked yesterday and today, and now Denise wants you to work tomorrow too? Does she expect you to work six days this week?"

"She needs the help." Alyssa took another bite of dumpling.

"But this is a part-time job," *Mamm* said. "Has Denise forgotten that we have chores here?"

"Christmas is next week," Alyssa said after swallowing. "It's almost over."

"But that's the problem." *Mamm*'s voice rose as she gestured around the kitchen. "Denise has been a *gut freind* to this family, but we have a lot to do. We haven't finished our Christmas cards or our baking. Your *schweschder* picked up a poinsettia for the *schtupp* today and she decorated the shelves and banister with greenery. You normally like to do that, but we were running out of time."

Alyssa sighed as her aching shoulders hunched. Why did *Mamm* have to bring up all this in front of Kyle? "I'm sorry."

"We haven't gone shopping yet either," Jenne Lynn added. "When are we going to do that?"

Alyssa swallowed and wiped her mouth on a paper napkin. "I don't know. As I said, I have to go in early tomorrow, and it might take all day to make enough *kichlin*."

Jenne Lynn's expression clouded with a frown. "But . . . we have so much to do."

"I'm sorry. Denise needs me, and I can't disappoint her." She moved a dumpling around on her plate. "I had no idea that following through on my ideas would make all this happen."

"Neither did we," *Mamm* said. "We need you around here. The bakery isn't your family."

Alyssa gritted her teeth and did her best to tamp down her swelling frustration. "I know, *Mamm*. This wasn't what I had in mind." She took a deep breath and searched her mind for a solution that would please her mother. "I can work on the Christmas cards later tonight."

"No. If you're going in to the bakery early tomorrow, you need to get to bed early tonight." *Mamm* pointed at the clock on the wall.

"I want to help, *Mamm*. I really do." Alyssa worked to keep her voice even despite the guilt churning in her stomach.

Mamm's expression softened. "I know. I'm frustrated with the situation, not with you." She looked at Kyle. "I'm sorry. I didn't mean to bring up this family business during supper."

"It's okay. I understand." Kyle's expression was warm as he turned to Alyssa. "I'm concerned about you too. You do look exhausted. I promise I won't stay too late."

The knot in the pit of Alyssa's stomach tightened as she took in his handsome face. Was she going to lose him? How could she have forgotten that they had supper plans?

When they finished eating, Alyssa helped her mother and sister remove the dishes before they had coffee and some of the lemon cake her mother had baked. After dessert, the women cleaned the kitchen, and then her parents and sister disappeared into the family room.

Alyssa breathed a sigh of relief after her family left. She could finally talk to Kyle alone and apologize again for her oversight.

She sat down beside him. "I'm so sorry for forgetting our plans for tonight. I never meant to take you for granted."

Kyle rubbed his chin and studied her. "I'm worried about you working so many hours."

"It's temporary." She touched his arm. "The Christmas rush is almost over."

He shook his head. "You're pushing yourself too hard."

"I'll be fine." She snapped her fingers. "I know what I meant to tell you. We ran out of *kichli* cutters today, and Denise asked me to see if you can make more."

Kyle made a noise in his throat as his mouth formed a grimace. "I don't think so, Alyssa."

"I have your money from the other *kichli* cutters." She retrieved her change purse from her apron pocket and pulled out a pile of bills. "Here. This is your part of the profit from the ones you gave us last week."

"*Danki.*" He took the money and slipped it into his pocket. "I'm sorry, but I can't make any more. I have to keep up with my work and chores."

"You can't make them after you finish your chores for the day?"

"No." He shook his head. "Christmas is next week, and I need to be with my family to help follow through on our traditions. *Dat* even turned down a last-minute order to ensure we're both available to *Mamm* and the rest of our family. I just don't have time for more work." He paused. "And I want to have time for you too."

Alyssa nodded as her hope sank—and as she realized her guilt was now a three-pronged monster. She'd made Denise's business nearly impossible to manage, she'd let down her family, and now she'd let down Kyle, who was willing to make time for her even as she let the bakery overshadow opportunities to spend time with him.

But again, helping Denise was only temporary. She'd make this up to her family and Kyle somehow—after the crisis she'd created was over.

She fingered the blue tablecloth. "I understand."

"I promise I'll make more cutters for next year." He touched her arm. "When can we go out again? I've been thinking about that ham loaf you liked so much at the Bird-in-Hand Family Restaurant."

"Can we wait until after Christmas? I'm sure I'll be working long hours until then." She looked away, unwilling to see more disappointment in his eyes.

When he didn't answer right way, she picked up her tote bag, pulled out a bag of cookies, and handed it to him. "I brought home peanut butter *kichlin*. Would you like one?"

"*Ya*, that would be great. *Danki*." He opened the bag and handed her one. "Have one with me."

She stifled another yawn before biting into the cookie.

"You look pale." He touched her face. "I think you should stay home tomorrow. Get some rest."

She sighed. "I can't. Denise needs me."

He shook his head. "I don't want you to get so worn-out that you wind up *krank* for Christmas. That would be awful."

She set her elbow on the table and rested her chin on her palm. "I created this mess, so I need to help Denise through it. I can't abandon her now."

His expression grew intense. "This is not your fault. At least promise me you'll get some rest tonight."

"I will." She nodded, and the concern in his brown eyes sent affection flowing through her. Her efforts might not have his full support, but he still cared about her.

"I should go." He pushed back his chair.

"You don't have to leave." She pulled his arm toward her.

"*Ya,* I do. You need rest." Kyle leaned forward on the table. "I've missed you."

"I've missed you too. I promise we'll see each other after this crazy Christmas rush is over."

"I'll keep you to that promise." They both stood, and when he kissed her, happiness buzzed through her.

"Please tell your parents and Jenne Lynn goodbye for me," he said.

As Alyssa walked Kyle to the back door, she asked God to protect their relationship through this challenging time. She needed him.

———◆———

Kyle's eyes widened as he entered Ronks Bakery Thursday afternoon and took in the crowd of people clogging the shop and rummaging through the shelves. Alyssa hadn't exaggerated when she said the bakery was busy. It resembled a grocery store on the weekend, not a bakery!

He searched the crowd for Alyssa, but he didn't find her. When he peered up toward the counter, he spotted Jenne Lynn and a young woman he didn't recognize checking out the customers. The line snaked from the back of the bakery to nearly the front door.

He made his way through the throng, excusing himself when customers stepped in front of him or failed to step aside.

When he reached the counter, Kyle waited for Jenne Lynn to notice him.

"Kyle," Jenne Lynn said after a minute or so. *"Wie geht's?"*

"Hi. Is Alyssa here?"

"Ya. She's in the back baking." Jenne Lynn stepped over to the door leading to the kitchen. "Alyssa! Kyle is here!" Then she stepped back to the counter. "She'll be right out," she told him before turning back to serve the next customer.

Kyle made his way to the doorway in the back just as Alyssa appeared. He grinned as he took in her appearance. Flour peppered her black apron, and a dot had landed on her cheek. He reached over and brushed it away with his fingertip.

"You've been busy," he said.

She gestured at the crowd behind him. "You could say that. Can you believe this?"

He shook his head. "No. I've come to check on you. I was hoping you'd let me know how you were doing."

"I'm sorry." She gestured around the bakery. "You can see what's been keeping me busy."

"Alyssa!" Denise poked her head out from the kitchen and looked at Alyssa. "We need to start baking more chocolate cakes. The shelf is empty."

"I'll be there in a minute," Alyssa said as Denise moved past her. Then she looked up at Kyle. "I'm sorry, but I have to get back to work."

"Wait." He held up his hand. "I know you said we'd have to wait to go out until after Christmas, but you have to eat sometime. How about I take you to supper tonight? I can wait for you as long as necessary."

"I'm sure I'll need to work too late for that." She grimaced. "I'll see you Sunday at church."

"At church?" He studied her, looking for the sign of a joke.

"I can't even visit you tomorrow evening? Or maybe Saturday evening?"

"Alyssa!" a voice called from the kitchen. "We need you back here!"

Alyssa touched his arm. "I'm sorry. I have to go. But *danki* for coming by."

Before he could respond, she disappeared into the kitchen, leaving him standing there with frustration boiling in his gut. He hadn't even had a chance to say goodbye.

He looked out at the chaos in the bakery, and his chest constricted with hurt. For years he'd liked Alyssa from afar, and now . . . Was he losing her? Why couldn't he manage to hold her attention even when she was busy? Or was her busyness just an excuse to pull away from him? The thought that she might have changed her mind about him was painful.

———◇———

Alyssa stepped into her kitchen Friday night and found her parents sitting at the table. Her heart felt like a lump of ice as she took in the deep scowls lining their faces. Had someone died?

"Was iss letz?" Her voice sounded thin and shaky to her.

"Why did you stay after your *schweschder* came home tonight?" *Dat* asked.

"Oh. Didn't Jenne Lynn tell you I had work to do?" Alyssa said, explaining as she sat down. "I spent all afternoon baking more Christmas *kichlin*, and then I had to put them in boxes to sell tomorrow. By staying later, I was able to get ahead on my work before—"

"You've missed supper with the family every night this week,"

Dat said. "Suppertime is when families come together after working hard all day. You're supposed to be here." He pointed his finger toward the wood tabletop.

Alyssa swallowed against her suddenly dry throat. "I know, but the bakery is so busy that I—"

"I'm tired of hearing about how busy the bakery is," *Dat* continued. "You're a part of this family, and I expect you to be here. We miss you." He pointed at her mother. "And your *mamm* needs your help."

Alyssa's lip trembled with guilt. "But Christmas is almost here, and that means the rush will stop. I'll make it up—"

Mamm shook her head. "No. You need to stop saying it will all be over after Christmas. We need to prepare for Christmas now. Your *schweschder* finished the Christmas cards while we were waiting for you to get home today. She and I also did our shopping and finished our baking on Wednesday while you were at work. Everything is done, and you haven't been a part of it. It's always been our tradition that we make the cards, bake, and shop together. But you weren't with us."

"I'm sorry." Alyssa choked on a sob as her tears broke free. "I didn't mean to miss out on it."

"We miss you." *Mamm* reached over and handed Alyssa a napkin before touching her arm. "The point of the season is to prepare for the coming of our Savior as a family. You've become so caught up in the hustle and bustle at the bakery that you've forgotten the point of it all."

Alyssa sniffed as she wiped at her eyes and nose.

"You need to take a step back and think about what's happened during the past few weeks. This is an important part of what makes us Amish: we work hard, but we always make time

for our family and togetherness. Our family is much more important than pleasing customers. Constantly putting family aside
hurts everyone, even when a *freind* needs help. I know Denise
would agree if she realized the toll this is taking." *Dat*'s tone had
warmed along with his expression. "You still have time to prepare
your heart for Christ, but you can't do it if you're rushing around
worrying about Christmas *kichlin*."

Alyssa struggled to keep more threatening tears at bay. "I
never meant to hurt my family."

"We know that." *Mamm* pursed her lips. "But we need you
to start thinking about us now."

Mamm stood and retrieved a bowl from the oven. The spicy
aroma of chili filled the kitchen, causing Alyssa's empty stomach
to growl. Lunch had been several hours ago.

"*Danki*," Alyssa said as *Mamm* set the bowl in front of her.
"My favorite."

Mamm smiled. "I know. I'm going to go help Jenne Lynn finish stamping the Christmas cards." She headed toward the family
room.

"I need to check on the animals." *Dat* stood and started for
the mudroom.

In a flash, both her parents were gone, and Alyssa sat alone
in the kitchen. Her spoon scraping against the bowl as she ate the
delicious chili provided the only sound filling the large room.

Her parents' words rolled over her as crushing guilt pressed
on her shoulders. She'd been so caught up in the excitement of the
window display and the needs at the bakery that she'd forgotten
the most important part of the Christmas season—preparing for
Jesus.

Then her thoughts moved to yesterday, when Kyle stopped

by the bakery. She recalled their quick conversation and how she'd rushed back to the kitchen when he'd suggested they spend time together, putting him off until Sunday to even see her.

Jenne Lynn told her later that Kyle looked upset when he left the bakery. At first Alyssa was confused and didn't understand why he would be angry with her. But then she realized she'd cut their conversation short and all but dismissed him. He must have felt just as forgotten as her family did. How could she expect God to protect their relationship if she wasn't willing to do the same?

Her heart squeezed as her eyes burned with more tears. She had hurt Kyle and she had to make it up to him—not later but now. How could she have done that to her sweet boyfriend? He deserved better. He'd gone out of his way to help her with the cookie nativity, and she had pushed him away in favor of the bakery. The tears spilled at the thought of breaking his heart.

She hoped her family and Kyle would forgive her for her mistakes. She couldn't lose them.

Closing her eyes, she sent up a silent prayer.

God, please forgive me for being too dismissive of the needs of my family and for how I've treated Kyle. Forgive me for neglecting to prepare my heart for the celebration that is Christmas. Help me fix the rift I created between Kyle and me, and please provide a way for me to spend more time with my family and Kyle without leaving Denise in the lurch. Only You can provide the solution I need.

As she opened her eyes, she felt the peace she'd been lacking for weeks. She'd finally turned to God for help, and she knew He would work this out—somehow.

8

"MAY I TAKE A LITTLE BIT OF AN EXTENDED LUNCH TODAY?" Alyssa asked Denise as they stood in the bakery kitchen the next morning.

"Of course." Denise looked over at her. "Why? Or am I being too personal?"

Alyssa fingered her rolling pin as embarrassment crept up her neck. "I just haven't done any Christmas shopping, and I'm running out of time."

Denise looked at her for a moment, then said, "I'm not surprised. You've been working so many extra hours for me." She glanced up at the clock. "It's eleven. Go now."

"Thank you," Alyssa said.

Denise shooed her away with her hand. "Get going while it's relatively quiet."

Alyssa pulled off her apron, and after putting on her coat, she rushed out the back door to the hardware store next door.

———◆———

Later that evening, Alyssa and Jenne Lynn walked up their farm's driveway together.

"*Mamm* and *Dat* will be so *froh* to see us walk in the door together." Jenne Lynn slung her arm over Alyssa's shoulder. "Supper hasn't been the same without you."

"*Danki.*" Alyssa smiled at her younger sister. "I'm glad to be home on time too."

They shucked their coats in the mudroom and then stepped into the kitchen, where the delicious aroma of beef stew tantalized Alyssa's senses.

"Hello," Alyssa sang as she set her shopping bags on the floor by the doorway. *Mamm* gasped at the sight of her. Then Alyssa walked over to the counter and hugged her. "How was your day?"

Mamm laughed. "It was *gut, mei liewe.* How was yours?"

"It was *gut* too." Alyssa walked over to the head of the table and kissed *Dat*'s cheek. "How was yours?"

"Fine." *Dat* raised an eyebrow. "You're awfully chipper."

"I'm just *froh* to be home with my family." Alyssa glanced over at Jenne Lynn, who studied her with something that resembled suspicion. "Do you need help, *Mamm*?"

"No, *danki.*" *Mamm* set the large pot of stew in the center of the table. "I have everything ready, so let's eat."

Alyssa took her usual seat across from her sister and bowed her head in silent prayer. Then she filled her bowl with her mother's amazing stew before smiling at Jenne Lynn.

"What did you buy today, Alyssa?" *Mamm* pointed to the bags in the corner of the kitchen.

"Christmas gifts." Alyssa pinned Jenne Lynn with a glare. "No peeking!"

Jenne Lynn held up her hands. "I won't look. I promise."

"How did you manage to get your shopping done?" *Dat* asked.

"I asked Denise if I could take a longer lunch today, and she agreed." Alyssa set her spoon on her napkin and took a deep breath. It was time for her to say the words she'd been practicing in her head all day. "I'm sorry for losing sight of what's important this time of year." She worked to keep her voice confident despite her swirling anxiety. "I realize now that I was too focused on the busyness of the bakery instead of on our family." She looked at her sister and then at her parents as fresh worry seemed to settle in the pit of her stomach. Was she asking too much? "Will you forgive me?"

"Of course we forgive you." *Mamm* reached over and rubbed Alyssa's shoulder. "We love you."

"Your *mamm* is right," *Dat* added. "You're our *dochder*. You're always forgiven."

"I forgive you too," Jenne Lynn said.

"Danki." Alyssa fought back her raging emotions. "We'll still have a wonderful Christmas."

"That's right." Jenne Lynn swirled her fork through the air, and Alyssa laughed.

"I have exciting news too," Alyssa said. "This afternoon Denise asked her cousin to help at the bakery until the Christmas rush is over—and even through the end of the year because some of her new customers have said they'll want baked goods for New Year's celebrations. Her cousin agreed! That means from now on I'll be home on time." *And it means God answered my prayer!*

Mamm clapped her hands. "That's *wunderbaar.*"

"I'm so *froh*." *Dat* beamed.

After cleaning the kitchen with her mother and sister, Alyssa climbed the stairs to her bedroom and then locked the door. She needed to create Christmas cards to go with her gifts for the family—undisturbed by her curious sister.

She breathed a sigh of relief as she recalled her family's forgiveness at supper. Now she just had to face Kyle. If only he'd be as happy to see her on Christmas Eve as she would be to see him.

Alyssa's hands shook as she stood on Kyle's front porch and knocked on the door. She glanced down at her bag of gifts and hoped he would invite her inside to spend time with him.

Five days had passed since she'd seen him at the bakery, and at church on Sunday he'd busied himself with setting up for lunch and talking with some of the other men. He seemed distant, and they'd hardly spoken. Now she was nervous about seeing him. Not only had she failed to apologize to him at church, but she also hadn't called before she asked her father's driver to take her to his house today. She was praying he'd be more prone to forgiving her on Christmas Eve, even if she didn't deserve it.

The door swung open, and Marietta smiled. "Alyssa!" she announced as she waved her inside. "It's so *gut* to see you."

"*Frehlicher Grischtdaag!*" Alyssa handed Marietta a bag. "I brought something for you and Abram."

"*Danki.*" Marietta pulled out the homemade fudge and box of assorted cookies. "These smell *appeditlich*! This is fantastic." She held out her arms to take Alyssa's coat. "I assume you want to see Kyle."

"*Ya.*" Alyssa hesitated. "Is he available?"

"Of course he is. Come on in." Marietta hung her coat and then walked over to the stairs. "Kyle! You have company!" She gestured toward the sofa. "Please have a seat here in the *schtupp*. He'll be right down."

"*Danki*." Alyssa sat down on the sofa.

"Would you like something to drink?" Marietta offered.

"No, *danki*."

"Okay. Well, please tell me if you change your mind." Marietta turned and walked toward the kitchen.

Soon footfalls echoed in the stairwell, and Alyssa stood. She fiddled with the handles on the bag in her hand as Kyle appeared at the bottom of the stairs. He stopped and studied her as she took in that same handsome face and honey-brown eyes. Her body trembled with worry.

"*Frehlicher Grischtdaag*," she said, her voice quiet and unsure as he studied her.

"Merry Christmas," he echoed in English as he walked over to her. "I didn't expect to see you today."

"I'm so sorry, Kyle." She tried to swallow against the lump in her throat. "The way I treated you at the bakery last week was wrong, and I don't blame you for avoiding me at church on Sunday. I never meant to hurt you. But I was so caught up in the craziness at the bakery that I lost sight of what Christmas is about. I've been taught it's about preparing for the coming of our Savior. About spending time with our family and remembering to thank God for all our blessings. About spending time with everyone we care about, but . . ."

He nodded, but his expression remained unconvinced, perhaps doubting her sincerity. Could she blame him?

"Please listen to me." She closed the distance between them and placed her hand on his chest. "My parents made me realize how lost I was. *Mei mamm*, Jenne Lynn, and I traditionally make our Christmas cards together, bake together, and shop together, but I missed out on all those things. Worse, I was forgetting Christ. And I failed to ask God to show me how He wanted me to help Denise. I also failed to honestly let her know all those extra hours were taking a toll."

She paused. "It's taken a toll on our relationship too. But you're important to me, Kyle, and I can't stand the thought of losing you."

His eyes seemed to warm as he looked down at her, spurring her on.

"I'm here to try to make it up to you. You are a blessing in my life, and I'm so thankful that God brought us together. Please forgive me."

He tilted his head and sighed. "I forgive you. I was never angry with you. I just missed you. Worse, I was afraid you were brushing me off because you regretted agreeing to be my girlfriend."

"That was never true, and I promise I won't put you off again. I very much want to be your girlfriend. And I'm not going to work long hours anymore. I asked God to find a way for me to return to my family and to you without leaving Denise without enough help. That's when Denise asked one of her cousins to fill in at the bakery for a while, and she agreed."

She paused, and then with a tremble in her voice, asked, "Are you sure you forgive me?"

"Yes, I do forgive you, Alyssa." He walked over to a table in the corner and picked up a cardboard box. "I have something for you. Despite my fears, I was going to take it to your *haus* tomorrow."

She smiled as she held up her bag. "I have something for you too."

"*Frehlicher Grischtdaag,*" he said as they exchanged gifts.

She opened the cardboard box and found a metal trinket box

with hearts etched into it. The design matched her candleholder. She opened the lid, and inside was a smaller metal heart.

"Kyle," she said as tears filled her eyes. "This is so *schee*. I love it."

"I'm glad. I thought maybe you could keep your bobby pins in it." He opened his bag of gifts and grinned. "Wow. Alyssa, these are perfect." He pulled out the safety glasses, safety mechanics gloves, and a hammer. "How did you know I needed all these?"

"I didn't." She laughed as she set her gift on the sofa. "I just went to the hardware store and asked the owner for ideas."

"This is exactly what I needed. *Danki*." He set his bag down on the sofa, too, and stepped closer. "This is the best Christmas I've ever had, because you're a part of my life now." He rested his hands on her shoulders. "I've never been happier."

"Neither have I." She gazed up into his eyes. "I'm so grateful that I can celebrate Christmas with you."

He lifted her chin with the tip of his finger and then kissed her. She looped her arms around his neck as euphoria flooded her body at the sensation of his touch.

When he broke the kiss, he leaned his forehead against hers. "*Ich liebe dich*, Alyssa."

Her eyes misted over at his words. "I love you, too, Kyle."

"*Frehlicher Grischtdaag, mei liewe*," he said.

As he pulled her in for a warm hug, she savored her overwhelming happiness and silently thanked God for bringing her someone to love. Kyle had made this Christmas so very special.

DISCUSSION QUESTIONS

1. Alyssa's Christmas family traditions include creating Christmas cards, baking, and shopping, all with her sister and mother. What Christmas traditions do you have in your family?

2. Kyle is hurt when Alyssa is too busy at the bakery to talk to him. Alyssa, however, is so caught up in her work that she doesn't realize she hurt his feelings until her sister mentions that he looked upset when he left. Have you ever inadvertently hurt someone's feelings? If so, did you apologize and make amends? How did that turn out?

3. Alyssa's parents are frustrated with the amount of time she's spending at the bakery. Do you think their feelings are valid? Why or why not?

4. Which character can you identify with the most? Which character seemed to carry the most emotional stake in the story? Alyssa, Kyle, Denise, or someone else?

5. At the end of the story, Alyssa realizes she was too caught up in the busyness at the bakery to remember the

true meaning of Christmas. What do you think caused her to realize she'd gone astray?

6. What role did the display window in the bakery play in the relationships throughout the story?

7. Some people may say Christmas has become too commercialized and that too much focus is put on material items instead of preparing for the coming of Christ. What are your thoughts on this issue? Share this with the group.

ACKNOWLEDGMENTS

AS ALWAYS, I'M GRATEFUL FOR MY LOVING FAMILY, INCLUD-ing my mother, Lola Goebelbecker; my husband, Joe; and my sons, Zac and Matt.

Special thanks to my mother and my dear friend Becky Biddy, who graciously proofread the draft and corrected my hilarious typos.

I'm also grateful for my special Amish friend who patiently answers my endless stream of questions. You're a blessing in my life.

Thank you to my wonderful church family at Morning Star Lutheran in Matthews, North Carolina, for your encourage-ment, prayers, love, and friendship. You all mean so much to my family and me.

Thank you to Zac Weikal and the fabulous members of my Bakery Bunch! I'm so grateful for your friendship and your excitement about my books. You all are awesome!

To my agent, Natasha Kern—I can't thank you enough for your guidance, advice, and friendship. You are a tremendous blessing in my life.

Thank you to my amazing editor, Jocelyn Bailey, for your

friendship and guidance. I'm grateful to every person at HarperCollins Christian Publishing who helped make this book a reality.

I'm grateful to editor Jean Bloom, who helped me polish and refine the story. Jean, you are a master at connecting the dots and filling in the gaps. I'm so happy we can continue to work together!

Thank you most of all to God—for giving me the inspiration and the words to glorify You. I'm grateful and humbled You've chosen this path for me.

LOAVES
OF LOVE

BETH WISEMAN

To Daddy

1

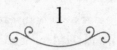

KATIE SWARTZENTRUBER SMILED AS SEVERAL *ENGLISCH* women browsed the various pies, loaves of bread, and cinnamon rolls she baked this morning. She'd topped the oval table with a freshly pressed white cloth, then carefully arranged the baked goods for sale.

Even though pride was frowned upon, Katie swelled with satisfaction over her accomplishments. She'd worked alongside her mother at their bakery for as long as she could remember, but this was the first day she had prepared everything on her own.

Her mother had surgery three days ago, and they'd made arrangements in advance for someone to help Katie. The hysterectomy and her mother's recovery went as planned. The procedure was necessary because of some tumors growing in her uterus. After returning to work yesterday, complications arose when she got a nasty infection at the incision site. It weakened her mother so much that the doctor insisted she stop working and rest to give herself time to heal, which he warned might not happen until after Christmas.

This meant Katie would be in charge of the shop—doing all

the regular baking, taking orders, and filling them—during their busiest time of year. Help was hard to find during the holidays, especially on such short notice. Katie had to convince her parents not to close, because she could run the bakery on her own. The first day had gone off without a hitch so far, but it was only eleven. She'd started at four o'clock, an hour earlier than she and her mother usually arrived, and she'd managed to open at the regular time, eight o'clock. There had been a few customers, and when her stomach began to growl, she looked at the clock on the wall and sighed, knowing she would have to cancel her lunch plans.

In a family of eight, Katie was the only girl. Three of her brothers were still in school, and the two older ones tended the land and worked construction part-time. They would be no help in the kitchen at home or here at the bakery, so the task was Katie's to fulfill.

"There are no better pies anywhere in the area," one of the older women whispered to her friend. "The fried raisin pie is my favorite, but you can't go wrong with apple or peach either. I usually get raisin for me and apple for Pete."

The individually wrapped fried pies were the biggest sellers, and some of the locals came every Saturday just for them. Tourists frequented her family's bakery, too, even though they were located in a remote area near Orleans. Word of mouth had spread, and folks often pointed visitors their way.

Katie opened the firebox a little to add warmth to the room since she didn't have to worry about maintaining the oven temperature right now. She would see how the morning fared before she baked anything else. Hopefully the weather wouldn't keep folks away. The snow was heavier than normal for this time of year, and even more had accumulated overnight. Thanksgiving was in three days, and business usually came with a big boom during this week. Sales would increase and remain strong through Christmas.

One of the ladies picked up a loaf of bread enclosed in plastic wrap, adding to the two fried pies she carried, then she joined her friend at another table against the far wall. They thumbed through crocheted pot holders, baby bibs, and other items for sale.

"Hon, did you make all of these?" The taller woman, whom Katie had seen before, lifted a green-and-white checked pot holder.

"*Mei mamm* and I made everything on the table." She smiled at the customer, eager to see how much the women would buy.

Katie's parents were skeptical that she could run the bakery by herself, but she'd assured them she could. An increase in sales would further prove that she was capable and could handle the workload.

As she waited for the women to make their selections, Henry Hershberger pulled up in his buggy. Through the window, she watched him tether his horse. His straw hat had been replaced with a black knitted cap, and he wore a big black coat. She could see his teeth chattering and wondered what brought him out in this weather. He may have a battery-operated heater in his buggy, but it was still too cold to be out. Even though Henry had practically grown up in the bakery, he seldom stopped in these days. He had a full-time job at the hardware store that also required him to work on the weekends sometimes. She was surprised he picked such a blustery day to visit.

Katie had known Henry since they were born. They had the same birthday and just turned twenty-one on August 17. Their families had always been close, and Katie helped Henry learn

Englisch when they started school. He'd had a hard time transitioning from Pennsylvania *Deitsch* to *Englisch*, especially when they started learning to read and write.

Henry was shy too. Even as a child, Katie never understood why. He was the cutest boy in school, and she was happy to spend her free time with him—and not just because of his mesmerizing blue-gray eyes and nice smile. Henry was kind and generous, especially to Katie. He carried her books when they walked to school together, and he always traded lunches with her when her mother sent something she didn't care for.

From the time they were children, Katie had thought their friendship would blossom into something more. She'd wanted him to ask her to a Sunday singing since they became teenagers, but he never had. Despite her attempts to flirt with him, Henry must not want to be anything more than friends, or so she was left to assume.

They were adults now, but Katie's heart still skipped a beat every time she saw him. The cute boy had grown into a handsome man. He was taller than most men, and his massive shoulders filled the heavy coat he was wearing. He had dark hair, and his eyes changed colors with the seasons. This time of year, they would be a bluish gray. In the spring, when the sun was full, they would brighten to more of a Nordic blue.

Katie and Henry had dated other people within their district and remained friends. With each person Katie dated, she hoped it would quell the affection she felt for Henry. Then maybe it wouldn't sting so much every time she heard he was seeing someone new.

———◆———

Henry brushed snow off himself under the awning outside the bakery. He'd made up his mind a couple weeks ago that he was going to ask Katie out on a date. Henry had dated on and off, and he'd even taken a woman to supper recently, but he continued to compare anyone he dated to Katie. He had to know, once and for all, if she harbored any feelings for him beyond friendship. Over the last two weeks, every time he headed to the bakery he lost his nerve and kept the horse going.

When they were kids, he and Katie did things together all the time, but when Katie grew into the prettiest teenager—and now woman—in their district, Henry had put some distance between them. She could have her pick of any eligible man in their community. Somewhere along the line, he'd become nervous and insecure around her. Today he was going to push past his fear and finally ask her out.

He took a deep breath, pulled off his black beanie, and walked into the bakery. Katie was accepting money from two older ladies, so Henry pulled off his gloves and began eyeing the items on the table. His mouth watered as he breathed in the aroma of freshly baked bread and pastries.

"What a nice surprise to see you, Henry," Katie said after the two women left. Then she stepped from behind the counter and smiled that same smile that won him over years ago. As she walked toward him, he was pretty sure she batted her eyes at him. Or maybe he read too much into it. Either way, he felt the familiar nervousness building, and he was determined not to let it get the best of him.

Henry saw Katie every two weeks at worship service, but he stayed with the other men while the women prepared the meal. There wasn't time to do more than greet each other in passing.

Although, he'd been tempted more than once to pull her aside and invite her to go out with him.

"It's nice to see you too." He continued looking at the baked goods, buying some time as she walked to where he was standing. He'd planned out exactly what he wanted to say, but now that he was here, his mind was hazy.

"You can have whatever you like." Katie nodded at the table of goodies.

He shook his head. "*Nee*, I'll pay." He wanted to tell her that she looked pretty, that her dark-green dresses brought out the color of her eyes. Instead, he reached into his coat pocket and found three dollars.

Katie brushed flour off her black apron. "You know if *Mamm* were here, she would never let you pay."

Henry knew she was right. He went through this drill with Katie's mother every time he visited the bakery over the years. Marie Swartzentruber always won the argument.

Katie smiled as she swiped at a loose strand of sandy-blonde hair that had fallen from her *kapp*. She was tall for a woman, which was another thing he liked about her. If Henry had to guess, he'd say she was close to six feet. He was six feet, five inches tall. Some of the women he'd dated didn't even reach his shoulder, which wasn't enough to rule out a relationship. It just hadn't worked out. Katie's height was a bonus in a perfect package that owned Henry's heart. If she declined his offer to go out, he would have to do his best to open his heart to someone else.

He held the money out to her, the same way he always did with her mother. "Take it. Your folks are counting on you to keep things afloat. You can't be giving away food."

"I'm not *giving* it to anyone but you." She stuffed her hands in her apron pockets, and Henry shrugged as he put the money back in his wallet.

"*Ach*, okay." He grabbed a fried peach pie. He wanted raisin, but there was only one left and he knew how popular they were with the tourists.

"Is that all you want, one pie? It's awfully cold outside to make a trip for one small pie." She raised an eyebrow and grinned. Henry wasn't sure if she was being friendly or flirting.

"It's not just any pie. You and your *mamm* make the best pastries, so it's worth the trip." He pulled back the plastic wrap and took a bite, savoring the flavor, as a new customer walked inside. Henry wanted to kick himself. He'd had less than a minute alone with Katie, and he'd talked about food instead of asking her out.

"Welcome." Katie waved an arm toward the two tables. "Thank you for coming. Everything was baked fresh this morning."

"This place is hard to find." The woman's teeth chattered as she spoke. She wore high-heeled shoes instead of warm boots. Her tan jacket looked more like a fancy accessory than something to keep her warm. And she had no hat.

"I'm glad you found us." Katie smiled as she folded her hands in front of her.

Frowning, the woman pointed a long red fingernail at the table with the breads and pastries. "Is that all you've got?"

"*Ya*, that's all I have for right now, but I take orders too."

The woman's expression softened a little as she shook snow from her white hair. Or maybe it was blonde. It didn't look like a natural color.

The lady narrowed her sculpted eyebrows into a frown. "Are you the only one working here?"

"*Ya*, I am. But I work long hours and can handle a large order. I can bake most anything you might need."

As the woman dug around in her purse, Katie waited patiently.

"Okay. I have a list." The woman slipped on a pair of red reading glasses as she studied the piece of paper. "I need two pecan pies, two apple, and a dozen fried pastries, a variety. And three loaves of bread—two sourdough and one white." She pushed the glasses up on top of her head. "I need to pick it all up by five o'clock tomorrow." The woman scratched her head, sending more snowflakes to the floor. "Is that where you bake them?" She pointed to the two wood ovens behind Katie. "Won't they taste smoky?"

Henry was sure Katie had fielded this question before, but he cleared his throat and waited until the lady looked his way before he spoke. "These are the tastiest fried pies you'll ever eat, better than the bakeries in town. I reckon part of the reason is because Katie uses wood ovens, not propane like other places. It's a distinctive flavor, but not smoky at all."

The woman turned back to Katie. "Don't you need to write down my order?"

"*Nee*, I've got it." Katie walked to the table, picked up the last raisin pie, and handed it to the lady. "Please, take this and try it."

Henry hoped Katie wasn't going to give away any more food, but the woman was placing a big order.

"No thanks. I don't eat sweets. But the herd coming for Thanksgiving will expect pies." The woman grimaced, then smiled a little for the first time. "I love them all, but they eat a lot." Shivering, she rubbed her hands together. "This is my first trip to Indiana. My sister relocated here with her family recently and invited everyone for the holidays. I could never live here, though. It's just too cold."

"You get used to it," Henry said. Southern Indiana enjoyed all four seasons. Even though Henry had never lived anywhere else, he loved that about his home state.

Katie set the pie back on the table and confirmed the order, promising to have everything ready on time. The lady was out the door again. They watched through the window as the woman stumbled to her car with her arms out to her side. It had to be difficult to keep her balance in the snow while wearing those high-heeled shoes.

"Can you really do all that by five tomorrow?" Henry rubbed his chin, thinking about all the other pastries she and her mother made daily.

She grinned. "*Ya*, I can have it ready by noon tomorrow, but just in case another big order comes in, I thought I better play it safe."

With half a pie in his hand, Henry decided he wasn't going to make the same mistake twice. He had promised himself that today was the day. He set the pie on the table and begged his pulse to slow down. He reminded himself that all she could do was say no, and they'd still be friends.

As he opened his mouth, the door swung open again, bringing inside another burst of cold air. They both turned, and a man Henry didn't recognize swaggered in. He was Amish, but not from their district. He was wearing black slacks, but they had pockets in the front, and his black running shoes had a checkmark on the side. Bishop Troyer only allowed black boots or standard black shoes that were selected by the elders. And they couldn't have pockets.

"You ready?" he asked, never even looking at Henry.

Katie cringed. "*Ach*, I can't go to dinner. I'm so sorry you made the trip. *Mei* cousin, Ella, was supposed to watch the bakery while we went to eat. She lives nearby, but she sent word this morning that her *dochder* is sick."

The man was older than Henry. He didn't know how much older, but the little bit of gray at his temples, along with a few lines feathering from the corners of his eyes, suggested he might be in his midthirties. His face was clean-shaven. Henry supposed the man was nice looking, although he wasn't sure he was a very good judge. *Why isn't he already married?*

The guy pulled a phone out of his pocket and held it out toward Katie. "I told you I'd get you one of these."

Katie's cheeks turned pink. "*Ya*, I know, and I appreciate your offer. But like I told you before, cell phones aren't allowed in our district."

Henry didn't want to encourage whatever was going on right now, but he did want to endear himself to Katie. He could plan out what he wanted to say when she returned. Feeling invisible, he cleared his throat again. "I can watch the bakery while you go eat."

Katie gave her head a quick shake. "Where are *mei* manners?" She introduced Henry to the man named David, then said, "I can't let you do that, Henry. I'm sure you have things to do."

Henry had the day off since he'd worked on Saturday. He wasn't sure when he'd be off again, and he could lose his nerve between now and then. A part of him wanted to bolt, to go home and lick his wounds. But maybe he would find out more about David when Katie returned. Perhaps it wasn't a romantic relationship. "I don't mind. Consider the pie as payment."

She smiled. "*Danki*. I'll be back in thirty or forty-five minutes." Maybe she had some sort of business with this man. But as

David put his hand on her back when they went out the door, Henry was pretty sure he'd just met his competition. Katie had dated guys in their district before, and it stung every time he found out she was being courted by someone new. None of them had given Henry too much concern since he didn't think any of them were a good fit for her. This man wasn't from their community. Henry should have known someone would come along—from another district—and steal her heart, eventually.

I waited too long.

2

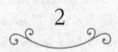

KATIE FINISHED HER BURGER AND FRIES IN RECORD TIME. Ella had filled in for Katie and her mother lots of times since she lived so close and didn't have a job outside the home. But how would Henry handle an onslaught of customers?

"Don't they feed you at home?" David grinned as he winked at her. Her date was incredibly handsome. She smiled at him, noticing the clear-cut lines of his profile and the way his coal black hair curled forward and backward, flattened on top where his hat had been.

"*Ach*, I'm sorry," she said. "I'm nervous about leaving Henry for too long." *Henry*. Now she would think about him for days, then have to reaccept the fact that he wasn't interested in her romantically. Then her emotions would eventually settle down until the next time he showed up, and another onslaught of feelings would bombard her again.

"Is he a relative?" David dipped a French fry in ketchup, took a bite, and waited for her to answer.

"*Nee*. He's a friend. We've grown up together. Our families are close." Katie tried to smile. She wasn't being fair to David by harboring feelings for Henry. She'd been doing pretty good until he came to the bakery today.

David nodded before eating another fry. Katie wondered if there was anything about Henry that made David jealous, but he kept eating and didn't mention Henry again. Katie didn't either. She didn't want David to be jealous. She was trying hard to give their relationship a chance to begin. This was the third time he'd picked her up for the noon meal, and she'd enjoyed herself each time.

David put his hat back on after he finished his burger and downed the rest of his root beer. Then he asked the waitress for the check. Katie had offered to split the bill after their first two lunch dates, but he'd declined the offers, so she didn't say anything this time.

She thanked David for dinner on their way back to the bakery. She had enjoyed her first two lunches with him more than today. She wasn't sure if it was solely because she'd left the bakery. Was just seeing Henry enough to distract her so much?

David lived near Shoals, and once a week he traveled to Orleans to pick up supplies for the roofing company he worked for. Katie recalled their first encounter, the day they'd met while waiting in line at the supermarket. They'd struck up a conversation about the weather that had led to a first date. She'd noticed the way his mouth curled up slightly on one side as he talked, almost like he was happy all the time. But it was a physical trait that hid the truth. She found out during their first dinner that David hadn't been happy for a long time. His follow-up words had been, "Until now, since I met you." She prayed he would be the one to shift her feelings away from Henry.

"Are you warm enough?" David reached for the heavy wool

blanket he'd draped around her shoulders and tucked it closer to her neck.

"*Ya*, I am." His dark eyes were masked in a serious expression in contrast to his half smile, which gave him a mysterious edge.

Light snow fell as they turned on the road to the bakery, and anticipation swirled in her stomach. She wished her anxiousness was based on whether or not David would ask her out again or how the bakery had fared during her absence. If she were truthful with herself, the swirling in her stomach was more about seeing Henry.

David slowed the horse after they'd turned, gently pulling back on the reins until the animal settled into a steady trot.

"I-I want to ask you something, but I'm not sure how you'll feel about it." David brought the horse to a stop at the bakery entrance, then twisted to face her. "*Mei mamm* has invited us to supper on Saturday. She takes the leftover turkey from Thanksgiving and makes it into a stew. It's kind of a family tradition. I know we've only been to dinner three times, and if it feels too soon for something like that, I won't hold it against you if you say no." Grinning, he shrugged. "But I like you, and you have to eat."

Katie knew it was a bigger deal than David was making it out to be. He'd told her that his only girlfriend died a month before they were going to be married. That was six years ago, and he hadn't dated anyone since. Katie wanted to bring him the happiness he deserved after going through such a tragedy.

"I'd love to meet your family." She folded her gloved fingers into his when he reached for her hand, then he leaned closer and kissed her on the cheek.

After discussing the plans for Saturday, Katie hurried beneath the awning, turned to wave, then rushed into the warmth of the bakery. Henry was sitting behind the counter with a clear view out the window and a scowl on his face.

Had something gone wrong while she'd been gone? Or was he unhappy to see David kiss her on the cheek?

As wrong as it was, Katie hoped for the latter.

———◆———

"How was dinner?" Henry forced a smile as he put his palms on the counter. His stomach churned, and it wasn't because he was hungry.

"It was *gut*." Katie came around the counter, took off her gloves, and stood next to him. "*Danki* for watching the place for me." She put a hand on his, which caused him to tense beneath her touch. She must have mistaken his reaction as unease since she took her hand away abruptly. "I-I appreciate it so much."

"*Ya*, you're welcome." He wanted to tell her that just the feel of her hand on his caused his pulse to pick up.

"Did everything go okay while I was gone? Any customers?"

"*Ya*, two ladies came in and bought some fried pies. One of them chose the last raisin pie. No problems, though."

An awkward silence followed as Henry pondered whether he should question Katie about her relationship with David. Was it serious? How long had it been going on? Or were they just friends? A kiss on the cheek seemed pretty friendly to Henry.

He lifted himself from the stool and rubbed his chin, wondering why this man in Katie's life was causing him such grief. Was it because he'd seen her being intimate with him? Knowledge of her other dates only played out as unpleasant scenes in his mind. Seeing her with this guy was different, more real, and felt like a significant threat. Henry had gone to great lengths to convince himself that now was the time to test the waters with Katie. That opportunity felt lost all of a sudden.

"Is something wrong?" Katie raised an eyebrow as she folded her arms across her chest and looked up at him. Her expression was a bit challenging, or maybe defensive.

He wanted to tell her that it upset him to see another man kiss her, even if it was just on the cheek. But he didn't have a right to tell her anything. He was the one at fault and should have told her how he felt a long time ago. If she'd rejected him, he could have forced himself to let go of his feelings for her. If that was possible. "*Nee*, I'm fine."

"I guess I better get back to work." She nodded to the half-empty table of pastries. "I need to make more pies for today and also work on that woman's order." She picked up two pieces of wood, added them to the firebox, and stoked the flames with a poker she kept nearby.

Henry was being dismissed, and after putting his nerves through a meat grinder, he still hadn't asked her out. Maybe it wasn't too late to throw his name into the hat. He shifted his weight and opened his mouth to force the words out, but Katie was already gathering bowls, flour, and a rolling pin, placing each item on the large counter behind her.

"Guess I'll see you around." Henry pulled on his black beanie, covering his ears, as he looked out the window at a fresh round of snow falling. He shuffled toward the door, hauling his defeated ego like a sled behind him.

"You could wait until the snow slows down."

He turned around and tried to decipher her intentions. His well-being? Or did she want to spend more time with him?

"I've got coffee." She smiled at him over her shoulder as she poured flour into a big bowl.

"*Ya*, sure." The snow was predicted to get worse, but something in Katie's eyes gave him enough hope to want to stay a little longer. He sat on one of three bar stools in front of the glass counter and pulled off his hat.

Katie stopped kneading the dough and put the bowl on the other counter, then poured two cups of coffee.

"*Danki.*" He sipped the warm beverage and watched the snow falling in blankets now. He took a deep breath and decided that asking her out wasn't off the agenda, but he wanted to know more about the guy she was dating before he decided for sure. "Have you been seeing David long?"

Her eyes met his right away. "Uh, *nee*. That was our third dinner." She stared at him as if waiting for him to comment. When he didn't, she refocused on the rising dough and dug her hands in. Maybe Henry wasn't defeated yet.

"Saturday, it's supposed to be warmer, and I've got to go shoe two horses at the Troyer place." His heart thumped in his chest. "Maybe, if you'd like to ride along, we could get dinner afterward."

There. He'd surprised himself and done it. Now it was Henry who was holding his breath as Katie looked across the counter at him and smiled. He knew a forced smile when he saw one, and he braced himself for the rejection he knew was coming.

———— ◈ ————

Katie couldn't tell if Henry was asking her out on a date or just asking a friend to keep him company. She'd been waiting for years for him to ask her out, and she wanted to jump on the opportunity. Then she remembered David.

"I'm sorry." She lowered her eyes and began kneading the bread, knowing she would have to toss this batch if she worked it anymore. "I'm meeting David's family on Saturday." She glanced up just in time to see Henry wince, and it warmed her heart to think he might be jealous, as awful as the thought was.

"I guess it must be serious." He pulled out his wool cap and put it on again.

"Uh . . ." Katie's emotions swirled and collided as she tried to figure out a way to cancel her date with David. It was an about-face, and she wasn't proud that the idea had come into her mind. She refocused her thoughts on doing the right thing.

Katie owed it to David to see where things were going. She'd sensed it had been hard for him to take that big step—to ask her to meet his family. As she stared into Henry's eyes, she just couldn't tell what his intentions were. She remembered Henry's scowl when she'd first returned from dinner. But maybe she'd read his expression wrong. She settled for the truth. "I think it's too soon to tell if it's serious. It's only been three dates."

Henry stood and pulled on a pair of black gloves. "Meeting the family sounds serious."

Katie searched his face again, but he wasn't giving away any hints about his feelings. Meeting the family did sound serious, even to her. Maybe she should have declined the invitation, but at the time, she really didn't have a reason to. Just because Henry had shown up today didn't mean she should let his presence dictate her decisions. He'd had a long time to ask her out, and he hadn't. She was trying to move forward and give things a chance with her and David. "I don't know," she said softly as she avoided his eyes.

"I guess I'll see you around. Have a nice Thanksgiving." He rushed toward the door.

"You too," she whispered, unsure if he'd even heard her.

She went to the table with the pies, chose a peach one, and pulled off the wrapper, then ate a large bite. After she'd soothed herself with sugar, she thought about God's perfect timing. Henry's timing certainly wasn't perfect. His attempt to spend time with her couldn't have come at a worse time. She might still think about him a lot and what might have been, but David was a nice man who cared enough about her to introduce her to his family.

Every time she resolved things in her mind, her heart bucked up against her, urging her to find out if there could be something more between her and Henry.

As she stared out the window, she reached for another fried pie.

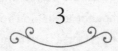

KATIE WAS STEPPING OUT WITH SOMEONE FROM ANOTHER district. Maybe Henry needed to broaden his search as well and quit pining about what might have been. Or did he owe it to himself to give it another try with Katie? Maybe wait and see what happened with her and David?

Thanksgiving had come and gone. Henry was glad to be off today since he'd worked last Saturday. Except, now he had idle time to torture himself even more with thoughts of Katie and David together. This was the slow time of year, following the harvest, and as he lounged on the couch, he wished he had something to keep him busy. He'd gone to shoe the two horses at the Troyers' place early this morning, but that hadn't taken long.

Lena walked into the living room carrying a box filled with Christmas decorations. His family always ran a strand of garland across the fireplace mantel during the Christmas season, and his mother had three small angels that would adorn the space as well. They never had a tree like the *Englisch*, but presents would begin to pop up here and there, wrapped and stacked in various places in the house. Henry hoped the festive decorations might lift his mood.

His sister sat beside him on the couch. She was only a year younger than Henry. At twenty, Lena still didn't have any prospects for marriage, at least none she was considering. She had been courted by nearly every available man in the district and turned down two marriage proposals.

"How is Katie doing, running the bakery by herself? I wish I could have helped while her *mudder* recuperates. But I'd already committed to volunteer at the women's shelter." She paused, cutting her eyes at Henry. "I'm guessing you didn't ask her out earlier in the week, or I would have heard about it." Lena and Henry confided in each other since they were the closest in age. Henry's four brothers were younger and all still in school.

He relaxed his shoulders and flicked at the straps of his suspenders until they dropped to his sides. "She's busy at the bakery, but she seems to be handling it. And *ya*, I did ask her out. It was an informal invitation, but she declined. She's seeing someone, a man from another district. She already had plans with him."

His sister clicked her tongue as she pointed a finger at him. "I'm sorry, but you should have asked her out long before now."

Henry didn't need another reminder, so he just stayed quiet.

"But . . ." His sister grinned. "I have someone I'd like you to meet."

"*Nee.*" Henry groaned as he shook his head. "I'm not interested in being fixed up." He kicked his socked feet up on the coffee table as he laid his head back and closed his eyes.

Lena nudged him with her shoulder. "Well, you're going to meet her anyway because she's coming for dinner today."

Henry opened his eyes and glared at his sister. "I won't be here. I already ate."

Lena pressed her lips together and shot him a thin-lipped smile. "I suggest you go change clothes. She'll be here in a few minutes. It's interesting that Katie is seeing someone from another district, because our dinner guest isn't from around here either. She is a cousin of Mattie Glick. Her name is Clara Zook, and I think you will like her."

Henry glanced down at his white undershirt, then frowned at his sister. "There's nothing worse than a blind date." He grunted. "And what if Katie had accepted my invitation? Your match-making plan wouldn't have worked."

Lena's shoulders slumped as she bit her lip for a few seconds. "True, but I was willing to chance it based on your history with Katie. You should make yourself available and look forward to meeting someone new."

"I'm not sure you're the one who should be counseling me about relationships." He nudged her with his shoulder. "No offense. But you've gone out with just about everyone in our district, and you're still single."

"I'm the perfect person to talk to you about this. I'm waiting for the right person. He's out there, and I don't plan to settle." She tucked a leg underneath herself and twisted to face him. "And you shouldn't either. What if you've thought Katie was the one for you all this time, but it hasn't come to pass, because she's *not* the right person for you?" She touched his arm. "Please. I've never meddled in your love life or tried to set you up before because I wouldn't want you doing that to me. But I feel strongly that you might hit it off with Clara. And she is anxious to meet you. It will be embarrassing for me if you disappear and don't join us."

Henry grunted again, then slowly rose to his feet.

"Keep an open mind. Clara is a beautiful woman," Lena said as he shuffled across the living room toward the stairs.

He'd do this for his sister, but his thoughts would be on Katie. And David. The latter causing his stomach to churn. He wondered how it was going.

———◆———

Katie sat across from David in his parents' dining room. It was odd to have only four people at a family meal. Katie was used to her family of eight eating together, but David was an only child. He lived in the *daadi haus*, the smaller house on the back of the property usually reserved for grandparents. If he married, he would likely take over this main house, and his parents would move to his place.

Katie glanced toward the kitchen, which resembled an *Englisch* kitchen. There was a full-sized refrigerator, a shiny white gas range on top of the oven, marble countertops, shiny wood floors, and decorative curtains adorning the windows. David told her the refrigerator and oven were powered with propane. Katie thought about the ice blocks they collected from their neighbor to keep food cold. She and her mother cooked in a wood oven at home, just like at the bakery. She wished she could open every cabinet and drawer to see what other fancy gadgets David's mother might have. Outside, she'd noticed solar panels that David said his father used for his power tools in the barn.

What if her relationship with David progressed? Would she be expected to embrace the modern technology that so many other Amish communities had succumbed to? She'd been raised to live as simply as possible.

After David's mother placed a loaf of bread on the table, she took her seat across from her husband, and they lowered their heads to say the blessing.

"It's so lovely to have you in our home, Katie." David's mother smiled. "We've heard a lot about you."

"*Danki* for having me." Katie wondered what David had told them about her. After three dinners, he knew she and her mother worked at a bakery, and it seemed obvious that he was attracted to her. But there was still so much they didn't know about each other.

Had he told his parents that her Old Order district was much more conservative than his? They probably assumed, since Katie's last name was Swartzentruber and she lived in Orleans. Old Order Amish groups as conservative as Katie's were often referred to as Swartzentruber Amish, even if a person didn't share the last name.

"Katie's running her family's bakery while her mother recovers from surgery." David reached for a slice of roast beef that had been making Katie's mouth water since she sat down.

"I'm sure this is a busy time of year for you," Caroline said, smiling.

"*Ya*, it is. *Mei* cousin, Ella, is watching the bakery so I could be here today." Katie hoped Ella wasn't having any problems. Katie had been able to keep up with the orders throughout the previous week, but she worried what she might walk into when she returned later. Ella had her six-year-old daughter with her, which would slow down production. Especially Ella's daughter, who was precious as she could be, but a bit hyper. Even so, Katie was grateful her cousin could help for a while.

"And how is your *mudder* doing?" Caroline took a small bite of peas before she raised an eyebrow.

"*Gut*. She is getting better each day." Katie thanked God for that often.

The remainder of the meal was filled with small talk about everything from the weather to what kind of crops they would plant in the spring. In addition to David's roofing job, his family farmed hay. Katie explained that her family grew only corn, while she and her mother kept a large vegetable garden.

David's father gave a courtesy nod of agreement from time to time but was mostly quiet. David didn't contribute much to the conversation either. Caroline kept the continuous line of questioning rolling forward with barely a pause.

"I've heard Bishop Lehman is very strict." Caroline glanced at her husband, but Enos didn't look up at her. He was busy cutting into a slice of roast beef.

"*Ya*, I suppose he is stricter than most." Katie liked Bishop Lehman. He might be strict, but he was fair. Then it occurred to her that, despite Caroline's politeness, she might not be in favor of her son choosing to date Katie. It was uncommon for the Amish to intermarry with someone from a more liberal district, due to the differences in their beliefs and lifestyles. Not that marriage had been mentioned in the short time she'd known David. But she was aware of at least one couple from vastly different districts who had married.

"I just can't imagine using a wood oven to cook." Caroline smiled as she tipped her head slightly to the side. "I'm surprised he hasn't bent that rule to allow some of the technology upgrades that other districts have embraced."

Katie dabbed at her mouth with her napkin as she tried to

buy herself some time. Her parents had stressed the need to stay detached from the outside world. They'd also explained that with every new piece of technology that was introduced and allowed, eventually they'd be no different from the *Englisch*. Katie thought it would be rude to tell that to Caroline. Her heart raced as she struggled to come up with a response.

"*Mamm*, quit interrogating Katie." David grinned at Katie as he spoke. Then shot his mother a smile as well.

Caroline chuckled. "Katie, *mei sohn* doesn't mince words, does he? I hope I haven't made you uncomfortable. I'm just curious about how other communities live, especially since we don't live very far from you."

Katie had been uncomfortable from the moment she walked into the Hostetlers' fancy house. The dinner conversation had only increased the feeling.

"*Nee*, not at all." She said a quick prayer and asked God to forgive the white lie. Meeting the parents under normal circumstances, following a much longer courtship, induced enough nervousness on its own. This meeting seemed too soon, and the family home was so different from what Katie was used to. Caroline's questions weren't helping.

After everyone finished the main meal, Caroline served peach cobbler with homemade vanilla ice cream. Katie savored every bite. She never had ice cream at home because it was too hard to keep frozen in the icebox.

"*Mamm*, *danki* for the great meal, but I should probably get Katie back to the bakery." David wiped his mouth with his napkin and stood.

Katie did the same. "*Ya*, Caroline, it was a wonderful meal, and it was very nice to meet you both."

David's parents stood as well and walked them to the door.

"We hope to see more of you," Enos said.

Katie nodded, thanked them again, and went with David to the buggy. She was grateful it wasn't snowing and the afternoon sun was warming things up.

"Your parents are nice." Katie pulled the blanket around herself when they turned onto the main highway and picked up the pace.

David glanced her way, grinning. "*Ya*, they're all right." He paused. "Do you have time to make a quick detour? I want to show you something."

Katie really didn't want to make Ella stay at the bakery any longer than necessary, but she supposed being a little late might be okay. "I-I can't leave Ella for too long."

"It's only about five or ten minutes out of the way."

"Where are we going?" She hoped it wasn't somewhere they would be alone. As it was, he was a little too affectionate for Katie's taste so early into their relationship.

He flicked the reins and picked up speed. "I just want to show you something."

"Show me what?" She playfully nudged his shoulder.

He glanced her way again, smiling broadly now. "You'll see."

As she pondered where David was taking her, she also wondered how Henry was spending his Saturday. Did he shoe the horses at the Troyer place? Did he dine alone? She wished she had gone with him.

4

HENRY'S BROTHERS WERE ALL OUTSIDE. LENA HAD FED them early, and their parents were gone to an auction in Shoals. It was just going to be Lena, Clara, and Henry for dinner—an awkward meal that was an obvious setup. Henry wished he hadn't agreed to this. He'd thought maybe it would stop him from thinking about Katie and David, but so far, the vision of them together continued to race through his mind.

When Clara arrived and was ushered into the den by Lena, Henry burst out laughing. Then Clara chuckled too.

"What's so funny?" Lena raised both eyebrows, looking surprised as she glanced back and forth between her brother and her new friend.

Henry extended his hand to her, and when she accepted his gesture, he put his other hand on top of hers. "*Wie bischt*. It's *gut* to see you." He finally dropped both arms to his sides and grinned. "I thought I'd never see you again."

Lena cleared her throat. "*Ach*, what's happening here? You two know each other?" His sister gave her head a quick shake. "How?"

"Well, not really." Clara laughed again, keeping her eyes on

Henry. "But I never forgot about the time I, uh, bumped into you."

Henry turned to Lena. "It's been a couple years, but Clara and I ran into each other at Dinky's Auction." He laughed again, and so did Clara.

"We literally slammed into each other so hard that we both fell down." Clara looked back and forth between Henry and Lena. "I was running through the crowd back to the table because I had forgotten my auction paddle, and I wanted to bid on some old books that were coming up." She paused and took a breath. "I got my paddle and took off running back to where my friends were." She turned to Henry, smiling. "This man, who I now know to be Henry, came around the corner carrying two trays filled with lots of hot dogs topped with chili, along with chips, drinks, and I don't know what else. But the timing couldn't have been worse. I knocked everything out of his hands."

Lena put her hands on her hips and laughed. "Well, I can see you must have had fun during your little mishap."

Clara held up a finger. "*Ach*, but here's what made it so memorable." She cut her eyes at Henry, grinning. "We were both covered in chili, and in all the commotion, when we got up, I threw my hands in the air." She mimicked the memory with her arms. "When my hands went up, so did my paddle." Laughing again, she finally caught her breath. "Those auctioneers are very unforgiving. If your hand is the last to go up, you own whatever it is you bid on."

Henry couldn't stop laughing.

Still giggling, Clara added, "And I became the proud owner of a portable generator for three hundred and fifty dollars."

Lena gasped. "Oh, *nee*. What did you do?"

"I had to call *mei daed*. *Mei* friends and I couldn't come up with that much money." She turned to Henry. "After I got cleaned up and paid for my new generator"—she paused, blushing—"I looked for you."

Henry couldn't take his eyes off her. She was so animated when she talked, and he'd always wondered what happened to her. He'd looked for her for over an hour. "I tried to find you too. But there are always hundreds of people at Dinky's."

"I didn't even know your name." Clara put a hand to her chest, smiling sweetly. "And now I do."

Lena let out an exaggerated sigh. "Goodness! What a story. And everything happens according to *Gott*'s plan." She folded her hands in front of her. "And here you both are."

Here we both are. Henry couldn't wipe the smile off his face even if he wanted to. He'd thought she was pretty when they knocked each other off their feet, even covered in chili. But he didn't recall her being this lovely. Her big, brown doe eyes grew even larger as she'd enthusiastically told the story, and her smile was flawless.

"Well, let's eat." Lena motioned for Clara to follow her into the kitchen, and Henry walked behind. When Clara looked over her shoulder and smiled at him again, Henry was sure this meal was going to go much better than he could have ever hoped.

———— ❖ ————

Katie wasn't sure why David wanted to take her to the bakery on Main Street, but he said she needed to see something. She'd been here plenty of times before, even though her last visit was a couple years ago.

"Why are we here?" She stared through the large window and saw two Amish girls sitting behind a counter. One had her head buried in a cell phone, and the other flipped through a magazine.

David tethered the horse and met her at the entrance. "Just look around and see how they do things."

Katie didn't appreciate what she thought he was implying and stifled a frown. Was David saying her way of doing things wasn't the correct way? He opened the door for her, and she walked into the bakery as the girls stowed the phone and magazine behind the counter.

"*Wie bischt.*" The older one, maybe about Katie's age, stood. The other girl didn't look like she could have been out of school for long. "Do you need something special?"

"*Nee,*" David said as he approached the counter. It was filled with four times as many baked goods as Katie had at her bakery. "We just came to browse, if that's okay."

Katie was sure the woman wouldn't deny David a look around. His charming smile and charisma would see to that. Her hair prickled on the back of her neck when the woman batted her eyes at him. She got over the jealousy quickly when David brushed off the gesture by turning to Katie and smiling before he whispered in her ear.

"You look beautiful today, in case I didn't tell you earlier."

A flush worked its way up her neck until she was sure her cheeks were a rosy shade of red. She was glad he didn't kiss her, even on the cheek, out in public. "*Danki,*" she whispered.

They looked around just enough not to appear impolite, then

made their way to the door. After they were back on the road, David turned to her.

"Did you see how those girls were just sitting around?" He pulled the horse to a stop, waiting for a car to pass. "I had to bid a job to repair their leaky roof last year, and I had access to the entire place. I've been in the back where they do all the cooking. They have two huge propane ovens. They're probably putting out four times as many pastries and pies as you are, and in half the time."

Katie stiffened beneath the blanket and took in a cool breath.

"I always see you rushing around. If you had a propane oven, even just one, it would speed up production for you. Especially now, while you're running the bakery by yourself."

Katie was no stranger to this subject. She'd asked her parents repeatedly if they should purchase a gas oven. Her mother always said they didn't need it, so Katie hadn't badgered them about it, suspecting it might be unaffordable. They weren't forbidden to use propane, but it was frowned upon, and most folks in Katie's area adhered to the unspoken rule and considered it part of the *Ordnung*.

For a few brief moments, she allowed herself to fantasize about what it would be like to put two or more pies in an oven that didn't require her to maintain the temperature constantly. How nice it would be to turn a dial and set a timer. Katie was pretty good at pulling out a perfect pie or sheet of pastries. But she'd had her fair share of burnt pies too.

"I-I don't think *mei* parents would allow a propane oven." Katie tucked the blanket tighter around her neck. "I've asked them about it before."

"I only bring it up because I hate to see you rushing around and working so hard."

128

"I don't mind," she quickly said. "Hard work is good for the soul." She remembered what Henry said about the wood ovens affecting the taste of the pies in a good way. "I-I think our pies might taste better because of the wood ovens."

David waved a dismissive hand toward her. "I don't think anyone would notice the difference. When I told *mei* parents you were using wood ovens in the bakery, *mei mamm* insisted I offer you our old one that's in the basement. It has double baking compartments." David chuckled. "*Mamm* loves to bake, and when she and *Daed* purchased that one years ago, she got it because it could accommodate a lot of food cooking at once—thinking they would have a large family. Since that wasn't in *Gott*'s plan, she downsized and bought a propane convection oven recently. The one in the basement is older, of course, but it would be a step up from what you're using now."

"*Nee, nee.* I couldn't do that." Katie felt herself blushing as she spoke.

"If it's about money, *Mamm* said you could have it. It's not doing anyone any *gut* in the basement."

Katie faced forward, wondering if her face was red again. It seemed David had a way of embarrassing her.

"*Nee*, it's not about money." She didn't want David to think finances were driving their decisions. "It's just that this is the way we've always done things, and I don't want to change anything while *mei mamm* is recovering."

David shrugged. "Suit yourself."

Katie slowly turned her head to face him. "Are you mad?"

"*Nee, nee.*" He put his hand on her knee, which caused her to jump a little, but he didn't move it. "I'm not mad at all." Grinning, he squeezed above her knee a little until she giggled and pushed him away. "I was just trying to make things easier on you."

He spoke with such tenderness that Katie was tempted to accept the offer. But it felt wrong, and she was sure her parents would disapprove.

When David pulled in at the bakery, he said he needed to come in to use the bathroom before he headed back to work.

They walked into the bakery, and Ella was nowhere to be found. Neither was her daughter, Susan. David excused himself to the bathroom, and Katie followed him, breaking off to the left when he went to the right down a short hallway to the bathroom. Katie wound around past the wringer washing machine, a worktable, and the sink. Finally, she saw Ella and Susan sitting on the floor. Ella's daughter was whimpering softly, and Ella was putting a bandage on her knee.

"*Ach*, she was running around back here when I told her not to, and she fell and skinned her knee." Ella put the last piece of tape across the white bandage and helped the little girl up.

"I'm sorry you fell, sweetheart." Katie leaned down and cupped Susan's cheek in her hand. "Is it anything a cupcake won't fix? Would you like one?"

Sniffling, Susan nodded, and they headed back toward the front of the bakery just as David emerged from the bathroom.

"Um . . ." He raised his eyebrows, then whispered to Katie, "That's another thing you might consider upgrading."

Katie didn't have to wonder whether she was blushing again. She knew she was. "I know." Her father insisted the bathroom was fine, even though Katie and her mother both felt like something needed to be done about it. It was basically a bench with two roughly cut holes. Most of the *Englisch* were appalled when they saw it, even though Katie was always waiting for any patrons outside the door near the sink. She pumped water for them to wash their hands and had a warm towel ready. In the end, Katie and her mother quit pushing her father to upgrade to something more comfortable. Their bathroom had become as touristy as the rest of the bakery. More than once, Katie had heard an *Englisch* person whisper, "And you have to go see the bathroom. You won't believe it."

David told them all goodbye, and Katie walked him to the door. "I'd say I'll call you soon, but . . ." He grinned.

"I know. I don't have a phone." Katie was tiring of David's reminders that she was living in the stone ages, as he'd once put it. He was kind, generous, and very handsome, so she tried to overlook some of his comments.

"But you're worth it," he whispered before he winked at her and left. She turned around to find Ella watching David leave, a dreamy-eyed look on her face.

"Forgive me for staring at your man, but he is easy on the eyes." Grinning, she lifted her eyes upward. "And forgive me, *Gott*. I'm a married woman."

Katie wasn't sure she knew a happier couple than Ella and Ben, so not an ounce of jealousy flared up when Ella gaped at David—unlike at the other bakery earlier when Katie's feathers had been ruffled.

"How was it while I was gone? Sorry I'm a little late." Katie glanced at the order pad and then at the dozen or so loose sheets next to it. She scooped them up and quickly began flipping through them. "What . . ." Her heart pounded.

"*Ya*, it was busy while you were gone." She nodded to the table with the fresh pastries. "A few sales, but mostly orders."

"This woman wants a dozen pies by Monday." Katie could have done that without a problem, but there were more orders. "Here's one for three dozen raisin fried pies, an apple pie, a pecan pie, and four loaves of bread." She swallowed hard. "By Monday." Her eyes widened as she looked up at Ella. "It's after Thanksgiving. Usually there is a lull before the Christmas orders pour in." She thought about all the hours she'd put in prior to Thanksgiving.

"*Ach, mei freind*, I'd come help you, but I have *mei* in-laws coming in next week for an early Christmas since they will be at Ben's sister's house the week of Christmas. I've got a lot of cooking to do in preparation for their arrival."

As Katie's heart continued to thud, she worried about disappointing her parents. She looked at Ella, then at the orders, then at David getting ready to leave.

"Be right back." She fled the bakery and ran to David's buggy, her arms shivering since she didn't even stop to get her coat.

"You're freezing." David rubbed her arms, then started to take off his coat.

"*Nee, nee*. Keep it on. I'm going back in, but I wanted to tell you that I'd love to have your *mudder*'s old propane oven. I just don't know how I'll get it here."

David smiled, then kissed her on the cheek. "I will make sure you get it."

She gazed into his eyes, trying to feel more than she did. He was a *gut* man. And no one would argue that he wasn't handsome. Maybe she hadn't spent enough time with him to really know how she felt. Perhaps her feelings would grow when they knew each other better.

Or had Henry unknowingly disrupted the natural progression of their relationship when he'd asked her out?

As David leaned down and kissed her gently on the lips, she forced herself to envision their relationship escalating. Still, she didn't think such things were meant to be forced.

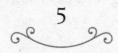

5

LENA INSISTED ON CLEANING THE KITCHEN AFTER SHE told Clara goodbye, leaving Henry to walk their guest to the door and help her into her coat.

"I had a nice time today. Your *schweschder* is a wonderful cook." Clara's brown eyes met his. "And it was fun spending time with you and reliving our adventure from a couple years ago."

Henry nodded. "I enjoyed myself too." His thoughts had drifted to Katie and David on and off, but Clara distracted him in a wonderful way. He liked how bubbly she was when she talked, and she smiled a lot. He wanted to ask her out, but he knew she would be his second choice, and that felt wrong. Then David's face came crashing to the forefront of his mind, reminding him that Katie was taken. Maybe he owed it to himself to expand his horizons. Maybe there was an opportunity for more than friendship with Clara.

"Would you like to have lunch next Saturday?" He held his breath, realizing again how long it had been since he'd had a real date.

"*Ya*, I'd like that." She pulled on thick black gloves, still smiling.

"What about the Railroad Café in Mitchell?" It wasn't anything fancy, but the food was good, and it wasn't far from where Clara lived. They would spend less time in the buggy and cold.

"That sounds *gut*."

After setting a time for the following Saturday, Henry walked Clara to her buggy and helped her in, thankful the snow had stopped for now.

When he walked back into the house, Lena was standing in the middle of the living room with her arms folded across her chest, grinning. "Ha. I did *gut, ya*?"

Henry looped his thumbs beneath his suspenders and chuckled. "*Ya*, I guess you did." He rolled his eyes. "But no more blind dates without asking me."

Lena dropped her arms to her sides, her eyes twinkling, as she bounced up on her toes. "Maybe you won't need any more blind dates. Maybe Clara is *the one*."

Henry wouldn't have thought it a possibility until the last couple of hours, but he was willing to get to know Clara better since Katie was involved with someone else. "Maybe."

Lena clapped her hands before she spun around and went back to the kitchen.

It had been a *gut* dinner, but now that Clara was gone, Henry's thoughts returned to Katie. He hoped it wouldn't always be this way. Maybe spending time with Clara was just what he needed.

Katie closed the bakery at three o'clock, as she always did on Saturdays, so she could go home and prepare supper. Even though tomorrow was a day of rest, she would have to come back to the bakery. Otherwise, there was no way she'd get all the orders completed by Monday. She wished she'd have that fancy propane oven on Monday instead of having to wait until the following Saturday. David said that was the soonest he could get it to her.

Her teeth chattered on the short ride home, despite being bundled up in a heavy blanket and using the small heater on the seat next to her. As thoughts of David and Henry battled for room in her mind, she tried to tune it all out and focus on what she had to do when she arrived at home—heat the supper she'd prepared late last night, sew buttons on two of the boys' shirts, and try to get to bed as early as possible.

It was only a half hour later when she put the large pot of chicken and dumplings on the table alongside two loaves of bread. After she set out the chow-chow, jams, and jellies, she joined her father and five brothers, never wishing she had a sister more than today.

After they bowed their heads in prayer, Katie's brothers dug in. Emanuel and Jonas were still in their work clothes, which consisted of overalls covered in paint, and she smelled the stench of hard work on them even from the other end of the table. Her mother never would have allowed them to gather for a meal looking and smelling that way, but Katie was too tired to enforce a rule her father had obviously chosen to overlook.

Katie's youngest brother, Reuben, wasn't a very good eater, and he was tiny for ten. She knew to keep a close eye on him and encourage him to eat enough. Mahlon and Vernon, twelve and fourteen, could eat almost as much as their older brothers, although Emanuel and Jonas ate faster and were usually the first ones to leave.

When the commotion of supper was over, Katie carried a plate of food up to her mother.

"*Mei maedel*, you look exhausted." Her mother positioned the tray on her lap, then looked up at Katie and frowned. "I hate being laid up like this. Maybe in another week or so I'll be able to get back to the bakery."

Katie caught a glimpse of herself in the bathroom mirror earlier. She had dark circles below her eyes, and several strands of hair had slipped out of her prayer covering.

"*Nee*, remember what the doctor said about staying in bed until Christmas?" Katie picked up the tray from her mother's lap and set it on the nightstand while she helped her sit up a little more.

"*Ach*, that's too long." Her mother flinched as she tried to lift herself up even more. Once she was settled, Katie placed the tray back on her lap, then sank onto the chair by the bed.

"*Nee*, it's not too long. You don't want to have another set-back." Katie waited as her mother prayed silently, then she said, "The dumplings aren't as *gut* as yours, but the boys didn't seem to notice."

"I'm so proud of you." Her mother smiled. "You've taken over the duties here at home, and you're running the bakery by yourself. You'll make a wonderful *fraa* someday."

Katie tucked her chin, feeling undeserving of the compliment. She was tempted to tell her mother about the propane oven that would arrive Saturday, but she decided to wait until the new appliance was already in place before she said anything. It would make it more difficult to return it if it was settled and in use.

"A lot of orders came in today. More than normal after Thanksgiving." Katie searched her mother's eyes for advice, but her mother was focused on her meal. Katie was glad to see her eating more than she had been lately.

"Can your cousin help you?" Her mother reached for a glass of water on the nightstand.

"*Nee*. I mean, I know Ella would if she could, but she has her hands full running her own household. Susan is a bit hyper, and they have Ben's parents coming for a visit."

"*Ya*, I remember that now." Her mother took a bite of the chicken and dumplings, and Katie waited, wondering again if she should tell her about the new oven.

"I can send your younger *bruders* to help you when they get out of school for the Christmas holidays." Her mother lifted an eyebrow.

"*Nee*. Absolutely not. Mahlon and Vernon fight when you and *Daed* aren't around, and Reuben would be bored silly and make me *ab im kopp*."

Her mother nodded. "True. I often catch them arguing with each other. It's the age. Twelve- and fourteen-year-olds don't believe themselves to be *kinner* anymore, but they aren't grown yet either." Pausing, she stared at Katie with sad eyes. "I don't like to see you so tired, but the Lord will surely reward your efforts. Just remember, don't try to rush the process by baking things too quickly. You'll end up with overcooked pastries and pies that aren't done in the middle." She took another sip of water. "Cutting corners won't produce the quality products we're known for."

Katie hoped she wasn't choosing quantity over quality, but there was no way to know until she tried the propane oven.

Even though it wasn't their way to discuss dating and relationships until things were serious, Katie was tempted to talk to her mother about David. Then she saw her mother flinch in pain, and decided not to. *Mamm* had enough on her mind—worrying about her household being run the way she liked and worrying that Katie would be able to keep the bakery going without losing business.

Katie thought again about the propane oven. She couldn't wait to see it. *I won't disappoint you,* Mamm.

Henry stopped by the bakery on Wednesday afternoon while his boss had him out running errands. He wanted to casually slip in the fact that he had a date on Saturday to see if Katie would have any kind of reaction to the news. Not that he wanted to use Clara to make Katie jealous. He really liked Clara.

When he got a look at Katie, he changed his mind. Walking toward the counter, he picked up the pace until he was on the other side of the glass enclosure. "Are you okay?"

Katie's *kapp* was lopsided, she had dark circles underneath her eyes, and there was something red all over the front of her blue dress. For a moment he wondered if it was blood, but after studying it for a second, he thought about Clara and if it might be chili. Although, he didn't think he'd ever seen Katie or her mother making chili in the bakery.

"What is that?" Henry pointed to the red splotches.

Katie rubbed a sleeve across her sweaty forehead, even though it was below freezing outside and not as warm as usual inside. "I caught my apron in the wringer earlier when I was washing towels, and when I tried to get it out, it ripped." She eyed her dress. "Then I spilled all the red food coloring I had left." Her voice cracked before she cleared her throat. "And I have an order for two red velvet cakes. I'm going to make two chocolate cakes and hope the woman will accept them for free."

Henry took off his hat and scratched his head, trying to figure out a way to take off the rest of the day so he could stay and help Katie. But even the hardware store was busy, and one of his errands was to pick up some Christmas tree stands from the warehouse in town. They'd already sold out.

Katie's bottom lip trembled, and Henry wanted to pull her into his arms, but he was afraid he'd never let her go. "Maybe you should try to hire someone to help you get through the holidays. It's clearly a two-person job, and you look worn-out."

Katie raised a hand to her chest and lifted her chin. "I can handle it. I'm just having a bad day." She rubbed her temples with both hands as she took a deep breath, then lowered her arms and blew it out. "I just have to make it until Saturday."

Henry narrowed his eyes. "What happens then?" *Besides another date with David probably.* Clara or no Clara, Henry's stomach lurched when he thought about the possibility.

"David is bringing me a propane oven that his family doesn't use anymore. I'll be able to bake more than just two pies at a time, and I think he said it has six burners, so I can add some other items to our menu too." She placed her hands on top of the counter and leaned forward. "I've been getting up at three o'clock in the morning so I'd be able to get all the orders filled."

Henry rubbed his chin. "What does your *mamm* think about bringing in a propane oven?"

Katie avoided his eyes as she began fumbling through a stack of orders on the counter. "I haven't told her yet."

"Doesn't your boyfriend know we don't use propane?" Henry

folded his arms across his chest. He couldn't even bring himself to say the guy's name.

"We don't use it, but it's not forbidden." She finally looked up at him, her lip trembling. "I can't do this by myself, and I can't afford to hire anyone." She went back to shuffling through the orders.

Henry realized she had let the boyfriend comment slide. He waited, hoping she would correct him and say David wasn't her boyfriend.

When she didn't, Henry told her bye and left.

6

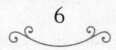

KATIE SAT ON THE STOOL BEHIND THE COUNTER, TEMPTED to throw all the order slips in the air, then fill the ones that landed right side up. She didn't know how she was going to have everything ready for customers, and she didn't want to disappoint them. She didn't even have a phone to let anyone know their orders wouldn't be ready on time.

As tears threatened to spill, she watched Henry untether his horse, then climb in the buggy and drive off. He never said why he stopped by, although Katie hadn't really given him an opportunity to say much. She'd avoided his comment about David being her boyfriend. After replaying the question over in her mind a few times, she still wasn't sure. It seemed as if David had slipped into the role of boyfriend without her knowing. He'd even gone from kissing her on the cheek to kissing her on the lips. Katie had been kissed before, but it usually didn't happen after three dates.

Fretting and worrying weren't going to get pies in the oven, so she added another log to the firebox and began rolling dough. She reminded herself that Henry had plenty of opportunities over the years to ask her out, and he hadn't until recently. At least David was making an effort to help her during this difficult time. Could she fault Henry for not offering assistance? He had a job, and he'd already watched the bakery once so Katie could go to lunch with David.

She set the rolling pin aside, then reached into the cabinet and pulled out a whoopie pie. After staring at it a minute, she eventually placed the wrapped dessert back in the cabinet. Gorging on sugar wasn't going to solve her problems.

I just have to make it until Saturday.

By the time Saturday rolled around, Henry was happy to have the day off and ready to see Clara again.

Lena walked into the living room just as Henry put on his hat and was about to leave. She stopped and sniffed the air. "Are you wearing cologne?"

He almost denied it, but he didn't want to lie. "*Ya.* But keep it to yourself."

Lena giggled. "You must really like Clara to be breaking a rule." She peered over her shoulder toward the kitchen where someone was clanging pots and pans. "You better hurry before *Mamm* gets a whiff of you. Even though you're still in your *rum-schpringe*, you know she wouldn't like it."

Henry tapped his hat into place, told his sister bye, and headed out the door. Even though he anticipated seeing Clara, he was equally eager to see Katie. He hoped she'd been able to find some help or get more rest. Or both. His mother had asked him to stop by the bakery since he would be out and about.

A short ride later, he picked up Clara and took her to the Railroad Café. They were about halfway through the meal when Clara picked up on the fact that Henry was present in body, but his mind kept drifting to other places.

"Are you okay?" She leaned her head to one side and pressed her lips together. "You seem distracted."

Henry looked down at his half-eaten plate of chicken tenders. Normally he would have downed those by now and been looking forward to dessert, which in this case would be off-site. Clara had carried most of the conversation, telling him about her sister who was due to have a baby any day, and she had told him about selling two quilts this past week at a co-op where she sold handmade items.

Henry had nodded and smiled. He'd looked forward to spending time with her, but his heart just wasn't in it today. "*Nee*, I'm fine." He picked up another chicken tender and saw that Clara had eaten most of her grilled ham-and-cheese sandwich. "Sorry I haven't been better company. I didn't sleep much last night." It was true. He'd tossed and turned most of the night. "I promise I'll do better next time." He stifled a yawn, realizing he'd just committed to another date.

Clara sighed. "I can see in your eyes that you're tired. It's times like this I wish phones were allowed. We could have rescheduled."

"*Nee*, I wanted to see you." He'd thought he had, and now he was just digging himself in deeper. He really wanted to give himself a chance with Clara, but Katie always found her way to the forefront of his thoughts.

Clara smiled, which lifted his spirits a little. She picked up the last of her sandwich. "It's cute how the food is named. I had trouble deciding between the caboose, the conductor, or the engineer sandwich."

Henry nodded since he had a mouthful. After he swallowed, he said, "I was thinking we could go by the Swartzentruber Bakery when we leave here and get a fried pie for dessert. The owners are friends of the family, and *mei mamm* asked me to stop by to see if everything is okay. Katie, the daughter, is running things by herself while her *mudder* recovers from surgery."

"*Ya*, sure. I'm fine with whatever you'd like to do." Clara was easy to look at, easy to be around, and she deserved someone who paid more attention to her. "I don't think I've ever been to that bakery, but I've heard *gut* things about it. The one in town is closer for us, so we just go there, though we do most of our own baking."

Henry nodded, then sipped his tea. His mind was awhirl with ways to introduce Clara to Katie. *This is* mei freind, *Clara. This is* mei *date, Clara. Clara and I just ate at the Railroad Café.* Would Katie care that he was with another woman? Part of him hoped she didn't care at all. Maybe that would put some closure on the ideas that had been formulating in his mind, notions of them as a couple. Then he could focus on getting to know Clara better.

Katie finished checking out three ladies who had come all the way from Bloomington. They were dressed in brightly colored Christmas sweaters, which reminded Katie that she needed to put up the holiday decorations. She was disappointed David hadn't shown up with her new oven yet. If plans had changed, he didn't have a way to get ahold of her.

Just then, he finally turned in, toting a small trailer behind his buggy. Katie felt lighter on her feet already. She thanked the women for coming, then followed them to the door, grabbing her coat from behind the counter first and putting it on as she walked.

"Sorry I'm late. *Mei* neighbor was supposed to come help me unload, but he didn't show up. *Mei daed* helped me load it, but it's much too heavy for you." David's breath met with hers in the frigid air, then he pulled her close and kissed her.

It caught Katie off guard, but she stayed in his arms until the clip-clop of horses got their attention, and they turned to their left.

Henry. And he'd surely seen the kiss. Katie strained to see who was in the buggy with him. When he came to a stop, a woman she didn't recognize stepped out and pulled a black coat snug around herself, her teeth chattering. Katie couldn't take her eyes off the woman as she walked toward them. She was beautiful with long dark lashes that swept down on high cheekbones. But her smile and big brown eyes captured Katie's attention. She immediately wondered what Henry's relationship was with this woman.

She extended a gloved hand to Katie. "*Wie bischt.* I'm Clara, a *freind* of Henry's."

Katie took hold of the woman's hand and introduced herself, then quickly turned to Henry. He walked toward David, and a few minutes later they had lowered the oven onto a rolling platform David had brought. Katie scurried ahead of them to hold the door open, and her heart pounded as she eyed her new appliance. It would easily hold the six pies she had ready to bake. She prayed they would taste the same.

"It's nice that you can use propane." Clara slipped out of her coat as she walked inside with Katie. "I didn't think this district used gas."

Katie forced a weak smile before she eased out of her own coat. "*Ya*," she said, avoiding Clara's curious eyes. "It's allowed in some instances." That was mostly true, but Katie's temples began to throb. Was she going against God, or just her parents?

"It's not going to fit without moving at least one of these wood ovens." David looked up at the ceiling, then ran his hand along the tubular chimney that trailed to the roof. "We can disconnect the chimney, then move it."

Katie was pretty sure that oven had been in the same place since her grandmother started the bakery decades ago, and it must have rooted itself to the floor by now. No matter how much Henry and David tugged and pushed, it wasn't budging.

There couldn't have been a worse time for six *Englisch* women to come walking in. Katie recognized one of the ladies. She was here to pick up pies—the six sitting on the counter waiting to be baked.

Katie wiped her hands on her apron. "Hello." She took in a deep breath. "I'm sorry the pies aren't ready yet, but you are a little early. Can you come back in about an hour? I'm sorry for any inconvenience."

The lady nodded toward the other women before she spoke up. "Actually, we were hoping to watch you bake them. My friends have never seen anyone cook with a wood oven. I was here once when you were baking, and it was fascinating to watch." She paused, then flinched when the wood oven finally budged, and the chimney broke off when it moved. "Oh, dear." Pointing to the other oven, she said, "Perhaps you can cook them in that other wood oven?"

Katie took a deep breath. "It's cooled down right now and would take a while to get the firebox up to the right temperature, but we should have this new propane oven in place soon."

Henry's hat fell off as he tried to move the broken chimney out of the way, but it wasn't moving either. David had already hit his head on it when he leaned over to try to move it.

"Will the pies taste the same? They had a very distinctive flavor the last time I was here."

"*Ya*, they will." Katie had no idea if they would. She'd never cooked with anything like this fancy oven. *Surely, I just set the temperature, put in the pies, then wait for them to bake.* She hoped God answered her prayer. He'd answered when the lady who ordered the red velvet cakes showed up. The woman happily accepted the chocolate cakes and even insisted on paying for them.

"Okay, then." The lady looked at her friends. "We can go do a little shopping, then come back. Does that sound okay?"

Katie breathed a sigh of relief when the women all chimed in and said that would be fine. After the women left, she finally turned to Henry, whose hat was still on the floor.

"Why are you here?" She rubbed her chin. "I mean, it was perfect timing to help with the oven, but did you need something else?"

"*Mamm* wanted me to stop by and check on you." He nodded at Clara. "I told her our families were *gut* friends. And we were going to get a fried pie. We just ate at the Railroad Café."

Katie glanced at Clara, who smiled. "Henry said the pastries here are the best."

"It doesn't work." David squatted down and jiggled the propane tank. "*Daed* said there was propane in it."

Katie stiffened and held her breath as she eyed the dangling vent, the propane oven standing diagonal behind the counter, and the other wood oven that was cold and useless at the moment. If David hadn't shown up, she would have gone ahead and baked the pies one at a time in her two ovens. It would have taken three hours, but she would've only been a half hour late on the woman's order. Now, she didn't know what to do as she stood staring, wringing her hands.

David stood, took off his hat, and ran an arm across his sweaty forehead. Then he looked at the clock on the wall. "I have to go. I have an appointment to bid a roofing job."

"What?" Katie walked closer to him. "We can't just leave it like this." She pointed to the oven that didn't work and waved a hand at the vent. "Are you sure it has propane?"

"*Nee*, I'm not. I can come back later and pick up the container, then go see if I can get it filled up." He groaned as he threw his head back before he looked at her. "*Ach*, I hate this. I know how much you need this oven working, but *mei* boss will go *ab im kopp* if I miss this appointment." He walked to her and kissed her gently. "I'm sorry. But I've got to go."

Katie's eyes darted to Henry, but he looked away. She wished David would stop with all the public affection. Her cheeks were warm, and she was too embarrassed to even look at Clara.

After David was out the door, Katie blinked back tears as she pressed her trembling lips together.

She turned to Clara when the woman put a hand on her arm.

"Don't worry." Clara looked at Henry, who had just picked up his hat and put it back on. "We don't have any plans, do we, Henry?" She turned back to Katie and smiled. "I don't know a thing about propane ovens, but I'm pretty handy with a wood oven. I think if we take the grill out of the oven they just broke, and put it in the other wood oven, we can get at least two pies in at one time. It might not be ideal, but we can give it a try. If the women are irritated when they get back, maybe you can discount the order or offer them some extra fried pies? Either way, let me help you get that grill removed." Clara began to roll up her sleeves, and Katie felt silly for not thinking of that herself. "And let's start getting that oven hot again."

Katie's people were happy to help one another, but she didn't even know this woman. When she subtly cast a glance in Henry's direction, he was smiling from ear to ear. Clearly, he knew her. Katie didn't know how well they were acquainted, but the way he was smiling, she suspected there was something between them.

She looked back at Clara. "I can't let you help me. You just came in for a pie, and I've got a big mess, and . . ." She paused when her voice cracked.

Clara touched her arm again. "As I said, we have nothing else planned for today." She glanced at Henry, then back at Katie. "Let us help you." Her face was aglow with a smile so bright that Katie wanted to hug her. It was impossible not to like Clara right away.

As she nodded, she glanced at Henry again. He wasn't staring at Clara, though. His gaze was fixed on Katie. Her eyes clung to his, and something about the way he looked at her caused Katie's heart to swell with emotion. She waited for him to look away, but he didn't.

7

HENRY RETURNED TO THE BAKERY ABOUT THIRTY MINUTES later with a full tank of propane. He got straight to work hooking it up.

Katie and Clara were side by side at a table they'd brought in from the back since Katie's normal workspace was occupied with the propane oven still at an angle and the wood oven in the way. Clara was rolling out dough, and Katie was mixing some sort of filling in a bowl. They both looked up when Henry opened the oven door and lit the burner.

"It works," he said, breathless. "What temperature?"

Katie rushed toward him, carrying the bowl with her and stirring. "Try 425. That's the temperature I try to keep the wood ovens at." She bent down, bracing the bowl against her stomach. She seemed in awe of the spacious new appliance. "Clara, we can put the other four pies in here and still have room left. Should we add the other two in the oven now? *Nee*, let's don't," she said, before giving Clara time to answer. "I wouldn't know how much longer to bake them."

Henry stepped aside as Katie put down the bowl and brought

one of the pies to the new oven, pushing it as far back on the rack as it would go. Clara handed her the next one, and once all four were inside, the two women stepped back, looked at each other, and smiled.

Henry had a queasiness in his stomach as he watched the woman he was dating standing next to the woman who made his heart flip. He could have kicked David for leaving Katie in a bind like this. David could have tried to reschedule his appointment and helped his girlfriend. He had a cell phone after all. Instead, he'd just taken off, seemingly unbothered by Katie's predicament as he rushed out the door.

Katie set the timer on the oven, smiled, and walked back to the temporary work area, chatting quietly with Clara. Henry wasn't sure what he should do now. Maybe try to get the broken oven out of the way and move the propane one in place, but he couldn't do that while the pies were cooking, so he leaned against the counter and sighed.

They all looked up when the door swung open.

"Jonas, what are you doing here?" Katie's jaw dropped as her oldest brother frowned, his eyes widening at the sight of the propane oven wedged sideways between the cabinet and where it needed to be up against the wall.

"Uh . . ." He slowed his steps as his eyes drifted up to the vent dangling from the ceiling, before he looked back at his sister. "What have you done?"

———◆———

Katie blinked a few times. "Jonas, what are you doing here?" she asked again. But her brother had noticed Clara, and his eyes were fixated on the woman. Katie glanced at Henry and wondered if he noticed the way Jonas was looking at Clara, but Henry only stared at Katie, grinning when he caught her looking at him. She smiled back, even though there wasn't one thing to be happy about at the moment. Maybe Henry needed to keep an eye on Clara since she seemed to be gazing back at Jonas in much the same way he was looking at her. Or maybe Clara just smiled a lot and had the same mesmerizing effect on everyone she met.

Jonas finally pulled his eyes from Clara after he'd introduced himself. He hung his head for a couple seconds before he looked at Katie again. "*Mamm* and *Daed* are going to go *ab im kopp* about this."

Clara set down the rolling pin she was holding. "I thought you said propane was allowed?"

Katie cringed. "It's not disallowed," she said before she squeezed her eyes closed, then opened them. "It's just frowned upon."

Jonas took off his coat. Her brother had a broad chest and muscular arms that filled out the blue long-sleeved shirt he was wearing. He grinned at Clara, showing off the efforts of his hard work from doing construction.

Again, Katie glanced at Henry, whose eyes were still on her. She wanted to tell him, "You better watch out for Jonas." Her brother was a good-looking guy and still unattached at twenty-four.

Jonas excused himself and headed toward the bathroom.

"What's this?" Clara squatted and fumbled through an open red suitcase on the floor. She pulled out stems of imitation holly that were mixed in with other Christmas decorations.

Katie looked at the timer on the propane oven. Thirty minutes left. The new oven was white and looked brand new. She couldn't imagine why David's mother would trade it for a smaller model, but she remembered him saying her new one was a convection oven. Katie was thrilled to have the hand-me-down.

She joined Clara by the suitcase, squatting beside her. "I have no idea where this suitcase originally came from, but *Mamm* pulls it out of the storage closet every year, so I took it out this morning. I've been meaning to get some of these Christmas decorations up since the day after Thanksgiving, but I've been so busy that I just haven't gotten around to it. I thought if I brought the suitcase out in plain view, I'd remember to make time."

Jonas emerged from the back and cleared his throat. "Um . . . there is a problem in the back. The sink is leaking. I think a strong arm and a screwdriver can fix it." He gave a quick wave before he turned back around.

Both women turned to Henry and smiled.

He rolled his eyes. "Give it to me. I'll take care of decorations."

Katie closed the suitcase, lifted it, and carried it to him. "There's a wreath for the door, and we usually hang the garland along the windows inside."

"I know," Henry said as he took the box from her. "I've seen it decorated since we were kids."

Katie smiled at him and fought the urge to tell him she'd had a crush on him since they were kids. A crush she was still trying to fend off. Clara had truly saved the day, and if Henry was going to be with anyone but Katie, it should be Clara.

"Isn't your boyfriend the sweetest?" It was a fishing expedition, but Katie couldn't resist the urge to find out for sure where things stood with Henry and Clara.

Clara's normally happy expression fell as her face turned as white as the new oven. "*Ach*, we, uh . . . we just had our first date today. So, we're not really, um . . . like that."

Katie's heart sang. "Oh." She tried not to smile as she looked back at Henry.

"Every relationship has to start somewhere." Henry looked past Katie at Clara, who smiled now.

Henry was smitten. They'd just started out, but Katie could tell by his flirty grin and her reaction that this wouldn't be their last date.

———◆———

Henry was going to need to pray extra hard tonight about the deceptions he was tossing around so carelessly. A better man would tell Clara he had strong feelings for Katie, even though Katie had never wanted to be more than friends. A better man would be happy for his dear friend, who had found someone who made her happy, even if Henry thought David was kind of a jerk. Maybe Henry's feelings for Clara would grow once he got to know her better. Then the sting of David and Katie might not hurt so much.

Katie and Clara hurried to the new oven when the timer buzzed. Henry carted the suitcase filled with decorations toward the glass plate windows and door. A screech almost caused him to drop everything. He spun around. "What?"

Clara covered her mouth with her hands as Katie pulled out one of the pies, and Henry smelled the problem before the women said anything. He set the suitcase on the floor by the window, then hurried toward them.

"Burnt!" Katie set the first pie on top of the oven, then retrieved the other three, each in the same condition. "I didn't smell anything burning? Did you?" She turned to Clara as she felt the color draining from her face, and Clara shook her head.

"Not until you opened the oven door."

Putting her hands on either side of her face, Katie's eyes rounded. "I should have been checking on them, but I thought opening the door might interfere with them cooking. And the interior light isn't working."

"Well, the other two that we baked in the wood oven came out nicely." Clara offered a smile, but it wasn't like the one that usually spread across her face.

Henry's heart hurt for Katie, and he wished he could hug her, then begged God to allow Katie to feel the love he carried for her.

The front door opened, and the six women from earlier came in smiling and talking about what they'd bought. They began to sniff the air, and their expressions fell. The leader of the group frowned as she approached Katie, the others following.

"Oh, dear." The *Englisch* lady shook her head, but when she looked at Katie and saw that she was about to cry, she took a deep breath. "I think we can make these work." Her friends nodded and smiled. None of the expressions were genuine, but Henry was ready to hug all of them for not making a big stink about the four burnt pies.

"*Nee.*" Katie sniffled but raised her chin. "These pies are unacceptable, and I cannot sell them to you. My deepest apologies." She waved an arm toward the table with all the fried pies and other pastries laid out. "Please help yourself to anything you'd like, to hopefully make up for *mei* blunder."

The speaker for the ladies' group took a couple steps closer to Katie. "Hon, these things happen." She turned over her shoulder and smiled at her friends. "Ladies, will your husbands eat these, even if they are a tiny bit overcooked?" The women all nodded, then the lady turned back to Katie. "Just box these up for us along with the other two, which look absolutely perfect."

Henry knew Katie prided herself on making the best pastries in town, and this was a blow, but she boxed the pies with Clara's help. He walked back to the window and started on the decorations, thinking this day hadn't gone anything like he'd planned. This was supposed to be a quick visit, but they'd been here for hours now. And Katie and Clara had become instant friends.

As Henry kept looking back at Katie, he knew there wasn't anywhere he'd rather be. He wouldn't be doing right by Clara if he went out with her again.

He'd just hung the wreath on the inside of the door when David pulled up in his buggy.

Henry opened the door for him and nodded as David stepped over the threshold. The guy went straight to Katie, pulled her into his arms, and kissed her passionately in front of everyone. Katie began to blush before the kiss was even over. Henry clenched his fists at his sides, wishing he could use them to pound David's face in. Clara looked away from the couple, her face turning a shade of pink too. David looked at Clara over Katie's shoulder, after he'd kissed Katie and still held her in his arms. He smiled at Clara in a way that made Henry want to smack him even more.

Does David want Clara too?

Henry wished he could start this day over again and do things differently, but he dutifully hung the Christmas decorations and tried to keep his thoughts on the task.

It was early evening by the time Henry and Clara left the bakery, but the sun hadn't quite set completely. Henry turned up the battery-operated heaters as high as they would go and wrapped a wool blanket around Clara. She was quiet for the first few minutes of the trip to her house. Finally, Henry asked if something was wrong.

She turned to him and smiled. "Henry Hershberger, you are a very nice man." Pausing, she held his gaze. "And a handsome one."

Henry prepared his ego for a giant blow. Maybe it was for the best since he already regretted placing Clara as runner-up to the emotions he felt for Katie. He'd never given her a chance.

"Hmm . . . I hear a 'but' coming." Henry took a deep breath. Perhaps he would feel relieved, but rejection tended to sting no matter the circumstances.

"A person would have to be blind not to see the way you look at Katie. There's more than a childhood history and friendship going on, whether you care to admit it or not."

Henry slowed the horse before he hung his head.

Clara stretched her arm out from underneath the blanket and placed a hand on his shoulder. "It's okay. I think Katie is lovely. Tell me if I'm right, Henry. Or did I misjudge?" She smiled. "Because I think I'm right."

Now it was out there. "I'm so sorry, Clara . . ."

"Don't be." She eased her arm back under the blanket, and when Henry looked her way, she smiled. He wondered if someone else had captured her interest. David, most likely. But what about Katie? "I'm right, aren't I, about Katie?"

Henry nodded. "*Ya.*" He turned to face her. "Clara, I like you, and I hoped that maybe we could grow into more than friends over time. But now it doesn't seem fair." He paused, a niggling feeling surfacing that there was more to this than just Henry and Katie. "Is there someone else you're wanting to go out with?"

Clara sneezed, then she sneezed again. When she was done, she looked at Henry. "I think Katie has deep feelings for you too. And I think you are both cheating yourselves if you don't explore what's happening." She tossed her head from side to side, avoiding his question. "I don't feel like David is right for her."

Ah, she does want to go out with David.

"Tell her how you feel, Henry."

"Right now, I feel like a louse." Henry picked up speed, anxious to get home and disappointed in himself. Clara giggled.

"Don't feel that way." She put a finger to her chin. "Besides, I have something I'd like you to do for me. Then you will have redeemed yourself."

Henry's jaw fell a little. This day just kept getting more bizarre.

"Relax, Henry. I'm teasing. No redemption necessary. But I would like to ask you to do this one thing for me."

"*Ya*, sure."

Then Clara confided in him about her request.

"Easy enough," he said as he nodded. What a whirlwind of a day it had been.

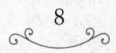

8

KATIE SKIPPED WORSHIP SERVICE, WHICH SHE NEVER DID, after confessing to her mother that she needed to work at the bakery today or she'd never get caught up on all the orders. She tried to downplay the situation so it wouldn't upset her mother.

By noon, she'd finally gotten the new oven figured out. Even though she'd been baking pies at 425 degrees Fahrenheit before, all the opening and closing of the firebox, combined with constantly checking on the pies by opening the door, had caused her to assume they were baking at a lesser temperature. When she baked a pie in the new propane oven at 350°F for an hour, they cooked properly.

But they didn't taste the same, and that was a huge disappointment after everything she and her friends had been through to make the propane oven functional. It was a fear Katie had all along. Henry and David had gotten rid of the dangling vent, moved both wood ovens to the back, and positioned the new appliance against the wall.

She'd been sure she could convince her mother to keep the new oven, but only if the quality of the baked goods was the same. And it wasn't. Whatever hint of smoke or magical power the wood ovens possessed had been a key factor that made their bakery a step above the rest. Katie had never been outwardly prideful about it, but there wasn't a woman in their community who didn't have a bit of competitiveness when it came to cooking and baking.

Now, it was the holidays, and Katie's food would be just like everyone else's. Even so, speed trumped quality right now, so she put three loaves of bread in the oven and set the timer, knowing she'd have to check them often until she became comfortable with the appliance.

She turned when she heard the door open.

"*Mamm* said you were here." Jonas closed the space between them, stopped, then shook his head as he eyed the new oven. "Did you tell her yet?"

"*Nee*. I thought it would be okay, that I could show her how much more efficient we could be." She turned to her brother and put a hand to her forehead. "But nothing tastes the same. I'm not sure why. Maybe wood ovens are like a cast-iron skillet—the more you use them, the more seasoned they become."

Katie wrapped her arm across her stomach when it started to knot with panic. "I wish I'd never accepted this new oven as a gift from David and his family."

"Give it back." Jonas shrugged. "Put the old ones back like they were. You might have to keep putting in long hours until *Mamm* is back to work, but at least you'd be putting out the quality of food folks have come to expect."

"I'd feel horrible returning such a nice, expensive gift. I thought it would save time and I'd be more productive, but with the learning curve, I've stayed backed up on orders."

"You'll feel even worse if *Mamm* comes back to a bakery that's

been in our family for generations, and you've messed things up."
Jonas stared at her. "That's something bigger at stake here than
hurting your boyfriend's feelings by returning the oven."

"He's not *mei* boyfriend." Katie rolled her eyes. "He's someone I'm dating."

Her brother grinned as he shed his coat and laid it on the
counter. "Does he know that?"

Katie recalled the few times she'd let David kiss her, but
it had happened so fast there wasn't much time to react. It was
much too soon, and she was going to have to talk to him about it,
especially the public displays. It might be fine for some women,
but Katie needed things to slow down. "We haven't been going
out for long."

"He's from a more liberal community, Katie. If it got serious,
you'd be expected to convert to his ways." Jonas walked around
the cabinet, opened it, and took out one of the cupcakes. "Can
you see yourself with a mobile phone, a house lit up by solar
panels, and fancy appliances?"

That lifestyle certainly allured sometimes, but Katie didn't
want to live like that. Her brother was thinking way too far in
advance.

"And . . ." He swallowed the chunk of chocolate cupcake in
his mouth. "I saw the way David looked at your friend Clara. That
doesn't seem right since he's dating you."

Katie wanted to tell her brother that everyone looked at Clara
that way because she radiated beauty inside and out. Katie still
felt no sense of jealousy where Clara was concerned, when it came
to Henry or David.

"How'd you meet her, anyway? Clara." He picked up his coat
and put it back on. "Is she Henry's girlfriend?"

"I thought so, but apparently they've only been out to lunch once, and that was yesterday."

Jonas buttoned his coat. "Lucky guy." His teeth started to chatter. "You better get some heaters now that you can't warm the place by opening the wood ovens." He shrugged, chuckling. "Might as well get propane ones so that when the bishop—and *Mamm*—gets hold of you at least you'll be warm during the scolding."

"Ha, ha." Katie folded her arms across her chest. Jonas was a good man, but he was still her brother and knew how to get under her skin when he wanted to.

After he left, Katie tried to peek at the loaves of bread cooking in the oven, but she couldn't see much with the oven light not working. She sat on the stool behind the counter and covered her face with her hands, determined not to cry.

Gott, what should I do? I can't tell Henry how I feel about him, because I like Clara too much to do that to her. I want to stop seeing David because I feel like I'm leading him on, even though he's been good to me. Gott, I don't think that's the best reason to stay in a relationship with someone. Please help me sort out my feelings and hear Your voice in my mind. I wish I hadn't made changes to the bakery. Please send me guidance about how to make it right.

She looked up when the door opened again, and just seeing Henry caused her to let the tears flow.

———◆———

Henry's breathing quickened as he hurried to Katie. He rounded the counter until he was standing right beside her. "What's wrong?"

She wrapped her arms around his waist and buried her head against his chest. They'd hugged lots of times as kids, but rarely as adults. He slowly eased his arms around her, cupping the back of her neck with one hand, and holding her close around the waist with the other.

He held her until she slowly eased away, then he gently pushed away loose strands of hair from her face and kissed her on the forehead. It came as naturally as breathing. "Whatever it is, we'll fix it."

As she gazed into his eyes, a tear trailed down her cheek, and Henry wanted to will away whatever was causing her pain. Instead, he prayed for God to give her comfort as he brushed away her tears with his thumbs.

She lifted her face, her mouth close enough to kiss, but Henry held back, moving only slightly away, still close enough to have an arm around her waist. *She is seeing someone else.* He wondered if Clara's advice to be honest would be the right thing to do while David was still in the picture.

"Can you just keep hugging me?" she asked as she laid her head against his chest again.

There's nothing I'd like more. "Ya, of course."

"Why are you here?" She was still crying, but she didn't lift her head again.

"You weren't at worship service today, so I went by your *haus*. Your *mamm* said you were here. I thought you might need help with something."

Sniffling, she looked up at him again. Henry was sure she wanted him to kiss her, and the temptation was overwhelming. He might have given in if the door hadn't swung open. Henry and Katie hastily stepped away from each other, as if they'd been caught committing a crime. By the look on David's face, maybe they had.

David didn't say anything until he got right up to the counter. "Am I interrupting something?" A bridled tension filled his voice as his nostrils flared a little.

Henry thought he should be asking Katie what was wrong. It seemed like that should be the priority.

"Nee, nee." Katie walked around the counter and put a hand on David's arm, still sniffling. "I've had a hard day, and I started to cry . . ." She hung her head and shook it before she looked back up at him. "Henry and I have been friends since we were children, so he was just giving me a hug."

David reached for Katie's hand and eased her toward him until he had an arm around her, then he leaned down and kissed her. Henry had to look away. He was sure he and Katie had a moment, but maybe it was lost forever. He'd just happened to be there to comfort her.

"I've got this now, Henry." David peered at him over Katie's shoulder.

Henry knew when he was being dismissed, but he wasn't going anywhere until he was sure Katie was all right.

"Danki, Henry, for stopping by to check on me. I'm just overwhelmed with orders, and I let it get the best of me." Katie gave him a quick smile as David kept her close to his side.

"Ya, okay." Henry tried to capture her gaze, but David was boring a hole through him, and Katie's head was down. He took a few steps toward the door but turned around. "I'll check on you tomorrow, Katie."

"She'll be all right." David spoke with an authority Henry hadn't heard before—a possessiveness that caused his chest to tighten. But Katie was a grown woman.

As Henry untethered his horse and readied his buggy, he

replayed the few minutes Katie was in his arms and pondered whether he'd made more of it than it was. Would she have fallen into anyone's arms the way she had his?

He thought about Clara, how honest she'd been, encouraging him to tell Katie how he felt.

Henry wasn't sure there was any point, especially when he looked back one last time and saw David kiss Katie. Again.

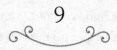

9

IT TOOK A WEEK AND A DAY, BUT KATIE FINALLY FELT LIKE she'd mastered the propane oven. Pies baked for thirty minutes at 350 degrees. Whoopie pies baked at the same temperature for eight minutes, and bread needed forty minutes. Maybe she would adapt to this new system after all.

Still, one element was missing—that special something the wood ovens had added to the flavor. She recalled her comparison to a cast-iron skillet, but she also wondered if the difference in taste had something to do with the process. With propane, she turned a knob, set the timer, and waited. When she used the wood oven, she had to tend the fire and monitor the temperature. It was a nurturing process. Whatever the reasons for the dissimilarity, her mother was going to be disappointed.

Around ten o'clock, Clara walked into the bakery, smiling in that way that warmed a person's heart. Katie barely knew Clara, but the woman had a gift. She could brighten a room with her presence. Katie's stomach twisted when she thought about how close she'd come to kissing Henry a week ago and how much she'd longed for it.

"*Wie bischt.*" Clara slipped out of her coat as she walked toward Katie. "I've come to offer *mei* help."

Katie stopped kneading the dough for the bread she was making. "I'm happy to see you, but I'm sure you have better things to do than to help me."

"We're out for the holidays, and I don't have anything else going on. I really don't mind giving you a hand." She giggled, eyeing the fried pies Katie had made earlier that morning. "I work for food."

Clara was a schoolteacher, a position she'd only hold until she married. Katie wanted to ask if she'd spent any more time with Henry, but it seemed forward.

"*Danki* for your kind offer," Katie said. "I'm still disappointed about the propane oven, but I don't have any choice but to keep using it during this busy season." She sighed. "And I don't want to hurt David's feelings by returning it, which is surely what *mei mamm* will want me to do when she is well enough to return."

Clara sat on the stool behind the counter and picked up a pen nearby. She twirled it in her fingers for a few seconds. "So, how are things going with you and David?"

Katie studied Clara's questioning expression. "Um, okay, I guess." She wasn't being entirely truthful. She'd dreamed up a dozen ways to tell David she didn't want to see him anymore, but it seemed unkind to break up during the holidays. She'd been drawn to his looks in the beginning, but the more she got to know him, the more she realized he wasn't the right person for her. He couldn't be when she was having such strong feelings for Henry. She thought about the intimacy she'd felt in Henry's arms a week ago, but then guilt wrapped around her, and she forced herself to let go of the memory.

"Do you think things will get serious with you and David?" Clara avoided Katie's eyes now as she continued to fidget with the pen in her hand.

Katie tried to understand Clara's expression, but after her friend set the pen back on the counter, she gnawed on a fingernail and wouldn't make eye contact. Then a light went on in Katie's mind. *Clara is interested in David. But what about Henry?* Maybe it should have been music to Katie's ears, but she wasn't sure David would be a good fit for Clara either.

"I am trying to think of a way to tell David that I think our lunches need to stop." She winced. "And all the kissing. Sometimes he makes me feel like a possession because he always wants to kiss when people are around, and it makes me uncomfortable." She was surprised she'd blurted out her feelings, but she didn't have any sisters, and she'd been too busy to visit the girlfriends she'd grown up with. It just seemed too personal to discuss with anyone else.

Clara's familiar glowing expression came alive. "You're going to break up with David?"

Katie's heart shriveled with disappointment. As much as she wanted Henry, she didn't want to see him hurt. It sounded like Clara was more interested in David than Henry.

"*Ya*, I guess I am going to slow things down, but maybe not until after Christmas." Katie opened the oven door and added a loaf of bread.

Clara smiled. "I don't think he's the one for you."

Katie didn't think David was good enough for Clara. He seemed self-absorbed, the opposite of this woman who'd offered to help someone she didn't know very well. Didn't she realize what a catch she had with Henry?

Whatever information Clara had come to gather, she'd apparently gotten, and she rolled up her sleeves and smiled. "Put me to work. Let me help you."

No matter their thoughts about David and Henry, Katie was happy to have Clara as a friend. For the next several hours, they knocked out a record amount of pastries, pies, and bread. The large oven, combined with another set of hands, allowed Katie to surpass what she and her mother had ever produced in the same period of time.

When the holiday season was over, Katie wanted to go back to the old way of doing things. Eventually, she would get used to Clara and Henry being together if they decided to continue seeing each other. She'd also be accepting if Clara chose to be with David.

Katie knew her time with David was coming to an end. Maybe Clara's interest should feel like a gift, but Katie felt like it was a gift Clara would end up wanting to return, regretting that she hadn't given Henry more time.

———◇———

Henry tapped his foot nervously at the Railroad Café as he waited for Clara. He only had an hour for lunch, and he was anxious to hear how Clara's conversation with Katie went. They were behaving like teenagers, but the anticipation of what might lie ahead had Henry feeling like a kid again. The thing about childish antics was that as a kid, hope reigned. Kids didn't usually feel defeated. For a while, Henry pretended to be that young boy again, braving his insecurities. Even as his confidence slipped away, he wasn't giving up until he heard what Clara had to say.

She finally showed up and slid into the booth seat across from Henry. "Sorry I'm late." She peeled off her black cape and laid it on the seat next to her. The temperature had warmed up over the past week, but it was going to get cold again by Christmas, which was only nine days away.

"I think Katie is going to break up with David, but I don't think it will be before Christmas."

Henry wanted to rid himself of the doubt he'd carried around for so long. But it remained, despite his best efforts. "That still doesn't mean she'll want to give it a go with me."

Clara smiled. "You just have to trust me about this. Katie won't say much about you because she doesn't want to interrupt anything that might be going on with us. I wanted to tell her that we weren't going to pursue anything romantic, but you said not to."

Clara had somehow slipped into the role of friend, and if he didn't have such strong feelings for Katie, maybe he would have tried harder with Clara. But then, he knew Clara's heart was being called in a different direction too.

Henry thought back to the embrace he'd shared with Katie, and as much as he'd like to think there was more to their relationship than friendship, he knew he could have just caught her at a bad moment, needing comfort.

"I just want to see what happens with her and David." He took a sip of water.

"Me too. But I'm rooting for you." Clara reached for her own glass of water.

"*Ach*, I took care of that errand you asked me to run." Henry smiled. Clara had come unexpectedly into all of their lives, and she'd been nothing but kind and giving. He was happy to do something for her, and he appreciated her honesty when she recognized his feelings for Katie. He would have dreaded telling Clara his heart belonged to someone else.

"*Danki*," she said. "I guess now we just wait."

Henry didn't think she would have to wait too long to see the results of Henry's errand.

———◇———

David came into the bakery just as Katie was taking out three loaves of bread. She'd turned the pans halfway through the baking cycle, but they were still lopsided.

"I don't understand why this keeps happening." She put her hands on her hips and blew a strand of hair from her face.

David walked up to the counter and leaned over like he might be expecting her to turn around and kiss him, but when she only took a quick look over her shoulder, he stood tall again. "*Ya, Mamm* used to have that problem too. I think it's why she got a new oven."

Katie gritted her teeth. As grateful as she was for the gift, maybe David could have shared that tidbit of information so she could have made a more informed decision. All she really wanted was her two wood ovens back, even if she couldn't produce as much. Hopefully, her mother would be back after Christmas to share the workload. A shiver ran the length of Katie's spine when she thought about her mother's reaction to the new oven.

"Lunch today?" David pulled his phone from his pocket.

Katie almost grunted, but she took a calming deep breath. "I can't. I have way too much to do." She was sure Clara would watch the bakery and keep things going when she got back from her own lunch with Henry. And maybe Katie shouldn't pro-long the inevitable. She'd made up her mind about David. Even though she'd planned to wait until after the holidays to break it off, maybe that was only leading him on further. What if he gave her a lavish Christmas present? Her family didn't exchange fancy presents, but David's family didn't live the way hers did.

Clara walked in right then, and Katie feared she wasn't going to get out of lunch now.

David put away his phone and smiled at Clara. "I bet your friend would watch the bakery, so we could go to lunch."

Clara gave David a curt smile as she passed by him. "What-ever Katie wants to do is fine with me, but I know she has a lot of back orders, and I'm helping her get caught up."

Katie was glad Clara was trying to deter David's efforts, but she was more confused than ever about Clara's intentions.

"Actually, I do need a break." Katie wiped flour from her black apron and reached for her coat on the rack. "You've done too much already, Clara, but if you could just give me this time with David, I won't be gone long."

Clara twirled the string on her prayer covering. "*Ya.* Sure."

Katie was certain Clara wasn't happy about her choice to have lunch with David. She could hear it in her voice. But Katie wanted to end this. Then Clara would be free to go out with him, and Katie would be able see where things led between her and Henry. As she gazed at Clara, she couldn't help but wonder if she would break Henry's heart when she started to see David.

And what if Henry remained uninterested in anything beyond friendship with Katie?

Either way, she was going to be truthful with David about her feelings.

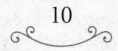

10

DAVID'S EYES ACTUALLY BECAME WATERY WHEN KATIE told him she didn't think she wanted to pursue a romantic relationship with him.

"Is it something I did?" He looked past the pizza on the table between them and stared into Katie's eyes.

"*Nee, nee.* It's not anything you did." It was, a little. He was too openly affectionate for her taste. She didn't like the way he constantly brought up her inability to embrace modern technology. He seemed to march to his own beat, instead of sometimes putting others ahead of him. Seeing him react like this made her feel compassion, and if Clara chose to date him, maybe it wouldn't be so bad. Katie wanted to stay friends with Clara.

"Is it someone else?" Neither she nor David had touched the pizza.

Katie swallowed hard. "I'm not sure." Looking down, she said, "And I'd like to give back the propane oven you gave me." She shouldn't have accepted it in the first place, for several reasons.

"*Nee.* You keep it. You need it." David finally put a slice of pizza on his plate and picked it up, but before it reached his mouth, he set it down. "Is it Henry?"

Katie was still pondering how she could get David to take back the oven when he hit her with that question. Avoiding his eyes, she said, "*Ya*, I think it might be."

"What about Clara? I thought they just started dating." David scooped up the pizza and took a large bite, keeping his eyes on Katie.

"*Ya*, I'm not sure where that's headed. I won't interfere or get between Clara and Henry." She reached over and put her hand on David's. "Either way, I don't have those kinds of feelings for you, although you have been wonderful to me and done nothing wrong."

David heartily finished the slice of pizza and took another one. He'd regained his appetite. "So, Clara might be free?"

Katie couldn't help but be offended that he'd gotten over her news so quickly and moved right on to Clara. Maybe it would be a relief once it sank in. "I-I don't know," she said. "She's only been out with Henry once that I know of."

David nodded with a mouthful of pizza. Katie finally took a bite of her slice as she recalled Clara's sudden interest in David. It could all be the perfect scenario if Henry had feelings for Katie. She'd sensed there might be something there, but she was not going to step on Clara's toes. She would need to put patience and prayer in the forefront of her mind.

By the time they'd eaten and gotten back to the shop, David had a bounce in his step that disturbed Katie. It only confirmed that she had made the right decision by cutting him loose. He'd gone from crocodile tears about the breakup to anticipation in less time than it took him to finish his pizza.

He's all yours, if you want him, Clara.

When they arrived back at the bakery, David followed her inside and went straight to Clara. If he asked her out right in front of Katie, only minutes after she'd broken up with him, she might smack him.

Katie decided to give them some privacy by excusing herself to go to the bathroom. She could hear through the wall if they didn't whisper. Clara would probably tell her if David asked her out. Or would she, knowing Henry was Katie's friend?

Sure enough, David asked if she'd like to go to lunch one day during the week. Clara's answer was like a knife to Katie's heart. "*Danki* for asking, David. But I'm seeing someone else."

Clara had made her choice, and she'd chosen Henry. As much as Katie wanted to stay friends with Clara, she wondered if her heart could take it.

Over the next week, Katie's patrons—many of them return customers—inquired about the new propane oven, which had become a huge thorn in her side. Loaves of bread were lopsided, the pies and pastries didn't have the same unique taste, and word seemed to be spreading through the district that Katie was using propane. It was only a matter of time before her parents got wind of the change.

Even though business had declined, she'd just received an order for a dozen loaves of bread, and the customer wanted to pick them up tomorrow evening. Christmas Eve. With one of the wood ovens still broken, and both stored in the back, she had no choice but to use the propane one for now.

She sat on the stool and looked around at her Christmas decorations, trying to drum up even the tiniest bit of holiday spirit. She'd been in the slumps ever since someone got word to her that Clara had a bad cold and wouldn't be able to help Katie as planned. She felt like a horrible person, but she questioned if that was really true. Maybe Clara was spending time with Henry since he hadn't been by either.

But it was a busy time of year, and Katie couldn't expect everyone to cater to her needs. She would allow a few minutes to feel sorry for herself, then she'd start on the loaves of bread and pray that at least some of them didn't come out lopsided.

When Jonas walked in the door, she sat taller. "Is *Mamm* okay?" Her brother hadn't been by since the day he visited and saw her new oven. She appreciated him not telling their parents, but if he was here to give her a hard time, she wasn't in the mood.

"*Ya, Mamm* is fine. She's anxious to get back to the bakery and said she is coming to work next week." Jonas shrugged. "You're going to have to face the music sometime, *mei schweschder.*"

Katie stood, put her hands on her hips, then gently kicked the propane oven. "I hate this thing. I'd do anything to have my wood ovens back." She turned to face her brother. "And not just because *Mamm* is coming back to work. Nothing tastes the same, and . . ." She put both hands on her forehead. "It's cold in here all the time, and I miss the smell of pies mixed with cedar burning."

"*Ya,* it doesn't have the same warm feeling in here." Jonas went around the counter, reached in, and grabbed a chocolate cupcake. He took a big bite, then finished it off with a second bite. "*Ach,* I ran into Henry. He asked if you could meet him here tomorrow night. He said he can't get here until late, like around nine, so I said I'd bring you since you don't like to drive the buggy at night."

Katie's stomach flipped a little. "But it's Christmas Eve. What could be so important that he needs to see me here that late on Christmas Eve?" She was going to be exhausted after baking and handling last-minute customers tomorrow, then going home to feed everyone. She had a lot of preparation to do for Christmas dinner.

"I'm just the messenger." Her brother snatched another cupcake and waved as he headed out the door.

Katie sat back down on the stool and tried to figure out why Henry wanted to see her tomorrow night. She wondered if Clara knew about this late-night meeting and how she would feel about it.

Katie was on edge all day Christmas Eve. Her stomach fluttered with anticipation and twisted with worry every time someone came in to pick up an order. None of the baked goods was up to the standard she and her mother had set years ago. Finally, there was only one order left to be picked up.

She'd just taken out the last of an order for a dozen loaves of bread when the lady walked in early. Six of the loaves were acceptable, barely, but the other half dozen were a bit lopsided. Katie hoped the woman was tolerant. She'd been very sweet when she came in to place the order a couple days ago.

Katie glanced at the clock, knowing she wouldn't be leaving by three today, even though she'd posted a notice on the door a week ago.

"Hello. The last loaves just came out of the oven and need a few minutes to cool off." She began wrapping the loaves on the racks nearby that had already cooled.

The older woman, dressed in a red pantsuit with gray hair tucked into a bun had already shed her coat and begun to look around. "No worries, dear. I'm not in a hurry." She glanced at Katie and smiled. "I don't have any plans for this evening or tomorrow."

Katie folded the plastic wrap over one side of the loaf, then looked at the woman, trying not to frown since she wore a full smile. "But you look so pretty and festive."

"Oh, aren't you sweet." The lady waved a dismissive hand as she chuckled. "I always wore this outfit when my husband was alive—only on Christmas Eve when we went to church." She paused as her eyes drifted somewhere over Katie's head. "And I guess I just keep up the tradition and think about the beautiful memories we made. We didn't have any children, but we had each other for fifty-two years."

Katie had stopped wrapping the bread altogether. "That's so wonderful," she said softly, wondering who the bread was for.

As the woman began to look at the handmade items Katie's mother kept stocked during the holidays, Katie finished wrapping the bread. When she had everything carefully packed in a bag big enough to hold all the bread, she told the woman she could check her out whenever she was ready.

"I'm sorry some of these loaves are a little lopsided. I've been working with a new oven, and I shouldn't have made the change during the holidays." Katie handed the woman her ticket with the total of her purchase.

"I'm not worried at all how the bread looks." She smiled before she began digging in her wallet. "I'm sure it will taste wonderful, although I'll never know."

Katie tipped her head to one side. "May I ask why? Who will all this bread go to?"

"I don't know yet." The small woman smiled again. "Did you know that the number twelve represents faith, the church, and divine rule? There are many examples of the number twelve in the Bible. Twelve apostles, for example." She handed Katie two twenty-dollar bills. "There are many more biblical mentions of the number twelve. So, each year my husband and I would get twelve loaves of bread. We'd purchase them from different bakeries each year, sometimes as far away as Bloomington or Indianapolis. Then we would ask God to point us in the direction of those He wanted us to offer up extra blessings for, and we gave them a loaf of bread. 'Loaves of love,' we'd call them."

"That's so nice." Katie thought about how stressful she'd allowed her life to become lately. She hadn't made time to soak up the spirit of the holiday.

The woman took out one of the loaves of bread. "And the Good Lord just told me that you are the first person I should give a loaf to." She pushed it toward Katie.

"*Nee*, I mean no. I baked it. I-I shouldn't accept it."

"Then there's double meaning in it. I will pray for extra blessings for you."

Katie feared she would hurt the woman's feelings if she didn't accept the bread, so she thanked her, then ran to hold the door open for her.

"Merry Christmas, child," the woman said, smiling as she carried her loaves of love to her car.

Katie quickly turned off the oven and cleaned up so she could get home, feed her family, then ride back to the bakery later this evening with Jonas. Every time she thought about Henry setting up this meeting, her stomach went wild, and she wondered if it would be something good or bad. Either way, she was going to do her best to remember the spirit of the season.

Katie's mother came downstairs for supper, her first meal with the family since she'd been prescribed bed rest. It was a special treat to have the entire family together for Christmas Eve supper, but Katie struggled not to yawn throughout the meal.

By the time she arrived back at the bakery with Jonas hours later, Katie could barely keep her eyes open. The shop was lit up with lanterns.

"I gave Henry a key in case he beat us here. I knew you'd have one." Jonas yawned along with Katie as they shuffled to the door.

He held the door open, and Katie covered her mouth as another yawn overtook her. Henry was standing behind the counter, grinning.

Katie's jaw dropped. Her wood ovens were back in place, the vent repaired, and everything looked exactly as it did before she'd installed the propane oven. "How did you do all this?" She finally got her feet to move, and she rushed to him.

"Merry Christmas," he said, smiling as she stopped on the other side of the counter. Her heart was alive and glowing with the Christmas spirit. *Thank you*, Gott.

"I'd heard rumors that you disliked that propane oven." Henry rolled his eyes, still grinning. "I've been putting in extra hours at the hardware store, or I would have gotten this done sooner."

"*Danki.* This means so much." She walked around the counter to hug him but changed her mind. It would be inappropriate in front of her brother, and the last time she hugged Henry, it hadn't gone well.

Henry cupped her cheek with his hand, which caught her completely by surprise. It felt wrong. Clara was her friend.

"I know how hard you've been working, and I wanted you to have a *gut* Christmas." Henry gazed into her eyes in a way that caused Katie's heart to flip. She wanted to ask where Clara was on this Christmas Eve, but she longed to savor the moment for a while longer.

"I thought I heard someone come in." Clara rushed out from the back, smiling from ear to ear and almost knocking Henry over to get to Katie. She threw her arms around her. "Are you surprised? Henry did most of the heavy lifting, but I wanted to be here to see your face when you saw everything back to normal!"

Katie nodded, speechless. Of course Clara would be here with Henry. How silly she felt. "It's all wonderful." She took a step backward and wound around the corner, leaving Henry and Clara side by side.

"*Ya*, okay. I'm glad everyone is happy." Jonas yawned. "Can we go now?"

Katie turned to leave, but Jonas held up a palm. "Not you." He chuckled.

Then Clara scurried over and stopped right in front of him. They shared a gentle hug, which was unexpected. "Two days is too long to go without seeing you." Clara's dreamy voice caused Katie's jaw to drop. Again. *What is happening?*

Clara eased out of Jonas's arms. "*Ach*, wait. I almost forgot." She hurried to the counter, reached around Henry, and pulled a sprig of mistletoe out of the cabinet. "I don't think you'll need this, but just in case."

Then Clara ran back to Jonas, latched on to his hand, and they were out the door before Katie had time to process what had just occurred.

"But I-I thought you and Clara were . . ." She searched Henry's eyes. "I thought you were a couple."

"*Nee*. She's had her eye on Jonas since the first day he walked in here. They've been seeing each other ever since she told me she didn't see us being more than friends. She knew I had my eye on someone else." He stepped closer to Katie, and her heart raced as he cupped her cheek again. "I wanted to give you time to see if David was who you wanted."

"It's always been you I wanted to be with, Henry. But I'd given up on you asking me out."

Henry brushed a stray hair from her face. "You take my breath away, Katie. You always have. I've always loved you, but as we got older, you blossomed into someone more beautiful than I could have imagined, inside and out. By the time we were teenagers, you seemed out of reach. I felt like you could choose anyone in our district, someone more handsome, smarter—"

She put a finger to his lips, shushing him. "I chose *you* a long time ago."

Finally, after years of waiting, Henry's lips met hers, and the feelings Katie had stored for so long were finally set free.

"Does this mean we're finally going to date?" Katie gazed into his eyes.

Henry took off his hat and held it to his chest. "Katie

Swartzentruber, would you like to go to supper with me next Saturday night?"

Katie tapped a finger to her chin, grinning. "Hmm . . . I believe I'm free that night, so *ya*, I would love to."

Henry slipped his hat back on, pushed back the rim, and kissed her again. Katie was sure she was floating. When she finally returned to earth, she noticed a loaf of bread on the counter. "Why is that there?" She pointed to the bread, wondering if she'd shorted the woman. She had put her loaf on the opposite counter by her purse before she left earlier. She was sure of it.

"A lady came into the hardware store just as I was closing up. She said she wanted to give me a 'loaf of love' and that she would be saying extra prayers for me."

Katie smiled. "Did she mention anything about the number twelve in the Bible?"

Henry's eyebrows drew together in confusion. "*Ya*, she did. How did you know that?"

Katie went to grab her own loaf of bread the woman had left with her, and she placed it next to his. "Maybe we need to find out if there's any biblical meaning to the number twenty-four since it sounds like we're going to have double the blessings."

Henry kissed her again, and Katie was sure God had an abundance of blessings stored up for them. She looked forward to a bright future with the man she'd always loved.

DISCUSSION QUESTIONS

1. Katie and Henry have always liked each other more than they let on. Do you think things would have worked out for them if they had gotten together when they were younger? Or, sometimes, do people grow and change into the person they were destined to be? Is this an example of God's perfect timing for Katie and Henry?

2. What did you think about David? He's a bit too affectionate for Katie's taste, but he also reveals some kind attributes. There were also some warning signs for Katie (and readers). What are some of the ways that David showed his true colors?

3. What were your thoughts about Clara? Was this also an example of God's perfect timing? Henry and Clara had bumped into each other at the auction, but they weren't able to find each other again. What if they had? Would they have gotten together then?

4. I suspect that cooking with a wood oven is tricky. This

story is loosely based on a bakery I visited in Indiana. I was impressed by the quality and amount of baked goods that came out of the ovens. Have you ever cooked in a wood oven, and if so, what did you think?

ACKNOWLEDGMENTS

THANK YOU TO MY PUBLISHING TEAM AT HARPERCOLLINS Christian Publishing. Special thanks to editors Kimberly Carlton and Jodi Hughes. You all rock, and I appreciate everything you do to make my books the best they can be.

To my agent, Natasha Kern, you're the greatest! Thank you for everything. ☺

I am grateful for my family and friends. I appreciate your continued love and support. Special thanks to Janet Murphy for always having my back and staying one step ahead of me.

Daddy, I love and miss you every day, but especially at Christmas. You left us before this "writing chapter" in my life began. I'm blessed beyond my wildest expectations and living my dream. I'll tell you all about it when I see you again.

God, all of the glory goes to You for gifting me with stories to tell. What an amazing journey You planned for me. Thank you with everything I am, in Your name Lord Jesus Christ. I am blessed.

*M*ELTING HEARTS

❖

KATHLEEN FULLER

To James. I love you.

1

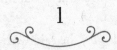

"MATTIE, ARE THE COOKIES READY?"

Mattie Shetler placed the last snickerdoodles specially wrapped for Christmas on a large tray. Each package, neatly tied with either a red or green ribbon, contained eight perfectly round cookies covered with sugared cinnamon. She handed the tray to her aunt Carolyn. "Here you *geh*. Fresh from the oven this morning."

"Bless you. These are going faster than we can make them."

"'Tis the season," Mattie said with a merry smile. Carolyn grinned before hurrying back to the front of the bakery she owned. It was still called Yoder's Bakery, even though she was now Carolyn Shetler, having married Mattie's uncle Atlee two years earlier.

Mattie picked up a clean dishcloth and started wiping crumbs from the stainless-steel worktable. She'd been in Birch Creek for two weeks, here at her uncle's request. When he asked her to come help Carolyn with the Christmas rush after his wife suddenly lost a couple of employees, Mattie caught the first bus from Fredericktown. Her uncle thought she was doing them a favor, but Mattie was benefiting just as much, if not more. She loved to travel, she loved to bake, and she especially loved Christmas. From the crisp, wintry weather to baking treats to celebrating Christ's birth, she always looked forward to this special holiday.

As if he sensed her thinking about him, *Onkel* Atlee strode through the back door.

"Something smells *gut*," he said with a grin. "Then again, something always smells *gut* in this kitchen."

Mattie shook out the dishcloth over the sink. "Snickerdoodles," she said. "I was just going to start another batch." She turned to him and said in a low voice, "Do you want me to save you a couple?"

He chuckled and nodded. "If you please." He leaned against the counter next to the sink. "Asking you to come out here was one of the best decisions I've made in a long time. Except for deciding to marry Carolyn, of course."

"Of course." Her uncle had lost his first wife years ago, when they were both around Mattie's age. He'd mourned her for a long time, even though he tried to be cheerful whenever he was around people. But a sadness had surrounded him, one he'd never been able to completely overcome.

Then he met Carolyn on a visit to Birch Creek, and his life changed. He was happy now—without even trying. Mattie was pleased for him, grateful he'd finally been able to move past his grief. She was staying at the couple's home next door to the bakery until a few days before Christmas, and then she'd return home to Fredericktown.

In their late forties, her uncle and aunt got along very well. Not all married couples did no matter their age, as Mattie had observed in her own community. But she was discovering that Birch Creek was a generally friendly place. It wasn't without its problems, as all communities had. But overall, she sensed a true togetherness here. That and a nice dose of Christmas spirit.

"You're home early," she said, referring to her uncle's work as a cabinetmaker.

"I took the rest of the day off. Those cabinets can wait another day. The plans are almost finished for the bakery addition," he said. "I came by to get some last-minute measurements. I wanted to wait until spring to build it, but Carolyn insists on doing it now. She says she has a feeling we shouldn't put it off until next year." He pulled out a tape measure from the tool belt slung around his waist. "I've learned to trust those gut feelings of hers."

Mattie nodded as she pulled a large bowl from underneath the worktable. When her uncle went back outside, she placed two pounds of butter, two cups of shortening, and six cups of sugar into it. She was mixing the ingredients with a mechanical beater when he returned. "Everything's set to *geh*," he said. "Just waiting for Peter Kaufmann to show up."

Her hands stilled, and the beater came to a halt. "Who?"

"Peter Kaufmann." He frowned. "Didn't I tell you I hired him to help me build the addition? I thought about asking a few folks around here to pitch in, and I know they normally would if I asked. But I also know how busy they are right now. *Yer daed* mentioned in his letter a couple of weeks ago that Peter was looking for extra work, so I decided to offer him a job. He'll be here for a few weeks."

She almost dropped the beater into the bowl of sugared butter. "Peter Kaufmann," she said weakly.

"*Ya.* You're around the same age, aren't you? Went to school and youth group together? Aren't you two friends?"

More like sworn enemies. "Not exactly."

"Oh. I didn't realize that." He frowned again. "He's arriving this afternoon. I told him he could stay in the second spare bedroom."

The one down the hall from her. Great. Not only did she have to suffer seeing Peter every day, but they would be living in the same house.

"Is this going to be a problem?" *Onkel* Atlee asked, his brow furrowing.

Mattie paused. If she'd known Peter would be here, she would have politely declined to come when her uncle called. "*Nee,*" she said. She'd just have to figure out a way to deal with Peter—unless she could somehow get her uncle to send him home.

Carolyn came dashing back into the kitchen, her cheeks flushed. "Mattie, where did you put the fruitcake loaves?"

Mattie pointed to a baking rack in one corner of the kitchen. "Over there, on the second shelf. I'll get some."

She'd spent nearly an hour chopping dried apricots and pineapple the previous morning, which had turned out to be a sticky task. But the results were worth it. Instead of dry and bitter tasting, these cakes were moist and filled with not only the chopped fruit but also candied cherry halves. Her mouth had watered when she pulled the loaves out of the oven.

"The packages look lovely," Carolyn said when she took a tray of them from Mattie. "Where did you get the bows?"

"At Noelle's in Barton." She'd visited the yarn and craft shop the week before and picked up some Christmas-themed ribbon spools, along with plenty of yarn for her own projects. These bows were made of red-and-white-checkered gingham.

Carolyn turned to her husband. "*Yer* niece is a jewel," she said. "I don't know what I would do without her. I was in such a pickle when Leah and Mandy left after Mandy's surprise wedding last month." She turned to Mattie. "*Danki* again for coming to help out." She glanced at the fruitcakes and made a face. "I can't believe people like these things."

"Hey," her uncle said, walking over to his wife. "*I* like these things."

"I'd question *yer* taste, but you had the *gut* sense to marry me." She smiled at him, winked at Mattie, and then rushed back to her customers.

Onkel Atlee shook his head and chuckled. "What am I going to do with that woman?" Then he once again left through the back door, this time before Mattie could talk to him about Peter.

But what would she have said? She stared at the chunks of sugar, butter, and shortening in the bowl. She couldn't ask her uncle to send Peter home. Not only would she have to give him a reason she didn't want to reveal, but it wouldn't be right—even though it was exactly what she wanted him to do.

She also couldn't leave Carolyn in a lurch. She worked hard, but she couldn't run the bakery with only part-time help, especially during the Christmas rush. Nor was it an ideal time to make new hiring decisions, which was one of the reasons her uncle had called her. And although their friend Joanna Beiler and Carolyn's sister-in-law Mary Yoder helped sometimes and were both excellent bakers, they had families to take care of. They couldn't work in the bakery any more than they already did.

Besides, Mattie realized, she didn't want to leave. She enjoyed working in the bakery, even more than she'd anticipated. And despite her feelings about Peter, she had to admit he was a good carpenter. *Onkel* Atlee had been smart to hire him.

Grimacing, she picked up the beater and continued preparing

the ingredients. She didn't have a choice when it came to Peter—she would have to put up with him for a while. And between working in the bakery and completing her own Christmas projects, she had plenty to keep her occupied. She'd have no problem avoiding him. She'd had plenty of practice.

———◆———

Peter Kaufmann slung his duffel bag over his shoulder, the weight of it slamming into his back. He'd brought his own tools and belt even though he knew Atlee would have everything they needed to build the addition. There was just something about the feel of his own tools in his hands. He always did a better job when he used them.

He was surprised when Atlee offered him the work, but his timing couldn't have been better. Peter had just finished a construction job in Fredericktown, no one in the area was hiring for other jobs until after Christmas, and he'd been growing a little concerned about being out of work that long.

He didn't even know Atlee very well. He'd been a kid when his wife died, and the man had kept himself at arm's length from the rest of the community for years as he grieved. When Atlee left Fredericktown to marry someone from Birch Creek, Peter was glad for him—and now he almost envied him too. The thought of leaving sometimes appealed to Peter, ever since . . .

He shook his head. He wasn't going to think about *her*.

Atlee had arranged for a taxi to take Peter from the bus station to the Shetler home, and he made small talk with the driver during the short ride. As the car pulled into a driveway that led to a small white house, Peter spied the bakery next door. He paid the driver, hoisted his duffel bag on his shoulder again, and walked to the front door.

He knocked and waited for an answer. No one came. He knocked again, and when he still didn't get an answer, he decided to go to the bakery. Maybe Atlee was there.

A bell rang as he opened the front door. The bakery was filled with simple decorations—baked goods decorated with colored ribbons, a large pine bow hanging over the top ledge of the window, a few rustic ornaments placed on the display tables and case. He breathed in a delicious mix of cinnamon, chocolate, and peppermint. His stomach rumbled. It was nearly four thirty, and he'd skipped lunch.

An older woman stood behind the long glass counter with a pile of receipts, a pencil, and a small notebook in front of her. "Hello. May I help you?"

"I'm looking for Atlee and Carolyn Shetler."

"I'm Carolyn."

"Hi. I'm Peter Kaufmann."

"Ah, Peter." The woman smiled and held out her hand. "Atlee's working with Solomon Troyer this afternoon. He should be finishing up anytime now, so it won't be long before he's home. It was a last-minute job or else he'd be here. It's already been a busy Christmas season for everyone in Birch Creek. I'm so glad you're able to help us."

He glanced again around the large room. It was a typical bakery, similar to one near Fredericktown he'd been to a couple of times. But it was quiet, and he didn't see any customers. From the taxi, he'd noticed the community itself was quiet, without a lot of tourists common in the larger districts.

Then again, most Amish businesses closed at five. "Is it nearly closing time?"

"Not yet." Carolyn had placed the receipts in a metal box, and she closed its lid and put it under the counter. "Right now I'm thankful for a break, but we stay open until six during the holidays."

"Six? Why?"

"You'll see."

As if on cue, the bell on the door rang, and he turned around. Six customers flowed through the entrance at once, and they were all *Englisch*. So Birch Creek had tourists after all. As he stood back and watched, two customers went straight to Carolyn and placed orders. The other four wandered around the store, inspecting the variety of baked goods on display tables and inside the glass case. Within the next minute, five more customers arrived.

Carolyn called over her shoulder in *Dietsch*, "I need you up front, Mattie."

Peter frowned. Ugh. Just hearing the name Mattie made his teeth clench. Although he managed to avoid the Mattie he knew as much as possible, at least he was sure he wouldn't have to deal with her for a while.

Now that he thought about it, though, he hadn't seen her lately.

One of the double doors he guessed led to the kitchen swung open, and Peter froze. He'd recognize that face full of freckles anywhere. What was Atlee's niece doing in Birch Creek?

Mattie Shetler had her head down as she brushed her hand against her dove-gray dress, leaving a faint trace of white powder on the fabric. Even her ears were covered in freckles. His stomach turned sour, and he fought the urge to flee. He would look downright foolish if he dashed out of here as though his pants were on fire.

Mattie lifted her head. "May I help . . ." Her cheeks turned pale, making the light-brown spots that dotted them stand out more than normal. "Peter." Her mouth twisted as she said his name.

"Mattie." He kept his expression blank. Or at least he hoped he did. "You don't look surprised to see me."

"I knew you were coming," she muttered.

She did? Now he frowned. "Atlee didn't say you'd be here."

She gave him a steady look as she said in a forced whisper, "I wouldn't have agreed to be here if I'd known you were coming."

Her barb bounced off him. He'd experienced her sharp tongue before. And even though they both knew he hadn't been talking about the bakery specifically, she obviously couldn't resist getting in a dig.

Mattie turned from him and rounded the counter toward a woman standing in front of a display of pies. "May I help you?" she asked, her tone shifting from the acidic one she'd used with him to one pleasant and helpful. Sweet. Nice, even. She definitely hadn't exhibited anything close to sweet when she was in his company over the last months. *Didn't know she had it in her.*

Realizing there was no sense standing there among the flurry of activity, especially not with Mattie around, he decided to go back to the house and wait for Atlee. He glanced over his shoulder as he opened the front door. Mattie was talking to the same customer and pointing to a sign that said *Buy three pies, get one free.* As the woman nodded, Mattie lifted her head and looked at him. Her face pinched into a scowl. That was the Mattie he was used to.

Irritated, he sneered back at her, and then he left.

This is going to be a challenge. Not the addition. He'd been working in construction since he was fourteen, both residential and commercial. He could build an addition in his sleep. But dealing with Mattie was a different story. Hopefully, she wasn't staying with Atlee and Carolyn too—although she more than likely was since she was their niece. Maybe he'd need to find another place to stay. But what would Atlee think if he did?

Once at the house, he dropped his duffel bag on the ground, sat down on the cold front porch steps, and put his chin on the heels of his hands.

Merry Christmas to me.

2

ALTHOUGH THE BAKERY CLOSED AT SIX, SEVERAL CUS-
tomers were still finishing up their purchases a few minutes after.
Mattie told Carolyn to go home, that she would ring up the last
sales and close up. Her aunt looked relieved. Mattie was still getting to know her since she and her uncle lived in Birch Creek, but
she thought Carolyn looked especially tired this evening. Maybe
the Christmas rush was really getting to her this year.

When Carolyn came back from the kitchen, having donned
her coat and placed a black bonnet over her *kapp*, she said, "Don't
work too late. Baking that pumpkin bread can wait until tomorrow morning." Mattie nodded, and then Carolyn opened the
front door, letting cold air into the warm bakery.

When the last customer had left, Mattie locked both the
front and back doors and then finished washing the rest of the
dirty pans, bowls, and utensils. Then she went to the front and
straightened the merchandise on the shelves. She neatened all
the displays as much as possible and made a mental note to
go back to Barton to buy some more ribbon and maybe some
other decorative Christmas items from Noelle's shop. While the

bakery did look festive, she thought it could use a few more special touches.

When the displays were to her satisfaction, she made one more check of the bakery. Then she put on her coat, locked the back door behind her, and walked home to the Shetlers'.

When she opened the Shetlers' front door, she inhaled the cozy scent of burning wood. She crossed the living room and held her hands in front of the woodstove. She'd forgotten her gloves this morning, and while the walk between the bakery and the house was short, the sun had set, dropping the temperature even further.

Once her hands were sufficiently warmed, she started to remove her coat. The garment was halfway off when she heard someone coming downstairs. Turning to see who it was, she groaned and then faced the stove again.

"Peter," she muttered, unable to look at him again.

"Mattie." She heard him start toward the kitchen, but then he stopped. "Looks like we'll be living in the same *haus* for a few weeks."

Might as well be an eternity. "I guess we are." She heard him moving closer behind her, but she refused to turn around.

"Since that's the case," he said, "I think we need to call a truce."

Now Mattie turned around. He was right, of course. Not that she wanted to admit it, but they couldn't be at each other's throats if they were both living here. "Fine. Truce."

He smirked. "Somehow I don't think it will be that easy."

"I don't care what you think." She pressed her lips together, cringing. She had a bad habit of smarting off, a habit she was trying to control—even if someone like Peter deserved it. She drew in a breath. "I'm sure we can be civil to each other. I don't want to make *mei aenti* and *onkel* feel uncomfortable."

"I don't either. *Yer onkel* was nice enough to give me this job." He stuck his hands into the pockets of his pants. "What happened with Lizzy was months ago. Let's just let bygones be bygones, *ya*?"

But Mattie couldn't bring herself to agree. Peter wasn't there when her friend Lizzy cried in her arms over his horrible treatment of her, finally confiding in Mattie after he broke up with her. "He's cruel," Lizzy had told her, her eyes red and puffy. "I've never met anyone so cruel in *mei* life. And to think I loved him!"

The only right thing Peter did in that relationship was breaking up with her—although he'd broken Lizzy's heart in the process.

She turned from him and stared at the glowing fire.

"I guess forgiveness isn't in *yer* vocabulary," Peter mumbled, and then she heard him leave the room.

Guilt prodded her. She was supposed to forgive him. She knew that. But every time she'd tried to, Lizzy had told her another story about how horrible he'd been to her. Peter might seem to be a nice person on the outside, but now Mattie wasn't fooled.

It didn't help that she'd always thought he was physically attractive, even before Lizzy and he started to date. Of course, it hadn't been a surprise to her that Lizzy—with her flawless skin, sparkling blue eyes, golden-blond hair, and always knowing exactly the right things to say to boys—had snagged Peter before Mattie even had a chance. That was okay, though. Lizzy was her best friend. They'd been friends since they were toddlers because their mothers were so close. Sure, over the years Lizzy had hurt her feelings at times, but no one was perfect.

Not even me.

She sighed. Peter was right. She needed to forgive him, for good this time. She hung her coat on the rack near the front door and then went into the kitchen. She glanced at Peter, but then she quickly fell back into the habit of ignoring him. She would deal with forgiving him later.

The delicious aroma of the chicken and noodles steaming on a platter in the center of the table made her stomach growl. She hadn't had time for a snack that afternoon. Not that snacking at the bakery wasn't tempting. The chewy date cookies had called her name, but she'd been too busy to try even one. "Supper smells wonderful, Carolyn," she said as her aunt put a big bowl of hon-eyed carrots on the table.

"It does, thanks to *yer onkel*." She looked at her husband and smiled. "He made most of the meal."

"I have a *gut* teacher."

"Do you need help with anything?" Peter asked as her uncle poured iced tea into a glass.

Mattie kept herself from frowning. This was what annoyed her about Peter. He could come across as kind and generous, but she knew deep down he was anything but.

Forgiveness, remember? She set her bitterness aside and said, "I can help too."

Onkel Atlee shook his head as he finished filling the last glass. "We're all set. All we need to do is pray." He and Carolyn sat down at opposite ends of the round table. It was a bit small since only the two of them lived there, but it did seat four.

Mattie sat down across from Peter and closed her eyes. Instead of praying for the food, she prayed for strength to get through the next few weeks.

After the prayer, Mattie and Peter reached for the rolls at the same time. He got there first and held out the basket to her. "Roll?"

She snatched one and set it on her plate.

No one talked for most of the meal, other than both Peter and Mattie complimenting the cooks. Carolyn was unusually quiet, and she hadn't even finished her meal before she started to yawn.

"Why don't you *geh* to bed?" *Onkel* Atlee said. "We can take care of the kitchen."

"*Nee.*" She rubbed her eyes. "I'm fine."

"You look exhausted. Please, *geh* get some sleep. You've been running *yerself* ragged these past couple of weeks."

After a pause, she nodded and pushed away from the table. "Okay. But I'll be up bright and early to make breakfast."

She was looking at Mattie, and Mattie nodded, but she'd tell her uncle to make Carolyn sleep in. She'd get up and make the meal. She hoped her aunt wasn't coming down with something. "*Gute nacht,*" she said as Carolyn left the room.

Her uncle started after her, but then he turned back. "There's cherry crumble for dessert. Somehow Carolyn had the energy to make it last night."

"You aren't having a piece?" Peter asked.

He shook his head. "I'm going to check on Carolyn." Concern etched his features. "She's been overly tired lately."

"I'll clean the kitchen," Mattie said.

"And I'll help," Peter added.

He gave them a small smile. "*Danki.* I gotta admit, it's nice to have extra hands around here." He stood. "See you both in the morning."

Mattie turned to Peter when her uncle was gone. "You don't have to help me," she said, keeping her tone as even as possible. She was tempted to add a sarcastic comment, but she held her tongue.

"I know." He calmly buttered a second roll. "Four hands are better than two, though."

She couldn't keep her gaze from narrowing. "I'm not fooled, by the way."

"Fooled by what?" He took a bite of the roll, looking completely unfazed by her words.

"This nice-guy act. I know it's for the benefit of *mei aenti* and o*nkel.*"

He swallowed, set down the roll, and then leaned forward. "Have you ever thought that maybe it isn't an act?"

She crossed her arms over her chest. "Lizzy says otherwise."

Peter scowled. "I don't understand the hold that *maedel* has over you." He scooted his chair back. "You want to clean the kitchen *yerself*? Be *mei* guest." He grabbed his roll and strode into the living room.

Mattie uncrossed her arms and looked at the table. There wasn't that much to clean up, and she didn't care that Peter left her to do it alone. But his comment about Lizzy bothered her. How dare he judge their friendship? Then again, he was probably still mad at her for the scolding she'd given him after he broke up with Lizzy, after Lizzy had told her he'd even cheated on her. When Mattie directly confronted him about his behavior, he'd made no denials. He'd refused to talk about his relationship with Lizzy at all. So no, she wasn't buying this nice-guy image.

She cleared the table, put up the leftover food, and washed the dishes. The cherry crumble would keep, and she didn't have the appetite for it anyway. She covered the baking dish with foil and left it on the kitchen counter, and then she went into the living room and sat down on one end of the couch. The basket with her crochet supplies was on the floor, and she picked up the scarf she was working on. It was a gift for her father, and it wouldn't take her long to finish.

She used a big hook and thick yarn, and the work kept her mind off Peter for a little while. When she finished the scarf, though, he came back to her thoughts. She hadn't seen him since he left the kitchen. Maybe he'd gone to bed too. She shrugged. She didn't care where he was. She also had to admit she didn't like the lump of bitterness sitting in her stomach like a cinder block. She couldn't blame that all on Peter, though. She was the one holding on to anger with all her might.

Mattie turned off the gas lamp, stirred the coals in the woodstove, and then went upstairs. She shivered as she entered her bedroom. The heat from the stove didn't reach the upstairs rooms, and even though she was used to cold winter nights, she didn't like them. As quickly as she could, she changed into her winter nightgown, took off her *kapp*, and braided her hair. Then she said her prayers and burrowed under the heavy quilts. It wasn't long before she was warm, and normally she would drift off to sleep right away. Instead, she lay awake, annoyed. She couldn't stop thinking about Peter.

Maybe she should call Lizzy and tell her Peter was here. But what would be the point? Lizzy had dated other guys since Peter.

She flopped over on her side, frowning. Meanwhile, Mattie had yet to go on even one date. What was wrong with her that no man in their community was interested in her? Could it be her freckles? She had tons of freckles, and she'd never liked them. She once tried to get rid of them by rubbing lemon slices over her cheeks, but that only made her eyes water.

Also, her slim figure was almost boyish, and she'd been extremely awkward during her teenage years. Lizzy had been both lovely and popular. They didn't have that much in common, especially once they were young adults. That's why Mattie thought herself lucky that their friendship had lasted so long.

But why didn't she miss Lizzy as much as she'd expected to?

———◆———

After leaving Mattie in the kitchen, Peter blasted out the front door. Clearly Atlee was worried about his wife, enough that he had forgotten about the evening chores, so Peter went to the barn to feed the horse and four pigs. He made sure they had enough hay, and then he swept the barn floor. He also tried to put Mattie out of his mind.

He had just put the broom away when Atlee walked into the barn.

"*Danki*," Atlee said, stopping in front of him. "I can't believe I forgot about the animals."

"*Nee* problem." And it wasn't, because he'd had an excuse to stay away from Mattie. Besides, he wasn't just going to do his job while he was here. He'd help out if he was needed in other ways. "How's Carolyn?"

"Sleeping." Atlee frowned. "She's exhausted, and she's been working too hard." He rubbed his chin through his salt-and-pepper beard. "But she says I'm overreacting. Maybe I am."

Peter nodded, but he understood why Atlee might jump to

conclusions. Losing his first wife had been hard on him. "I'm sure she'll be fine with a *gut* night's sleep."

Atlee nodded, but he still looked worried. "Guess I'll *geh* to bed now."

Peter started to leave the barn with Atlee, but then he stopped, picked up a curry comb, and began brushing the horse. He was still avoiding Mattie, which wasn't exactly mature of him. They were both twenty-two and should be past these childish games, but Mattie had gotten under his skin. If she only knew the truth about Lizzy. But Peter wasn't going to be the one to tell her. It probably wouldn't make a difference anyway. Mattie Shetler had blinders on when it came to Lizzy Miller. She always had.

More than an hour had passed before he finally ran out of things to do. He closed up the barn, and then he shoved his hands into his pants pockets and looked up at the night sky. It was cloudless, but the moon was bright. It was also bitterly cold. He'd been so irritated with Mattie that he'd left the house without a coat, wearing just a navy-blue pullover sweater and denim pants. The work in the barn had warmed him up enough, but now that he was outside, his breath was coming out in puffy clouds. Shivering, he hurried back to the house.

He entered the back door and turned on the battery-operated lamp in the center of the kitchen table. The room was spotless, as he'd expected. Except for that bit of flour he'd seen on her dress at the bakery, Mattie was the tidiest woman he'd ever known. In school she kept her desk neat at all times, and her handwriting was perfect. She never had a hair out of place or a stain on her clothes. Since he was also neat, he kind of admired that quality in her. He just wasn't as fastidious about it.

Spying the cherry crumble on the counter, he decided to have some before he went to bed. He had just put a piece on a plate when he thought he heard someone behind him. He turned to see Mattie standing in the doorway, wearing a plain robe belted at her slender waist. Instead of a *kapp*, a light-green kerchief covered her hair—except for the long braid draped over one shoulder. He was about to say hi, but he didn't bother. He wasn't in the mood for another conversation that would head south faster than he could snuff out a candle. He put the foil back over the crumble, found a fork in a drawer, and then sat down at the table.

Mattie didn't move, and when he glanced at her, he saw indecision on her face. Then after her gaze landed on his crumble, she marched to the counter and got herself a piece. As she passed by him on her way out of the kitchen, he blurted, "There's room enough at this table."

He groaned inwardly. Why couldn't he keep his mouth shut? He'd also wondered that earlier tonight, when he'd approached her while she was warming her hands. But something had made him try to make peace with her. It lasted about as long as he should have expected. He plunged his fork into the sweet crumble crust and focused on something pleasant—the delicious-looking dessert.

Mattie paused, and then she surprised him by sitting down. Across from him, of course. She kept her head down as she took the edge of her fork and neatly cut off a corner of the crumble.

In the dim light of the kitchen, he couldn't see the auburn tones he knew were in her hair, but for some reason he kept looking for them.

"Stop staring at me. It's rude."

"I wasn't staring." He ducked his head, avoiding her brown eyes, and scooped up two cherries.

He heard her set down her fork. "Why did you ask me to sit here?"

He put down his fork, too, and looked up at her. "Why did you agree to?"

"I don't want to get crumbs in *mei* bed."

Peter couldn't argue with that. He wouldn't want crumbs in his bed either. "What are you doing up?"

"Not that it's any of *yer* business, but I couldn't sleep."

"Why not?"

Her nose scrunched, turning the individual freckles on it into one brown clump. "Like I said, none of *yer* business." She took a large bite of the crumble.

"Milk helps with insomnia." When she didn't answer him, he got up, went to the gas-powered refrigerator, and took out a quart of milk. He poured some milk into a glass and then set it in front of her. "Here."

"*Danki*," she said quietly, and then she took a small sip. Her eyes had narrowed when she looked up at him. "Why are you being nice to me?"

He sat down. "Because I'm a nice guy?" *Sometimes too nice.* That's what his father had said after the Lizzy nightmare— "You're too nice for *yer* own *gut, sohn*." But Peter couldn't help it. That's the way he was, and some people took advantage of that.

She smirked. "Humble, too, I see."

"You know," he said, pointing at her with his fork, "you should try it sometime."

"What?"

"Being nice." He scraped his plate for the last bite.

"I am." She lifted her chin. "To people who deserve it."

Good grief, she could be insufferable. He stood. "I'm going to bed." After rinsing off his fork and plate, he set them in the sink. Then without saying another word, he left the kitchen—again.

As he made his way upstairs, he grew even more annoyed. Mattie was overly nice to Lizzy, who didn't even deserve her friendship, but she couldn't be bothered to be decent to him. He'd never done anything to her. Women didn't make sense, which was why he swore off them after dating Lizzy. It would take a special *maedel* to make him want to date again, and the last thing he wanted was another romantic entanglement. He'd had enough with Lizzy to last a lifetime.

3

THE NEXT DAY, *ONKEL* ATLEE CONVINCED CAROLYN TO see her doctor. She'd been able to make a same-day appointment, so Mattie was thankful that Joanna could work in the bakery a little later than usual. They'd had a steady stream of customers, and Mattie couldn't have made so many sugar cookies cut into Christmas shapes and sprinkled with green and red sugar without Joanna's help.

Mattie was also tired. She'd slept very little after her encounter with Peter the night before. She hadn't expected him to invite her to sit down with him, although it could barely be called an invitation. And then when he poured her a glass of milk, she was confused. She had to remind herself that Peter wasn't who he presented himself to be. He might say he was a nice guy, he might act like a nice guy, but she knew otherwise.

She hadn't thought much about Peter all day, though. She also hadn't seen him since breakfast that morning, and even then he'd merely grabbed two slices of bread and left the house without a word.

At the end of the workday, she turned the sign to CLOSED, counted the money for Carolyn, and made sure everything in the kitchen and the storefront was spotless. She hoped Carolyn was okay. She seemed fine when she told Mattie they were headed to Akron to see the doctor. "I'm sure I'm all right," she'd said.

"I just want to be sure too. You've been so tired lately," her uncle had added.

Now Mattie locked the front door of the bakery behind her and then put the key in her purse. She was pulling on a glove when she turned around and found Peter standing there on the bakery's porch. "I left *mei* tape measure in the kitchen."

He was wearing a winter jacket and a knit cap that covered his ears. Light-brown hair peeked out from under the hem of the hat, and his pale-blue eyes signaled impatience.

"Mattie?" He peered at her. "You can give me the key. I'll lock up."

"*Nee.*" She retrieved the key and inserted it into the lock. Carolyn had entrusted her with this business, and she wasn't going to let Peter be here alone. She opened the door for him, the scents of cinnamon and cloves mingling with the cold air. "I'll wait out here."

"Fine." He went inside, and she peeked around the doorjamb. He marched straight into the kitchen and then came out a few seconds later. He held up the tape measure so she could see it. She jerked back and frowned. It wasn't as if she didn't believe him. She just didn't trust him.

He came back out, shutting the door behind him. She expected him to immediately head for the house, but he stood there, his hands in his pockets. She'd noticed he didn't wear gloves, even though it was winter.

"You don't have to wait for me," she said, lifting her chin.

"I know. But I'll walk home with you anyway."

The key slipped from her bare hand and clattered on the cement in front of the door. Peter swiped it up before she could get to it. He put it in her hand, and his skin was ice cold against hers. "Why don't you wear gloves?" she blurted.

"It's hard to do *mei* job wearing them, so I often forget. I even forgot to pack them for this trip." He shrugged. "*Mei* pockets keep *mei* hands plenty warm."

They didn't, judging from how cold his hand had felt when he gave her the key. She turned around and locked the door again. It wasn't her business if Peter wanted to freeze his hands off. She didn't care. She put the key back in her purse, and then she pulled on her other glove and walked past him and down the steps as if he weren't there.

As she strode toward the house, Peter caught up with her, his hands still in his pockets. But he didn't say anything as they walked side by side. When they arrived, he bounded up the porch steps and opened the door, motioning for her to go through. If she didn't know any better, she would think he was a gentleman.

Once inside, Mattie saw her uncle and Carolyn sitting next to each other on the couch. That was strange at suppertime. Usually one or both of them were in the kitchen cooking. She knew Carolyn gave her husband cooking lessons while they were dating, which Mattie thought was sweet. But right now they looked anything but sweet. They looked stunned. What had the doctor told them?

"Carolyn?" Mattie moved to her aunt and uncle, swallowing concern, hoping the looks on their faces didn't mean bad news. "Is everything all right?"

"I don't know," Carolyn whispered, looking up at her. "I really don't know."

Her uncle ran his hand through his hair, and then he leaned forward with his elbows on his knees. Mattie's stomach grew queasy. "*Onkel?*" she said, looking at him. "Is something wrong with *Aenti* Carolyn?"

He turned to her, his expression dumbfounded. He paused, and then he shook his head. "She's going to have a *boppli.*"

———◇———

Peter watched with a mix of shock and amusement as the newly expectant parents grappled with the news. Mattie seemed just as stunned as she sat down on the coffee table in front of them. He knew she'd never do that otherwise. "Are you sure?" she asked.

"Positive." Carolyn gripped the edge of the light-blue throw pillow on the couch. Her face turned red when she glanced at Peter. Then she leaned toward Mattie and whispered, "I'm due in June."

Peter could barely hear what Carolyn said. Talking about pregnancy openly wasn't usually done in mixed company. Then again, a couple in their late forties having a baby wasn't usual either. He'd never known it to happen.

"Let's *geh* to the bedroom," Carolyn said, getting up. She took Mattie by the hand and led her to the back of the house, leaving Peter alone with a mute Atlee.

Peter still stood, unsure what to do. Atlee just stared straight ahead. Peter waited a few moments, and then he joined the man on the couch. "Congratulations," he said.

"*Ya.*"

"Guess this is a surprise."

"*Ya.*"

Peter frowned. At this point he was more concerned about Atlee than about Carolyn. "Are you all right?"

Atlee turned to him. "I never thought it would happen, being a *vatter*. After May died, I accepted that *kinner* would never be in *mei* future. And Carolyn and I accepted that we'd never be parents." He shook his head. "How did this happen?"

Peter didn't say anything. If Atlee didn't know how it happened, the situation was worse than he thought.

Atlee waved his hand. "We're too old to have a *boppli*."

"Apparently God has other ideas. Remember Sarah and Abraham?"

"But we weren't praying for a *kinn*."

Peter clapped Atlee on the shoulder. It was strange to be comforting an older man over something like this. "Are you happy?"

The question seemed to pull Atlee from his fog. "*Ya*," he said slowly, and then he smiled. "I am. At least I think so."

"Then I'm happy for you."

Atlee slapped his hands against his legs and bolted up from the couch. "I need to heat up those leftovers from last night. After all, Carolyn's eating for two now. Not enough time to make supper from scratch."

"*Gut* idea." Peter stood next to him. "I'll help."

"I think it's going to be okay," Atlee said, turning to Peter. "I think we're going to be all right."

Peter grinned. "I'm sure you will, *vatter*."

———◆———

She wasn't sure whether pacing at a rapid rate was bad for the baby, but Mattie didn't dare try to keep Carolyn from marching back and forth in the master bedroom. Mattie stood in the corner, unsure what to say. She didn't know anyone who'd had a baby in their late forties. The oldest new mother she knew was forty-two, considered an advanced age for pregnancy. All the other mothers she knew had had their babies in their twenties and thirties, and one when she was in her late teens after marrying early.

"I don't know what to do," Carolyn said, wringing her hands. "Pregnant? How is that possible? I'm forty-eight. That's too old."

"Apparently not," Mattie said quietly.

Carolyn didn't seem to hear her. "I can't have a *boppli*. I have a business to run. And what about Atlee? He'll be nearing his seventies by the time this *kinn* is an adult." She gasped. "So will I!" She started to pace faster. "The doctor also said this is a high-risk pregnancy because of *mei* age. I don't have time to be high-risk anything!"

Mattie decided to intervene. She stepped in front of Carolyn, which stopped her in her tracks. "God has a plan, *aenti*," she said. "Every *kinn* is a miracle from the Lord. You know that, right?"

Tears came to Carolyn's eyes. "*Ya.* I do." She put her hand over her abdomen. "I can't believe I'm going to be a *mutter*," she said, her voice thick. "I never imagined I'd be one."

Mattie held her hand. "Do you want to be a *mutter*?"

Carolyn nodded. "*Ya*, Mattie. I do." She looked down at their hands. "I really do."

Mattie put her arms around her aunt. "You're going to be a great *mamm*," she said, feeling a lump in her throat. "And don't worry about the bakery. I'll stay here as long as you need me."

Pulling away from her, Carolyn said, "I can't ask you do to that. You have a home in Fredericktown."

She did, but the thought of returning there didn't hold much appeal. Lizzy was busy with her new boyfriend and her job at an Amish diner in the next town over. And, of course, she didn't have a boyfriend of her own to go back to. She also had to admit it felt good to be more independent.

"I don't mind," she said. She'd found more purpose in Birch Creek than she ever had in Fredericktown. "Don't worry about me."

"All right." Carolyn sniffed, and Mattie handed her a tissue from the box on the dresser. "I better *geh* make something to eat," Carolyn said. "The men are starving by now, I'm sure."

"I'll do it."

"But you made breakfast. And took care of the bakery today. How were sales, by the way?"

Mattie almost chuckled. Leave it to Carolyn to be concerned with business, even after today's news. "Very *gut*. You'll be pleased. We're running low on sugar, though."

"That's not surprising. I underestimated the amount we needed. I'll send Atlee to purchase some. I promised the doctor I'd rest for a while."

"*Gut*. Now let's *geh* to the kitchen and get you something to eat. You have to keep up *yer* strength."

When the women walked into the kitchen, they were surprised to see the men putting last night's leftovers on the table. "It's not a fresh meal," her uncle said, looking at his wife. "But it's hot."

"That's all that matters." Carolyn touched his arm and smiled before sitting down in the seat opposite him.

Mattie had to hold back a sigh. Would she ever know that kind of love?

Peter tapped her on the shoulder. "Ahem."

"What?" She whirled around, annoyed that he'd interrupted her thoughts—although it was probably good since they were on the brink of being depressing.

"Aren't you going to sit down? We're hungry." Peter moved past her and sat down in his chair.

"Oh." She quickly sat down in her own seat. "I didn't mean to keep everyone waiting."

After they ate supper, Peter insisted on doing the chores in the barn. Her uncle protested, but when Carolyn tried to stifle a yawn, he promptly escorted her to her room. *Oh boy. If* Onkel *Atlee was overprotective before, he'll be downright smothering now. How sweet.* Although Mattie couldn't imagine Carolyn putting up with that for long.

"So." Peter took a toothpick from the small container in the middle of the table and put it between his teeth. "You're getting a new cousin."

Mattie hadn't even thought about that. "*Ya*," she said, staring at the glass of tea in front of her. Would the baby be a boy or a girl? Have Carolyn's features or her uncle's? She just hoped the baby wouldn't have her freckles. Neither her older brother nor her older sister had them, but some distant cousins did. She just had the lion's share of them.

"I'm sure Atlee and Carolyn will be *gut* parents," Peter said.

"How do you know?" Mattie narrowed her eyes. "You just met Carolyn, and you and *mei onkel* aren't exactly close."

"I'm a *gut* judge of character." He frowned. "Had to learn that the hard way." He dropped the toothpick onto the edge of his plate. "I'm going to do the chores outside," he said. "Clean the kitchen, will ya?"

"Ooh," she said as he strolled out the back door. The nerve of him ordering her around. While smirking too. She shoved back from the table and started clearing the dishes. *Not because he told me to.* Because she had given Carolyn her word, and she wasn't going back on that.

4

FOR THE NEXT TWO DAYS, MATTIE BAKED ALL THE SPE-cial orders—six dozen red-and-green sugar cookies—a treat becoming more popular by the day—twelve nut rolls, ten pound cakes, and a yule log. She'd never made a yule log before, but she found Carolyn's recipe and followed the easy directions.

The doctor had actually insisted that Carolyn rest not for "a while" but until at least January. That's when she'd know if she could approve light duty at the bakery. So her uncle had decided to manage the front of the store himself. That meant he'd been too busy to go buy more sugar, and by the second afternoon, Mattie had finally run out of it. She decided to go herself.

When she went to the front of the bakery, she found it sur-prisingly empty. The chance of snow reported in the newspaper might have had something to do with it, but when she looked out the window, she didn't see any sign of snow.

"I need to purchase some more sugar," Mattie said to her uncle.

He opened the cash box and handed her a twenty. "That should be enough for a couple of bags at Schrock's Grocery."

Mattie shook her head. "I need more than a couple of bags." She explained how Carolyn usually ordered in bulk but had under-ordered the last time. "There's a store in Barton where I can get at least fifteen bags. They always have plenty in stock. I'll call a taxi to take me there. It won't take too long."

"That's fine. Mary already went home, but I can handle any customers who come along." He grinned as he gave her another twenty and more for a taxi. "It's not half bad, working here. Pretty easy if you ask me. Then again, I don't have to bake anything, which is a *gut* thing for everyone concerned."

The front door opened, and Peter came inside. She hadn't seen much of him over the past two days, although she knew he'd been laying the groundwork for the addition. Eventually they'd have to tear down the wall between the kitchen and addition, but that wouldn't be until the new space was almost completed. Until then, that wall would separate her and Peter. She'd never been so grateful for wood beams and dry wall.

Peter walked toward them, his cheeks red from the cold. His pale-blue eyes looked almost like glass, and his light-brown eyelashes were ridiculously long. That wasn't fair. She barely had any eyelashes at all.

As Peter spoke to her uncle, she pretended to be busy straightening up the display of individually wrapped brownie squares at the end of the checkout counter.

"I'm ready to take a trip to Barton to pick up those supplies we talked about. The cinder blocks are arriving in the morning."

"What a coincidence," her uncle said. "Mattie was just telling me she has to *geh* to Barton too. Why don't you two share a taxi?"

Mattie's head jerked up. "I'm sure Peter doesn't want me tagging along while he goes to the hardware store."

Peter looked directly at her, his expression deadpan. "*Of course* I don't mind."

"She just has to make a stop at a store for sugar," *Onkel* Atlee said. "I have an account at the hardware store, so have them put the supplies on *mei* tab."

"Will do." Peter stood there, now looking at Mattie with an expression she couldn't read. What was he up to?

"Mattie, you want to *geh* ahead and call that taxi? You can call Carl again." Her uncle handed her the cell phone Carolyn kept for her business.

"Maybe I should just stay here," she said. "I can *geh* tomorrow."

"But you said we're all out of sugar."

"*Ya*, but . . ."

"Besides, Peter can help you carry the bags to the taxi."

"Yep," Peter said, still looking at her. "I'll help you."

Mattie grimaced, but then she took the cell phone and punched in the taxi driver's number, almost sorry she remembered it. Now she was stuck spending the rest of the afternoon with Peter. After she made the arrangements, she pressed the off button on the phone. "Carl will be here in five minutes. He said he's nearby."

"I'll wait outside," Peter told her as he went out the door. Once again Mattie noticed his hands were bare, and so did *Onkel* Atlee.

"That *bu* needs some gloves," he said, shaking his head. "I've been meaning to give him *mei* spare ones."

"You do have a few things on *yer* mind," Mattie said. Carolyn had started experiencing morning sickness, which in turn made her husband nauseated. This morning at breakfast they had both turned a little green when Carolyn put her hand over her mouth.

"True." He took the pad of paper next to the cash register, and then she saw him write *gloves for Peter.* "There. That might help me remember. Now, *geh* on. The taxi will be here any minute."

Mattie complied, but she dragged her feet as she went into the kitchen for her coat and purse. She even paused to retie a perfectly tied ribbon on a package of eggnog bread on her way back through the store. When she saw the taxi pull into the parking lot, she went outside, breezing past Peter. She started to put her hand on the handle of the front-seat door, but Peter dashed in front of her.

"You can get in the back," he said, pulling open the door and getting inside. Before he closed the door, she heard him say, "Hi, I'm Peter Kaufmann. Thanks for picking us up on short notice."

Mattie scowled as she got into the backseat. How rude. Why was it such a big deal that he sit up front? Not that she cared, really. But he had *told* her where she would sit, and she didn't like that one bit. Not that she was surprised. She'd known Peter's real personality would come out sooner or later. He was showing his true colors.

———◇———

Peter halfway tuned out Carl, the friendly taxi driver who clearly never met a stranger. He was probably in his midsixties and the kind of guy who always had a story. He also had the radio on low, and Christmas music hummed in the background. Normally Peter would listen and engage in conversation, but right now he was too busy trying not to laugh. He was getting Mattie's goat, all right, and he loved every minute of it.

He could tell she was appalled when Atlee suggested they go to Barton together. Mattie could never hide her feelings, which had worked against her more than once as they grew up together. When the kids picked on her for her freckles and skinny body, she tried to hold back the tears. But everyone could see she was upset, which made them tease her more. Peter hadn't engaged in any of that. He'd thought it was cruel, especially when Lizzy joined in. Her supposed best friend would turn on Mattie every once in a while, and Peter never understood why Mattie put up with it.

The memories made him frown. Wasn't that what he was doing now? Annoying her on purpose, making her mad for his own amusement? When he grabbed the front seat from her, her face had turned bright red, and she was biting her bottom lip with her two front teeth as her eyebrows flattened into a line. He had to admit that angry Mattie was a little bit . . . cute. In her own coltish way. And up until now, that had been funny.

He glanced over his shoulder and looked at her. She was staring out the window, her brow still flat but her face back to its normal color. Guilt hit him. He shouldn't have made her upset . . . but it had felt good. He was tired of her righteous attitude toward him. *If she only knew the truth.* But he wasn't going to tell her. That was Lizzy's responsibility.

He faced the front and tried to focus on Carl's story about the history of the area, which was mildly interesting. But all he could think about was how he owed Mattie an apology.

A brief time later Carl pulled up to the store where they were going to buy the sugar. "I'll park over there and wait in the car," he said, pointing to a parking lot. "Take your time. I've got my book to read."

"Aren't you going to be cold?" Mattie asked as she opened her door.

"Nah. This isn't bad. I grew up in Manitoba. Nothing compares to Canadian cold."

After Carl drove off, Mattie had just turned to go inside when Peter called her. "Mattie."

She took a few steps, but then she turned around. "I want to get this over with," she said, a spark in her brown eyes.

Yeah, she was still mad, and she had a right to be. He went to her. "I'm sorry."

"For what?"

"For taking the front seat." He shifted on his feet. "And, um, annoying you in the bakery."

"You weren't annoying me," she said, averting her gaze.

"*Ya*, I was, because I meant to."

Her eyes flew to him. "You were *trying* to make me mad?"

"Stupid, I know."

"Ugh. You're worse than I thought."

His contrition turned to anger. "Is that even possible? You've accused me of some awful things in the past, and you've treated me like I'm worse than the manure in a barn."

She lifted her chin. "Because you are."

He flinched. That was it. He was finished with her. She was mean, plain and simple. *Lizzy taught her well.* He blew past her and went into the store. He didn't have a clue where the sugar was, but he didn't care. He just had to get away from her before he said something he would regret.

Mattie watched Peter leave. She had crossed a line this time, and guilt hit her like a tractor trailer. She had no right to say that to him, even if she thought he was a jerk. But other than his behavior in the last hour, he hadn't been acting like a jerk. *Maybe he is a nice guy.*

She shook her head. Being nice for a short time didn't make up for what he did to Lizzy. Despite that, she needed to apologize. She went into the store, passing the bundled-up young man wearing a Santa hat and ringing a bell. Normally she would put some change into the dangling red kettle next to him, but she had to catch Peter.

She spotted him struggling to pull out a shopping cart that was stuck to another one. That might have been humorous if he wasn't so angry and she wasn't so contrite. By the time she walked over to him, he had dislodged the cart and was shoving it through the automatic doors.

"Peter," she said, following him.

But he didn't slow down. Then he stopped a woman who was wearing a vest with the store's name on it. "Where's the sugar, please?" His voice was low and uncharacteristically tight.

"Aisle eight," she said, pointing to the other side of the store.

He took off again, and Mattie hurried after him. Christmas music played from the sound system, and holiday glitter, lights, and sparkle were everywhere. Normally she'd saunter through the wide aisles to enjoy it all, but right now she had to catch Peter. "Stop," she said just as they got to the aisle where the sugar was kept.

He turned to her. "What?"

She moved to stand close to him, looking around to make sure no one was watching them. "I'm sorry."

"Fine. You're sorry. Let's find the sugar and get out of here."

He pushed off again, and she trailed after him. Great. She'd have to repeat her apology, because he clearly hadn't accepted it the first time. She started to get mad at him all over again, but this time she knew she was at fault.

"How many bags?" He was crouching in front of the sugar on the bottom row of shelves. He didn't look at her as he crammed three five-pound bags under one arm.

"Ten," she said meekly. "That should do it."

He put the three bags in the cart, and then he put in seven more before pushing it toward her. "*Geh* pay for these. I'm going to find Carl." He took off, leaving her gripping the handle of a cart half full of sugar.

All right. Let him stew. He had a right to. She would tell him she was sorry again later, when they were alone. Until then, she would take care of business. She decided to add two more bags of sugar to the cart and then went to check out. By the time she had the cart outside, Carl's car was waiting along the front of the store, parked away from most of the crowd.

Mattie pushed the cart to the car, and Peter got out. The trunk lid flipped open, and somehow he grabbed all the bags of sugar at once without dropping a single one. Wow. She hadn't realized he was that strong. He dumped them all into the trunk, and then he shut the lid before getting into the backseat. She quickly slid into the front seat and shut the door.

"The hardware store is next, right?" Carl said, glancing at Peter in the rearview mirror.

"Yes," he ground out.

Mattie sank into her seat. It was going to be a long ride back to Birch Creek.

Carl drove to the hardware store and pulled up in front of it.

"How long do you think you'll be?" he asked as Peter was getting out of the car.

"Not sure. Twenty minutes or so?" Peter leaned back in. "Depends on how busy they are. But I'll have most of the stuff delivered."

"I might come in with you, then. I need a few things myself. I'll pull around back and park."

Peter shut the door, and Carl parked behind the building. "Care to join us?" Carl asked with a good-natured smile, apparently oblivious to the tension between her and Peter.

"Sure," she mumbled with little enthusiasm. As she got out of the car, she realized Noelle's shop was only a few doors down. "Actually, I have another errand to run. I'll meet you back here."

As soon as Mattie entered Noelle's store, the scent of cinnamon and pine reached her, calming her a little. The small diffuser in the window next to the door had to be the source of the wonderful smell. The warmth of the small shop, which was packed to the brim with yarn, fabric, and other crafting materials, made Mattie smile. She loved shopping in craft stores, especially at Christmas, and right now she needed a respite from her feud with Peter.

"Hi," Noelle said, coming toward her. She was a pretty lady, with tortoiseshell glasses and dark-red hair, the shade Mattie had always wished she had. "Merry Christmas! Mattie, right?"

"I'm surprised you remembered."

"I'm pretty good with names. How can I help you?"

Mattie realized she shouldn't take too much time looking for candles and other Christmas decorations as she'd once planned, so she just asked for holiday ribbon. "Do you still have some in stock?"

"A few rolls. We're almost sold out, so you came just in time." She tilted her head toward the checkout counter. "They're in a bin over there." She led Mattie to a wicker basket.

Mattie selected three rolls of ribbon, all red with a thin gold stripe down the middle. The design was nothing too fancy but it was still Christmas-y. She put the rolls on the counter and then spied a large box on the floor next to the register. She hadn't noticed it when she was here before. On the front was written *Donations Appreciated*, and inside was a variety of winter outer-wear. Many of the items looked handmade, but a few coats and jackets were obviously store-bought.

"Do you know someone in need?" Noelle asked as she picked up one of the rolls.

"No. I was just wondering what you were collecting."

"Winter clothing, as you can see. I've had this box out all fall. When it's full I take the donations to local shelters." She shook her head. "They always seem to need the help when it gets cold. I'm taking this box to Akron before too long."

Mattie thought about the scarves and hats she was making as gifts while she was in Birch Creek. "How long will you be collecting donations before you go?" she asked.

"Up until Christmas Eve."

That would give her plenty of time. Mattie held up her hand. "Can you wait to ring those up? I have some more purchases to make."

The hardware shop wasn't too busy. Peter arranged his deliv-ery, and then he purchased nails, screws, shims, and a bucket of mortar for the foundation to the addition. He had to dig it out first, which would take a while since he was working by himself now that Atlee was working in the bakery. He didn't mind doing the work alone, and he would be happy to have a shovel in his hand to burn off a little steam right about now.

The clerk rang him up, charging the purchases to Atlee's account. Carl had already finished shopping and returned to the car, first reminding Peter where he'd parked. Peter took the bags and the bucket of mortar and headed out the front door, ready to get home. He didn't want to spend another moment stuck with Mattie.

When he pushed on the glass door, he struck something. Then he saw Mattie sprawled on the sidewalk, large plastic bags strewn all around her. "*Gut* grief," he said, lowering his own bags and the bucket to the ground.

As he knelt beside her, she sat up, clasping her shoulder and then slowly moving it.

He helped her up, making sure to lift her under her other shoulder. She was so slight that he didn't have to strain at all to pick her up. He set her on her feet and bent down to look into her eyes. "Are you okay?"

"*Ya.*" She bent to pick up her packages, but he beat her to it. He hung the two large bags, which didn't weigh much either, on his right forearm, and then he picked up the bucket and his bags. "I'm sorry about that," he said. "I didn't see you there."

"It's all right. I wasn't paying attention." She looked sheepish. "I was admiring some of the *schee* yarn I just bought."

Well, if that wasn't the girliest thing he'd ever heard. It almost made him laugh, but then he remembered he was supposed to be mad at her. Yet his anger had disappeared the moment he realized he'd slammed her with the glass door. They headed for Carl's car. "What are you going to make with it?"

"Things. I can carry *mei* bags, Peter." She reached for them, but he wouldn't relinquish them.

"*Yer* shoulder might be hurt more than you think." He expected her to fuss at him, but she only nodded, and they continued toward the car.

Carl had already opened the trunk for them, and Peter placed their purchases next to the bags of sugar. He shut the lid and saw that Mattie was already in the front seat. At least they wouldn't be bickering over where to sit—which in hindsight seemed childish. He got into the backseat.

Dusk rapidly descended as they drove back to Birch Creek. By the time they reached the bakery, the CLOSED sign was already on the door. "It's only a little after five. *Onkel* Atlee must have closed up early." Mattie pressed some bills into Carl's hand. "Thank you for taking us."

"My pleasure. Do you need some help with your bags?"

"I've got it," Peter said.

Mattie unlocked the bakery while Peter got the bags of sugar. He put them on the bench by the front door and then went back for the rest. Carl drove away as Mattie grabbed one of the bags of sugar.

"I've got that." Peter reached for it, and his hand brushed hers. He looked at her. "Mattie, just let me carry this stuff inside, all right?"

"All right. I'll hold the door open."

He made quick work of putting the sugar on the worktable in the kitchen. "I'll put those away in the morning," Mattie said, coming up behind him.

Turning, he faced her. "How's *yer* shoulder?"

She moved it and winced a little. "It'll be fine."

"Maybe you need some ice on it." He didn't see disgust in her eyes when she looked at him. Maybe it hadn't been there earlier either.

"Peter, I'm sorry for what I said. I didn't mean it."

It was on the tip of his tongue to make a joke out of her apology, but he could tell she was serious. "I know. And I acted badly trying to get you riled up. I shouldn't have done that."

"I haven't been treating you very well," Mattie said, looking away again. The tips of her ears turned bright red. "I guess I deserved a little push back."

He was surprised. This wasn't the Mattie he was used to. Had the door knocked her in the head too? "We really do need to come to an understanding," he said.

"I agree." She met his gaze. "I promise I won't be so rude from now on."

"And I promise not to try to get *yer* goat." He held out his hand. "Truce? For real this time?"

She took it. "Truce."

She'd removed her gloves, and as he shook her hand, he noted how soft and delicate it was. It was nice. Very nice.

Mattie released his hand. "I need to start supper," she said. "Although I'm sure Carolyn already has. She's going stir-crazy staying home all day, and *mei onkel* is only going to let her do so much." She left through the double kitchen doors.

Peter stared at his hand, still feeling the warmth from hers.

5

THAT EVENING, MATTIE SPREAD SOME OF THE YARN SHE'D bought on what space was left on the coffee table in the living room. Carolyn had decorated it earlier that day with a pine bough and a candle for Christmas. Then she put the rest of the skeins on the couch cushion beside her. She had a variety of yarn—some bulky, some baby fine, some dark, some light. It was enough to make quite a few hats, scarves, and mittens for Noelle's charity box. Now she needed to roll the yarn into balls. It was tedious work, but if she didn't do it, the yarn would tangle as she used it. And she'd rather make the balls all at once to get it over with.

She was on her third skein when Peter walked into the room, eating an apple. He paused at the foot of the stairs and watched her. She was aware of him, which annoyed her, just like she'd been aware of the feel of his hand as she'd shaken it. It was cold, as expected, and roughly calloused, which she'd also expected. What she hadn't expected was the shiver that traveled down her spine when they touched. The *pleasant* shiver. Maybe that was what every girl felt when she shook a boy's hand.

Not a boy. Peter was a man, and for some reason she'd become more aware of that too. Not to mention becoming more aware that her shoulder did hurt. He was right. She might have to put some ice on it.

Peter held his apple in midair. "What are you doing?"

"Making yarn balls."

"Why?"

"Because it's easier to crochet that way."

"You going to do all of them?"

"*Ya.*" She continued to wind the forest-green yarn in her hands.

"You realize you'll be here all night."

He was exaggerating, but it would take her a couple of hours to wind them all. "*Nee*, I won't." She focused on her task, and then she heard him crunch another bite of his apple before she heard footsteps. He'd gone into the kitchen, not up the stairs.

A few minutes later he was back and sat down in the chair near the couch. He picked up a skein of baby-pink yarn. "How do you do this?"

She looked at him. "You want to help me?"

"Why not? Atlee and Carolyn might turn in early, but that doesn't mean I have to." He started to pull on one of the yarn ends.

"Wait." She took the skein from him. "Don't do it like that. You'll get it tangled." She proceeded to show him how to wind the yarn into a ball, and then she handed it to him, certain he'd get bored with the process soon and leave.

He took the ball and the skein and started winding. The doors to the woodstove were open, and although the flames inside were low, she could hear the crackle of the fire, and the cozy scent of burning wood filled the room. Outside, the wind had picked up, and she heard a distant howl as they wound yarn in the low light of the gas lamp.

Peter finished the pink yarn and set the ball on the couch. Then he picked up a skein of bulky beige yarn and tore off the paper wrapper around it. "What did you say you were going to use these for again?"

She hadn't said, but she didn't see any reason not to tell him. She explained about the charity box at Noelle's store.

"So you're going to give away everything you make?" He looked surprised.

"Except for a few things I've already made or started for *mei familye*." And Lizzy, but she didn't mention her name. She and Peter were getting along for once, and she didn't want to ruin that.

"That's generous of you," he said, his blue eyes still filled with surprise.

She shrugged as she wound a ball of sparkly red yarn. This one had been on special, and while it was too fancy for her, she imagined some woman or even a teenager enjoying the pretty color. "I'd have bought more, but I didn't have enough money with me. I think it's wonderful that Noelle is so dedicated to making sure as many people as possible have something warm to wear during the winter. She told me several yarn shops in the greater Akron area do the same thing." She smiled and looked at him. "I'm just doing *mei* small part."

"Not so small," he said, glancing at all the yarn. "How will you get it all done?"

"I'm fast." She grinned.

He grinned back. "That I can believe."

They rolled in silence, and to Mattie's amazement, Peter stuck with it until the very last ball. It was past ten o'clock when Mattie stood, and she winced as she moved her shoulder.

"Did you put ice on that?" Peter asked.

"Nee." She touched it. It did feel a little swollen.

"Geh into the kitchen and get some ice," he ordered. "Or I'm going to unwind all these balls, and you'll have to start over."

"All right," she said, unable to keep from smiling. "I'll *geh.*"

Peter turned toward the woodstove as she was leaving, no doubt to stir the embers and close the doors. In the kitchen, she put some ice in a clean dishcloth and then sat down. After placing the ice pack on the table, she pushed her dress off her shoulder a little to take a look. She had to lift her shoulder a bit so she could really see, and she grimaced when she saw a purplish bruise had already formed.

"That's a doozy."

She looked up to see Peter standing there, in his sock feet so she hadn't heard him approach. She let go of her dress so it once more covered her shoulder.

His expression was somber as he moved one of the chairs closer to hers and sat down. "It must hurt a lot."

"It's not bad." Although now that she'd seen the bruise, she felt more pain. That had to be psychological, because she hadn't felt much discomfort while she was winding the yarn. Then again, she'd used her wrists more than her shoulders.

"Here." Peter picked up the ice pack and put it against her shoulder. When she moved to take it from him, he shook his head. "I'm so sorry I did this to you."

"It was an accident, Peter."

"Still." He gently pressed it further.

She wasn't sure what to do. She'd never been this close to a boy before, unless she counted that time in fourth grade. All the kids were playing baseball, and of course she hit the ball straight to the pitcher. But he didn't catch it. She ran, and Samuel Beachy knocked into her when he tagged her out.

She fell down—and come to think of it, Peter had been the boy who helped her up.

"Feeling better?"

She didn't notice any difference, but she nodded anyway.

"*Gut.*" He smiled. "That makes me feel better too."

Mattie noticed a sparkle in his eyes when he said that, and she shivered. But surely that was because the wind had picked up outside, and because the cold ice against her shoulder coupled with the chill of the kitchen.

Peter took her hand and put it against the ice pack. "Be right back." He disappeared, leaving her to wonder where he was going. He returned right away with the quilted blanket Carolyn kept on the back of the couch, and he wrapped it around her shoulders. "This should help."

"*Danki,*" she murmured as he went to one of the cabinets. He pulled out two glasses and then took the milk out of the fridge. He poured them each half a glass and then set one glass in front of her. She watched him as he sat down next to her, taking a long drink of milk.

She was so confused. How could he be this *nice?* She didn't detect anything pretend about it. The concern over her shoulder seemed real. She hadn't asked for milk, but he gave it to her anyway, knowing it would help make her sleepy. He'd also rolled at least six balls of yarn, one of the most boring activities she'd ever experienced, and he'd done it without one word of complaint or sarcasm. The man in front of her was nothing like the one Lizzy told her about.

She put the ice pack down and took a sip of milk.

Then she looked at Peter, hiding a frown. How she could trust him? Lizzy wouldn't have lied about him. Or had she?

———◆———

Peter had always thought Mattie was an odd duck. That was one of the jokes going around in school, even in youth group—that she was weird. But never had she seemed like the shrew she turned into after he and Lizzy broke up, almost as if she *were* Lizzy. She was still a shrew when he showed up in Birch Creek, still believing the lies Lizzy had told her and anyone she could.

But now he saw Mattie differently. She wasn't odd or weird. She was generous, as he'd discovered when she told him her plans for the yarn. She was loyal too. She'd offered to stay in Birch Creek as long as Carolyn and her uncle needed her, even though that meant she probably wouldn't see her family at Christmas. And she hadn't complained about her shoulder. Surely she'd winced more than once when they were working in the living room, though, and he felt bad that he hadn't noticed.

Then again, he'd been focusing on the yarn and trying to reconcile the Mattie he'd known with the Mattie he was getting to know.

It was all very strange.

He picked up the ice pack, ready to put it back on her shoulder, but she shook her head. "I don't need it anymore."

"Mattie, the longer you keep it on, the more the swelling will *geh* down."

She set down her glass and took the ice pack from him. "Then I'll do it myself." Her tone had a new edge to it, but he chalked that up to pain. When she pushed back from the table and got up, she said, "*Danki* for the milk and the quilt. I'm going to bed now."

"Are you sure you don't want some pain reliever? I can get that for you."

"Just stop!" she said, her voice definitely sharp now. "What *is* all this?"

He was confused. "All what?"

"*Yer* being nice to me. I already said you don't have to feel guilty about *mei* shoulder."

"I don't."

"Then why the milk? The quilt?" She started to shake, and he didn't know if it was because she was cold or angry. "Or are you making fun of me?"

"What?" He stood. "How is taking care of you making fun of you?"

"Because . . . because . . ." Her bottom lip trembled. "Because *nee* one has ever been this nice to me before."

Peter was shocked. "*Nee* one?"

She looked away. "You don't have to feel guilty, and you don't have to be nice to me. I gave you *mei* word that I would treat you with respect. I don't *geh* back on *mei* word." She started to leave the kitchen.

He couldn't stop himself from touching her arm. "What if I want to be nice to you?"

Mattie whirled around. "Why? I've been *nix* but horrible to you."

That was true. However, he'd seen a different side of Mattie tonight, one he found appealing. "I'm always nice to *mei* friends," he said.

"We're not friends."

"But maybe we could be?"

6

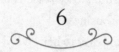

MATTIE WAS DUMBFOUNDED. PETER WANTED TO BE friends? It was one thing for them to be civil to each other, but friends? "We don't even like each other."

"Ouch. You sure know how to wound a guy." But he didn't look all that wounded. "Friendship isn't hard, Mattie." He frowned a little. "At least it shouldn't be." He paused. "Have you heard from Lizzy lately?"

"Nee." Her eyes narrowed. "Is that why you want to be friends? So you can try to get back together with her?"

He scowled. "Absolutely not. I'd rather have a root canal. Make that three." He met her gaze. "I will never, ever, *ever* get back with Lizzy."

"Don't worry," Mattie said, lifting her chin. "She's already moved on."

"I'm sure with several other guys." He paused again. "I shouldn't have said that."

Although it was true that Lizzy had dated and discarded several suitors in a matter of months, Mattie didn't want to listen to him disparage her best friend. "I'm going to bed," she repeated, again turning to leave the kitchen.

"You didn't answer *mei* question."

She let out a sigh and spun around. "What question?"

"Have you heard from Lizzy since you've been here?"

"That's none of *yer* business."

He stood and walked over to her. "Maybe not, but since you're evading the question, I'll take that as a *nee*." He hesitated, but then he said, "You've been away from home for weeks. Wouldn't a friend have contacted you? At least once?"

"She's busy." That's what Lizzy's mother said when Mattie called just after she arrived in Birch Creek. And the letter she sent soon after had gone unanswered. Mattie understood being busy since she was busy herself. *But I made time to get in touch with her.* Familiar disappointment went through her. This wasn't the first time Lizzy had let her down, and she always had an excuse. She was *busy* or she *forgot* or she *misunderstood*. Like the time she was supposed to meet Mattie at the diner for dinner, bringing along her current boyfriend and his cousin. It would have been Mattie's first double date . . . actually, her first date ever. None of them had shown up, and Lizzy had brushed it off, saying she'd mixed up days. She never offered to reschedule.

"Mattie," Peter said, his tone gentle. "Lizzy's not *yer* friend."

She swallowed the lump in her throat, unwilling to consider that statement as truth despite her disappointments. "And you are? We barely know each other."

"That's true. We grew up together, but we don't really *know* each other." He shook his head and looked down at the floor. "How did we let that happen?" he said, sounding as though he were talking to himself more than to her. Then he looked up at her again. "Let's give this friendship thing a chance. What do you think?"

She didn't respond right away. She'd spent so much time believing the worst of Peter, and before that she'd seen him as the handsome boy who would never give her the time of day because she wasn't like Lizzy. Now he was shattering everything she'd believed about him, had expected of him. "What would Lizzy think?"

He rolled his eyes. "Who cares what she thinks? You have a mind of *yer* own. You decide, and then let me know in the morning." He lightly turned her around, avoiding her bruise. "Now, *geh* to bed, and make sure you rest that shoulder."

In a daze, she left the kitchen and climbed the stairs, trying to understand what had just happened. Peter wanted to be her friend. Even stranger, the more she thought about it, the more she liked the idea. But was she betraying Lizzy? She could never do that to her best friend. And Lizzy *was* her friend, no matter what Peter said, no matter how Lizzy sometimes disappointed her.

But what if Peter could be a friend too?

When Peter came downstairs for breakfast the next morning, the mouthwatering aroma of bacon frying and biscuits baking made his stomach growl. Both Carolyn and Mattie were excellent cooks, and Atlee wasn't too shabby himself. Peter had never eaten so well in his life. When he came to the kitchen doorway, he saw Carolyn and Mattie standing side by side near the stove. To his surprise, they were also bickering.

"You *know* I'm going stir-crazy being home all day." Carolyn turned over thick strips of bacon in a cast-iron frying pan. "It won't hurt for me to work in the bakery for a couple of hours each day."

"*Aenti*," Mattie said, frowning. "You're supposed to rest."

"*Ya*, but the doctor didn't say I had to turn into a couch potato. Make that a big Christmas potato."

"I don't think there is such a thing."

"Well, if there is, I'll turn into one if I don't find something more to do besides light housework and cooking."

"Wouldn't being a couch potato be worth a healthy *boppli* and *mamm*?"

Carolyn turned to face Mattie, the bacon sizzling beside her. "Of course it would." She sighed. "You're right, not to mention that Atlee would have a fit if I tried to work at the bakery. But what else can I do? I can't just sit around."

"How about I teach you how to crochet?" Mattie said. "It's easy, and you'll be making something in *nee* time. That's a *gut* skill to have for making Christmas presents! I can show you how to make scarves and hats, if you want."

"I tried crocheting when I was younger. I didn't have the patience or the time." She shifted and turned off the heat under the bacon. Then she picked up tongs and started placing the strips on a plate covered with a paper towel.

"You have the time now." Mattie put her hand on Carolyn's shoulder. Peter couldn't see her face, but he could clearly detect her encouraging tone. "And you'll need patience when the *boppli* gets here. Why not gain some now?"

Carolyn turned around, gave her a hug, and then released her. "You're a wise *maedel*, Mattie. Word about our *boppli* is already spreading because I'm not at the bakery, and *mei* friends want to get together when I'm ready. Maybe sometime soon I can have them over to do crafts. Cevilla crochets, and Abigail Bontrager knits. Naomi Beiler and Rhoda Troyer like to do cross-stitch."

"That sounds like a great idea."

"When can you teach me?" Carolyn asked, now sounding excited about learning something new.

"Tonight, after supper."

Atlee came through the back door, his cheeks red from the cold. "Those pigs were greedy things this morning." He started to take off his coat, but then he stopped and squinted his eyes at Mattie and Carolyn. "What are you two plotting?"

"Us?" Carolyn said as both women faced him. "We're not plotting anything. But if we were, how dare you risk spoiling a Christmas surprise!"

He tilted his head and looked at them a bit longer. "Something's up, and I don't think it has anything to do with Christmas," he said as he took off his coat and hung it on a peg near the door. "But I'll let you keep *yer* womanly secrets."

Peter chuckled, and they all looked at him standing in the doorway. "What's so funny?" Atlee asked.

Not wanting them to realize he'd been eavesdropping, he said, "*Nix.* Just thought about something funny. Wow, breakfast smells *appeditlich.* Can I help with anything?"

"It's all taken care of," Carolyn said. "Just sit down."

Peter did as he was told, and Mattie and Carolyn set out the food as Atlee washed his hands. Mattie didn't look at Peter, and he wondered if she'd thought about what he'd proposed the night before. He'd surprised himself by suggesting they be friends, but now that the idea was out there, it wasn't a bad one. Better friends than enemies since they saw each other every day.

Yet his suggestion was about more than proximity. He was starting to like Mattie, which threw him for a little loop.

After they'd all said a silent prayer, Peter placed a biscuit on his plate, and then he looked up to see Atlee staring at him just before he snapped his fingers. "I remember what I wanted to tell you, Peter. I've got a spare pair of gloves. I noticed you don't have any."

Peter took three slices of bacon. "I'd appreciate borrowing them. It's going to be cold today."

"It already is."

Carolyn told the men about Mattie teaching her how to crochet, and then Atlee and Peter discussed their work plans for the day. Peter was going to start digging out the foundation for the addition, and Atlee wanted to help if business was slow at the bakery. "Business hasn't been slow for a while, though," he said, "so I'm not sure how much help I'll be."

"I'm sorry, Peter." Carolyn pushed her plate away, finished with her meal. "We didn't mean for you to do such a big job by *yourself*."

"I can't think of a better reason for it," he said, meaning the words. A surprise baby—and some might say a miracle baby—was worth a little extra work. He and Mattie were on the same page about that.

He looked at Mattie. She'd avoided eye contact throughout the meal, and he had the sinking feeling she was going to refuse his offer of friendship. He couldn't blame her, in a way. Lizzy had been in Mattie's orbit much longer than she'd been in his, and he realized now that she had manipulated Mattie as much as she'd manipulated him, if not more, which he really resented. He also wouldn't push Mattie into a friendship she didn't want.

Carolyn insisted on washing the dishes so Mattie and Atlee

could get to the bakery. When Peter offered to help her, she shooed him away. "I promise I'll rest after," she said. "None of you need to worry. I'll be fine."

Atlee nodded, but there was still a bit of concern in his gaze. As he and Mattie left for the bakery, Peter headed for his tools and the supplies he'd bought the day before.

When the brutal cold hit him, he realized Atlee had been right. It was downright frigid today. He also realized Atlee had forgotten to give him the gloves. Peter shrugged and headed for the back of the bakery, where the cinder blocks had been delivered early that morning and stacked. He couldn't set them until he dug out the foundation. The digging would be a lot of work, especially without help, but it wouldn't be impossible. At least they hadn't had a long, protracted freeze yet.

He set his tools to the side, grabbed a shovel, and went to work.

"Peter."

He looked up to see Mattie a few steps away. He leaned on the shovel's handle as she came closer and handed him some work gloves. "*Danki*," he said, putting them on. "Tell Atlee I appreciate it. Wonder why he didn't bring them himself?"

"Because I wanted to." She snuggled into her jacket, but she didn't have any gloves and she was wearing only her white *kapp* on her head. "I . . . I thought about *yer* question last night."

"About friendship?"

She nodded. "*Ya.*"

Her voice was soft and uncertain, which made him want to reassure her. "I won't be mad at you," he said. "Whatever you choose."

"Somehow I knew you'd say that." She smiled.

She really had a nice smile, with a dimple on the right side. Right now her nose and cheeks were red, which muted the freckles there. He'd never minded her freckles anyway. They were unique.

"I"—he had to lean forward to hear her—"I'd like to be friends, Peter."

Then she turned around and hurried inside the bakery. That made him grin. He'd seen Mattie a lot of things—angry, mouthy, and more than a little rude, especially recently. But he'd never seen her shy. It was sweet. Cute. And he was surprised at how her accepting his friendship made him happy. Very happy.

———— ❖ ————

The next week sped by. Mattie's uncle was still proving to be so good with customers that she was completely free to work on orders and replenish the bakery's empty shelves. Carolyn said she was thankful for such a prosperous Christmas season for her store.

Mattie had all the baking down to a science, especially whenever Joanna and Mary were lending a hand. "Just don't let Mary make any donuts," Carolyn had warned. "We don't want anyone breaking their teeth."

Carolyn was pleased and grateful for all the help, but sometimes she came to the bakery anyway. Her husband always sent her home.

"I'm just going to watch," Carolyn said.

"And then in five minutes you'll be working away." Atlee shook his head and pointed toward their house. "*Geh* on home," he said. "Please."

She huffed a little, but then she always nodded and left. Mattie knew once they were assured everything was all right at their next doctor's appointment, her uncle would relax. He had a deep faith, and even though he worried, that faith kept him from being a complete basket case.

When she wasn't trying to sneak to the bakery, Carolyn stayed busy learning to crochet. She was a fast study, and she was already working on her first scarf after only three lessons. The edges were crooked, and the stitches were too tight in some areas and too loose in others, but it was good practice. She was hoping she'd be able to make some scarves and hats good enough for Noelle's charity box before Christmas Eve. In the meantime, she didn't seem to get frustrated. "I can see why you like this," she said to Mattie one evening. "It's relaxing."

At that moment Peter walked into the living room after helping her uncle with the outside chores. Mattie could see the weariness on his face, and his normally confident stride was a little slower since he'd started on the addition. But he hadn't complained, and she was amazed at how hard and efficiently he worked.

Rather than taking the extra time to go indoors for lunch, Peter liked to eat in the addition—despite the cold. Mattie didn't mind taking him food and hot coffee out there, and she had every day for the last week. Now that they'd agreed to be friends, there was no awkwardness between them. She found herself looking forward to seeing him. And one day he suggested she eat with him sometime, if she wasn't too busy and could stand the temperature.

Peter yawned. "I'm heading to bed," he said as he went to the staircase. "*Gute nacht*, Carolyn." He paused and smiled at Mattie. "*Gute nacht*, Mattie." Then he went upstairs.

"Hmm," Carolyn said, unraveling a stitch. "What's going on between you two?"

Mattie quickly finished a row of the green scarf she was working on. She already had ten scarves completed, and she hoped to have another ten done the day before Christmas Eve, when she planned to get them to Noelle so she could take them to Akron. She also wanted to have some hats finished by then. She didn't pause in her crocheting as she looked at Carolyn. "There's *nix* between me and Peter."

"I've noticed otherwise." Carolyn was still pulling out stitches. "And yet I had gathered you two didn't like each other very much."

"We don't," Mattie said, but then she realized her knee-jerk response wasn't true. "I mean, we had a misunderstanding. We're now . . . friends." It seemed weird to say that out loud. It also felt right. She was still a little confused, but as each day passed, she realized she'd been wrong about Peter in many ways. Neither of them had brought up Lizzy, and Mattie didn't want to. Whatever went on between Lizzy and Peter was their business, although now she was having a tough time believing he'd done the things Lizzy accused him of. But why would she lie about him? And to her best friend?

"Being friends is nice." Carolyn smiled. "I'm thinking there's a little bit more there, though. Especially on his end."

"Oh, that's not possible."

Carolyn put down her crochet. "Would you like it to be?"

Mattie's hands stilled. The truth was she had thought about Peter as more than a friend lately, but she'd put up a mental stop sign every time. Anything she felt for him other than friendship was obviously left over from before he'd dated Lizzy. And Peter was handsome, no doubt about it. But he wasn't just good-looking. He was nice, caring, and smart.

She also admired how devoted he was to his faith. She'd seen him read from his Bible, and last Sunday they'd discussed the sermon, something she'd never done with anyone. She'd seen him concerned over how Carolyn was feeling and available for anything her uncle needed him to do. Those qualities were what made her heart flutter whenever she saw him smile, which he did quite often when they were together.

But Peter wasn't romantically interested in her. She wasn't pretty, like Lizzy, or popular, like Lizzy, or confident, like—

"Mattie? You didn't answer *mei* question."

"*Nee*," she said, knowing she was lying. But she needed to be realistic. "I'm happy being friends." She started to crochet again. "That's enough for me."

They worked on in silence. The scent of pine boughs filled the room, and Carolyn had lit the cinnamon-scented candle on the coffee table before they started crocheting.

"Speaking of friends," Carolyn said, breaking into the peaceful silence, "I'm sure they miss you back home. You're missing all the fun of Christmas preparations."

Mattie shrugged. "I don't have too many friends."

"Really? I'm surprised, a sweet *maedel* like you. I figured you had lots of friends."

"Just one really close one. A lot of the *maed* I went to school with are already married."

Carolyn nodded. "It gets a little tough when *yer* friends are married off. I understand that well." She stopped crocheting, and then she frowned. "Now I've done it." She held up the scarf, which was starting to look more like a triangle. "Unlike you, I can't talk and crochet at the same time."

After Mattie showed Carolyn where she'd made her mistake, her aunt wrapped the scarf around her ball of yarn and put her crochet hook through it. "I'll fix it tomorrow," she said, and then she yawned and stood. "Atlee must have gone to bed already. I think all this worrying and fretting over me and the *boppli* has gotten to him." Her smile was warm. "Guess I'll join him. *Gute nacht*, Mattie."

"*Gute nacht.*"

Mattie kept crocheting, but her conversation with Carolyn made her think about Lizzy again. Why hadn't she heard from her? Surely her friend could have at least called her after all this time.

She set down her yarn and hook. Maybe something had happened to Lizzy, something serious—although Mattie would have thought her own mother would let her know. A little worried, she closed the woodstove doors. Then she grabbed her coat and a knit hat and slipped them on along with her shoes. She had a pocket flashlight, so she didn't need to take a lamp.

Once outside, she shoved her hands into her coat pockets and walked down the driveway toward the phone shanty. A few sparse snowflakes floated from the sky. She hoped they'd have a white Christmas, but she was glad she didn't have to wade through inches of the stuff tonight.

It wasn't much past eight, so she knew Lizzy would still be up. Once inside the shanty, she shined the pocket flashlight on the phone keypad and punched in the Millers' number. The phone rang several times, which was odd since Lizzy's family kept their phone in the mudroom and Lizzy was always quick to answer it.

Finally, she did. "Hello?"

"Lizzy." She let out a long breath. "It's me. Are you all right?"

"Of course I'm all right. Why are you calling at this hour?"

Mattie flinched. Lizzy didn't sound happy. That was never a good sign. "I didn't think it was that late."

"I don't have long to talk. What do you want?"

"I . . . missed you."

"Not enough to tell me Peter is there. You didn't even mention him in *yer* letter."

Mattie paused at the ice dripping from Lizzy's tone. She shouldn't be surprised that she knew Peter was helping her uncle. She always seemed to know what was going on in their community.

Mattie twirled the phone cord tightly around her finger. "He arrived after I did. After I wrote the letter."

"And you couldn't be bothered to write again?"

Mattie felt anger rise inside her. "You couldn't be bothered to write me back?" she snapped, surprising herself.

Lizzy sniffed. "We're not talking about me. I can't believe you would betray me like this. You know what he did to me."

Mattie gripped the phone receiver. Betray her? How? Besides, she couldn't reconcile the man who had become her friend with the man Lizzy had described. "He's changed, Lizzy."

"Changed? What's he been telling you? Whatever it is, it's all lies. You can't believe him over me. Not after we've been friends all these years!"

But you didn't write me or call me. Seems like a friend would. Mattie also noticed Lizzy didn't say *best* friends. That's how Mattie had always referred to Lizzy. Her throat grew tight. "I'm . . ." For the first time, she couldn't bring herself to tell Lizzy she was sorry. Mattie was always the one apologizing, not Lizzy. *Never Lizzy.*

"I can't talk to you right now," Lizzy huffed. "I'm too upset.

You need to think about what you've done to me, Mattie. Think long and hard." She hung up.

Mattie froze. Her fingers were stiff with cold when she finally put the receiver in its cradle.

Think long and hard.

Mattie trudged up the driveway, tears stinging her eyes. Inside the house, still in her coat and hat, she sat down on the edge of the couch, pain and resentment filling her as she thought about times Lizzy had been mad at her over the years. She'd been mad quite a lot, actually, and usually when she didn't get her way. When they were six she'd torn the head off Mattie's one and only doll, the one her grandmother had made for her, because Mattie wouldn't let her go first when they played checkers. When Mattie had gone crying to her mother, *Mamm* had simply said, "You should have let her *geh* first." Lizzy always seemed to come first, even in her own home.

Her chest ached as her past flew by. The time Lizzy taunted her when she was fourteen and had an outbreak of acne on her face, saying she was gross in front of all the boys. The time she had to walk home by herself because Lizzy let Andrew Kurtz drive her home in her buggy—without Mattie, who'd come with her. She even knew everyone else had already left.

More recently, when she'd mentioned that she thought Peter was *schee*, and Lizzy had told her not to be stupid. She'd said, "*Schee bu* don't date *maed* like you." Lizzy and Peter had started dating soon after, and now she suspected Lizzy had pursued Peter, not the other way around. Why? To cruelly put Mattie in her place?

Tears flowed down her cheeks, and she started to sob. What kind of friend did those things?

———————⬦———————

Exhausted, Peter had put on a pair of sweatpants and a long-sleeved crew neck shirt, climbed into bed, and dozed off. But then he woke up, his stomach growling. He'd eaten a full supper, but he was working hard in cold temperatures, burning up calories. That last piece of the chocolate cake they'd had at supper sounded good.

He grabbed a miniature flashlight and turned it on. The house was quiet as he crept down the hall. He was almost at the top of the stairs when he heard a noise coming from the living room. He tiptoed down the steps, stopping on the bottom one, and saw Mattie sitting on the couch, her head in her hands. Was she crying? "Mattie?" he said quietly.

She looked up and wiped her cheeks with the back of her hand. *"Ya?"*

"Are you all right?"

"Ya." She cleared her throat. "I'm fine."

She didn't sound fine, and she was wearing her coat and a hat. When had she gone outside? He descended the last step and went to her.

Mattie turned from him and grabbed a tissue from the box on the table next to the couch. She blew into it, and then she said, "I told you. I'm fine."

"You're crying. That's not fine in *mei* book."

"Nee. I must be getting the sniffles." She took a deep breath, and then she shuddered.

He sat down next to her. "Do you have the chills? Is that why you're wearing *yer* coat?"

"Ya . . ." She looked down at her lap, and then she shook her head. *"Nee.* I'm not sick."

"What's going on, Mattie?"

She turned and looked at him. Her eyes were red-rimmed and full of tears, but she didn't look sad. She looked angry. "Am I stupid, Peter?"

The question surprised him, but he shook his head. "Absolutely not. Who told you that?"

"I did." She yanked off her hat, which he realized was one of Atlee's. The bobby pins holding her *kapp* in place caught on the knitted fabric, and she yanked those out too. Then she took off her *kapp* and tossed it on the coffee table. "I can't even take off a hat," she muttered.

Peter was confused and concerned. Her hair was bound in a thick, pretty, coiled braid. But her hair wasn't foremost on his mind. "You're not stupid," he said, making sure she understood him. "We've been around each other for a while now, and I haven't seen you do one stupid thing."

"But I feel like a *dummkopf*."

"Why?"

He listened as she told him about her phone call with Lizzy. Just hearing that woman's name got a rise out of him, but when he heard how Lizzy had treated her, he was furious. "Mattie," he said, measuring his words. He knew how much she'd counted on Lizzy as a friend. "She shouldn't have treated you that way."

"I know."

His brow lifted. That wasn't the answer he'd expected. In the past she would defend Lizzy against anybody and anything.

"I'm so angry," she said, angling her body toward him. "I've never been this mad before."

Normally he wouldn't want anyone to be upset. But seeing Mattie angry about how badly Lizzy had treated her gave him hope that she was finally seeing the light. "You have a right to be."

Her shoulders slumped, as though the anger had already slipped away. "Do I? Sometimes she hurts *mei* feelings, but she's *mei* best friend."

"Why?" Peter asked.

"What do you mean?"

"Why is she *yer* best friend? What has she done for you? How has she showed she cares about you? When has she been there when you needed her?"

"I . . . I don't know." Now her head was hanging down. "Maybe I don't deserve all that."

"Everyone deserves to be treated with respect." Without thinking, he took her hand. "Especially you. You've always been there for Lizzy. She couldn't have a more loyal friend than you. What I don't understand is why you give her that loyalty."

Mattie glanced down at their hands. But instead of letting go, she held on more tightly. "*Mei mamm* and Lizzy's *mamm* are best friends. I don't know if you knew that."

"I see them together a lot," he said. "Like you and Lizzy, actually."

"Our being friends made *mei mamm* so happy." Mattie averted her gaze. "She wanted me to be more like Lizzy, and so I tried. 'Why can't you make straight *A*s like Lizzy?' she'd say. 'Why can't you be graceful like Lizzy?' 'You're never going to get a date unless you're more like Lizzy.'"

"She actually said those things?" Peter couldn't believe any mother would, but he was beginning to understand what Mattie had faced growing up.

Nodding, Mattie let go of his hand. "I think she's right. I

should be more like Lizzy." She paused. "At least I used to believe that. Lizzy is smart, and she's *schee*, and she always knows the right things to say—"

"She's awful." Peter's anger made him throw caution out the window. "She's a liar, she's selfish, and she's a user." He tried to hold back his temper as he waited for Mattie's reaction.

"Then why did you date her?"

He rubbed his temple. That exact question had run through his mind a thousand times during the six months they dated and even after their relationship ended. The answer was simple and didn't say much for his character at the time. He dated her because she was pretty, and because, like Mattie said, she knew the right things to say. She had fed into his pride, and he had paid a price for being such a fool. "Because I'm the *dummkopf*," he admitted. "She was never the right *maedel* for me. And none of those things she told you about me are true."

Instead of tearing into him like she used to, Mattie met his gaze. "You didn't cheat on her?"

"*Nee*," he said, firmly.

"You didn't break up with her?"

"*Nee*. She broke up with me." He hesitated. Now it was his turn to confess. "We'd been having problems for a long while. Then when I found out about the other guys—"

"What other guys?"

"Pick one." He scowled. "She flirted with every *bu* in the community. Didn't you notice that?"

"I thought she was just being friendly."

"Is she friendly with any of the *maed*? Other than you?"

Mattie frowned. Lizzy didn't really have any female friends other than Mattie. "Lizzy says all the *maed* are jealous of her."

"They know the truth about her." Peter faced her. "Listen. Lizzy is poison. I don't like saying bad things about people, but it's true. I know she's *yer* friend, even though I'm still having a challenging time understanding why." He softened his tone. "I was just as sucked in as you were. When Lizzy turns on the charm, she turns it up high. She can be nice. She just chooses not to be when it suits her. I don't know why she's the way she is, and I pray that someday she'll realize she can't treat people the way she does.

"Mattie, Christ tells us to love one another, and that's what I see in you. You dropped everything to help *yer onkel* and *aenti*. You're making scarves and hats for people in need. Atlee told me you put an extra cookie in each package he sells at the bakery. You're making sure Carolyn doesn't *geh* stir-crazy, and you're doing the heaviest housework so she doesn't overdo it. If that isn't loving others, I don't know what is."

Mattie looked down at her lap again. A wavy tendril of hair rested against her cheek. He couldn't help himself from brushing it back behind her ear. When she looked up, his breath caught. She was still the same Mattie on the outside—thin, freckled, plain faced, the exact opposite of Lizzy's stunning beauty. But the inside of Mattie Shetler was more beautiful than anything he'd ever seen, and it sent a jolt of attraction through him.

"I'm sorry," she said, her voice barely above a whisper. "I've treated you so badly, and for *nee* reason."

"You thought you knew the truth."

"But that's not an excuse for the things I said to you. You just said that I love others." Her troubled eyes met his gaze. "I haven't shown that love to you."

At the word *love*, he felt another jolt. Of course, she was talking about the loving-your-neighbor kind of love. Yet for a slight moment, his heart had believed something else. *Or had wished for it.* He brushed the thought away. Here she was giving him the apology he'd wanted, and all he could think about was how he was starting to want something more from their friendship. But she needed his reassurance right now, not his mixed-up feelings. "You bring me hot *kaffee* and lunch every day while I'm working."

"That's hardly enough to make up for what I've done."

"You don't have to make up for anything. I forgive you. And while you're the one saying sorry, remember, I've snapped back at you plenty. Can you forgive me for that?"

She smiled. "There's *nix* to forgive." Then she chuckled. "You're really kind of perfect, Peter. Did you know that?"

He blushed at the compliment. It was so good to hear something positive from her. "I'm far from perfect," he said, and then he smirked. "But if you want to think so, I'm not going to stop you."

She batted his arm and laughed. Then she sobered. "*Danki* for helping me see things more clearly."

"What are you going to do about Lizzy?"

"I don't know." She started to take off her coat. "I'll have to pray about it. I don't want to fly off the handle anymore, the way I did with you. I want to follow God's lead."

"You're not mad at her anymore?"

"Oh, I'm mad." Her arm got stuck in her coat. "But a sharp tongue doesn't help anything."

"I know *that.*" He leaned over and helped her out of her coat. Their faces were only inches apart, and his heart went into overdrive.

Then his stomach growled.

She laughed as he put his hand over his middle. "Hungry?"

"Very. I was just going to get the last piece of cake." He scooted back. Being close to her wasn't a good idea. But he wasn't ready to leave her just yet. "Want to split it with me?"

She paused as if she were thinking it over. Then she shook her head. "I'm really tired all of a sudden. I'm going to bed."

"All right." He was disappointed, but he also understood. It wasn't every day that you realized *yer* best friend wasn't a friend at all. It would take her time to get over the hurt, like it had taken him time. He started to get up from the couch.

"Peter?"

He looked at her. *"Ya?"*

"Why did you let everyone think you cheated and broke up with Lizzy?"

Her question was easy to answer. "The people who know me knew she wasn't telling the truth. As for everyone else . . . What could I do about it? I didn't want to get into a war of words with her. It wasn't worth it. She moved on, and so have I. I'll see you in the morning."

"Gute nacht, Peter."

He went through the kitchen doorway, but then he peeked to make sure she was really okay as she walked up the stairs. He wasn't sure what had happened between them tonight, but he knew their relationship had changed forever.

7

THE FOLLOWING SATURDAY, A WINTER STORM HIT, SLOW-ing progress on the bakery addition by a day. After the weather cleared, everyone was back to work. Joanna and her sister Abigail had offered to work a little extra so Mattie's uncle could help Peter. The men wanted to get the walls up before the heavy snow set in.

Mattie enjoyed baking. She never thought she would look forward to rolling out dough, decorating cookies, and making fruitcakes every single day, but she did. There was also the bonus of lunch with Peter as often as she could get free, something else she never thought she would look forward to. But she definitely did.

Today she'd prepared leftover fried chicken from the night before, tangy potato salad, crisp apples, and fresh-baked oatmeal raisin cookies for them. She bundled up in her coat, and then she picked up the lunch cooler and a thermos of hot coffee and went outside.

Peter was nailing down plywood flooring. The trusses for the roof had been put in place the previous Saturday with the help of several men in the community, and the rest of the addition was already framed in. She waited while he finished nailing. Then he looked up. "Hi," he said, grinning. He set down the hammer and took off her uncle's gloves. "*Gut* timing. I'm starving. Let me *geh* inside and wash up."

While he was gone she spread one of Carolyn's old tablecloths on the floor. Then she knelt and prepared Peter's plate before pouring coffee into a Styrofoam cup. When he returned, she was almost finished preparing her own plate, adding an apple to the rest of her lunch.

He smiled when, she assumed, he realized she was staying. Then he sat down and crossed his legs. They both bowed their heads for prayer before digging in. "I'm hungry too," she said before taking a bite from a chicken leg.

"*Nix* better than cold fried chicken." Peter bit into his own piece.

"Except hot chicken."

"Nah." He wiped his lips with one of the napkins she'd brought. "Cold is better."

She burrowed into her coat and kept nibbling. It was snowing a little, but the light flurries didn't bother her, and they didn't seem to bother Peter either. "How long before you can start putting up the walls?"

"Next week. It's going well. We should be finished before Christmas as planned."

"Oh. Then you'll be going back to Fredericktown?" She would be here at least until after the doctor gave Carolyn the go-ahead for light duty at the bakery. That could be at least the middle of January, and it could be even later.

"*Ya.*" He met her gaze. "Unless there's reason for me to stay."

Her heart skipped a beat, and it wasn't the first time since they'd had their conversation last week. She couldn't stop thinking about Peter and her feelings for him. Yet she kept those to herself. She and Peter were friends—good friends. But that was all. She had no reason to expect anything more.

Yet the way he was looking at her now, a mix of questioning and pleading in his eyes, made her wonder about a new possibility. *What if I could have more?*

"Peter!"

At the familiar voice, Mattie dropped her chicken leg on the tablecloth. Her stomach turned as Lizzy walked toward them.

Mattie looked at Peter. He was sipping coffee and peering at Lizzy over the rim of his cup as if she hadn't just showed up out of the blue.

"What are you doing here?" he asked calmly.

"I need to talk to you," she said, and then she turned to Mattie. "Could you leave us alone for a few minutes?"

"Don't move, Mattie," Peter said under his breath. Then he looked up at Lizzy. "You're wasting *yer* time. We have *nix* to talk about."

"But, Peter," she purred, "we have unfinished business."

Mattie's stomach turned again. Lizzy looked perfect, as usual, and her large blue eyes were wide with flirty innocence—although Mattie wasn't sure if that was an accurate description. Leave it to Lizzy to invent a move so contradictory. She picked up her plate of food, dumped it into the cooler, and stood. "I'll leave you two alone," she said, pain squeezing her chest. With Lizzy looking at Peter like that, Mattie was sure she'd soon be forgotten. Lizzy always got what she wanted, and if she wanted Peter back, Mattie could do nothing to stop her.

Peter stood and placed his hand on her forearm. "I want you to stay."

Her heart thumped in her chest, and then it took a flying leap when he slid his hand to hers and clasped it.

"Lizzy, whatever you have to say, you can say it in front of Mattie. She's *yer* best friend, remember? The one you haven't bothered to say hello to?"

Lizzy rolled her eyes. "Hello, Mattie," she said, impatient, as if saying the words was a monumental task. Then her gaze dropped to their clasped hands. "What are you doing, Peter?" she snapped.

"Holding Mattie's hand." He bent down and snatched up the piece of fruit from his plate. "Apple?" he said, offering it to Lizzy.

Lizzy's face turned red. "*Nee*, I don't want a stupid apple. I came here to discuss our relationship."

"There is *nee* relationship." He turned to Mattie. "Want a bite?"

"Ugh." Lizzy stomped her foot, and then she turned her blazing gaze on Mattie. "What is going on with you two?"

Lizzy was acting like a spoiled brat. "We're friends," Mattie managed to say. Lizzy was acting like a spoiled brat.

"Friends don't hold hands like that."

Mattie looked at her hand in Peter's. She'd been so caught off guard by Lizzy's arrival that she only now realized how this must look. Why was he holding her hand?

Lizzy scowled. "I can't believe you would do this behind *mei* back."

"Do what?"

"Don't act stupid, Mattie. I know you've always liked Peter."

He turned and looked at Mattie, surprised. "You have?"

269

"That was a long time ago," she mumbled, her face heating at the lie. She *had* always liked him, even though she'd only told Lizzy shortly before they started dating. Now Lizzy was using what Mattie had told her to humiliate her. And this wasn't the first time she'd humiliated her.

Lizzy let out an ugly laugh. "You're jealous of me, just like everyone else. You always have been. It's sad, really, how you're so desperate for a man that you think Peter would be interested in you."

Peter let go of Mattie's hand and took a step forward. "Lizzy, I'm warning you—"

"Enough!" Anger flamed inside Mattie—even more anger than she'd felt after that phone call with Lizzy. And she was angry with Peter too. He had to be using her to make a point to Lizzy, holding her hand like that. What that point was, she couldn't fathom, but she was finished having her emotions toyed with, by both of them. "I know why you're really here, Lizzy. You couldn't stand the thought of us being together after I told you Peter had changed. And you realized I was getting close to the truth."

"I'm sure you're hardly together," Lizzy huffed.

"That's not the point." Tears gathered in her eyes, and Mattie tried to blink them back. She often cried when she was angry. She'd cried the night she spoke with Lizzy on the phone and got mad about how stupid she'd been. But this was the worst time to melt into a puddle of tears.

"Now I've realized he's the same as he always was. You lied to me, Lizzy. You lied about what happened with you and Peter. You let me defend you when you knew you weren't telling the truth." She started to shake. "You've always made me look stupid. You took advantage of me in so many ways. What kind of friend are you?" Her throat constricted. "What kind of *person* are you?"

Lizzy took a step back, her face filled with shock. "How dare you accuse me of those things? If it wasn't for me, you wouldn't have anyone."

"That's not true either." Peter moved closer to Mattie. "She has me, Lizzy. You're the one who's going to end up alone if you don't change *yer* ways."

Lizzy's face pinched, making her look downright ugly, something Mattie had never seen. "You'll both regret this, you pathetic losers." She turned away with clenched fists and stormed away.

When Lizzy had run off like this in the past, Mattie had always chased after her, begging for forgiveness, apologizing for some slight she hadn't even realized she'd committed. This time she didn't move. She was finished running after Lizzy. She didn't have to beg anyone to like her—or to be her friend. But despite that realization, her body began to shake again.

Peter put his arm around her shoulders. "Are you okay?"

She shrugged him off and moved away. "I won't let you use me either, Peter."

———◇———

Peter grabbed Mattie's arm as she tried to leave. She looked up at him, tears streaming down her face. "Let *geh* of me," she said.

He did, not wanting to hurt her. But somehow, he had anyway. "What did I do?"

"Holding *mei* hand." She sniffed, her nose turning red.

"Telling Lizzy that I have you. You can't use me to make her jealous, Peter." Her shoulders slumped. "As you can tell, she doesn't believe it anyway."

"You think I held *yer* hand to make Lizzy jealous?"

"What other reason is there?"

True, he had probably taken advantage of the moment. He wanted to make it clear to Lizzy that he had moved on. Unfortunately, he had sent the wrong signal to Mattie. "I'm sorry," he said, wanting to brush the tears from her cheeks. "I didn't mean for you to get the wrong idea."

"It's . . . it's . . ." She put her face into her hands and spun around, her shoulders shaking as she sobbed.

Oh boy, he'd made a mess of things. But unlike Lizzy's tears, used as a weapon whenever she wanted him to feel guilty, Mattie's tears born of pain reached his soul. He went up behind her. "Mattie, listen to me. I shouldn't have held *yer* hand when Lizzy was here."

"It's okay," she said, her voice muffled.

"*Nee*, it's not. I should have held *yer* hand long before now."

She stilled, sniffed, and then turned around. "What?"

"I didn't hold *yer* hand to make Lizzy jealous. I don't care how she feels about me. The fact that she even thought there was a chance for us to get back together proves that she doesn't care anything about me." He couldn't resist wiping Mattie's cheek with his thumb. "I care about you. That's why I held *yer* hand. Because I wanted to."

"Oh." Mattie's gaze held his. She blinked. "Wait. You did?"

"*Ya*, I did. Mattie, I can't say I understand everything I'm feeling, because I don't. This has hit me from out of left field. I didn't expect to fall for you—and certainly not so fast."

She shook her head. "You're just rebounding from Lizzy, that's all. You're—"

He took her face in his hands and kissed her. "Does that feel like a rebound?"

Her eyes were wide, no doubt with shock. "*Nee*," she said softly.

Peter stepped back, now feeling both contrite and confused. "I'm sorry." He shoved his cold hands into his pockets. "I shouldn't have kissed you so suddenly. I'm messing this up big time. It's just that I . . . I really like you, Mattie. Please believe me."

She smiled. Then she shocked him by standing on her tiptoes and giving him a kiss. Sweet, sincere, and everything he'd always wanted. *Lizzy who?* When she pulled away, his heart felt like it was going to explode. "Mattie?"

"I like you too." She looked at him shyly. "Was it all right to kiss you?"

He wanted to laugh, but he held it in since he didn't want her to get the wrong idea. She was the perfect *maedel* for him. Suddenly his vow to avoid any further romantic entanglements flew out the window. "Mattie, you can kiss me anytime you want."

———◆———

Three days before Christmas, the addition was finished. The next day Peter accompanied Mattie to Noelle's shop to drop off the scarves and hats she and Carolyn had made. They'd added boxes of Christmas cookies and banana and pumpkin bread for the Christmas dinner Noelle had told Mattie the shelter was also giving for the needy.

When they arrived back in Birch Creek, it was almost

suppertime. Peter paid Carl, once again their taxi driver, and when they started for the house, Mattie stopped him. "Peter?"

"*Ya?*" he said, taking her hand. They hadn't kissed again. They were staying in the same house, and they decided to keep their behavior completely aboveboard. They hadn't given up on their lunches together, but even then they'd kept their distance. Now it felt good to have Peter's hand in hers.

"I have something to give you," she said, her heart feeling heavy. He would be leaving for Fredericktown tomorrow, and she wasn't sure what the future held for them. She wouldn't be back home until her uncle and Carolyn no longer needed her. Had this just been a magical time? Would Peter have forgotten her by the time she went home—or would he have changed his mind?

Those questions plagued her, but right now she wanted to focus on the present—and the present in her coat pocket. She pulled it out. It was wrapped in plain brown paper tied with twine. "Merry Christmas," she said, handing him the gift.

"Wow," he said, his brow going up. "I wasn't expecting this."

That left her a little disappointed. What kind of relationship did they have if he didn't think she was going to give him a Christmas gift? "Open it," she said, trying to be optimistic.

He tugged at the string, and it came undone. He opened the paper and revealed a pair of crocheted, dark-blue wool mittens.

Peter put the paper and twine under his arm and slipped on the gloves. "They fit perfectly," he said, bending his fingers. "I haven't had mittens since I was a *kinn*. They're really warm too."

"You can't use them for work, obviously," she said, pleased that he liked them. "But I figured you could wear them other times. The weave is really tight."

"I can see that." He looked again at the mittens, and then he looked at her. "*Danki*," he said. Then he grinned. "Great minds think alike, by the way."

"What?"

He slipped off one mitten and put his hand in his pocket. He pulled out a wooden crochet hook. "I was going to give this to you later, which is why it's not wrapped. I checked the size of the one you use for *yer* scarves, and then I asked Martha Yoder to make this for you. I hope we got it right."

She held the hook in her hands and examined it in the fading daylight. "It's perfect," she said, looking at him. "*Danki*."

"I have something else I want to give you." He took her other hand in his. "A promise." He pressed her hand against his heart. "I promise that even though we're apart for a little while, we'll still be together. I'll write to you, and I'll come visit you when I can. I don't want you to wonder about us while you're still here helping Carolyn and Atlee."

Mattie breathed out a sigh. *Us.* How did he know that was exactly what she was worried about?

"When you return to Fredericktown, I'm going to spend so much time with you you're going to get sick of me." He chuckled. "Or you'll want to marry me." He leaned forward and kissed the top of her head. "Not that I'm trying to rush things."

She couldn't help but smile. She didn't want to rush, either, but his words warmed her heart. "Merry Christmas," she whispered.

"Merry Christmas." He drew her into his arms, and she wished she could stay there forever.

EPILOGUE

SEVEN MONTHS LATER

THE TAXI PULLED INTO THE DRIVEWAY NEXT TO YODER'S Bakery, and when it came to a stop, Mattie stepped out into the summer heat. When she left Birch Creek at the end of January, five inches of snow had been on the ground. Now the sun's midday rays warmed the back of her neck, and she removed the light sweater she'd worn on the air-conditioned bus ride from Fredericktown.

Mattie smiled. She was glad to be back here. She'd missed not only her uncle and aunt, but everyone in Birch Creek. Staying an extra month after Christmas had given her the opportunity to make *real* friends. She already had plans to get together with Abigail and Joanna tomorrow.

But today was about her aunt and uncle . . . and their new baby boy.

A car door shut behind her, and she turned to see Peter approaching the trunk. Her smile widened. He'd been eager to meet Atlee Jr. and to see her uncle and Carolyn again. Although his time here had been shorter, he'd missed Birch Creek too.

Peter paid the driver, and then he lifted both their bags. "Ready?" he said, grinning.

She nodded. "Ready."

When Mattie knocked on the front door, it immediately opened. "Right on time," *Onkel* Atlee said, his smile wide. Mattie was glad to see him looking relaxed. When she left, the doctor had assured Carolyn that she and the baby were fine and healthy, but Mattie knew her uncle wouldn't fully set his worry aside until after the baby was born.

Once they were inside, the men shook hands as Mattie spied Carolyn sitting in a rocking chair, Junior in her arms. She waved Mattie over.

"He's just fallen asleep," Carolyn said as she cuddled her son.

Mattie sat down on the couch as Carolyn stroked Junior's soft black hair. He had a lot of it for such a tiny baby. "He's *schee*," Mattie whispered.

Carolyn nodded, accepting the compliment with humility. "It's *gut* to see you again. Let me set him in his cradle, and I'll be right back."

A little later the four of them were settled in the living room, glasses of iced tea and a tray with thick slices of apple-carrot bread in front of them. Both parents looked tired, as new parents tended to be, but they also looked happy. Mattie glanced at Peter, but he was busy putting a slice of the bread on a small plate.

"We're sorry we couldn't attend *yer* wedding," *Onkel* Atlee said. Mattie and Peter had been married in late March when Carolyn couldn't travel and her husband wouldn't leave her side. The whole community—including their parents—had been supportive. But not Lizzy. She hadn't come to the wedding, even though Mattie had invited everyone. Her rejection had hurt a bit, but Mattie wasn't going to let Lizzy spoil their happiness. She could only pray for her former friend.

"We understood." Mattie picked up her glass of tea.

"You missed a great wedding, though," Peter said between bites. "If I do say so myself."

Mattie elbowed him, but she couldn't keep from smiling. Peter grinned at her, and then he nodded. She drew in a big breath. "We have some news," she said, looking at Carolyn and then her uncle.

"You're having a *boppli*!" Carolyn said, clasping her hands together.

Onkel Atlee gave her a stern look. "Don't spoil it for them."

"Actually," Peter said, "we're moving to Birch Creek."

"You are?" Carolyn's smile widened.

Mattie nodded. "Peter got a job working for a construction company in Barton." She glanced at him. "He started looking as soon as we realized this is where we want to live."

"I had *nee* idea."

"We both like it here." Peter set down his empty plate. "And we figured this would be a great place to start our future."

"That's wonderful!" Carolyn exclaimed. "A lovely little *haus* is for sale down the street. Just came on the market yesterday."

"We'll take a look at it," he said.

They all heard Junior whimper. Instead of getting up from her rocking chair, Carolyn said, "Mattie, why don't you check on him?"

Mattie blinked. "Are you sure?"

Carolyn's expression grew soft. "I'm sure."

Mattie went to the master bedroom, where a simple but lovely cradle sat in the corner next to the bed. She leaned down and looked at Junior, who had already fallen back asleep. She couldn't resist lightly touching his hair. Then she felt a hand on her shoulder. She turned her head to see Peter smiling at her.

"Should we tell them?" she whispered.

He put his hand over her abdomen. "We'll tell them later. Then Carolyn will really be surprised." He kissed her forehead.

Mattie's heart squeezed with happiness as she looked down at the baby. She was deeply in love with her husband, and soon they would have a new home.

And come Christmas, we'll have a boppli *too.*

DISCUSSION QUESTIONS

1. Why did Mattie have so much animosity toward Peter?
2. Why did Mattie believe Lizzy was her best friend, even though Lizzy was cruel to her at times?
3. Peter let everyone believe a lie about his relationship with Lizzy. Was he right to do this, or should he have told the truth at the start?
4. What qualities did Mattie and Peter have that attracted them to each other?
5. Do you think there's hope for Lizzy? Why or why not?

ACKNOWLEDGMENTS

A BIG THANK YOU TO MY EDITORS, BECKY MONDS AND Jean Bloom, for their invaluable input and editing expertise.

CAKES AND KISSES

---◆---

KELLY IRVIN

To my sweet uncle Duane, may he rest in peace

So God created mankind in his own image,
in the image of God he created them;
male and female he created them.

GENESIS 1:27

1

AMBROSE HERSHBERGER COUNTED THE CHANGE AGAIN. The last time his boss sent him to the Jamesport Grocery Store to buy extra food for the café, the change hadn't matched the receipt. Ambrose wasn't good at math, but his boss, Burke McMillan, never complained. He never yelled at Ambrose. He simply pointed out the mistake. Then he gave Ambrose a cup of coffee, sat him down on a stool at the front counter of the Purple Martin Café, and went over the numbers with him, like he was a regular guy who understood these things.

Like he cared about Ambrose knowing how to count change.

Jonnie Parker's forehead furled. The cashier's dark eyebrows, mismatched to her blonde-and-blue hair, rose and fell. "Is everything okay, Ambrose?"

"Yes, ma'am."

"I keep telling you, don't 'ma'am' me. I'm only twenty-nine."

"Sorry, ma'am."

Jonnie giggled. "You're holding up the line, sweetie."

Ladies always called Ambrose names like sweetie and honey. He had no idea why. "Sorry."

"You shouldn't apologize so much." She handed him a chocolate Tootsie Pop. "On me. See you next time."

"Thank you." He liked chocolate. A lot. He unwrapped the sucker and popped it in his mouth. The cashier held out her hand. He deposited the wrapper on her palm. "See you next time."

"Not if I see you first."

That wasn't very nice. How did a man answer that?

"I'm joking, sweetie. You're welcome here any time."

"Oh. Okay." He laughed. He liked a good joke, even if it was on him. "Take care."

"You too. Don't take any wooden nickels."

He glanced at the change in his hand. Three dollars, a quarter, two dimes, and two pennies. No nickels. Wooden or otherwise.

"It's a joke, Ambrose."

"I know." Of course he knew. No wooden nickels. Careful not to jostle the two twenty-four packs of eggs nestled on top, he scooped up three large paper bags and headed for the door.

"Do you need some help?" Louis, the stock-boy-slash-janitor, set aside his push broom and rushed to open the glass door for Ambrose. "I can carry some of those bags out for you."

Louis was a nice kid, but Ambrose topped six four and weighed at least two hundred pounds. He had lots of muscles from working on his little farm, doing handyman jobs for folks around town, and delivering for the Ropp family's bakery. "Thank you, but I got it."

"Take care."

"You too." Louis closed the door after Ambrose.

They were such nice folks. Most people in Jamesport, Missouri, were. It was one of the many reasons Ambrose was content to live in the place he'd been born thirty years earlier.

Contentment felt good. Like hot coffee on the front porch as the sun crept over the horizon each day.

He'd parked the wagon in the only open spot, near the corner. He didn't mind the short walk. The chocolate sucker tasted good. The sun shone on this first day of May. A breeze blew and only a hint of summer's heat touched his face when he lifted it to the sun. Spring was by far the best time of year. He tilled the soil for his garden, planted vegetables and flowers, filled the bird feeders, and sat on his front porch to drink his coffee and share his breakfast with Samson, Jasper, and Amelia, his cats, and Pirate, the one-eyed dog who acted like he owned the place.

Sometimes Aunt Mae joined them, but she didn't talk much, so Ambrose didn't mind.

He had a good life. It lacked a wife and children, but he'd given up the desires of his heart long ago. A simple man like himself couldn't expect to be a husband and father. He wasn't smart enough to be in charge of anything.

A group of English boys clustered around a bench outside the store. They bellowed over something on a phone.

Ambrose zigzagged to avoid their sprawling legs and feet that wore fancy, expensive sneakers.

A second later, his boots encountered an obstacle he couldn't see over the bags. He teetered and pitched forward.

Don't let go, don't let go.

He had no choice. He let go of the bags, flailed, and tried to catch himself.

Too late. The sucker went flying. He flopped facedown in a quart of fresh strawberries.

A jar of artichoke hearts shattered. Cans of tomato sauce rolled into the street. Heads of lettuce scattered.

"Oops!" One of the boys squatted next to him. Conner Benson, the middle school principal's oldest son. A squinty look on his pimpled face, he patted Ambrose's face and grinned. He had a mouth full of braces. "You fell."

"It's okay. I'm fine." Ambrose struggled to rise. "I'm clumsy."

Another boy Ambrose didn't recognize planted his cowboy boot in the middle of Ambrose's back. "Don't get up. You might have broken something. You shouldn't move."

"You lost your hat." Jason Mick, one of Conner's buddies, picked it up. Instead of putting it back on Ambrose's head, he plopped unbroken eggs, one after the other, into the straw hat. "Here you go."

He slapped the hat on Ambrose's head.

Slimy egg yolks and pieces of shell trickled down Ambrose's forehead and into his eyes. "That's not nice." He slid his hands forward, palms down, and hoisted himself up. A nasty pain sliced through his palm. Broken glass. *"Ach!* It's okay. Let me up."

"Sure thing."

Laughing, Jason and Conner moved back a step. Ambrose stared at their fancy shoes. A foot remained shoved into his back.

The word *idiot* floated over him, mixed with snorts and chortles.

"Get away from him right now," a familiar voice yelled from a distance.

The laughter died. The pressure on his back disappeared.

The scents of cinnamon and vanilla tickled his nose. Soft fingers touched his cheek.

No one ever touched Ambrose. Not even Aunt Mae.

It felt so nice.

2

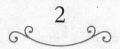

"I SAW WHAT YOU DID!"

Yelling at the fleeing boys did no good and likely would've caused the bishop to wince at the public display of ire if he were present, but Martha Ropp wanted them to know their meanness had not gone unnoticed. She saw it. So did an omnipotent, omnipresent God, if she understood Bishop Ben's sermons.

Which, truth be told, she often didn't.

Martha crouched next to Ambrose. She used her apron to wipe egg yolks mixed with broken shell from his forehead and eyes. "That boy Conner stuck his foot out and tripped you." She peered at Ambrose's face, looking for wounds. "They need to be taught a lesson. Preferably in the woodshed."

"They're just being boys." Ambrose drew up his knees and rose on all fours. He grunted. "I'm so clumsy. I've ruined Burke's groceries."

"You're not clumsy. They did it on purpose."

"Ben would say to forgive them."

Indeed the bishop would say exactly that. "You're right, but he would also say children need to sow what they want to reap in order to become God-fearing adults."

"Did they plant seeds?"

Ambrose's penchant for literal-mindedness tickled Martha sometimes, but she never laughed at him like the others. "None that will grow."

He swiveled, sat on his behind, and swiped at his eyes. A streak of blood mixed with the eggs, strawberries, and dirt on his face.

"*Ach*, you're bleeding." Renewed anger coursing through her, Martha grabbed his hand. A gaping cut seeped blood on his palm. She applied pressure with her apron. "I should tell Deputy Dan. He'll have a word with their parents. And the high school principal. He'll stop letting them leave the campus for lunch."

"*Nee! Nee.*" His smooth, dimpled cheeks were cherry red. Ambrose tugged his hand back. He ducked his head and grabbed the closest paper bag. It was wet and dirty. "It'll be fine. Burke is waiting for the groceries."

"You're covered with eggs and produce." She'd touched him without thinking. Now heat toasted Martha's cheeks. With the exception of her father, God rest his soul, she'd never touched a grown man. A single Plain woman didn't take a man's hand—or any man's hand. The bishop wouldn't like that either. Nor would Martha's parents if they could see her now.

Martha didn't think of Ambrose like that. He was sweet and kind and ready to help at the drop of a hat. He'd give a person his favorite clean shirt along with his last dollar. Why would anyone be mean to him? "You can't go back to the restaurant looking like this. Come to the bakery. You can clean up in the back."

Ambrose scooped up a head of iceberg lettuce and laid it

gently in the bag. Still on his knees he corralled cans and jars. "Burke is waiting."

"He'll wait a little longer, I promise." Martha plucked a large container of pepper from the detritus on the sidewalk. "I reckon this is just stopgap until he does his big grocery shopping on Friday. Come on. Come with me."

She stood. Ambrose did the same. Martha was short and round. Ambrose towered over her. He had broad shoulders, big hands, and not an ounce of fat on his body. Despite his size, he had a child's face. Smooth, fair skin, eyes the color of maple syrup, curly brown hair, and not a line around his eyes or mouth. He was the same age as her oldest brother, Henry—thirty. His sweet smile always made Martha smile in return.

Not that she would tell him that. She grabbed a sack and started filling it. Louis stuck his head out the grocery store door. She explained the mess and he promised to take care of hosing it down. After a glance back to make sure Ambrose followed, Martha trotted across the street to the Sweet Tooth Bakery, owned by her family since before she was born. She unlocked the door and pushed through. "Come around the counter into the back." She set her bag on the table behind the counter. She didn't want that mess on her sparkling-clean glass countertops.

His expression meek, Ambrose deposited his sacks and lumbered past her without speaking.

"First things first." She pointed to a chair tucked into a table by the room's only windows. "Have a seat so I can take a look at your hand."

"You don't have to do that." He shuffled his scuffed, worn work boots. "I'm okay."

"You keep saying that, but you don't want that cut to get

infected, do you? Raw eggs have germs in them." She tugged the first aid kit from the shelf and moved to the table. "Sit."

He sat.

"Let me see your hand."

He kept it tucked in his lap.

"It won't hurt. Not much. And you're a big guy. You can handle it."

He sniffed and scowled. Slowly, his hand slipped on to the table. Palm down.

"Ambrose."

He turned it over. The piercing wound was deep, but not too long. Martha took a quick breath. She loathed to hurt him. Still, it would hurt worse if it got infected. Sighing, she poured hydrogen peroxide on a piece of clean gauze and dabbed gingerly until the cut was clean.

His hand jerked once or twice, but Ambrose didn't speak. Martha let her gaze sideswipe his face. He seemed mesmerized by her hands. His fingers were twice as long as hers with calluses representing years of hard work. His fingernails were clean but jagged.

She touched a scar near the inside of his ring finger. Now he'd have another to match it. Something about holding his hand in hers and tending to it made her throat tighten. He was like an injured animal, scared but trusting.

Their heads were so close she could've leaned forward a bit more and kissed him.

Whatever made that thought rise to the top?

Goose bumps tap-danced on her arms. The pancakes she'd eaten for breakfast decided to somersault from one end of her stomach to the other. She was a silly goose who spent too much time reading mail-order bride books. That's what Mother would say.

If she were here. But she wasn't. She was gone.

First to faraway Mexico for special treatments that were supposed to make her better. But didn't. And then simply gone. A phone call from Uncle John said so. The bishop said so at her funeral only weeks before Christmas. Yet, it still didn't seem real. Couldn't be real.

For the thousandth time, the question of why darted around in Martha's head like a mosquito that wouldn't die. Why Mother? Why cancer? Why their father first, and then Mother? *Why, Gott?*

Ambrose began to hum in a low, singsong fashion that reminded her of something. She couldn't put her finger on it. "What's that song you're humming?" She fashioned a bandage from a clean piece of gauze and white tape. "It's pretty."

"Nothing."

"You made it up?"

He nodded.

"It's nice."

"You're nice."

He uttered the words without innuendo or flirtation. A simple observation. A statement. Still they hung in the air, a lilting tune all their own. No one ever complimented her, least of all a man. Not that Martha needed compliments, but still it seemed exceedingly sweet of him to offer the kind words. "Th-thank you." Her own words came out in a semi-stutter. *Why?* "I try."

He shrugged, his expression matter-of-fact. "You don't have to try. You just are."

People like her father who had thought Ambrose to be simple

were wrong. He was smarter than a lot of people—especially those boys who entertained themselves by harassing him. He managed to say just the right thing. "So are you."

Again he shrugged, but this time his face turned brick red.

She stared at the floor. What would Mother say if she were here? Surely she'd say help thy neighbor. Even if he were a man and they were alone in the back room of a bakery, just the two of them.

She glanced at Ambrose again. He didn't seem bothered by their proximity. In fact, his hum had resumed. It had a pleasing calm to it.

She rose and went to one of the two enormous, stainless steel sinks. She turned on the water, stuck her hand in the flow, and waited. "Okay, it's warm, but not hot."

Ambrose frowned and looked from her to the faucet. He didn't move.

"Come on. You need to wash your hair."

"I could go home."

"I thought you wanted to take the groceries to Burke and explain what happened."

His nodded vigorously. His hat slipped. A piece of eggshell escaped, plopped on his nose, and then fell to the floor with a faint crackle.

He chuckled. Surprised, Martha laughed with him. His chuckle turned into a deep-bellied laugh. His shoulders shook. He rocked. Tears escaped the corners of his eyes. The more he laughed, the more Martha laughed. Her ribs ached and her nose started to run.

He removed his hat. Eggshells plummeted to the cement floor. *"Ach."*

More gales of laughter. Martha clutched her middle and bent over. "Stop."

He covered his mouth with both hands, muffling his chortles.

She took a deep breath, in and out. *No more laughing.* A tiny giggle escaped. *Stop.* It must be nerves. Or simply how cute he looked with his wild curls and eggshell decorations and dimples. She'd never noticed the dimples before.

"Let's get you cleaned up before Burke's groceries spoil."

He remained in his chair as if glued to it.

He reminded her of her brothers. They hated bath time. "It won't hurt any more than cleaning the cut did, I promise."

He laid his hat on the table, rose, and trudged to the sink. Still, he didn't look convinced. She offered her best smile. "Go on. Lean your head down."

He did as she instructed and stuck his head under the faucet. He swished his hands through his hair and straightened. "There."

Eggshells remained stuck to his wild curls, mixed with fruit. Dirt had turned to mud.

"*Nee,* not there." Not even close. Martha grabbed the bottle of dish soap and squirted some into her hands. Tiny bubbles floated in the air. "Back you go."

Scowling, he resumed his position with his head under the faucet.

Martha ran her hands through his long, auburn curls until they were thoroughly wet. They were silky and soft and such a pretty color. Ignoring the thought, she began to scrub. Suds cascaded into the sink. She drew water into her cupped hands and wiped soap from his face like she often did when she helped her little sisters and brothers with their baths. This was different somehow. She couldn't put her finger on it. His skin was warm and soft. His eyes were closed. He trusted her completely.

It was just hair, but the act of washing it plucked at her heartstrings.

Ambrose said nothing. Nor did he move.

Her breath caught in her throat. She turned up the water and began to rinse.

"What are you doing?"

Martha whirled, flinging sudsy water in all directions. Bubbles floated toward the ceiling as if seeking an escape.

Her older sister Elsie, hands on her hips, stood in the doorway. Her expression of wide-eyed surprise and irritation said it all.

3

THE LITANY OF SINS MARTHA HAD COMMITTED, ACCORD-ing to Elsie, left her sister speechless. Which made no sense because Elsie's loudly whispered monologue continued in a frenzy of words. Martha had no opportunity to defend herself or explain. Elsie had quite the lung capacity and apparently no desire to pause for air.

The front door was unlocked. Two customers were pacing out front, wondering why no one appeared to wait on them. Hadn't Martha heard the bell? And someone had tracked in nasty-looking garbage on the plank floors. Did Martha know who had done such a thing, and why hadn't she mopped it up? Plus, a message had been left on the phone for a three-layer red velvet cake with cream cheese frosting for Mr. and Mrs. Polanski's thirtieth anniversary. Shouldn't Martha be working on the cake, which was needed the very next day?

If it weren't for the waiting customers out front, Elsie surely would have exploded.

"And what are you doing back here with Ambrose? Alone?"

On this last question, Elsie's voice rose above a whisper. She clapped her hand over her mouth and shook her head. Ambrose edged toward the door. Water dripped down his face onto his dirty, faded blue shirt. "I'll go."

"*Nee.*" Martha snatched a towel from a nearby hook and handed it to him. She stepped between Ambrose and her sister. "I closed up to run an errand after the lunch-hour rush—which I told you I planned to do. I happened to see Conner Benson trip Ambrose on purpose. He stuck his foot out and tripped him—"

"I'm okay." Ambrose sidestepped two more paces closer to the door. "*Danki*, Martha. I'm okay."

"Wait. Dry your hair. Wipe off your shirt."

"I'm okay."

He grabbed the bags and clomped past Elsie.

"He's the one with the garbage on his boots." Elsie darted to the corner and retrieved a mop, which she thrust at Martha. "Why is his hair all wet?"

"I washed it."

"You washed a man's hair?" Elsie's face turned white. Her eyebrows rose a foot. Her mouth opened and closed like a hooked fish gasping for air. "What possessed you? If *Daed* were here he'd take you to the woodshed."

"He would say we should be kind and help our neighbors."

"Don't be sassy, *schweschder*!"

Exactly the point. Elsie was her sister, not her mother. She was twenty-three to Martha's twenty, but that didn't put her in charge. She had no right to boss Martha around, but since Mother's death, she'd become more anxious. The more anxious she became, the more she nagged. Martha had no doubt it was because she was exhausted from playing mother and father to their six younger brothers and sisters. And because she was overwhelmed with so many responsibilities between the house and the bakery. Uncle John and their older brother Henry helped, but Elsie felt responsible. And she grieved deeply. Afraid of saying something she would regret, Martha gritted her teeth and accepted the mop.

"Don't give me that look." Elsie sighed. "I'm only trying to do what's right and stay true to the *Ordnung*. I wish you would too. Mother would tell you to listen to me if she were here. I know Henry will say the same thing."

Henry was busy running the farm and raising his own five children.

Mother would have told them to work together. To take care of the bakery and their younger siblings. Mother would've made it sound so simple. So organized. Instead, chaos seemed to reign supreme.

"Didn't you say customers are waiting?"

Shoulders slumped, Elsie trudged from the room. Mopping up Ambrose's trail as she went, Martha started in the same direction. Her head throbbed. *Please,* Gott, *I don't have time for one of my headaches.*

Fierce, piercing headaches that forced her to lie down in a dark room for hours, sick to her stomach and unable to withstand the light, had plagued Martha for years. Before Mother's illness and death, she only had them occasionally. Now, they interrupted her busy schedule at least once every two or three months.

The simple action of swishing the mop caused the pain to flare. Her stomach heaved. The muscles in her legs threatened to buckle. *Not now.* Forcing a smile, she grabbed a bucket, dunked the mop, wrung it out, and swished her way into the main bakery.

Perplexed customers milled around in front of the counter.

Adelaide Mitchell scowled at Elsie and tapped one long, red fingernail on the glass. *Tap, tap, tap.* "I've been waiting forever. I need to pick up the two dozen cupcakes for the pinochle tournament tonight. I'm in a hurry."

"I'm so sorry, Adelaide." Elsie flung a worried glance at Martha. "Martha, did you box them up?"

"I did." Martha pointed to the table behind the counter. "All ready to go. Made fresh this morning."

"Chop-chop. I'm running late for my hair and nail appointment." Adelaide tapped harder. "It's not like you girls to be so lax. If your mother were here, she'd be so ashamed."

If Mother were here, life would be different. Elsie would be married by now, and Martha might actually have a special friend. But family came first. The children came first.

Please, Gott. *I know You have a plan for us. Please show us the way through these trying times.* Martha prayed the same words she'd prayed every day since Mother's funeral. *Thy will be done.*

The last words were added hastily in deference to her upbringing. God had a plan. It was her job to obey, submit, and above all else, be humble.

If only it were that easy.

The other customer turned out to be Carina Lopez, a friend of Burke McMillan. She stood at the front door talking to Ambrose, who had his head down and his arms full. She patted the big man's arm and held the door for him. Then she turned back. A wide smile on her face, she started toward Martha. Martha wracked her brain. On top of everything else, had she forgotten one of Burke's regular orders? Bread? Pies? Cakes? The restaurant owner baked his own pastries when he had time, which wasn't as often as he liked.

"Martha, thank you so much for helping Ambrose. Poor guy feels terrible that he fell and messed up the groceries." Carina's tawny brown skin had a healthy glow. Unlike most of the English ladies who came into Sweet Tooth, she wore no makeup or jewelry and her silver hair was cropped short against her head. She still managed to look more beautiful than any woman Martha had ever seen. Mother said her beauty came from being lovely inside. "He's such a sweet guy. He hates to disappoint Burke."

"He didn't fall. Conner Benson tripped him on purpose."

Carina's smile disappeared, replaced by an icy stare that would strike terror into a hardened criminal. Sometimes the Episcopalian priest looked more like a policewoman or a mother.

"Funny, he failed to mention that little piece of information. Don't you worry, Burke and I will make sure Conner rues the day he messed with Ambrose."

"Good." Martha chewed her bottom lip for a few seconds. Might as well cut to the chase. "Did you have an order pending? I'm so sorry. I seem to have totally forgotten it."

"No, no, no. You haven't forgotten anything." She held up an issue of *Brides* magazine. The headline on the cover read, "Wedding Cakes A to Z."

Carina grinned. "Can you keep a secret?"

4

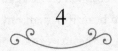

A DECEMBER WEDDING. THAT GAVE MARTHA SEVERAL months to design Carina and Burke's cake and practice making it. Good thing, too, because Carina seemed to be in the throes of indecision about every aspect of the cake.

"Are you sure you want me to do the honors?" Martha asked for the third time as she poured more cold peppermint tea in Carina's glass. "There are bakeries in Kansas City that specialize in fancy wedding cakes."

"Of course we're sure." Carina flipped through the magazine pages again. "You make beautiful cakes. And they're moist and yummy. Some people think how the cake looks is more important than what it tastes like. That would not be Burke and me. We're all about gorging ourselves. There will be no saving of the cake for us."

Mother had spent years teaching Martha to bake. She said Elsie had a head for numbers and management, but Martha's special gift was decorating cakes and making fancy pastries. Martha held that thought as a shield against the pain in her heart—and in her head. Three ibuprofen had reduced the second to a dull throb behind one ear. But the nausea in the back of her throat tipped her off to its intent to return.

Ignoring it, she summoned her best smile, poured herself more tea, and settled into the chair across from Carina at one of two tables situated in front of the bakery's floor to ceiling windows. The tables were intended exactly for this purpose, although Martha rarely received a special order requiring this much preplanning. Plain weddings had simple cakes and pies. No piping or fondant flowers or fancy decorations of any kind. "I'm so excited for you and Burke. Aunt Mary Katherine and Uncle Ezekiel must be over the moon."

"We haven't told anyone yet." Carina dumped artificial sweetener in her tea and stirred. "We're having them over for supper next week to share the news. They've been so good to Burke since he showed up here. Nobody else would've taken him in and given him a job after he broke into Mary Kay's house. Such good people."

They were good people. Mary Katherine had been married to Martha's uncle Moses before he died, and then she'd married Ezekiel. The Ropp men seemed to die young. "We try. Mary Kay is special, though. I don't think everyone in our community would feed a strange man a ham sandwich after he broke in."

"He was a lost soul in those days." Carina's smile faded at the memory. "He's come so far since the death of his wife and daughter. I can't believe we're getting married. I can't believe *I'm* getting married. I'm forty years old. I figured it wasn't in God's plan, and I was good with that. Being a navy chaplain gave meaning to my life. I didn't need anything more."

"How did you know?" The question was one Martha never had a chance to ask her mother. Plain folks didn't talk about such things much and the right time never presented itself in the day-to-day job of keeping the bakery doors open, keeping the farm going, and then, praying for Mother to stay alive. "I'm sorry. I know that's a personal question. You don't have to answer."

"No, no. It's a good question." Carina patted Martha's hand. "At first I wanted to help Burke as his colleague. I was concerned for him. He was a chaplain who helped others in their times of need, but he couldn't help himself. Then he disappeared for so long I thought I would never hear from him again. When a postcard showed up from Jamesport, I was so relieved I came out here to check on him. The more we talked, the more I felt drawn to him. Even though I didn't want to be."

"Why not? He's nice and smart and a hard worker. He's old, but he's pleasing to look at." Martha cringed. She had no business expressing an opinion about Burke's looks. It had to be the throbbing headache or lack of sleep. She was used to getting up early to start the breads, doughnuts, pies, and cakes, but keeping up with the laundry, cooking, and cleaning at home meant she, Elsie, and her younger sister Annie, who was fourteen, often worked far into the night. "I'm so sorry. I don't know what's wrong with me."

"Honey, there's nothing wrong with you. He is good-looking. I think he looks like Kevin Costner, the actor. Of course, you don't know who that is, but take my word for it. I'll be sure to tell Mac you think he's old. He *is* old—fifty to my forty." Carina chuckled. She always called Burke Mac. She said that's what the chaplain corps called him—when they didn't call him commander. "I didn't want to be drawn to him, because I knew his wounds were deep and raw and he needed time to heal. A lot of time."

"But now he's better."

She smiled. "Much better. He'll never be the same, but God sewed those wounds together and made something new of his heart and soul. He's not so ragged and bewildered anymore."

Like when Martha's dad died of a heart attack at age fifty. Mother had been ragged and bewildered, but she soldiered on for three more years before she became ill. Tears at the funeral had been few, but her hand on Martha's tightened so much her fingers left red marks. "Will you work at the restaurant?"

"I'm substituting as a cashier right now and I could fill in as a waitress if needed, but I won't be cooking. I can barely fry an egg. I'm a terrible cook."

"I could teach you."

More giggles. Carina's tinkly laugh made Martha laugh. The corners of the slender woman's eyes crinkled and her dark chocolate eyes lit up. "Honey, don't you think people have tried? My mother, my aunties, my sister. I'm a lost cause." She bent closer and lowered her voice. "I think it's better to let Mac be the cook in the family. He's good at it and he likes to cook for me. It makes him feel good."

Such an arrangement boggled a Plain woman's mind. Men worked in the fields or made furniture or shoed horses or built barns. Women cooked, sewed, cleaned, cared for children, gardened, canned, and managed a hundred other household chores. The only time Father had cooked was to roast the meat at big weddings. "Will your family be here for the wedding?"

"My mom and dad, who are in their seventies, plan to stop in Omaha and pick up my sisters and my younger brother on their way here from Fort Myers, Florida. My older brother will fly in from Seattle. A whole bunch of aunts and uncles and cousins will descend on this place like bees on honeysuckle. I just hope we don't have snow and ice. That's the big challenge of having a Christmas wedding."

"Why did you choose Christmas?"

"Because it's a time of new beginnings. It suits how we feel about each other and the world right now. Shiny and new and wonderful. It's the perfect time of year to marry in this season of our lives. We want all our family, related or not, to join us in this celebration."

"Then it better be a big cake, I reckon. What about Burke's family?"

The smile flickered. "Mac doesn't have any family left. That's one of the reasons he fell so hard after his wife and little girl died."

Again, hard to imagine. "Even so," Carina went on, her smile reappearing. "You're family; the entire community is family. We're inviting everyone. That's why we need a big cake and why we're having the wedding at the café."

The tinkling of the bell over the door signaled another customer entering the bakery. Martha checked over her shoulder. Yep. Elsie's anxious look said, *"Help me."* She pointed at the clock on the wall over the display of teas, coffee beans, and mugs. Martha nodded encouragingly and mouthed the word *"Soon."* Elsie's shoulders sagged.

Wedding cakes were great revenue for the bakery. Especially for Sweet Tooth. They did little advertising, so word of mouth was the best form of marketing. Mother would agree. Do a good job for Burke and Carina, and everyone in the county would know the next day. Elsie was so overwhelmed with the day-to-day nuts and bolts of running the business, she couldn't see the importance of spending time simply talking with a customer and making her feel special.

They did a good volume of business, but they needed to do more. The *Gmay* helped with Mother's medical bills that didn't go away when she died, but the family had to pitch in as well. The bills were mind-boggling and stretched over more than two years.

Martha's headache ratcheted up a notch. Her cake would be an important part of the festivities. "What did you have in mind, exactly?" She bent over the magazine and read, "'A seven-tier classic with garlands and latticework piped into the fondant in royal icing and delicate roses and bunches of grapes.' Or, here's another one, 'A tiered cake with monogram in pale green fondant and fresh hydrangeas.' Or, 'A garden of roses in pink, peach, and yellow on buttercream with sugar paste roses to look like fabric flowers.'"

They were all so gorgeous, far too beautiful to eat, and a stretch for Martha's skills. *You have lovely piping skills, dochder. And such patience. You'll do well.* Mother's words resounded in her head like a sweet song that buoyed her. She never overdid compliments, but she didn't mind handing out a few now and then. She offered them as gifts wrapped in a shiny smile and delivered with a pat on the back.

"These are all so fancy." Carina wrinkled her petite nose. "It's a winter wedding. I was thinking something dense and warm and filling, like spice cake or carrot cake or cinnamon spice cake with a buttercream frosting. You could pipe some poinsettias and garlands as decorations. Or maybe snowflakes or Christmas tree ornaments. I'm sure you'll have more ideas than I do. You're so creative."

Martha's imagination drew pictures in her mind. "I know just the recipe."

"Can you design something?"

"Sure I can." She would do her best. That's what Mother always told her, *"Just do your best, dochder."* Martha tugged her sketchbook from under the magazine. "How many layers do you want? Round or square?"

"Lots of layers because we'll have lots of people. Round, I guess. No, rectangular. It's easier to cut. Or round. Whatever you think is best. You're the expert." Carina rubbed her eyes and sighed. "Who knew planning a wedding could be so hard? And it's just getting started. My sister is coming to visit for a week in September so we can go dress shopping in Kansas City."

"What about your job as a chaplain?" When Martha first learned Carina was a priest, she'd been sure the woman was up to no good, courting Mac. It turned out an Episcopalian was different from a Catholic priest. "Will you still travel back and forth?"

"I resigned my commission." Carina leaned back in her chair and let her arms fall to her sides as if the thought made her tired. "I realized life was slipping by. It's so short. I love Mac and he loves me. Why miss out on all life has to offer?"

How amazing to be able to say those words aloud and with such freedom. To have a special someone to be with for however many days they had left on earth. With her father's death, then Mother's, Martha had jumped from childhood to womanhood in a single enormous bound. No one knew better how short life could be.

"What about you?" Carina gave Martha a sideways glance. "Do you have someone special in your life? Wedding bells on the horizon?"

"No. No one." Recently, the only bachelor in her life was Ambrose and he'd never shown any interest in her. Still, he was sweet and kind. The memory of his wounded hand in hers and his trusting gaze sent a soft tremor up her spine. "I'm too busy with the bakery and the children."

"That's understandable and admirable." Carina's tone was kind. "But don't let your youth slip away. I imagine there's a limited supply of suitable husbands in your community." A sly look on her face, she smiled. "So, what do you think of Ambrose?"

"Ambrose?" Did the woman read minds? Martha covered her cheeks with both hands. Surely they were the color of vine-ripened tomatoes. "Why would you ask me about Ambrose?"

Because she washed his hair in broad daylight in a public place? Because she held his hand while she tended his cut? How much had Ambrose told Carina?

"Because he's such a nice, sweet man. There's a lot to be said for simple and straightforward." Carina's gaze wandered out the window. She seemed lost in thought for a moment. "There's also something to be said for delving beyond the obvious into deeper, more complex waters. You know what I mean?"

"Not exactly."

Carina giggled. "Sorry, I didn't mean to get all metaphysical on you."

Meta-what? Martha tapped her cheek with her index finger. "He's a hard worker. He's dependable. He never misses a day. He's kind. He never raises his voice."

"That's quite a list. You've given this some thought."

Martha saw Ambrose every day. She was what her mother called a people watcher. What made people the way they were? Such thoughts occupied her mind while she kneaded dough or frosted cupcakes or wove a pastry lattice on a pie. Ambrose was different. Special. "He also loves animals and he takes care of his *aenti* Mae. He builds birdhouses and birdbaths. He likes to garden."

"Wow, he has all kinds of wonderful qualities and you, my friend, have cataloged them all. Why do you suppose that is?"

"I have lots of time to think while I make pie filling or bake cookies."

"So those are the pros. What are the cons?"

"Cons?"

"Why wouldn't you pick Ambrose to be your soul mate?"

Soul mate. What a nice word to describe a husband. "He's old."

"Old?" Carina giggled. "He's all of thirty."

"I'm only twenty." Usually Plain people married long before thirty and had four or five children at least. "And he's not very . . ."

"Smart?" Carina frowned. "Book learning isn't everything."

Indeed, it wasn't. "We don't hold a lot of store by book learning ourselves."

"I know. I'm sorry. I don't mean to be prickly." The frown faded, but Carina's dark eyes remained somber. "I have a brother with special needs. He lives with my sister. I'm a bit touchy about these things."

Strange phrases flitted through their conversation today, making it all the more surreal. Sitting in the bakery talking about soul mates and love—or the possibility of love. That's what impending weddings did to a person. "Special needs?"

"He has a developmental disability."

"We just say they're special gifts from *Gott*." Because they were. If God had given Mother a special child, she would've loved him exactly the same—maybe more—and so would everyone in the family. "They go to school and church and play with other children as if there were no difference."

"I like that. Special gifts from God. But Ambrose isn't like that, really. He's very high functioning." A thin wrinkle carved its way across Carina's normally smooth forehead. Her eyes squinted as if she looked for someone in the distance. "He never lets Mac write out a list for him. He says he can remember it all in his head. Mac just paces and spouts off the list and Ambrose remembers it."

"He does the same thing here." Once, Martha had written down names and addresses along with the item each person ordered, but Ambrose handed the list back to her. "He says he likes to keep his memory sharp."

"I suspect it's more than that." Carina leaned closer. "I don't think he can read. And I think you would be the perfect person to teach him."

The image appeared in her mind's eye. Hours spent sitting at this table, heads bent close together. The opportunity to talk. Then the little Elsie twin that sat on her shoulder whispered in her ear. *Don't you have enough to do already? The bakery. The* kinner. *The house. Don't we have enough responsibility?* "Me?"

"Yes, you. It's perfect."

The grating sound of Elsie—the real one—clearing her throat for a third time forced Martha to swivel and look at her. "Did you get something caught in your throat?"

Elsie made a show of looking at the clock hanging above the table. "You'll have to come back after supper and make the cake for the Polanskis. I've been so busy with customers I haven't had time to restock the supplies or start on the pies Lorelei Maynard ordered or clean up."

The steady stream of customers meant a steady stream of funds, which usually made Elsie happy. A fancy wedding cake would surely add a tidy sum to their coffers. Today, however, Elsie simply looked ragged.

Carina stood and scooped up her magazine. "No worries. We're done for now. I can scratch cake off my list."

"A four-tier cinnamon spice cake with butter cream frosting." Martha rose. "A Christmas theme. I'll sketch something for you to look at in the next few weeks."

"Think about what I said." Carina winked. Then she turned and stalked to the door. Hand on the knob, she paused. Her forehead furled. Her nose wrinkled. "Hmm. I'm thinking . . . Mac's favorite cake is German chocolate with dark chocolate frosting and raspberry mousse. That would be a great Christmas cake. Let's do one of those too."

Two fancy wedding cakes. Funds to keep the family afloat and pay bills. The possibility of teaching Ambrose to read and the challenges that entailed.

Silver linings inside blessings.

See, dochder, *you don't have to look for blessings. They just show up.*

If only Mother were here to share in them.

5

HOME LOOKED GOOD. REAL GOOD. AMBROSE MADE IT AS far as the closest hickory rocker on the front porch. With a grunt, he dropped a stack of mail on a wicker table and plopped down in the rocker. It creaked under his weight. Amelia, a skinny gray cat with enormous eyes, hopped in his lap. Her purr filled the late-afternoon silence. A soft breeze rustled the leaves in the half-dozen oak and elm trees that shaded the two-story A-frame home with its pert white paint and cheerful evergreen shutters. Pirate stuck his graying snout on Ambrose's knee. His whimper held a question.

"I'm fine, *hund*." Ambrose patted both animals. He let out a long breath. Fine now that he was home. Nobody would trip him here or laugh at him or tell him what to do. He could simply be. "How was your day?"

Pirate growled deep in his throat.

"That *gut*, huh?" Ambrose leaned back and closed his eyes. The memory of the boot on his back made him wiggle. Then he remembered the gentle look on Martha's face and the way her hands felt in his hair. Soft hands. A sweet touch. "Mine had its moments."

A man couldn't help but long for a touch now and again, but it wasn't right to think of Martha like that. She had a helper's heart. She saw he needed help and was kind enough to offer it. Nothing more.

Still, being so close to her had stoked the longings he'd worked so hard to banish. He might be stupid, but not so stupid as to think a learned, pretty woman like Martha would settle for the likes of him. Day after day he watched her and thanked God for giving him a job that allowed him to be close to her. That would have to be enough.

No point in thinking about it. He riffled through the stack of envelopes. Why did so many letters come to this address? He never sent any mail. Neither did Aunt Mae. He ran his fingers over the big red letters on the top envelope. O-V-E-R-D-U-E. He sounded them out. "O-v—v-v-rrrr-dd-ewww. Overdue."

That couldn't be good. He dumped his hat on the table and scratched his head. "What do you think, Pirate? Is that *gut* or bad?"

Pirate whined.

"Agreed." Ambrose tore open the envelope like a man ripping off a bandage. The single sheet of paper was covered with dense English sentences. He recognized his name. The rest was alphabet soup.

He tossed it aside the way he always did. For later. At least, that's what he told himself. He could figure it out. Eventually. He didn't need anyone's help to read. Not much.

Jasper and Samson scampered across the wood slats of the porch and joined the party. The two were inseparable. They tolerated the other animals, but none were permitted to come between them.

"Come on, you two. There's room for everyone." He patted his lap and the cats joined Amelia. But not without a warning hiss. Just so everyone knew where they stood.

Hands occupied spreading love around, Ambrose studied the flowers he'd planted the previous weekend in long swathes across the front yard. His eyes feasted on the riot of colors. Purple and pink and red pansies, petunias, and impatiens along with yellow marigolds on one side. The perennials—salvias, lantanas, sunflowers, and Pride of Barbados—on the other. God provided natural medicine for what ailed a man. Beyond the flower garden stood the purple martin birdhouses—an apartment complex Ambrose had built and painted himself. The birds joined him every year in March and April to start new families. They fussed over their babies, and he made sure the baffles on each twenty-foot pole kept the critters like raccoons and snakes from bothering them.

At the moment, a fancy cardinal all dressed in red sipped dainty-like from the birdbath he'd made out of teacups, saucers, and a serving spoon. Nearby, two robins shared supper at the birdseed wreath he'd hung from a tree branch. "Looks like everyone is having supper but us." He scratched behind Pirate's ears. The dog's tail thumped. "I haven't forgot about you. Let me rest a minute."

"Ambrose, is that you?"

Careful not to jostle his menagerie, he craned his head and looked back at Aunt Mae, who stood at the open screen door. "*Jah*, it's me. How was your day, *Aenti*?"

She pushed the door open and used her cane to tap her way

onto the porch. Not that she needed it. Aunt Mae had lived in this house most of her fifty-some years. She knew exactly how many steps took her to the rocker closest to the door. "The girls came by and took me to the quilting frolic at Laura's."

The "girls" were a handful of women friends in their fifties, sixties, and seventies who included Aunt Mae in all their activities. She might be blind, but she was a wealth of information that came from listening and remembering. She also told a good story.

"That's *gut*."

"You sound down." What she lacked in sight, Aunt Mae made up for in hearing.

"Long day."

"Hard work makes you happy, not sad."

"I'm not sad." Not in a million years would Ambrose complain to a woman who had been born blind, married at twenty, lost all her babies before their birth, and become a widow at thirty. "I'm content to sit here and be quiet, that's all."

"Point taken."

They rocked in silence for a goodly time. Ambrose stole a glance at his mother's younger sister. Her pale lilac dress and white apron were clean and neat. Her *kapp* covered her bun without a single gray hair out of place. Small lines around her pale blue eyes and full lips were the only signs of aging on her face. Compared to her, he looked like a bum who hadn't taken a bath in a month of Sundays. At least she couldn't see his dirty pants and shirt.

Or the bad attitude surely written all over his face.

Rubbing stubby fingers knotted with arthritis, Aunt Mae began to hum. She did that sometimes. The hum grew until it became a full-out song. An English hymn with pretty words. "Trust and Obey."

Was it her way of reminding Ambrose that God always had a plan and they were expected to go along with it? Or just her way of celebrating her contentment?

After the first stanza, he joined in on the chorus. Songs sung many times were easy to remember. Unlike written English, which was a mishmash of letters hard for Ambrose to make heads or tails of.

She stopped, leaving Ambrose to finish the last few words in his wobbly tenor. His voice sounded puny without hers.

"So, tell me what's really bothering you."

He made quick work of the story. No sense in belaboring the point. Aunt Mae's lips pursed. She nodded a few times and *tsk*ed once or twice.

"I'd like to do something nice for Martha." The thought ran out the gate before he had time to shut it. "She was nice to me."

"You should. She's a *gut* girl."

Not a girl anymore. A woman. The feel of her hands in his hair returned. His brain cramped for a second. "What could I do for her?"

"Don't sell yourself short." Aunt Mae rocked harder. "It pains me when you do. Make her a bird feeder or a birdbath. The things you create are nice, and the birds would bring more of *Gott*'s beauty to her life."

Ambrose sometimes took his finished pieces to Aunt Mae so she could run her hands over them. She said she could picture them in her mind, even though she'd never seen a single bird in her life. "She and Elsie work all week in the bakery. Maybe I could weed their garden for them someday when they're not home. It could be a surprise."

He liked nice surprises. Would Martha?

"That's a nice idea." Aunt Mae sat up straight. "Someone is coming."

Ambrose stared at the road. He strained to hear. Aunt Mae's ears were far more attuned than his.

Eventually, an olive-green van came into view. It crawled along through the gate and up the rutted dirt road, dust billowing behind it.

"Were you expecting someone?"

"Nee." In fact, the last thing Ambrose wanted was company. "I don't recognize the van."

"It's a *gut* thing I put a roast in the oven." Using her cane, she stood. "I thought we would have leftovers and you could take sandwiches for your lunch, but instead we'll feed our company."

She sounded delighted at the prospect.

Sighing, Ambrose joined her at the railing. "I suppose."

She smacked his chest with unerring accuracy. "Be kind, *suh.* It'll be nice to share our supper."

"You're right." He forced himself to shed the whiny tone of an eight-year-old. "Too bad I ate the rest of the cherry pie yesterday."

"Laura sent an apple pie home for you and two new novels in braille she ordered through the library for me."

"That was nice of her." Laura Stutzman was a kind, thoughtful person and an old friend of Grandma Hershberger. And a good cook. "I reckon I can share."

Aunt Mae chuckled. She knew what a sacrifice that would be. Ambrose could eat an entire apple pie—or any pie—by himself in one sitting. Along with a pint or two of vanilla ice cream.

The van halted. A tall, skinny guy with black curls escaping from under his straw hat burst from the van. He dragged a large duffel bag from the middle seat. Waving his hat, he strode toward them. His long legs ate up the space with amazing speed. "*Aenti* Mae, Ambrose, it's me," he hollered. "It's so *gut* to see you."

Aunt Mae's hand touched Ambrose's sleeve. "Who is it?"

"I don't know." Ambrose studied the stranger, whose wide smile, square chin, dimples, and long nose reminded him of someone. He had a long neck with an oversized Adam's apple. "He looks familiar. Like someone from *Onkel* David's family." David, Aunt Mae's husband, became good friends with Ambrose's dad after David and Mae married. His family lived in Kansas but came to visit often. "He looks like a young David."

Uncle David hadn't lived to be old. Aunt Mae had to go on living for years and years without her husband. Father and Mother were parted by death for a mere two years. Father passed away peacefully in his sleep the previous year. Aunt Mae always said he couldn't wait any longer to shed his achy, gout-ridden body and get to work for Jesus alongside Mother, who surely planted a vegetable garden in heaven exactly like the one she'd shown Ambrose how to plant when he was a little boy.

Which was fine, except they left Ambrose, their only living child, born late in life, alone.

"It's me, Joshua." The stranger bounded up the steps. He opened his arms as if inviting Aunt Mae into a hug. When she didn't move, his arms dropped. "Didn't you get my letter?"

Aunt Mae's hand squeezed Ambrose's arm. "It must've gotten lost." She'd never asked outright, but she knew Ambrose's secret as surely as if he'd announced it. "You're Noah's son."

"Your nephew." He chortled as if this were somehow funny, gave her a big squeeze that lifted her off her feet, and then turned to Ambrose. "Which makes us cousins."

Noah was David's brother. He and his family lived in Haven,

Kansas. Ambrose hadn't seen Joshua since he was three or four. He looked to be about twenty or twenty-one now. "Welcome to Jamesport."

"Danki." He dropped his bag on the porch with a thud. "I can't wait to get started."

"Get started at what?"

More chortling. "Farming, of course. You could have knocked me and my *daed* over with a feather when we found out your *daed* left the farm to you and me together." He pulled a slim envelope from his bag. "My *daed* held on to your *daed*'s letter until I turned twenty-one. Which was last week. Your *daed* wanted me to be full-grown before I left home. It's *gut* of you to be so understanding about it. I don't know if I would've been."

Aunt Mae's fingers wrapped around Ambrose's hand in a warning squeeze. "Maybe we should go inside. You must be hungry and thirsty."

"Lead the way." His grin unwavering, Joshua grabbed his bag and swept his arm out in a huge flourish. "I can't believe I own this house—half own."

Ambrose clamped his mouth shut, but every bone in his body shouted in chorus. *Neither can I.*

6

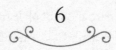

THE DISH SOAP BUBBLES ENCHANTED THE CATS. SAMSON and Jasper took turns batting at them while Ambrose stood at the sink washing the breakfast dishes. If they could see the pretty blue birds preening in the oak tree out front, they would've jumped right out the window. He didn't tell them. He liked watching the birds while he washed the dishes. Aunt Mae sat at the table finishing the bacon and eggs he'd made for her. He dried his hands, grabbed a pot holder, and picked up the coffeepot from the gas stove burner. He went to the table and poured a second cup for Aunt Mae and another one for himself.

"Are we going to talk about it?" Aunt Mae ran her finger along the edge of the cup, then picked it up. She didn't spill a drop on the path from the table to her mouth. "Or are you planning to sulk all day?"

"What is sulk?"

"Throw a pity party." She settled the cup back on the pine table. "Your father wanted to do what was best for you."

"He didn't think I could take care of you and the farm."

"Do you remember what it was like around here after your mother passed?"

Sad. No silly jokes. No singing while weeding the garden. Pirate curled up on a blanket in the corner. Dark even when the sun shone. *"Jah."*

"You may not be smart about book learning, *suh*, but you feel what people feel. Your heart is big." Aunt Mae placed her hands over her heart. "You received that gift from your *daed*. After Josie died, he had no will to live. He knew he must go on, but when he buried your *mudder* he buried his heart."

Ambrose went to the cemetery once a week to place flowers on Mother and Father's graves and the graves of the four little babies who were born and died before he came into the world, a beloved only child. "He still had me."

"He did. That's why he asked Joshua's *daed* to send Joshua to you. He didn't want you to be alone."

"I'm not alone. You're here."

"Not forever."

"You can't go."

She smiled. "I'm not planning to go anywhere, but when it's my time to go, I will go with a joyful heart. Having Joshua here will allow me to do that."

"Do what?" *The Budget* newspaper under one arm, Joshua sauntered into the room. "It smells *gut* in here. I love bacon."

He slid into a chair across from Aunt Mae, laid the newspaper on the table, and looked around. Ambrose managed a smile. *"Gude mariye."* He pointed at a plate covered with a napkin on the counter next to the stove. "You can heat your food in the oven or set it on top of the stove for a few minutes to warm it. I've already cleaned up."

"I have reading to do until Ruby comes for me." Aunt Mae stood and picked up her cup. Ambrose took it from her before she could take it to the sink. "*Danki*. I'm helping her weed her vegetable garden today. I'll let you boys get acquainted. I'm sure you have lots of plans to make."

"So how come you do the dishes? Can't *Aenti* Mae do them?" Joshua made quick work of getting his plate and placing it in the oven. He stopped by the open window and stared out. "What exactly does she do all day? What do you do?"

"I work in town, making deliveries for the bakery and doing odd jobs at the café." Ambrose went back to scrubbing the skillet. "Ruby Eicher's daughter LeeAnne comes over on Mondays and does the laundry. She cleans the house, too, and *Aenti* Mae helps. When there's a frolic, *Aenti's* friends pick her up and take her. Some days they go to the library and get braille books. Hannah Yoder comes over and sews for us when we need clothes. People help us out."

"That's *gut*." Joshua turned and leaned against the counter. "My *mudder* wanted to ask you to move to Haven, but *Daed* said the *Gmay* would take care of you."

"For the most part, we take care of ourselves." Ambrose grabbed a towel and dried his hands. He folded it and carefully hung it back on its rack. He went to the table to push in the chair Joshua had left, then returned the salt and pepper shakers to their spot next to the napkin holder.

"You sure are fussy." Joshua wrinkled his long nose. "You're a lot like my *groossmammi*."

"We have a system." Ambrose pointed at the open cabinets to the left of the sink. "Plates, saucers, cups, glasses—they all have a place." On the right side, the doorless cabinets held pots, pans, lids, bowls, and other cookware. "That's so *Aenti* Mae can find what she needs. The furniture always stays the same, too, so she can get around without help."

"Makes sense." Joshua straightened and returned to the table where he picked up the newspaper. Underneath it was an envelope. The envelope. The one with the word *overdue* stamped in big red letters across the top. "What's this all about?"

Ambrose froze. Sweat dampened his armpits. His heart did a loop-di-loop. He stared at the offending envelope. "What do you mean?"

"You opened it. I reckon you know what it says. Did you take care of it?"

"Why are you reading my mail?"

"It's from the county tax office so I figured it was about the farm, which I own half of . . . I was right." Joshua's nose wrinkled as if he smelled something bad. "Why didn't you pay last year's taxes?"

"I guess I forgot."

"Forgot?" Joshua's laugh had a scoffing tone to it. "Like you forgot to open the other letters? There's a whole stack of them that have never been opened. Including the letter my *daed* wrote saying I was coming. I can see why *Aenti* Mae didn't open them, but why didn't you?"

"I was busy."

"Doing what? You haven't planted any crops." He pointed in the general vicinity of the tall windows that looked out on the front yard. "Instead you planted a bunch of flowers and some vegetables."

"I like cucumbers."

"Me too." The scoffing tone gone, Joshua looked truly puzzled. "But this is a farm. It's a business. I may be young, but I know how to do it. I figured you did too. You worked with your *daed*, didn't you?"

"Until he died."

"I'm sorry about that." Joshua scratched his smooth chin. "They said you was slow, but I reckon I didn't really get what that meant."

Slow. His father never used that word. He often told people Ambrose was special in a way that made Ambrose feel special.

Not less than.

Joshua picked up the envelope and slapped it against the open palm of his other hand several times. "Do you have money?"

Ambrose nodded. "I put money in the grocery jar yesterday."

Shaking his head, Joshua sighed. "I don't think your grocery money will do." He held out the envelope. "Your mess. You clean it up."

Ambrose accepted the envelope. It didn't look messy. "Okay."

"You understand? You have to go to the county courthouse and ask them about a payment plan before they foreclose and put the farm on the auction block."

A whirlwind of fear raced through Ambrose. It left him breathless. His lungs didn't like that. No part of him did. He couldn't go to the courthouse. They would want him to read papers and sign papers. But the farm was all he and Aunt Mae had left. It was their home. Where would Jasper, Samson, Amelia, and Pirate go? Who would fill the bird feeders and birdbaths? Who would water the flowers? "They can do that?"

"That's what I'm telling you, cousin."

"I'll go."

"You do that. I have to plant the milo and corn you didn't before it's too late."

He tromped out the back door, leaving Ambrose holding the envelope by its corner.

It felt as if it might turn into a rattler any second.

7

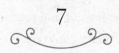

MORNING CAME FAR TOO SOON. THE SUN PEEKED IN Sweet Tooth Bakery's windows just as Martha slipped the second batch of bread into the massive commercial ovens. The heavenly scent of freshly baked bread served as medicine. Her eyes were bleary, but the headache was gone, leaving her feeling weak and tired. No rest for the weary had been Elsie's proclamation as she rousted Martha from her bed and plied her with coffee, bacon, eggs, fried potatoes, and toast.

The predawn feast came as a surprise. So did Elsie's offer to bring the horse and buggy up to the house. Something was going on. Something that put a smile on Elsie's face and giddy-up-and-go in her step. She had to stay behind to feed the children and get them off to their last day of school. Then Elsie would do laundry. She would complete a full day's work before she set foot in the bakery. To still be cheerful was a gift.

Elsie didn't bring up her concern over Ambrose. A double blessing. Martha had no regrets about helping him. Maybe she should, but she didn't. In fact, Carina's certainty that Ambrose couldn't read only stoked her desire to help him.

The Bible was full of admonitions to help those who can't help themselves, to love thy neighbor. The meek shall inherit the earth. Ambrose was definitely meek.

In the meantime, Martha had orders to fill. First the birthday cake for six-year-old Tammy Clark. She wanted a strawberry cake with confetti butter frosting and cowgirl decorations. Martha whipped up the batter, then went to check on the cinnamon rolls. The lovely fragrance of cinnamon permeated the air when she opened the oven door. Puffy, oversized rolls with brown swirls glistened in the oven light. She donned mitts and pulled out four pans. The rolls were best sellers—at the bakery and the café. Once they cooled she would slather them with buttery powdered sugar frosting. The lovely rhythm of her morning routine soothed Martha. The muscles in her neck and shoulders relaxed. Whatever ailed her the previous day had disappeared.

The front door bell tinkled. Martha glanced at the clock: 7:38 a.m. Too early for a customer. She trudged to the front. The object of her musings stood before her. Ambrose wiped his feet on the welcome rug. He seemed intent on getting every last speck of dirt off his boots.

The sun peeking through the double-glass doors glowed around him. His hat hid his expression.

"*Gude mariye.* You're early. The rolls aren't ready yet." She said the first words that came to mind. Not the best beginning for her mission. The vivid memory of her hands touching his face rocked Martha. Sudden heat toasted her cheeks. Her breath caught. This was why Elsie frowned on her sister washing a man's hair. Martha sent her unruly thoughts packing and rushed to offer a welcome. "But that's okay. Do you want *kaffi* while you wait?"

"*Gude mariye.*" He ducked his head. "*Kaffi* would be *gut.*"

"Have a seat. I'll get it."

"I can get it. Carina sent me to see how you're doing." He sounded weary, but he shuffled to the oak cabinet that held the coffeepot, mugs, and all the necessary condiments. He had a large manila envelope in one hand. "How are you?"

"*Gut*." Uncertainty flooded Martha. Would now be a good time to offer reading lessons? How did a person bring up such a delicate subject? He might be embarrassed and that would break her heart. "Why did Carina think I wasn't *gut*?"

"She said you had a headache yesterday." He laid the envelope on the cabinet and poured steaming coffee into the largest mug in the collection.

Martha hadn't said a word to Carina about her headache. How had she known? "It's not necessary to check on me. If you have other errands to run, you should do that. Swing back by later."

"*Nee*. Carina said to check on you."

And Carina was marrying the boss. Of Ambrose. Not of Martha. Still, the Purple Martin Café was one of the bakery's best customers. And those who ate her desserts at the café often came by the bakery later to buy more. "Come on back, then."

Ambrose poured a liberal stream of sugar into his coffee, added a huge dollop of milk, and began to stir. Coffee slopped onto the envelope. "*Ach!*" Irritation—no, it was more like fear—darkened his normally sweet features. "Such an idiot."

He grabbed a wad of paper napkins and swiped at the spreading stain.

"You are *not* an idiot." Martha went to him. She tugged the napkins from his hand and blotted the coffee. "I don't want to hear that kind of talk from you. Understand?"

"I keep messing things up."

331

"Which makes you human. At least, that's what *Mudder* always says—said." Martha dumped the napkins in the waste bin and picked up his mug. "You just filled it a little too full. I'll carry it for you."

Acutely aware of his lumbering form behind her, she led the way to the back. Here they were once again. Alone in Martha's favorite part of the bakery. The heart of it, where she labored over sweet-smelling cakes, pies, breads, cookies, and more. Most often alone, she could sing to her heart's content or pray and daydream about the life she would share some day with a loving husband and many children.

A strange shiver of anticipation ran up her spine. She turned to Ambrose. His gaze locked with hers. Almost as if he could read her mind.

Read. Concentrate on the mission. "What's that envelope you're carrying? Do you need to go to the post office this morning?"

"*Nee.* To Gallatin."

"What's in Gallatin?" She set his coffee on the prep table and picked up a ladle to give the frosting one more stir before she handed it over to Ambrose to top the rolls. "Besides the sheriff?"

Ambrose looked everywhere but at her. His features tightened. It almost looked as if he were afraid.

"What is it, Ambrose? What's bothering you?"

"What do you need me to do?"

"Can you frost the rolls? Just a light coating." Martha held out the bowl. "They're sweet enough as it is."

"I can do that."

She handed him a rubber spatula and tugged the envelope from his hand. Daviess County Assessor's Office. *Overdue* stamped in big, fat red letters.

"Do you owe some taxes?"

"That's what Joshua says."

"Who's Joshua?"

Ambrose's fair skin reddened. "Cousin. He's living with us now."

Help for the farm would be good, but Ambrose didn't look happy. "What does the letter say?"

Ambrose studied his boots. "I owe taxes."

"Ambrose." Martha touched his arm. "Could you look at me?"

His gaze sideswiped her face and then meandered toward the ovens behind her.

"It'll be okay. I promise." She tapped the envelope. "Do you know how to read?"

"Some." His begrudging tone said he did not want to talk about this. "A little."

Her opportunity handed to her just like that. "Why didn't you learn in school?"

"Too many letters. Too fast." He turned his back, stuck the spatula in the frosting, and began to frost the cinnamon rolls with a surprisingly gentle stroke. "I'm a *gut* cook. I cook for me and *Aenti* Mae. She likes my bacon and scrambled egg sandwiches."

"That sounds *gut*." Martha reached in front of him and stilled his hand. The back was covered with fine, auburn hair. Her fingers looked so small next to his. "May I read your letter?"

"If you want. Joshua read it. He says I need to pay money for taxes."

"Let's see." She worked her way through the pages. Even for her, always a good scholar, it was tough going. Bottom line, Ambrose did indeed owe money to the county for the farm. A lot of money. The envelope also held a checkbook. A good sign. "Do you have the money to pay this?"

"*Daed* left money. For me and *Aenti* Mae." He hung his shaggy head. "I don't know how much."

He sounded like a child in trouble for not doing his chores.

"It's okay. You can stop at the bank before you go to Gallatin. They'll tell you how much you have."

His woebegone face tugged at her heart. He needed someone to go with him to the bank and to the courthouse. If only it could be her. Elsie would have a heart attack if Martha closed the bakery. If she waited until Elsie arrived and left her alone in the bakery, she'd faint. For all her bluster, she depended on Martha to stay on top of the orders while Elsie handled the customers.

Besides, Ambrose needed someone who knew about these things. Who understood about taxes and money and property. Someone like Burke. "I have an idea."

Ambrose's expression lightened. "A *gut* one?"

"I think so. Two ideas, actually." In her excitement, Martha squeezed his hand. The anxiety on his face fell away, replaced by the sweetest grin. "First, I'll call Burke and ask if he can get away from the restaurant long enough to go with you to the courthouse. He's *Englisch*. He knows about these things, with the restaurant and his house."

"I can't ask him to do that."

"He'll want to do it. He's your friend."

"My friend?" At that, Ambrose's smile broadened. It was so infectious no one could keep from smiling in its presence. Then it died. "He can't leave the restaurant."

"He has help he can rely on. You said yourself Carina is there."

Ignoring Ambrose's protests, Martha made the call. They were allowed to use the bakery phone for business and this was business—Ambrose's business. Carina answered. After all the preliminary chitchat about Martha's health, she launched into Ambrose's problem.

"Absolutely. I'm on it," Carina said before Martha could finish explaining. "The bank doesn't open until nine. Burke will pick Ambrose up from the bakery at eight thirty, take him to the bank, and then to Gallatin. It'll be much faster in his truck."

"What about the restaurant—"

"He has backup—me."

Martha hung up and explained the plan to Ambrose. Now to present her idea—Carina's and hers. "Tonight, you can come back to the bakery and I can start teaching you to read while you help me with the baking."

Trepidation in his eyes, he slid back a step. His fingers plucked at his shirt buttons. "You don't have time to do that for me."

"I'll make time for a friend."

"You're my friend too?"

"*Jah*, I am."

His smile returned, even more brilliant than before. Like his friendship, it was a gift. Martha smiled back.

They stood there, smiling. The seconds ticked by.

The shrill shriek of the oven timer broke the silence.

They both jumped. Martha's hand went to her heart. She giggled. Ambrose guffawed.

"What is so funny?" Elsie strolled into the kitchen. Frowning, she stopped and stuck both hands on her hips. "You again?"

Martha laughed harder, which seemed to make Ambrose laugh even more too.

"Don't you have errands to run?" Elsie pointed to the door. "Deliveries to make?"

"We have to finish frosting the cinnamon rolls." Martha

stifled a giggle that turned into a snort. "Burke is coming by in a little bit to pick up Ambrose. He'll take the cinnamon rolls and the rest of the café's order then."

His face earnest, Ambrose returned to his chore.

Elsie sighed and trudged from the kitchen.

Martha grabbed another rubber spatula and joined Ambrose. He didn't say anything, but he looked up and winked.

Martha didn't even stop to think about it. She winked back.

A half hour later, she sent Ambrose packing with forty-eight cinnamon rolls, ten loaves of bread, and six pies of various flavors for the Purple Martin. He and Burke would also deliver the cake to Tammy Clark's mom. Then they would go to the bank and on to Gallatin to the courthouse.

It felt good to help a friend.

Martha loaded the commercial-size dishwasher, added the soap, and turned it on—one of several concessions to the English business world. They didn't have time to wash dishes by hand. After a quick look around at a tidy, clean workspace that would impress even the finickiest health inspector, she went out to the front. Elsie stood at the cash register counting bills. She glanced up and went back to her task. "Are you done back there? I need you up front while I run to the bank."

"*Jah*. Unless new orders come in."

Elsie slid a wad of cash and checks into a canvas bank deposit bag and locked it. She laid the bag aside and turned to face Martha. "I know you think I'm being overbearing."

"I-I don't." Martha faltered. "Not much, really. You mean well."

"Which means you think I'm wrong." Elsie wrapped her arms around herself. Her eyes reddened and she sniffed. "I just keep thinking of what *Mudder* would say. I want to live life the way she and *Daed* taught us. To do right in the eyes of *Gott*."

"I know. Me too." Martha went to her sister and wrapped her in a hug. "We're both trying to be so grown-up. We can't forget, though, that we're still in our *rumspringa*, both of us. We have to think about our futures too. As wives and mothers of our own *kinner*."

"I haven't forgotten." Elsie managed a watery smile. "I have been out and about in case you haven't noticed."

Martha had noticed. Sometimes Elsie wasn't home when she returned from the bakery. She knew her sister was courting—a realization that made Martha more than a little envious. A sin for which she immediately begged forgiveness. "*Gut* for you. If you're as tired as I am at the end of the day, it's a wonder you can manage."

"I'm not tired." Elsie's smile grew. Her grim visage disappeared, replaced by the girl who had the prettiest voice at the singing. Her blue eyes were bright and her cheeks pink. "I have a special friend."

"That is *gut*."

"It is *gut*, but it also means I don't get much sleep." Elsie picked up the bag and strolled to the door. "Which makes me cranky. But I know in my heart he's right for me. He loves the *kinner* and wants to help us. It'll be all right. I know it will."

From Elsie's lips to God's ears.

8

ONLY PRIDE KEPT AMBROSE FROM POUNDING HIS FIST ON the dashboard. *Danki, Gott, for gut freinden.* With that small prayer, he swiveled in the seat and offered his best smile to Burke, who seemed relaxed behind the wheel of his pickup truck. "Thank you."

"My pleasure. If you ever need help with business matters, don't think twice. Ask me." Burke pulled in to the parking lot behind the Purple Martin and put the truck in Park. "Like I said before, you wouldn't believe the rigmarole you have to go through when you deal with the government."

"But we're okay?" The entire morning and part of the afternoon had been taken up with going to the bank, driving to Gallatin to the courthouse, and dealing with a fussy person in the tax assessor's office. It turned out Father had provided funds for the taxes. If Ambrose had read the monthly bank statements, he would've known this.

"You're okay. I promise." Burke touched the envelope that sat between them on the bench seat. It must not look like a coiled

338

snake to him. "I've put the correct balance in the checkbook register. That tells you how much you have in the bank. On the first of each month, you'll write a check to Daviess County and subtract that amount from the total. If you have any problems, ask me or Carina. We're glad to help."

"I don't want to be burden."

"You're not. You're a friend."

Ambrose looked at the restaurant's pretty purple door. A knot made his throat hurt. Maybe he was getting a cold. "Martha says she's my friend too."

"That's good." Burke's voice held a hint of laughter. "A man can never have enough good friends. Especially a nice female friend."

"She is nice. And pretty." Should a Plain man say such a thing aloud? Burke would understand. He told Carina she was pretty all the time. Only he said beautiful and gorgeous. Carina was pretty—inside and out. "She's going to teach me to . . . to read. She makes a good friend."

"Good friends help each other. You should definitely take her up on that offer. But you like her more than just as a friend, don't you?"

No one Ambrose knew talked about these things. At least not with him. The men in the *Gmay* treated him like one of the schoolboys. If he weren't so tall, they'd probably pat him on the head and tell him to run out and play when they started their discussions of farming, the cost of land, and the price of crops.

Burke leaned against the seat and drummed a rhythm on the wheel. "It's okay to like her. In fact, it's a good thing, in case you haven't figured that out."

"It's not good."

"Why?"

"Because my heart hurts."

Burke frowned as he turned on the seat so he half faced Ambrose. "Did you ask her to take a ride with you and she turned you down?"

"No."

The frown changed into a smile. Burke's smile always made Ambrose want to smile. Burke cocked his head. "Then why?"

"She's smart. I'm not." That was an understatement. She read recipes and made fancy dishes that were hard, not like scrambled eggs and toast. She knew how much everything cost and rang up orders on the cash register. She made change like nobody's business. And she read books—fat books, not the ones with pictures. "She won't like me like . . . I like her."

"Number one, you're smart in your own way." Burke pointed that index finger at Ambrose. "Number two, you don't know if she likes you until you ask her out."

Burke thought Ambrose was smart. Amazing. The thought that Martha might like him made the muscles in his shoulders knot. How could she like a man she had to teach something he should've learned years ago? Something everyone else learned in the first grade? "You really think she would go for a ride with me?"

"She offered to help you with reading." Burke's words were gentle. "Accept the offer. Spend some time getting to know her. That's always the first step in a relationship. For most everyone. You're no different."

"I am different."

"Every single one of us was made in God's image. I'm His image bearer. You're His image bearer. You and I are no different in God's eyes. He simply gave me different gifts than He gave you."

Ambrose nudged that idea around in his head for a few seconds. "I can lift heavy boxes. And build bird feeders."

"And plant gardens. And take care of sick animals. And eat a whole pan of cinnamon rolls in one sitting."

"That's a gift?"

Burke grinned. "I envy you the ability to do that. You never get fat either."

Ambrose patted his belly. "Maybe a little."

"I'd wager you've never done a mean thing or hurt a single living creature in your entire life." Burke's grin faded. "Very few people in this world can say that. Martha is blessed to have you in her life. I also envy your ability to see the good in people and to forgive when they don't treat you the way they should. Of course, envy is yet another sin for which I must seek forgiveness."

No response occurred to Ambrose. No one had ever said such nice things about him or to him. He hunched his shoulders and studied the cars on the street beyond the parking lot.

"You haven't said much about this cousin Joshua who's come to live with you. Are you close to him?"

"He moved in the bedroom two doors down from mine."

"I meant, do you like him a lot? Is he a close family member?"

"Not like you."

Burke's smile returned. It split his entire face. "That's one of the nicest things anyone has ever said to me. I don't have much family anymore. It's good to have family close." He leaned over and clapped Ambrose on the shoulder. "Brother, go get your buggy. Go find Martha. Start getting to know her better tonight."

"What about *Aenti* Mae? Who'll make her supper?"

"Carina and I will stop by on our way home to make sure all is well. We'll take care of the animals too." Burke smoothed the wheel with both hands. "Although, I suspect Miss Mae can take care of herself."

She could indeed. Ambrose trusted the Lord with his aunt's care. It was Joshua who worried him.

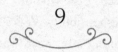

9

MARTHA THUMBED THROUGH THE WORKBOOKS, STUDY guides, and picture books Carina had dropped off at the bakery after the lunch-hour rush. Carina had a good heart, but she might be overestimating Martha's ability to teach. Ambrose would like the stories. One was about a dog, and the other one featured a family of cats. Anything with animals would pique his interest.

The workbooks, at least, were simple. They would help her teach Ambrose the letters and the sounds they made. Worksheets focused on words adults needed to recognize—about medicine, the bank, grocery shopping, and driving—would be especially handy. Martha could use the white erase board they had for posting specials as a place for Ambrose to practice sight words. If he showed up. If he really wanted to learn. If he really wanted her to teach him. He might think it was too embarrassing. Or he might not think it was worth it.

Her new role as teacher would also serve to take her mind off Elsie's announcement. That she had a special friend. Her good mood suggested they would marry soon. She would have her own children. They would likely live in the Ropp home so Elsie could continue to care for their younger brothers and sisters. What a blessing that would be. A father figure for their siblings.

But when it came to the bakery, that's where change reared its ugly head. Once married, Elsie wouldn't want to work. Martha would shoulder that responsibility. Was she ready for that? She loved baking, but running a business wasn't her strong point. When would it be her time to court? In God's time. That's what Mother would say. In the meantime, she should keep her chin up and do her very best. That's what Mother would want.

Buoyed by the thought, Martha went to the dry erase board and wrote the first four letters of the alphabet, uppercase and lowercase. Next to the letters she wrote *Ambrose*, *bird*, *cat*, and *dog*. Four words Ambrose would want to read and write.

The bell tinkled. She turned. Ambrose wiped his boots on the welcome rug. He had a large box wrapped in brown paper in his arms.

"You came."

"You said to come." His forehead wrinkled. "Didn't you?"

She rushed to the table where she'd spread out the school supplies. "Of course, I did. Have a seat and we'll get started."

Package outstretched, he ambled toward her. "I brought this for you."

"For me? It's not my birthday." Puzzled, she accepted the package. "It's not Christmas."

"For being nice to me. Open it." He still had one hand on the box. "Do you need help?"

Laughing, she shook her head and ripped away the paper. His gift was a wooden bird feeder shaped like a blue jay. "It's beautiful. I like it very much."

He clapped his hands as if he'd received the gift. "You open the bird's head and the bottle comes out so you can refill it."

He demonstrated. Birdseed scattered in the bottom of the box. "Sorry. I'm making a mess."

"I don't mind. It's a *gut* idea. Did you make it?"

"I painted it blue too." He nodded vigorously. "Do you like it?"

"I do. I can't wait to put it in the yard. *Danki*." She smiled up at him. His eyes shone with excitement. He was so happy to give her this homemade gift that took his time and effort. "You didn't have to do this."

"You're nice to me. You don't have to be."

"I like you. I don't want you to be hurt."

He touched the bandage on the palm of his hand. "You like me?" His voice filled with surprise and pleasure. "I like you too."

She should move. She should start the lesson. Instead, she stood transfixed by the simple joy on his face. The joy of giving. Martha raised her hand to his cheek and stroked his skin. His eyes widened. His hand covered hers and held it there.

"You're smart." His voice had turned gruff. Gently he lowered her hand. "I'm not."

He edged beyond her reach and turned toward the pile of books on the table. "You teach. I learn."

"You're smart in your own way, Ambrose."

His expression filled with a sadness that broke Martha's heart. He ran his fingers over the first workbook. "You teach. I learn to read."

"And nothing more," his tone said, even as his touch had asked for more. His fingers on her hand had been strong and callused. She wanted them back, but she couldn't have what he wasn't willing to give. She set the workbook on the table and went to the

white erase board where she pointed to the word *bird*. "What does this spell?"

Ambrose stood next to her. He smelled of sawdust and dish soap. He said nothing. She looked up at him. His face scrunched in a frown, he cocked his head, then shook it.

"Sound it out."

"B-b-b . . ."

"That's right. What sound does *r* make? Then *d*."

"B-b-b, i, rrrrr, duh, duh, duh. Bird."

"*Jah!*" It was Martha's turn to clap. "You *can* read English words."

Grinning, he clapped with her. "I can read. Are we done?"

If only it were that easy. "*Nee*, we still have a way to go."

They returned to the table where Martha opened the first workbook and got down to business. Together, they bent over the page as she pointed out the letter *A* and asked him to write it. His head was so close to hers she could've touched his curls. His scent enveloped her. What would it be like to be married to this man?

The question made her sit up straight. She was his friend and teacher. His reaction to her touch had been undeniable. He was a righteous Plain man. She would match his self-restraint.

Ambrose could pick out many individual words. He knew the sounds made by most of the letters, but when asked to put them together and read sentences, he simply couldn't. Martha returned to the basics. They practiced letters and sounds together and then read the story of "Little Red Riding Hood."

"Wolves don't look like *groossmammi*." He frowned. "It's a silly story."

"It is. Can you read it for me?"

He stared at the page and began to read. The singsong way

346

he spoke and his squinted eyes gave Ambrose away. He was reciting the words from memory.

"That's cheating."

His eyebrows lifted. "I don't cheat."

"You remember the story. You're not reading it; you're reciting it."

Ambrose ducked his head and sighed. "Isn't that just as *gut*?"

"Well, it shows you have a *gut* memory and you're smart, but you still need to be able to *read* the words."

"I'm smart?"

"Don't fish for compliments." She closed the book and offered him her best smile. "I think that's enough for tonight."

"But I need to be able to read."

"It'll take time, but you'll get there."

His face crumpled. "I don't have time to get there."

"Why the hurry?" Did he not want to take lessons with her? Spend time alone with her?

"I need to be smart now."

"Reading is important, but it's not the only way a person can be smart."

"I need to be smart now."

"Because of your cousin Joshua?"

"*Nee*. Because of you."

"Maybe just a little bit longer then." Martha couldn't stop the smile his words evoked in her. She didn't want to.

Or a lot longer.

10

"B-B-B-O-B-B. BOB M-M-M-I-LL-E-RRRR. BOB MILLER SOLD the f-f-ar-m-m. Bob Miller sold the farm!" Triumphant, Ambrose leaned back in his chair on the front porch and grinned at Pirate, who lounged at his feet. The dog raised his head and grinned back. He didn't seem quite as excited as Ambrose about reading *The Budget*.

After three months of Martha's patient, steady tutoring, Ambrose could read short books with lots of pictures. He practiced at home, reading for Aunt Mae every night after he returned from his lesson. He also read grocery lists and lists of homes where deliveries were needed. Plus, newspapers, highway signs, menus, and fliers. In fact, he read everything he could get his hands on.

It didn't matter what it was, Martha always smiled and cheered. "Good job," had become his favorite phrase. Seeing her smile was like winning a race or the volleyball game—only better. The more he practiced, the better he read. He bent over the newspaper and put his index finger on the next line. "A young couple . . . were un-i-ted in m-m-m-arr—iage."

Marriage. A hard word. To read and to do. Elsie and her friend Stephen had married in June. Martha was one of her sister's witnesses. She seemed very happy for Elsie. But also sad because her mother and father weren't there to celebrate with them. Now Martha ran the bakery with help from her younger sister, Annie. Martha never complained, but sometimes she looked sad. Ambrose wanted to make her happy, so he worked hard. He sighed. "Marriage."

All these evenings spent with Martha. Every minute of every hour, the urge to take her hand or brush back a curl that had escaped from her *kapp* or ask her to go for a ride had nearly burst from him.

Instead, he kept his hand on the book in front of him and his gaze on the page for fear one wrong word would end the sweet time they had together. They didn't just read. They ate peanut butter cookies and drank iced tea. They talked about the day behind them and the one coming.

"Did I hear you talking to yourself?" Joshua bounded around the corner and up the steps to the porch. "Has it come to that now? Surely you have friends you can talk to."

"I have friends." Ambrose counted in his head. One, two, three, four, five. Martha's lessons hadn't stopped at reading. He could also make change now. Add and subtract simple numbers. Not so simple for him. Why did he care what Joshua thought? "I'm not talking to myself. I'm reading."

"It's *gut* that you can read now. Not that we have to worry about getting behind on our taxes with me here to go through the mail." Joshua dropped a pile of mail on the table between the two hickory rockers. He nudged at Pirate with his dirty boot. "Move, you lazy *hund*." He settled into the rocker, picked up the top envelope, and held it out. "This one is addressed to you. Why don't you read it for me? It'll be good practice."

His voice held a note of kindness that hadn't been there before. Joshua hadn't been exactly a nuisance since his arrival. He worked hard and whipped the farm into shape. He didn't cook or clean up after himself, but he liked to make popcorn in the evening and listen to Aunt Mae tell her stories. He hadn't heard them before, and with Ambrose gone more now, he provided company for her.

With each passing week he seemed more like family and less like a guest. He seldom challenged Ambrose—not since a visit from Burke and Carina the day of the trip to the courthouse. What had been said Aunt Mae refused to share, but whatever it was, it shut Joshua up.

"I'm done reading. I'm tired." Ambrose accepted the envelope but laid it back on top of the others. He patted Pirate's head. The dog snuggled closer to his leg. Ambrose refused to rise to his cousin's bait. "How was your day?"

"*Gut*. And it's not over yet." Joshua removed his sweat-darkened straw hat and slapped it on his knee. "I have some courting to do. 'Course, you wouldn't know about that sort of thing."

"Why do you say that?" People always underestimated Ambrose. Usually he let them. Martha's encouraging words and her gentle smiles over the past few months had given him a different perspective on himself. To his unending surprise. "I know about courting."

"You know about it. But you've never done it."

As much as he wanted to lie, he couldn't. *"Nee."*

"A man has to be able to be the head of a household. To earn enough to take care of a family." Joshua swatted a persistent fly with his hat. "That's the kind of *mann* a *fraa* wants and needs."

His tone said what he thought of Ambrose ever fulfilling

that role. He was likely right. One day Joshua would bring his bride home to this house. They would have children. What would Ambrose do then? The house was half his, but he couldn't imagine living here with Joshua's family. The cat brigade—all three of them—scampered across the porch. Amelia scooted into his lap, beating Jasper and Samson to the best spot. They yowled in disappointment and plopped down beside the rocker.

Even his family of animals would leave him eventually.

Amusement written across his face, Joshua stood. "At least you'll have your animals to keep you company. Me, I'm going to get cleaned up and go find myself a *fraa*."

How did this young man know what went on in Ambrose's head?

"I can be a *mann*." Ambrose surprised himself with the words. He looked around to make sure he'd been the one to say them. "I have a job. I have *freinden*. People like me."

A look of mild surprise on his face, Joshua paused at the screen door. He scratched his head and squinted at Ambrose as if seeing him for the first time. "Carina and Burke sure do like you. They let me know they were around to help you and Aunt Mae with anything that comes up. It's *gut* to have *freinden* like that. Now all you need is a *fraa*. You should work on that."

"I will. I am." Ambrose pronounced the words with more certainty than he felt. "Don't you worry."

"*Gut* for you." His expression sly, Joshua walked back toward Ambrose. "I'll tell you what. Let's agree on something. Let's agree that whoever marries first will live in this house and take care of *Aenti* Mae. The other man must build a new house for his *fraa* and live there. It can be down the road, on this property. What do you think?"

Resolve overcame fear in a heartbeat. This was Ambrose's

home. He and Aunt Mae had lived together most of his life. "I think it's for the best. You and me can't live together forever."

"*Gut.*"

"*Gut.*"

Joshua grinned. He swiveled and ambled back to the door. A second later he disappeared into the house.

Ambrose blew out air and hugged Amelia close to his chest. He patted the cat's soft fur and stared at the words on the envelope. He recognized his name and address. Easy-peasy. The return address was a feedstore. Two easy words. *Feed* and *store*. An advertisement. He should've opened it.

No. Don't take the bait. That's what Martha would've said. He'd let Joshua bait him. But his cousin was right. A man needed a wife. Cats and dogs were good, but not the same. "Sorry, my *freinden*." He hoped the cats didn't read his mind. "You're my *freinden* too. Where I go, you go. I promise."

The squeak of the screen door told him Joshua was back. "I can read this—"

"I know you can read and you do it really well." Aunt Mae's cane went *tick-tick-tick* on the wood. Her warm voice covered him like a toasty quilt on a winter night. "I heard what Joshua said. He's right. You should think of your future."

She eased into the rocker. Jasper immediately joined her, followed by Samson.

"What future?"

"Don't play addled with me, *suh.*" Her unseeing eyes turned toward the setting sun as if to let it warm her wrinkled face. "You're smart about the important things. Go to her."

He didn't bother to pretend not to know who she meant. "I don't want to spoil it."

"You won't."

"What if she doesn't like me like that?"

"I reckon she'll always want to be your *freind*, but you won't know unless you ask. Don't let the naysayers keep you from having everything in life you want. If *Gott* wants it for you, you will have it. Make no mistake. *Gott* knows what is best for you. He brought Martha into your life. Follow His lead."

Ambrose considered Aunt Mae. She was blind and widowed and childless but still much smarter than the Joshuas of the world.

"I'll try."

"And just so you know, I decide where I live—and with whom."

"I'm sorry—"

"Go. Now."

He went.

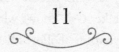

11

WEEDING WAS GOOD FOR WORKING OUT PROBLEMS. Martha wiped sweat from her forehead with her sleeve and rocked back on her knees. After a full day at the bakery, she knelt in the deepening dusk of a hot July day pulling thistle, dandelions, and crabgrass determined to choke out cucumbers, lettuce, tomatoes, radishes, green peppers, and carrots in the family garden.

Annie had slipped into the house to get them some cold tea, and after fifteen minutes she still hadn't returned. She couldn't be blamed. She was still getting used to the long days in the bakery and returning to help Elsie with work around the house. Elsie glowed with newlywed happiness until last week when Martha discovered her bent over the kitchen sink vomiting on the dirty breakfast dishes.

Already in a family way after two months of marriage. What a blessing. Martha gave herself a stern talking-to when envy tried to creep in and take hold of her heart. A niece or nephew on the way was a wonderful gift. She dug her hands into the warm soil and ripped more ragweed from between two plants heavy with tender green peppers. "Be content," she whispered to herself. "Be happy."

Her disconnected thoughts were weeds determined to choke out her delight in the blessings God had supplied in abundance. She had a good life. She loved working at the bakery. She loved teaching Ambrose.

She loved Ambrose.

"Ach." Martha looked over her shoulder. Had she said those words aloud? She hadn't even said them to herself until this moment. Did she love him? How could she not love his outrageous smile when he mastered a new word or the way he crinkled his nose when another one stumped him until he figured it out? The way he brought flowers from his garden and arranged them in an oversized pickle jar that sat on the table in her workroom. To brighten up the place, he'd said. She even came home one day to find him weeding the flowers in front of the house.

How could she not love a man who looked at her the way he did, with such undisguised happiness when she praised him?

Not that he'd said a single word to indicate his feelings. She had no more idea what he thought of her now than she had at the beginning of May when she started tutoring him.

She stuck her spade in the dirt with more force than necessary. A mosquito buzzed around her face. She slapped it away. If Mother were here, she'd say be patient. In all things, God works to prosper not to harm you. Be still and know that He is God.

She had a thousand more verses at her fingertips.

Mother, I miss you. I need you. Why did you have to go?

The dull thud of horse hooves on the dirt road penetrated her reverie. She stood and peered into the dusk. For a scant second, it seemed as if it might be her mother waving at her.

Nee, my child, but ask and ye shall receive, not only what you want, but what you need.

Ambrose.

She dropped the vanquished ragweed into the pile and wiped her hands on her already dirty apron. The buggy slowed, then halted a few yards from the garden. Ambrose hopped down, light on his feet for such a big man. For a few seconds he lingered near the pretty strawberry roan he called Berry. Then he seemed to make up his mind. He trekked toward Martha.

Relieved, she smiled. "You're here."

"Should I leave?" He turned as if to do exactly that.

"*Nee, nee.* Stay." She rushed over to him. "It's just that I was thinking of you and then you were here."

"You were thinking about me?"

He shook his head. His straw hat slid back, revealing shaggy hair. He needed a haircut. Which made her think of washing it that day months ago. "Why did you come?"

"I brought you a birdhouse to go with the feeder."

He pulled the small rectangular house from the buggy. It was painted blue to match the feeder. "It's very cute. *Danki.*" She turned the house around in her hands. He'd painted a little door and windows on the front. It even had red and purple flowers on one side. The workmanship was delicate and sure. "You did a nice job."

"Like the painting you do with frosting."

A nice compliment of sorts. Martha's hand touched his of its own volition. She pulled it back. *Behave yourself.* "I guess it is a similar technique. Shall we go hang it up next to the feeder?"

Ambrose shuffled his feet. "I thought maybe we could . . . I mean, I wonder if . . . if you might . . . if we could—"

"It'll be time for me to make the pies again if you don't hurry up and spit it out." She smiled to soften the words. "I'd like to go for a ride with you."

"You would?" Surprise mixed with delight filled his response.

"Of course I would."

To prove it, she slipped around to the other side of the buggy, laid the birdhouse in the backseat, and climbed in the front. Ambrose still stood rooted to his spot. She cocked her head and smiled. "Are you coming?"

"Coming." He heaved himself onto the seat next to her and picked up the reins. His grin split his face in two. "Where shall we go?"

"You're in charge."

For the next hour they wandered the back roads of Daviess County at a leisurely pace. Conversation was soft and sporadic. Ambrose seemed content to simply sit next to her and enjoy the ride. The silence didn't bother Martha either. They were comfortable, content, and peaceful after months of turmoil and busyness and missing Mother. What would she say if she could see Martha now, riding through the dark countryside with their deliveryman?

She'd be happy. She liked Ambrose. She'd said so on more than one occasion. She'd say, *It's about time.*

Were you trying to tell me something, Mudder?

No answer. If she were here, she'd say Martha was all grown-up and should act like it.

"Burke says there's no shame in liking someone even if it makes your heart hurt." Ambrose glanced her direction for a split second, then back at the road. "He says it's worth it, especially if the person likes you back."

"I reckon he's right." Martha examined Ambrose's words and then his tone. An important nugget was no doubt hidden in the observation. "Why would it make a person's heart hurt?"

"The other person might not like you back." Ambrose's voice trailed off. The squeak of the buggy wheels mingled with the *clip-clop* of hooves on the asphalt for a minute or two. "That would feel bad."

"If you're talking about yourself, everyone likes you."

He ducked his head so all she could see was his hat and the hair that hung down over his ear. "I'm not worried about everyone."

"Ambrose, you're hippity-hopping around some point, that's obvious." He had to say it first. Women didn't. That much she knew. "I'm here, aren't I? You came to take me for a ride, which tells me you like me. I'm riding with you. That should tell you something."

He hunched his shoulders and winced as if waiting for a blow. "You like me?"

"Of course I like you." *I might even love you.* Martha clasped her hands to her mouth. That last sentence had come precariously close to escaping. What did she know about love? Plain women shouldn't go around proclaiming their love, of that she was sure. "Do you like me?"

Ambrose seemed to contemplate his hands, the reins, his horse, the sky. "I do."

"*Gut.* I'm glad we got that figured out." She heaved a long breath. "This is hard."

"I thought I was the only one who thought so."

"*Nee.*"

"Maybe we can figure it out together." Ambrose slowed the buggy and pulled over to the side of the road near the Bontragers' milo field. "You're real smart."

"*Danki.*" She held her breath. Maybe he would take her hand. Or kiss her. Or both. "So are you."

His smile disappeared. He snapped the reins and the buggy started up again.

No more words were spoken for at least a mile. Martha tried a few times, but her efforts were rebuffed by silence.

They turned onto the road to her house. She tried one more time. "Did I say something wrong?"

"People who like each other don't lie to each other, even if they don't want to hurt their feelings. That's what *Aenti* Mae says."

"I didn't lie to you."

"I know I'm not smart."

"There's book smart and then there's life smart." She measured her words with care. "That's what *Mudder* always said and *Mudder* was really smart."

"I suppose there's truth to that."

"*Mudder* knew things, just like *Aenti* Mae."

"I want you to be happy." His face scrunched up tight as if thinking that hard hurt. "Even if it means you like somebody else."

"I don't like somebody else so stop making this so hard." She breathed in and out, trying to get a handle on her feelings. Everything had been so hard for so long. Love shouldn't be. "You make me happy."

His face relaxed. He laughed. Not a little chuckle, but a great chortle. A belly laugh filled with surprise and delight. She had no choice but to join him.

He took her hand. "My heart doesn't hurt anymore."

"*Gut.* Mine neither."

He leaned closer. She met him halfway. His eyes warmed her through and through.

"I want to kiss you."

"I wish you would."

"Are you sure?"

"Ambrose!"

His face full of wonder, he came the rest of the way. He closed his eyes. Wanting to memorize everything about his face, she waited until the last second to close her own. Her first kiss. His too. Their first kiss. Sweet and delightful and full of surprise. And far too short.

He leaned back, his eyes large and bright. "Your lips are soft." He sounded like a child whose curiosity had been piqued. His finger brushed against her lips. "And warm. Nice."

She could say the same about his lips. A shiver traveled up her spine. The hair on her arms stood. Wave upon wave of warmth enveloped her. "Would you like to try it again?"

He nodded. "Very much."

"Me too."

So they did.

12

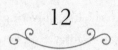

THAT THE SUMMER MONTHS PASSED SO QUICKLY INTO autumn, which quickly gave way to winter, didn't surprise Martha. She hadn't had time to miss either season. Staying busy at Sweet Tooth. Reading lessons with Ambrose. Buggy rides. Hugs. Kisses. More hugs. More kisses. Fixing supper for Ambrose's Aunt Mae and his cousin Joshua. The man had needed lessons in kindness and caring, but he would gradually come around under Aunt Mae's patient tutelage. She had him following her around like a grateful puppy. Which made Ambrose and Martha feel less guilty about the time they spent together. Life filled her days full of a contentment she hadn't thought possible. Only one thing was missing—Mother's presence.

Martha tore November from the wall calendar and stared at the December page where she'd drawn a big, fat, yellow circle around the first Friday of the month, the day before Carina and Burke's wedding.

The day had another significance as well—one she didn't want to dwell on. No matter how hard she tried to build a dam against them, the memories flooded her. This day one year earlier she'd bustled into the bakery's workroom ready to make a cake for Mrs. Cartwright's annual book club Christmas party. The red light blinked on the answering machine. She assumed it would be more orders. They were abundant during the holidays. So many Christmas parties, so many sweet goodies needed.

Instead, Uncle John's hoarse, quivering voice greeted her. His message would be engraved forever on her brain.

"Your mudder has passed. Her body was too weak. The treatments didn't work. She died during the night. The will of Gott be done, as hard as it is for you—for all of us—to understand. It will take a while for the paperwork to go through the Mexican Consulate. Then I'll bring her home on the train."

Martha sank onto the three-legged pine stool next to the workroom table and touched the offending tape recorder as if it were to blame for the unhappy memories. Grief, as fresh as if Uncle John had just left the message, wrapped itself around her body, weighing her down. She had so much to do, but her arms and legs refused to move.

After an entire year, the same question fought its way to the front of the pack that hounded her. *"Mudder . . . Mudder,* how could you?" Her own high, tight voice filled with wild notes of hysteria shamed Martha. Mother couldn't be blamed for the disease that took her. Their days were numbered. God gave and He took away, according to His plan. His grace and mercy covered them even when they fell short—which was every day. Martha swallowed tears and reached for a tissue. Pain shot like white-hot lightning from her temple down the left side of her head. The headache that had hovered on her periphery all afternoon used her moment of weakness to gobble up more ground. *"Nee, Gott.* Not now. Please, not now."

She closed her eyes and lowered her head into her hands. *Breathe, breathe. One, two, three. One, two, three. In and out. In and out.*

Mother wouldn't be happy to see Martha acting like this. She would've expected more. *Enough with the pity party. You have work to do.*

Mother's days were done, but Carina and Burke were celebrating a new season in their lives. A season that promised to hold joy, love, and contentment. Martha had a role to play in that celebration. Mother would be happy for them and happy that her bakery and her daughter had been chosen to participate.

Martha wiped her face and stood. Time to get to work. The layers for Burke's cake were in the freezer. She'd already piped all the poinsettias for it. Next would be Carina's cake layers. While they were in the oven, the filling for the German chocolate cake needed to be mixed, along with the frosting for the cinnamon spice cake. Then the garlands, the mistletoe, and the Christmas tree decorations for Carina's cake.

So much work to be done. No time for tears.

Rubbing her stiff neck, Martha grabbed the broom from its spot in the corner and began to sweep the workroom. Her head throbbed. *Think of something else.* She inhaled the scent of warm chocolate and cinnamon. The image of her mother making hot chocolate on a cold winter morning flooded her. The steaming hot liquid on her tongue. The warmth spread through her body. She breathed in the steam and the sweet aroma. Mother brushed Martha's hair in long, even strokes. She braided it with deft fingers. Martha trusted her completely. She never pulled her hair. She never became impatient. She sang "Jesus Loves the Little Children" as she wound the braid into a bun and pinned it. Then she added the *kapp*, more bobby pins, and a pat on Martha's shoulder.

"There you go." She'd always patted Martha's shoulder and said the same thing. *"There you go."*

No matter how many children pushed and pulled at her, she always had time.

Martha forced a smile and lined up the ingredients for the spice cake. Flour, baking powder, salt, butter, sugar, ten room-temperature eggs, milk, vanilla, cinnamon, nutmeg, allspice, ginger, cloves, cocoa.

Pain drummed in her temples. A wave of nausea joined in. "Focus. Focus."

The light hurt her eyes. She began to sing "Jesus Loves the Little Children" as she squinted and measured the flour, baking soda, salt, spices, and cocoa into one bowl. The familiar routine calmed her. The words calmed her.

Time to beat the butter and add the sugar. Her arm and shoulder ached. Elsie drew the line at an electric beater. Mix hard for two minutes. Martha closed her eyes and counted to sixty twice.

She opened her eyes and Ambrose stood in the doorway. He held a Purple Martin Café bag in his hands. "I brought you supper." He smiled. "Your favorite. Burke's fried chicken, coleslaw, creamed corn, and iced tea."

Martha swallowed tears and laid the spatula on the prep island. "You're so sweet."

She didn't dare say more or the tears would spill over and flood the bakery.

"What's wrong?" He set the bag on the table and strode to her prep island. "Is it the cakes? It's okay. I'll help you. I know all my numbers now. I can read the recipe."

His reading was on par with most fourth graders now. "It's not the cakes." Although, the intricacies of a four-layer cinnamon spice cake with buttercream cheese frosting and a Christmas display of poinsettias around a red bow on top and silver snowflakes on the side seemed more daunting than it had an hour ago. Not to mention the four-layer German chocolate cake with its toasted coconut-pecan filling. "My *mudder* passed a year ago today. I was here in this room when I found out. I thought I was okay, but I can't stop thinking of her."

"I'm sorry." His face crumpled. "I know how that feels."

"I know you do." She sighed and turned back to the batter. The cakes had to be made, no matter the circumstances. As a season of life ended for one family, it began for another. Carina and Burke deserved their special day. Especially Burke, who had suffered devastating losses in the past. "We need to make this extra special for Burke and Carina. Our *mudders* would like that."

His expression puzzled, Ambrose wrinkled his nose. "Dead people like cake too?"

"I like to think cake tastes even better in heaven." Embarrassed at how silly the words sounded spoken aloud, she ducked her head and focused on the cake. She added the dry ingredients alternately with milk and vanilla to the eggs, starting and ending with dry ingredients. "I need to get this in the oven. The layers have to cool completely before I can put them together."

"I'm sorry about your *mudder.*"

"Me too. I was always so sad that we didn't get to say goodbye, but *Gott* took her home for reasons we can't understand. She is better off. No more pain. No more cancer treatments."

"But you don't understand."

"I try."

"Me too." Ambrose pulled paper plates from the bag and began setting out the Styrofoam serving containers, biggest to smallest in a neat row. "But I'm not smart enough."

"No one is smart enough to understand *Gott*'s plan. He's way smarter than any of us."

"*Gut* to know."

She gestured at the cake pans. "I have to get these cakes made."

"Eat first."

The thought of food made her stomach pitch, but Ambrose had been so kind to think of her. The pounding in her head ratcheted up another notch. "A bite or two."

"Or three or four." He chuckled and began doling out generous portions on paper plates he produced from the bag. "Or five or six or seven or eight."

"You're showing off your counting skills."

She placed the cake pans in the oven and set the timer for thirty-five minutes. Together, she and Ambrose sat at the small round table where he'd prepared the food. They prayed silently, Ambrose pronounced "amen," and they dug in.

At least, Ambrose did. Martha took a few bites of corn and watched as he devoured everything on his plate. By the time he finished, he had creamed corn on his chin, and his fingers were greasy. He smacked his lips and sighed. "Burke's food is *gut*."

Martha clenched her jaw. "It is."

She handed him a napkin. He patted his cheek. The corn remained on his chin. She leaned over and wiped it for him. His hand came up and caught hers. "You didn't eat."

"I can't."

"Is it your head?"

She nodded.

His face full of concern, he cocked his head and stared. Finally, he rose and trotted around to her side of the table where he put both hands on her shoulders.

"What are you doing?"

"What my *mudder* used to do."

He massaged her shoulders and neck with strong fingers and steady pressure. At first, it hurt, but gradually her muscles relaxed and she let her head hang down.

A soft humming sound floated on the air. Notes of a song she'd never heard. His baritone soothed her. Her eyelids fluttered. They wouldn't stay open. She demanded they cooperate, but they simply wouldn't.

The massage stopped. The feel of something soft and warm touched her nape. His lips. A kiss. A light, feathery kiss.

"Ambrose?"

"Hmm?"

"I . . ."

"You need to sleep." A rustling sound. She opened her eyes and he handed her a dish towel he'd rolled up. "A pillow. Lay your head down."

There needed to be more kisses. The perfect antidote for a world where she no longer had a mother or a father. Ambrose was older and in his own way, wiser. He knew how to navigate this world. He'd done it himself with kindness and grace and care. There needed to be more love. She needed to know if he loved her. "Ambrose, please. I want to know—"

"You sleep. We can talk later."

"I can't sleep. I have to make the cakes."

"They still have twenty minutes. And then they have to cool, don't they?"

"*Jah.*"

He took her plate. "I'll save this for later when you're feeling better."

The thought of resting her eyes beckoned her. Leaving Ambrose in charge of her job was wrong, the mini-Elsie perched on her shoulder argued. "For a few minutes. Wake me if the timer doesn't. The cakes need to cool, and then I have to put them in the freezer for a while. I need to start making the filling for the German chocolate cake and the decorations—"

"I promise. Sleep."

She laid her head on the towel and closed her eyes. For a few minutes. Just a few minutes.

13

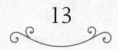

SOMETHING WAS VERY WRONG. CHEWING ON HIS LOWER
lip, Ambrose studied the four layers of the cinnamon spice cake.
They smelled good, but they looked funny. Like overcooked pancakes. They were flat. Maybe Martha made a new, fancy English
wedding cake he'd never seen before. His cooking skills stretched
as far as goulash, hamburgers, hot dogs, and tacos, but he didn't
bake. Aunt Mae's friends kept them supplied with all the baked
goods they needed.

He touched the cake. It didn't bounce back. It just laid there
looking sad. He should wake Martha. She hadn't budged when
the egg timer went *brrriinnnggg*. She looked uncomfortable
slouched over the table with her head on her forearms, but the
occasional dainty snore said she slept.

The temptation to kiss her neck again stalked him. It was
wrong. He shouldn't have done it the first time, his father's voice
nagged him. A good man didn't take advantage of a woman sick
with a headache so bad it turned her face white and kept her from
eating a perfectly good fried chicken leg and Burke's creamed corn.

But the soft skin of her nape and the fine wispy blond hairs that escaped her *kapp* called to him. His fingers wanted to touch them and trail down her arm to her hand so he could entwine his fingers with hers.

What would Aunt Mae say? She'd say to work. Work cured what ailed a person.

Martha said the cakes had to be placed in the freezer after they were cool enough to take from the pans. He could do that. He slid a knife around the edges the way he'd seen his mother do and turned the cake pan over. The thin disc plopped out on his huge palm without a murmur of distress.

Not so with the second one. He turned the cake over. Nothing happened. He tapped the bottom of the pan. Nothing. He tapped harder. Half of the cake fell from the pan and landed just beyond his outstretched fingers. The edges were jagged. Crumbs fell on the table and the floor. "*Ach*, no!"

Martha bolted upright. "What is it? What happened?" Her wide-eyed gaze swooped from Ambrose's face to the pan in his hand to the floor and back. "What did you do to my cake?"

"It's flat. It stuck."

"Flat? What do you mean flat?" She popped up from her chair, then froze. Her hand went to her forehead. "*Ach*." She panted. "My head wants to explode."

She took a deep breath and let it out slowly. Then, as if she walked on broken glass, she eased her way over to the prep island. Her mouth fell open. "Flat and burnt. They're flat and burnt."

"And this one stuck to the pan. When I tried to get it out, it broke and part of it fell on the floor."

She sank to her knees and swept up the pieces with her hands. "I have to start over. What time is it?"

"I'm sorry."

"It's not your fault. I left something out—one of the ingredients. What time is it?"

"Eight thirty."

"Why did you let me sleep?"

"Because you needed to sleep and you said it had to cool."

"I planned to make the frosting and the filling and decorations while they cooled."

"You still can."

Still on the floor, she closed her eyes and bowed her head.

"I'll help you." He grabbed the cookbook that lay open on the counter. "See, it says here, 'Crack all the eggs into a bowl. Your eggs should be at room . . . tem . . . temppppu, tempera . . . temperature.'"

She opened her eyes and looked up at him. "Very *gut*. Your reading is *gut*."

Which didn't mean he would be much help, but he could try. He held out his hand. She took it and he pulled her to her feet. Her skin was so soft. He didn't want to let go. He pulled her closer. She didn't resist. He let go and her arms slipped around his waist. Her head leaned on his chest. He rubbed her back.

She sighed. "I have to make the cake." Her voice was a whisper. "But *danki*."

"For what?"

"For being you."

"I'm sorry you're sad."

"I know."

He cleared his throat. "I can make the cakes. I can read the recipe. You make decorations. I can help."

"You're right. You can." She raised her head and looked up at him. She looked relieved. She believed in him. The realization was like a warm spring breeze after a long, icy winter. "I'll be right here to oversee."

They went to work. Ambrose used his index finger to follow each line of the recipe. Fractions were easy because he could use measuring cups and spoons. Dry ingredients. Then wet ingredients. Then mixed together. In the meantime, Martha swallowed ibuprofen and began creating tiny, delicate branches from melted dark chocolate squeezed onto wax paper, followed by lacy vines that made a green garland. Small wrapped gifts were next. Then pine cones squeezed onto small straws. Everything went into the freezer while she made more green frosting for the leaves and stems.

The minutes ticked away. Hours passed. Twice Martha urged Ambrose to go. Twice, he refused. The new cakes were in the oven. He helped with the cleanup so she could start the filling for Burke's cake. The smell of toasted pecans and coconut filled the room, mingling with the mouthwatering scents of cinnamon, ginger, cloves, allspice, and nutmeg. It smelled like autumn and Thanksgiving and Christmas all rolled into one happy day.

If only it were. The lines around Martha's mouth deepened. Dark circles like bruises smudged the spaces under her eyes. Her hands shook.

He took the ladle from her and stirred the pecan-coconut concoction. "Rest."

"I can't. I need to put the cake together."

"You can't until it cools completely."

"It's after midnight. You should go."

"Sit." With both hands on her shoulders, he marched her to

the closest chair. She sank onto it with a sigh. "Tell me how to make the frosting for Carina's cake."

"You've done enough. Go home. Get some sleep. Tomorrow—later today—you have to help with the setup and serving. You're a groomsman."

What exactly a groomsman was remained a mystery, but to be asked by Burke was clearly an honor. Ezekiel's grandson Kenny, who supervised the restaurant from his wheelchair, would be the best man. "This is where I want to be."

"Why?" Her red-rimmed eyes swam with tears. Her hands fluttered. "Why would you want to be here with me? I made a mistake. I messed up Carina's cake. I want my *mudder* back even though I know she belongs to *Gott*. Why can't I be like Elsie?"

"Because you are you." Ambrose knelt next to her chair. "I like you the way you are."

"'Because you are you.'" She took his face in her hands. "'I like you the way you are.' You're the kindest, sweetest, gentlest, most special man I've ever met."

Joy struck Ambrose dumb. He couldn't speak so he did the only thing he could. He kissed her.

She tasted better than the most delicious cookies she could bake. She smelled like cinnamon and nutmeg. Her hands crept up and stroked his hair. These moments were the best in Ambrose's entire life. "I love you."

The words were out of the box. No putting them back.

She opened her eyes and smiled. "I love you too."

Danki, Gott, danki.

She leaned her head against his chest. He put his arms around her and held her close. Life was good and complete. He would never need more than this. His whole world was right there in his arms. He kissed her *kapp*. "We have to finish."

"I know. I don't want to move."

"Me neither."

Two more minutes. Time was running out. She pushed away. "I should make the frosting." She rose and went to the counter. "We need three sticks of butter, twelve ounces of softened cream cheese, three cups of powdered sugar, vanilla, and salt."

They made the frosting together. Ambrose brought her the ingredients. She mixed and smoothed until the creamy goodness was perfect. Then she created a little piece of Christmas beauty. And she allowed him to help.

They placed the first three round layers on a silver platter and then added a smaller cake on top, which received a thin layer of the white frosting. The bottom layers were covered with cream cheese frosting piped out in a texture that looked like tiny snowflakes. Placing the white chocolate lacy collar around the smaller top cake proved to be challenging. Because his hands were bigger, Ambrose was allowed to gently place the lace against the frosting. His hands warmed the wax paper, so the collar stuck to the cake without breaking.

"Beautiful. Good job!"

Her pleasure at his success made him feel ten feet tall.

Together, they added the poinsettias, pine cones, and branches, and Martha piped on the greenery.

The sun shone through the far window by the time they stood back and stared at their creation. The long night had turned to day. Their time together, alone, was over. They'd made it. They would go to the wedding where a few hundred people would celebrate the union of two people who loved each other.

Ambrose held his breath.

Martha's hand slid into his. He let out his breath and wrapped his fingers around hers.

"It'll do," she said finally.

"It's too pretty to eat." He cleared his throat. "I want to ask you something."

She glanced at the clock over the door. "Can it wait? We still have to finish Burke's cake."

It could wait, but not for long.

14

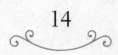

THE PURPLE MARTIN CAFÉ HAD NEVER LOOKED MORE festive. Martha tucked her coat on a shelf behind the counter, smoothed her wrinkled, vanilla-stained apron, and tried to fix her hair. She and Ambrose had finished the cakes with less than an hour to spare. Ambrose went to change into his church clothes at Burke's house while she delivered the cakes to the restaurant.

The smaller cake sat on the table covered with a lacy white tablecloth next to Carina's bigger cake. Someone had festooned the wooden beams overhead with tiny white lights intertwined with garlands. They had pushed aside the tables and lined up the chairs in two rows on each side with an aisle down the middle. Mason jars filled with red and white mums sat on the tables. Large poinsettias decorated the counters and booths.

Mother had loved Christmas. She loved making cards and sending them to family and friends scattered across the country. She loved making gifts for the children, finding just the right one for each of her eight boys and girls. She loved the school program on Christmas Eve and making gingerbread men and popcorn balls and fudge and divinity. Most of all she loved the gift given to the world by their Lord.

A pain so sharp she almost doubled over pierced Martha's heart.

Don't be sad, dochder. *I'm resting now. No more pain. No more treatments. Just sweet repose.*

Jah, *but you're not here to see how happy Ambrose makes me.*

I see.

Elsie would think her fanciful. So would the bishop. But those words echoing in Martha's head kept the searing pain of loss from swallowing her whole. She closed her eyes and breathed. Gott, *thank you for helping me through this.*

A small platform in the front with a podium would be the center of the ceremony, which would be performed by one of Burke and Carina's chaplain friends. After the service, the podium would be whisked away and replaced by a sound system for a band that would play a mix of music representing the bride and groom's diverse tastes. Martha knew all of this because Carina had kept her informed every step of the way.

A low hum grew as guests flowed into the restaurant in a steady stream. The Plain folks wore their usual Sunday service clothes while the townspeople and out-of-town guests dressed in dark suits and fancy dresses in bright seasonal colors of red and green.

Martha went first to her family, seated on one of the back rows. Elsie, looking so much like *Mudder* with her blue eyes and dimples, offered a wordless hug as a somber Stephen looked on. "I can't believe she's been gone a year." Martha whispered in Elsie's ear. She gritted her teeth to keep the tears at bay. She counted to ten twice. "Will every Christmas be like this?"

"It'll get better. She would've loved a Christmas-themed

wedding. She'd be so happy for Burke." Elsie's voice quivered. She sniffed. "We must enjoy it for her."

"I know."

Martha stepped back and repeated the hug with each of her siblings. Annie clung to her an extra minute. "How did the cakes turn out?"

"They're nice. Ambrose helped."

"He's such a *gut* man." Her younger sister managed a watery smile. "You are blessed."

"You'll find someone like him one day."

"I hope so."

Annie's expression left no doubt that she thought she would be blessed to find someone like Ambrose. Her sisters saw what Martha saw. A special man made in God's image.

The bride, dressed in a long-sleeved, tea-length dress of lace and silk in a deep autumn red, rushed toward Martha full tilt, arms wide open. "I can't believe you're here. You look exhausted." She wrapped her arms around Martha in a sweet hug. She smelled of flowers. "The cakes look gorgeous. You've outdone yourself."

"I didn't want to let you down." Carina need never know how difficult the task had been. "I keep thinking how much my mother would've enjoyed this day. She'd be so happy for you and Burke. And she loved Christmas. It's such a joyous time of year, made happier by your wedding."

"She'd be proud of your beautiful handiwork today. The cakes are perfect." Carina patted Martha's shoulder. Her fingernails were painted the same shade of red as her dress. She wore a silver locket and small antique-looking silver hoop earrings that matched her hair. "She'd be proud of how well all of you have handled yourselves over the last year. Elsie and Stephen,

Annie, but especially you. You're a bakery owner with a successful business."

"We've all worked together to make it happen." Martha pointed to the empty chair between Annie and her youngest brother Thomas. "It's been hard, but there's been joy in the journey."

"You're such sweet examples of faith." Tears trickled down Carina's face. "You truly walk the walk."

"Don't cry, you'll mess up your makeup." Martha wiped at her own face. So much sadness mingled with deep happiness for her friends. "Today is a day for laughter, not tears."

"There's room for both," Carina whispered as she surveyed the crowd. "Life is like that. Bitter and sweet often dance together."

Smiling and laughing, Burke wove his way toward them, stopping to welcome guests every few feet. He looked sharp in a dark-blue suit and red tie. "He cleans up good."

Carina wiped away more tears. "I'll need another packet of tissues just to get through the ceremony."

"It's time." Burke held out his hand to his bride. Smiling, she took it without hesitation and they turned to make their way to the podium.

"I'll get the tissues," Martha called after her. At this rate, she'd need an entire packet for herself too. She scurried into Burke's office, a temporary makeshift dressing room, grabbed the tissues, and returned.

By that time, Ambrose stood next to a woman who could be Carina's twin, except that she was younger, had dark chocolate hair, and was undoubtedly in a family way. She wore a simple frock the same color as Carina's dress. The maid of honor. Next to Ambrose, Kenny, Burke's young best man, had parked his wheelchair. A small, but perfect wedding party.

Carina had chosen no procession or music. She and Burke had written their own vows. They were brief, simple, and so heartfelt, more sniffles could be heard throughout the throng of guests that filled the space to standing room only.

"A man doesn't often get a second chance at love so astonishing it rocks him down to the soles of his feet not once, but every single day, from the time he opens his eyes in the morning until he closes them at night," Burke said. He had a piece of paper in his hand, but he didn't look at it. "That's why my feelings for you, Carina, took me so by surprise. I didn't deserve it once. I certainly don't deserve a second chance. I don't deserve you. But our God is gracious and merciful and loving, so here I stand promising to honor you and respect you and most of all, love you with every atom of my being for as long as I shall live."

To have such big words to describe big feelings would be nice. Martha squeezed between two couples standing along the wall so she could get closer. A kaleidoscope of emotions played across Burke's lined face. He couldn't hide his feelings. Happiness, uncertainty, joy, longing.

So like the feelings running through her own heart.

"I now pronounce you husband and wife. You may kiss the bride."

Such beautiful words. Mann *and* fraa. Nothing would be sweeter than to spend the rest of her life with one man.

Ambrose's gaze met hers across the expanse of people.

His smile held a question and a promise in equal measure.

Martha needed to get to him. As soon as possible.

She moved forward. Burke and Carina were still kissing. They acted on the chaplain's instruction with great enthusiasm and thoroughness. The crowd clapped, then laughed, and finally cheered. Martha paused, waiting.

After a bit, Burke looked around. "Oh, you're all still here. Thank you for coming. Give us a few minutes and we'll get the place set up for dinner and dancing."

Everyone began to move at once. A man jostled Martha. Then another. She couldn't seem to make any traction forward. An army of volunteers moved quickly and like a well-oiled machine, re-arranging chairs and moving tables. Good-natured guests pitched in while the band set up. Burke and Carina made it to her before she could get to the front. By then, she couldn't see Ambrose.

"The tissues. Do you have them?"

Martha glanced down at her hand. She still clutched the for-gotten tissues. She held out the packet.

"Thank goodness. I needed those." Carina dabbed at her tear-streaked face. "And you, my friend, need to find Ambrose."

"Why? Is something wrong?"

"No, honey, everything is fine. He congratulated us and then said he had something to do. I had the distinct impression he was looking for you."

Martha swiveled and stood on her tippy toes. He was tall. She should be able to see him in a crowd. There. By the counter. He nodded and smiled. "I have to go."

"You sure do." Carina pressed her bouquet of red and white mums into Martha's hands.

"I can't take this. Aren't you supposed to throw it or something?"

Carina shook her head. "Nope. They're my gift to you. Go, run."

Running was impossible but Martha zigged and zagged until she made it to the swinging doors that led to the kitchen. Ambrose cocked his head toward the back. She grabbed her coat from under the counter and put it on as she followed him past the busy bees who were preparing a serving line that featured lasagna, caprese salad, green beans almandine, and bread sticks. The smells were heady, but food wasn't her priority. That belonged to the man in front of her. They slipped through the back door and out into the parking lot. A section had been set aside for buggies and horses using hay bales as the boundary lines. Ambrose took her hand. "Come with me."

The cold December air nipped at her cheeks after the heat of so many bodies crowded into the restaurant. Berry lifted her head and nickered a welcome. Martha laid the bouquet on the buggy seat and patted the horse's long, graceful neck. With a long sigh, she ran her fingers through the horse's thick mane. Berry's body warmed her.

"How are you?" Ambrose's hand pressed against her back. "You look very tired."

"I'm fine. Let's sit."

They sat side by side on the bale closest to the horse. "Are you okay?"

"I'm tired. Happy for Carina and Burke. Sad for me. Sad for my *bruders* and *schweschders* who will grow up without their *mudder*. Happy to be here with you." She leaned against his shoulder. He slipped his arm around her and they huddled against the cold, their white puffs of breath mingling. "Is it possible to be so many things at once?"

"*Jah.*" Ambrose took her hand and traced the lines on her palms with his big thumb. "It feels big to me. Like my heart will blow up."

"But it's *gut*?"

"It's *gut*." His forehead wrinkled. "Is it bad that I want to ask you a question on a day of celebration for Burke and Carina? It's also a sad day for you, made for thinking about your *mudder*."

"*Mudder* loved her *kinner*. She wanted all of us to be godly, hardworking, and happy. She told me so before she left for Mexico a few months before she died."

Martha had read and reread the memories like the pages of a favorite book that wrapped themselves around her heart. Mother had hugged and kissed each one of her children and whispered something in their ears just for them, from eight-year-old Thomas to her oldest son Henry who, at thirty, was running the farm. Mother barely had the strength to put her thin arms with bony wrists around Martha. Instead of a *kapp*, she wore a white scarf wound around her smooth, now hairless head. Her gaunt face still shone with the light of love when she leaned close and whispered in her ear.

"*Be content, my* dochder, *be happy. Whatever life brings, follow* Gott *and you'll never go wrong.*"

"She knew she wasn't coming back." Tears choked Martha. *Be happy.* She breathed. "She left us content knowing we have everything we need."

She swiveled so she could look Ambrose in the eye. "Including you. She hired you, knowing you would watch over us and help us."

"You think so?" He shook his head. "I only deliver the pastries."

"And look at you now. Holding my hand and comforting me."

"I want to do more."

"I'm *gut* with that."

"You are?"

"Haven't you figured that out by now? I don't kiss anyone but you, Ambrose."

His expression lightened. "That is *gut* to know." He took a big breath and released it slowly. "Will you marry me?"

The joy of new beginnings mingled with the pain of loss until the two became one bittersweet gift. "I will."

"You said *jah*!" Ambrose sprang to his feet and shouted. "She said *jah*!"

Berry stomped and whinnied. Nearby horses sidestepped and neighed. Birds nestled in trees barren of leaves took flight. Ambrose threw his arms in the air and clapped. Had he not been a Plain man, the average person might have suggested he danced a jig.

His sheer delight cloaked Martha like a warm shawl. Clapping her hands and laughing, she rose.

Ambrose swooped down, lifted her into the air, and swung her around.

Their laughter mingled like a song of celebration.

His kisses stole her breath and her words. She threw her arms around his neck and hung on. "She said *jah*, world! Did you hear her?"

Laughing and crying, Martha kissed his forehead, nose, and lips. "Why are you so surprised? I love you."

"I love you, I love you, I love you!" He kissed her again, then settled her on her feet. "When? When do we get married?"

She leaned against his chest and considered. "We have a lot to do first. Elsie will need my help when the baby comes. We'll need to make changes in your house so *Aenti* Mae will still have her own space—like a *dawdy haus*. How about in the spring? Early May. When the flowers are blooming. My mother loved that time of year."

"So did mine." Ambrose nodded so hard his black Sunday hat shifted. "I can grow the flowers for the tables and you can make the flowers for the cake. Do you think Joshua might want to be my witness?"

That Ambrose wanted to include his cousin in this special day proved what Martha already knew. He was a good man. "I'm sure he will. It will be a beautiful day."

"I don't have to wait until then to kiss you, do I?"

The concern on his sweet face made Martha giggle. "I should hope not."

"*Gut.*"

Their kisses sealed the promise and spoke of so many more to come. One day soon they would become *mann* and *fraa* and their new season of life together would begin.

A person couldn't ask for a more special love.

A NOTE FROM
THE AUTHOR

I HOPE YOU ENJOYED AMBROSE'S STORY. IT'S ONE CLOSE to my heart. I grew up visiting with my uncle Duane, who had a developmental disability greater than the one that challenges Ambrose. Duane was my mother's older brother, but growing up, she took care of him. She told us stories about defending him against kids who bullied or mistreated him. She was a child herself, but he was her responsibility when her parents were working. As an adult he rode his bike around my small hometown and all the shop owners knew him. They gave him coffee and donuts and looked out for him. I remember my dad saying that Duane was the only person he'd ever known who had never done a mean or bad thing in his life. As a child, I found that to be amazing. As an adult, I still do. One of the many aspects of the Amish faith that I respect is their acceptance of children with disabilities as special gifts from God. They would never consider them burdens. The secular world could learn so much from their reminder that we are all made in God's image. Those of us who have disabilities are God's image bearers too. We have spiritual gifts to offer too.

As always, my thanks to my team at HarperCollins Christian

Publishing for their hard work in making this novella collection shine from the editing of the stories to the gorgeous cover. It's a joy to work with every one of them.

To my family, love always, and thanks for putting up with me.

None of this would be possible without the grace of my Lord Jesus Christ, who makes all things possible. May He bless and keep you.

DISCUSSION QUESTIONS

1. Did you ever experience bullying as a child? How did you deal with it? Why do you think children and even some adults engage in bullying? How did you react to seeing other children bullied? What is the best way to deal with it in all its forms in today's era of social media?

2. Ambrose doesn't want people to know he can't read. He doesn't ask for help and it causes him problems with his property taxes. Are there times when you know you should ask for help, but you don't because you're embarrassed for your shortcomings? What are the consequences?

3. Martha lost both of her parents while they were still relatively young and had children at home. She can't understand why God would let this happen to her family. How would you answer this question? What does Scripture say about her grief and suffering over their loss?

4. When Martha lists Ambrose's good qualities, she includes hard worker, dependable, kind, even-tempered.

Carina says these things are more important than book learning or "smarts." Do you agree? What would you say to people who might question Martha's decision to marry a man categorized by many as "slow"?

5. What does the phrase "God's image bearer" mean to you? What does it mean that we were made in God's image? How does it affect the way you live your life?

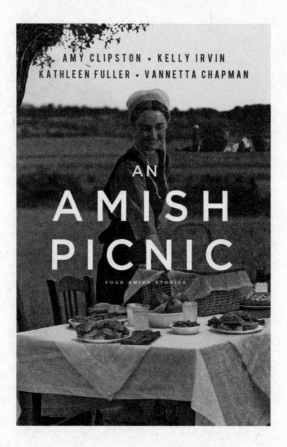